The New Moon

IN THE SAME SERIES

The New Moon
and Other French
Imaginary Voyages

translated, annotated and introduced by
Brian Stableford

A Black Coat Press Book

Visit our website at www.blackcoatpress.com

TABLE OF CONTENTS

Introduction

La Nouvelle Lune, ou histoire de Poequilon par M. Le
B***, here translated as "The New Moon," was originally
published in Amsterdam by J. B. Henry in 1770. The author
was subsequently identified by Antoine Alexandre Barbier's
Dictionnaire des ouvrages anonymes as Alexis-Jean Le Bret
(1603-1779).

The Bibliothèque Nationale's data file relating to the author in question gives his place of birth as Beaune and his profession as Advocate and Royal Censor but two of those data
are probably incorrect. Georges May, who wrote an excellent
essay on the book, published in *Essays on the Age of Enlightenment in Honour of Ira O. Wade* (1977), edited by Jean
Macary, sorted out the various confusions of identity that led
to the false attributions, understandable given the profusion of
Le Brets and Lebrets active at the relevant time. According to
May, the birthplace of Beaune was that of the author's cousin
Louis Lebret, whereas Alexis-Jean Le Bret was actually born
in Dijon, and the Advocate of that name was Francois-Xavier
Dardin Le Bret. On the other hand, May confirms, perhaps
surprisingly, that the author of *La Nouvelle Lune* really was a
royal censor, from 1759 onwards, who presumably spent a
good idea of his time barring the way to publication—in Paris,
at least—of licentious satirical works like *La Nouvelle Lune*.
May also records among the reliable biographical data that he
was able to locate that Alexis-Jean Le Bret adopted that form
of his name (having previously termed himself Lebret or
Lebreth) when he married Ann Binet in 1732.

La Nouvelle Lune is a relatively late addition to the tradition of lunar satires spectacularly launched in France by the
posthumous publication of Cyrano de Bergerac's *L'Autre
monde, ou Les États et empires de la Lune* (1657; tr. as *Comi-
cal History of the States and Empires of the Moon*) and more

7

recently carried forward by Charles-François Tiphaigne de Le Roche in "Zamar" (1754 in the second edition of *Amilec*; tr. as "Zamar")[1], *Le Voyageur philosophe dans un pais inconnu aux habitans de la Terre* (1761; tr. as *The Philosophical Voyager*)[2] signed "Monsieur de Listonai," and one of the episodes in *Voyages de Milord Céton dans les sept planètes* (1765-66; tr. as *The Voyages of Lord Seaton to the Seven Planets*)[3] by Marie-Anne de Roumier-Robert. Between the first cited works and the 18th century cluster the tradition had taken on many of the pretentions and sophistications of the *conte philosophique*, sometimes becoming quite sober in the process, but Le Bret's work, while maintaining many of those sophistications, also retains in full measure the exuberance and—in the broadest possible sense—licentiousness of Cyrano's work.

Unlike the great majority of its predecessors, *La Nouvelle Lune* it does not take the narrative form of a journey undertaken by a human from Earth to the Moon, describing instead the elaborate odyssey of a uniquely-favored lunar native, but that alternation only serves to emphasize that the Moon depicted here, like those featured in the earlier works, is not really the Earth's satellite at all but a distorted mirror image, displaced in order to put on a blatantly false pretence of not wanting to give offense to its various targets. The odyssey in question first allows the narrator to explore the potentials of his own natal society, then takes him on a kind of world tour of nations paralleling those of Earth, and finally concludes his epic journey in the most delightful of all imaginary locations, the island of Eutoquia, the fictional Moon's equivalent of the Earthly Eutopia—without which, as Oscar Wilde once pointed out, no map of the world can really be reckoned complete. Although couched as a pure fantasy, giving its protagonist a seemingly-inexhaustible but carefully spaced-out series of

---

[1] Included in *Amilec*, Black Coat Press, ISBN 978-1-61227-033-3.
[2] Black Coat Press, ISBN 978-1-61227-367-9.
[3] Black Coat Press, ISBN 978-1-61227-444-7 (forthcoming).

wishes, the story nevertheless maintains the kind of rational skepticism typical of Voltairean *contes philosophiques*, and its breezy hybridization of the attitudes and methods of Cyrano and Voltaire makes it one of the most lively and interesting works of the pre-Revolutionary era.

The text placed before *La Nouvelle Lune* in the present volume—in order to maintain the chronological order of publication—the anonymous *Relation d'un voyage du pôle arctique au pôle antarctique par le centre du monde avec la description de ce périlleux passage et des choses merveilleuses et étonnantes qu'on a découvertes sous le pôle antarctique*, here translated as "A Journey from the Arctic Pole to the Antarctic Pole via the Center of the Earth," was first published in Amsterdam by Etienne Lucas in 1721. Its publication in Amsterdam was not the result of a refusal of approval by the royal censors in Paris; they issued a certificate of license bearing dates ranging between August 1722 and October 1722, used for at least three editions issued by different publishers in Paris in 1723, which were presumably pirated from the original. The story was reproduced from one of the latter editions in Charles Garnier's set of *Voyages imaginaires, songes, visions et romans cabalistiques* [Imaginary Voyages, Dreams, Visions and Cabalistic Romances] (1787-89). It is also reproduced, under a slightly different title and dated 1780 in the contents page and on the back cover (inexplicably, as the introduction to the story gives the correct date), in the Robert Laffont "Bouquins" omnibus of *Voyages aux pays de nulle part* [Journeys to Nowhere Lands] (1990).

No one, including Garnier, has been able to provide any information regarding the authorship of the text. It has certain similarities to the much more elaborate imaginary voyages written in the same era by Simon Tyssot de Patot (available in English translation in a Black Coat Press edition as *The Strange Voyages of Jacques Massé and Pierre Mésange*),[4] and might well have been inspired by them, but is a much less

---

[4] Black Coat Press, ISBN 978-1-61227-370-9.

considerable work in literary terms, and is primarily interesting for its eccentricity, in being written mostly in the first person plural and entirely devoid of dialogue. Like Tyssot de Patot's works, it reflects an era in which interest in the reports brought back by voyagers to remote and still-unknown lands was shifting from a context of purely economical interests to a context of scientific interest in which exotic variations of natural history became a fascination in their own right.

To that fundamental shift of interest the author adds the remarkable narrative device of the journey from one pole of the Earth to the other via its center. All fantastic voyages are, in a technical sense, "portal fantasies" in which the narrative moves from the known to the unknown, transporting the narrative viewpoint from familiar to exotic surroundings, and many such fantasies introduce material portals in the interests of abridging the transition, but very few imagine such an extravagant portal as the one employed in this text. It was produced not long after the English astronomer Edmond Halley had published an article, in 1692, arguing that the Earth might well be hollow—a serious speculation based on an error in Isaac Newton's *Principia* (1687), which had miscalculated the relative densities of the Earth and the Moon. Halley was also attempting to account for variations in the Earth's magnetic field, by means of an internal body contained within the Earth's hollow interior, so his structure of cavities is much more complicated than the simple one imagined in *Relation d'un voyage du pôle arctique au pôle antarctique par le centre du monde*, but might nevertheless be considered an endorsement of sorts. At any rate, the idea cannot have appeared as absurd then as it does now, and does not disqualify the work from being considered as an early item of *roman scientifique*.

The change of perspective illustrated by *Relation d'un voyage du pôle arctique au pôle antarctique par le centre du monde* with regard to the essential interest of accounts of actual voyages was, of course, lavishly illustrated in the second half of 18th century by a considerable number of expeditions sent forth specifically to gather scientific information and to report on discoveries in a scrupulous scientific manner. The great exemplar was set in France by the expedition undertaken by Louis-Antoine de Bougainville, which set off in 1763 and returned to France, after circumnavigating the globe, in 1769, the report of which had a considerable influence on the French Encyclopedists, eager to incorporate its results into their project and to extrapolate its implications.

Bougainville's expedition and subsequent ones had a considerable impact of imaginative fiction across a broad spectrum, extending from the earnest to the satirical, enabled the development of utopian and philosophical fictions that would make the Cyranoesque extravagance of *La Nouvelle Lune* seem a trifle old-fashioned, and helped paved the way for a dramatic sophistication of the kind of roman scientifique sketched in a primitive fashion in *Relation d'un voyage du pôle arctique au pôle antarctique par le centre du monde.* Inevitably, however, the stylized mode of reportage of such expeditions became a topic for satirization itself, and the most extravagant and Cyranoesque of such satires was the remarkable *Voyage pittoresque et industriel dans le Paraguay-Roux et la Palingénesie australe, par Trédace-Nafé Théobrôme de Kaout't'tchouk, gentilhomme Breton, sous-aide à l'établissement des elyso-pompes, etc. etc. etc.* by the humorist Henri Delmotte, first published in 1835, ostensibly in Meschacébé [Mons, in Belgium] by Yreled-Sioyoh [Hoyois-Delery], here translated as "A Voyage to Paraguay-Roux."

The text in question was reprinted in 1841 in an omnibus of *Les Oeuvres facétieuses de Henri Delmotte* [The Facetious Works of Henri Delmotte], by which time it had acquired a wider, if slightly paradoxical, celebrity by virtue of a substantial review-article published in the *Revue de Paris* under the pseudonym Docteur Néophobus and subsequently reprinted under the name of its prestigious author, Charles Nodier. The celebrity won for the story by that article was "paradoxical" because Nodier somehow forgot to mention the author's name, with the result that many subsequent writers interested in the text referred to his paraphrase of the text rather than to the

11

original, so that Nodier effectively usurped much of the credit awarded by subsequent commentators to the quasi-futuristic sections of the text describing the technological innovations encountered in Polynesia on Civilization Island.

Seen in the original, as translated here, Delmotte's account is much more obviously a parody of scientific reportage than of utopian fantasy, but the description of Civilization Island remains by far the most interesting section for the modern reader. As in several other satirical works poking fun at euchronian dreams, the exaggeration inherent in the narrative method require a great imaginative reach than the objects of parody, and thus to bring them much closer to the actual extravagance of technological achievement since the early nineteenth century, which adds to the interest of the text. Part of the joke is the fact that the potentially-interesting locations mentioned in the title are not reached by the text itself— something that the modern reader will perhaps regret more than contemporary ones, for whom the whole endeavor was an exercise in calculated silliness. Indeed, as the name of the ship featured in the story implies, the story is a deliberate exercise in the production of nonsense, and modern readers— especially English readers—familiar with the works of Edward Lear and Lewis Carroll are more likely to be attuned the esthetics of calculated nonsense than Delmotte's contemporaries.

The text translated here as "The Aerial Journey" by Edmé Rousseau was originally published in Limoges by Barbou et cie—the publisher of all the author's works—in two small volumes, as *Le Songe, ou voyage aérien* [The Dream; or, Aerial Journey] (1864) and *La Rêve, ou Promenades dans les espaces imaginaires* [The Dream; or, Excursions in Imaginary Spaces] (1876). The Bibliothèque Nationale catalogue also lists a reprint of the former work issued in 1885, and it might be the case that there were other editions of either or both. The Bibliothèque Nationale refuses to identify their author with the artist Edmé Rousseau (1815-1868), who was best known as a miniaturist, presumably because the publication dates of the editions it possesses of the works credited in its catalogue to "*Edmé Rousseau, romancier*" are mostly later than that of the artist's death, but their publication pattern is strongly suggestive of some posthumous publication, and the two individuals might well be one; if not, nothing at all is known about the writer—and, indeed, very little is known about the artist, except that he worked for a while in America, although his works are nowadays very collectible.

The composition of the two texts, the first of which indicates that it was written in 1859, predates the boom in the popularization of science and its extension into works of fiction—including the first significant flowering of interplanetary fiction in France—that occurred in the 1860s. It is, therefore, not entirely surprising that it is primarily remarkable for its eccentricity. In fact, the episodic story told in the two texts fully justifies the original titles describing them as dreams; the visits to the various major and minor planets, especially the exceedingly strange "imaginary" planets featured in the latter half of the narrative, do indeed have something of the texture of dreams, and Freudians will have no difficulty finding material there for interpretation in accordance with Freud's theory of dreams as wish-fulfillments laden with sexual symbolism. Although the final section of the narrative clearly reflects the modifications to the city of Paris then being carried out under the aegis of Baron Haussmann, the translation of a similar project to an exotic other world and its concentration on the erection of a colossal symbolic column make it far stranger than any of the other utopian fantasies provoked by that endeavor.

As with Delmotte's story, Rousseau's must have seemed to contemporary eyes to be monumentally silly, without the saving grace of the silliness being entirely deliberate, but as with Delmotte's, the passage of time has lent it a slightly different gloss, and it can now be viewed as an exotic exercise in proto-surrealism. It is deliberately old-fashioned in using "*génies*" [genii, or perhaps genies in the sense of djinn] as a method of interplanetary travel, after the fashion of Voltaire

13

and Tiphaigne de la Roche a hundred years earlier, in addition to the second layer of apology provided by dreaming, but that does help to license a certain flamboyance that has something in common with the blithe extravagance of *La Nouvelle Lune*, which is interesting, and perhaps admirable in itself.

Rousseau's story remains highly original, in presenting an image of the solar system far more bizarre and complex than any other work of interplanetary fiction, refusing to be fettered by the inconvenient detail of astronomical observation. Like the other three stories in the present volume, it is unique, albeit within the framework provided by the rich tradition of fantastic voyages, and the four works provide a striking illustration the broadness of that spectrum by selecting from its most unusual extremes. If the first and fourth conspicuously lack the literary sophistication of the second and third, they do provide compensation in the matter of their sheer bizarrerie—the appreciation of which is, after all, one of the cardinal purposes of imaginary voyaging.

The translation of *La Nouvelle Lune* was made from the version of the Henry edition available on the world wide web via Google Books. The translation of *Relation d'un voyage du pôle arctique au pôle antarctique par le centre du monde* was made from the version reproduced in the 1990 Bouquins omnibus. The translation of the Delmotte story was made from the edition of *Les Oeuvres facétieuses de Henri Delmotte*, reproduced on the Bibliothèque Nationale's *gallica* website. The translation of the Rousseau composite was also made from the *gallica* versions of the Barbou volumes, that of *Le Songe* being the 1885 reprint and that of *La Rêve* being the 1876 original.

Brian Stableford

Anonymous: *A Journey from the Arctic pole to the Antarctic pole via the Center of the World*
(1721)

I

Having always had a very great passion for voyages in my youth, I have traveled, in order to content my curiosity, all the principal parts of the old and new worlds. At the end of my last journey I found myself in the great and famous city of Amsterdam, where I made the acquaintance of three or four prosperous businessmen, who told me that they were fitting out a vessel to send to Greenland to fish for whales. At that news, I felt my natural inclination reanimating, and I immediately conceived the design of making the voyage, having not yet seen the icy climates of the cold zones. I therefore began to purchase all that I thought necessary, and, having put my modest equipment in order, I embarked on the third of May in the year 1714.

We departed with a favorable wind, and had ideal weather for several days, but on the tenth, in the evening, the sky darkened and was covered in a short time by thick black clouds. The wind began to blow with such vehemence and impetuosity that the crew was alert all through the following night. That tempest carried us westwards with such rapidity, in spite of all our maneuvering, that in the morning, at about four o'clock, we found ourselves within sight of the coast of Iceland, from which we were only about three leagues distant.

The wind dropped then, and was succeeded by a twelve-hour calm, after which we resumed our route with a slight south-easterly wind. We sailed fortunately thus until the fourteenth, when we perceived two vessels that appeared to us to be coming from Greenland and heading for Holland. We were then at sixty-seven degrees seventeen minutes of latitude; but we soon lost sight of them because the weather suddenly changed and we saw a terrible storm forming to the east, which approached us in the space of a few minutes.

First, we were surrounded by an infinite number of lightning flashes, which were followed by frightful thunderclaps, and rain so heavy, so forceful and so long-lasting that the sky seemed to be menacing the earth with a second deluge. The obscurity was so great that we could not distinguish objects from the poop to the prow; the waves were so high, and the winds intersected so furiously, that our pilot, although very experienced, no longer had any idea what action to take.

Finally, after we had been within an inch of death for a long time, the horrible tempest began to dissipate; daylight reappeared and we found ourselves in an expanse of sea filled with large blocks of ice, which, as they collided with one another, caused us to fear being overturned or crushed. It was very cold, and we could see no coast or island in any direction. We had lost our route. Having taken a bearing we found that we were at seventy-six degrees twenty-two seconds.

A gentle south-westerly breeze was still pushing us northwards, and we eventually reached a place where the sea seemed to us to have a slight slope, and where a current seemed always to be drawing us, albeit quite slowly, in the direction of the pole. Then an old matelot told us that he had once been told by a famous pilot who had traveled a great deal in the northern seas that there is a frightful whirlpool at the North Pole, which can be seventy or eight leagues in circumference. He deemed it to be the most dangerous reef in the world, in the middle of which there had to be a frightful bottomless gulf, into which all the waters of the seas precipitated, communicating via the center of the world with the seas at the Antarctic Pole.

That story chilled us with fear, and made us shiver in every limb, for we saw that the watercourse was taking us along, and that it was impossible for us to turn back.

With that, we held council, and it was concluded that, although there was almost no likelihood of salvation for us, it was nevertheless necessary to take all imaginable precautions, and block the openings of the vessel in order to prevent any passage of water. We did that immediately, in haste and with incredible diligence.

After that, we went up on deck, in order to see collectively whether we could find any means of avoiding the frightful peril by which we were menaced. The sun was no longer setting then, and we saw it rotating around us perpetually on the edge of 'the horizon, but it was a trifle pale. To the west we perceived a rather long coast, which had three capes, of which the middle one advanced much further into the sea than the other two. We could see several high mountains there, completely covered in snow and ice; the passes between them all seemed to be on fire.

On the same coast, toward the right, we saw a large mass of clouds, almost green in color, mingled with a very dark gray, part of which descended so low as almost to touch the sea. An infinite number of birds emerged from it, flying toward us, whose number increased so prodigiously that all the air in the vicinity was obscured by them. A flock detached itself from the mass, passing immediately over our heads, attacking one another furiously, pecking one another cruelly, with the result that three of them fell dead at our feet. Their plumage was very black and their break as red as blood; from the head to the extremity of the tail they had a stripe as white as snow. However, we soon lost sight of all the birds. One might perhaps wonder how they are able to cross those vast seas, but it is presumed that they rest from time to time on the large blocks of ice that one finds in various places in the northern seas.

Meanwhile, we were following the penchant of the waters, in spite of ourselves, until our vessel made a sudden turn to the left, and then we began to sail in a circle. That circumstance told us that we had entered the whirlpool. The rotating sea was swarming with an incalculable number of small fish, about the same size as a herring. From the middle of the body to the tip of the tail they are a beautiful golden color; as they almost always swim close to the surface, head down, and when the sun is reflected from all those tails, which are entirely out of the water, the whirlpool resembles a watery sky covered with an infinite number of golden stars, which are in perpetual movement. An object of that nature would doubtless have charmed people able to contemplate it with a tranquil gaze.

After having made several circuits, we perceived in the middle of the whirlpool a kind of floating island whiter than snow. However, as our circular movement was bringing us ever closer to the center, we realized that the supposed island was nothing but foam, which formed at the surface of the waters, as they precipitated into and were engulfed by the abyss.

We judged then that it was time to retire inside the vessel, which we did immediately, all descending into the depths of the hull to wait there for whatever heaven had ordained for us.

II

We had only been enclosed for ten or twelve minutes when we felt ourselves sinking into that profound abyss with an inconceivable rapidity. The horrible whistling and buzzing that we heard around us incessantly, importing terror into our souls, gradually sapped our confidence, and we fell into a kind of faint, which left us in no state to measure the time that we remained within the frightful torrents that flow so impetuously through those frightful subterrains.

We awoke, however, from the torpor into which we had plunged, and, without knowing as yet whether we were alive or dead, we soon came round. Straining our ears, we could no longer hear anything. It seemed to us that our vessel was almost motionless. Our pilot, the boldest of us all, decided to go up on to the deck; he opened the poop hatch and went up.

One by one, we followed him, and we saw, with the utmost surprise, that we were on a calm sea, surrounded by a mist so dense that it was impossible to discern any object round us. The mist and the sea were the same color, with the consequence that our vessel seemed to be suspended in midair. Gradually, however, the atmosphere cleared, and daylight appeared, almost as it is in our climes about half an hour after sunset.

It is easy to imagine the joy by which we were all penetrated, after having thought that we were doomed without resource, on seeing that we could still hope to return to our fatherland.

However, we did not know where we were. Our pilot having taken a bearing, we found that we were at seventy-one degrees eight minutes of south latitude,[5] which informed us that we were in the southern seas, near the Antarctic Pole.

For the moment, there was not the slightest wind. We occupied ourselves in repairing, as best we could, all our rigging and all of our sails. We still had provisions aboard the vessel for some time.

After some four or five hours, a slight north-westerly wind rose, but so terribly cold that the sea was entirely frozen in the space of a few minutes. I can say that I have never felt a cold so penetrating, and I doubt that we would have been able to resist it if it had continued for long. Fortunately, a gentle rain soon began to fall, which caused us to pass in a few minutes from the harshest winter to spring. Sage providence, in order to substitute for the lack of sunlight, which is absent

---

[5] In 1720 the privateer George Shelvocke set a new record in reaching a south latitude slightly in excess of sixty degrees, but that information was not publicized in Europe until two years later, so it would not have been known to the author of the present story; it was not until 1774 that James Cook first reached seventy degrees, so the imaginary territories features in the story are located in a region that was entirely unknown at the time, and remained so for more than half a century..

for so long from those dismal climes, tempers their extreme cold with warm exhalations, which conserve even in winter the grass, the plants and the bushes that one sees there.

We sailed under full sail toward a broad coast that we perceived to the east, in the hope of being able to land some-where along it. At one of its extremities, which advanced to-ward the Antarctic Pole, there was a light reminiscent of the dawn, but we knew that it was not the forerunner of the sun, since several months would pass before it reappeared in those regions. We were no longer able to make a distinction between day and night, morning and evening. Even so, the light was bright enough to prevent us from seeing the stars. Luminous exhalations rise into the air during the absence of the sun; oth-erwise the two cold zones would be buried alternately, for six months, in frightful night.

As we were sailing slowly toward that coast, we saw in four or five places, about the range of a musket-shot apart, accumulations of seething foam that rose up impetuously to a height, forming something akin to small hills on the surface of the sea. Those broths of water and foam had sufficient force for our ship, passing close to one of them, almost to be cap-sized. We were never able to understand what they might be, but we saw many others thereafter.

The light that I have just mentioned having gradually dissipated the clouds that hid it from us, it brightened sudden-ly, with such visual force that it threw us into admiration. It was a marvelous meteor,[6] which formed a perfect oval of very dark blue, which was speckled with stars; the one in the mid-dle, which was the largest, appeared dominant over all the others. That admirable phenomenon augmented the light by half on the coast, so that we were able to see all the objects distinctly, as we were already very close. Having finally reached it, as we had the design of going ashore, we dropped anchor.

---

[6] In 1721 the term *"météor"* [meteor] signified a bright atmos-pheric phenomenon, not a spacefaring lump of rock.

III

At the place where we moored, the coast was entirely bordered by tall reeds, which appeared to extend out of the water to the height of a pike, at least as stout as an arm, terminating in exceedingly sharp points. They had nodules at intervals, beneath which hung large yellow leaves, as broad as a large hand-span and about as long as a Dutch yard. We lowered the launch into the water in order to go ashore, but we had a great deal of difficulty passing through the reeds, because they were very densely packed. We all took firearms, as much to defend ourselves against wild beasts as to kill any game that we might encounter.

After having climbed up, for the terrain was steep, we found a beautiful plain covered with thin, short grass that exhaled a pleasant odor. It was limited by three broad chains of mountains, which extended as far as the eye could see to the left and right. Those mountains appeared to us to be arranged like an amphitheater, the second range being higher than the first and the third much higher than the second. The first range—which is to say, the closest to us—was really only a series of large hills, entirely clad in green moss; the mountains of the second range were covered in snow, and those of the third appeared in the distance to be flame-red, which produced one of the most beautiful views imaginable.

When we had traversed the plain and reached the foot of the hills we pushed on forward, and saw that in that area they formed a great ring or enclosure a full league in diameter, full of grass so long that if the tallest man in our party had gone into it, we would scarcely have been able to perceive the top of his head.

We observed that all around that enclosure there were large holes or dens in the hills, which we judged to be the retreat of some sort of wild beasts—and, indeed, a few minutes later, we saw three white bears of prodigious size emerge from the long grass two hundred paces away from us. Without turn-

21

ing to one side or the other they went into the lair in front of them.

We did not think it appropriate, after that, to stay in a place that seemed so perilous. We immediately left and, still heading toward the mountains, found a little stream of clear fresh water, on the banks of which we saw a large number of birds walking, about the size of quails, so unintimidated that they allowed themselves to be picked up. We killed a few of them and sent them back aboard.

As we followed the stream it led us gradually between two high, steep rocks, covered in ice from top to bottom.

We were very surprised to feel an intense cold there, and could not understand how, having emerged from very mild air that as almost warm, that which we had just entered could be so harsh. We were then waking on exceedingly hard snow, and our little stream had entirely frozen over in that pass. The mountain to our right received on its icy surface all the light of the meteor that I have mentioned, and reflected it on to the opposite mountain, both of them shining in such a fashion that our eyes were dazzled by them, and we had difficulty seeing what was in front of us.

As soon as we had emerged from between those mountains, we felt a mild and temperate atmosphere, and the stream flowed and snaked as it had on the other side. Two hundred paces further on we saw it disappear into the ground facing a rock that had the shape of a stout round tower.

Nature had hollowed out a kind of grotto there, which had three openings arranged vertically, in the form of arcades, in the middle of which and within which we could see a large pool into which we saw that the stream ran by way of a subterranean channel. There were several niches in the grotto in which we found birds' nests. In some of them the eggs were a very pale green, three times as large as the eggs of our ducks. The top of the rock was flattened in the form of a terrace, covered with a herb very similar to our purslane but much larger, the leaves being very broad and about the thickness of a little finger, and the stems so long that some hung down all the way to the bottom.

After having admired that work of nature, we judged it appropriate not to push on any further forward for the time being, and we headed back toward our vessel, but not by exactly the same route. We deviated a little to the left, and after we had been walking for some time our ears were suddenly struck by a bellowing and horrible howling that were coming from the same direction in which we had seen the three white bears. The air around us was resounding with it in such a way that we thought there must be a large number of the ferocious animals in that place.

We arrived gradually on a rough and stony terrain that led us toward a mass of large, densely aggregated rocks. They had red, green and blue veins similar to marble. As we could see a kind of marsh to the right and left we were obliged to pass through them; we found various routes that intersected with one another as in a maze, with the result that we went astray for some time, but one of us finally found the exit and we emerged from it.

Scarcely had we taken four steps when a monstrous beast launched itself toward us from behind a small rock. It had the shape and the color of a toad, but was infinitely larger; it had a large crest on its head of a vile pale blue, and dripped yellow and green foam from its mouth from time to time. It turned in the direction of the marsh, threw itself in to it with a single leap and dived, with the result that we did not see it again. We had no doubt that there were many others of the same species in the locality, and that the animals were very venomous.

We continued walking, with considerable difficulty, along the stony path, until we reached the beautiful plain where we had come ashore, and returned to the ship gladly, where we cooked the birds we had killed. The flesh was very tough, but tasted quite good, not unlike that of a duck.

We formed the design of making a second excursion soon, in order to capture more of those birds and any other species we could find, in order to conserve our supplies of biscuit and other provisions that would keep. We then saw, with chagrin, the beautiful meteor that had appeared when we arrived on the coast fade away.

Afterwards, there was a shower of rain mingled with snow and large hailstones, which lasted for more than fifteen hours. We were then measuring time by means of a sand-glass that we were fortunate to find aboard the ship. The air became so cold that it was impossible for us to remain on deck even for half an hour, but, when the rain had stopped, the air became so mild that we seemed to be breathing an autumnal air as in temperate climes.

Another phenomenon was manifest in the west, which was not nearly as bright as the first, but was nevertheless very beautiful. It formed an irregular zigzag, and closely resembled a constellation. In its lower reaches it had a kind of tail that was very broad at its extremity.

It is necessary to remark that since we had anchored, our view had always been limited to the south—which is to say, in the direction of the Antarctic Pole—by large thick clouds, which were finally dissipated by one of the beautiful luminous exhalations so frequent around the poles, with the consequence that we suddenly discovered a island, which appeared to us to be floating on the surface of the water, and which we did indeed see approaching us, to within the range of a cannon-shot.

The island was almost round, and was undoubtedly nothing more than an assemblage of the large pieces of ice that one sees in those seas, which had joined up and been frozen together. In the middle of it was a mountain of ice that rose up to a great height in the shape of a pyramid. The pieces that formed it were, by virtue of a surprising artifice, disposed in such a manner that they appeared to be cut into facets like a diamond, with the difference that the facets were proportionate to its size. The island was entirely covered in snow, and one could see on its shores, at intervals, something akin to little trees of ice that put forth branches laden with snowflakes, which took the place of leaves and fruits. On the mountain, however, there was no trace of snow; all of its ice was as clear and transparent as crystal.

We considered all these things for some time, and then went to bed. After sleeping for several hours, wanting to go up on deck, we were alarmed to see the entire atmosphere ablaze. Having looked in the direction of the island, however, we realized that the great illumination in question proceeded from six marvelous meteors suspended in the air, at almost equal distances, all around the mountain, like so many large and magnificent chandeliers. They were all the same in form, each composed of four large globes of fire; the one at the bottom was the largest, the second, third and fourth diminishing by degrees. All those luminous globes were multiplied infinitely by the facets of the mountain, making it appear that fire was everywhere.

All these great and surprising objects had a collective effect by which the eyes were delighted and enchanted, with the result that, struck by admiration and astonishment, we stood as motionless as statues for several minutes.

While we were still contemplating them attentively, we perceived three huge birds high in the sky, which suddenly plunged straight toward the nearby coast. Their plumage was a mixture of gray and brown; on the head of each one there was a large plume of three snow-white feathers, whose extremities were a beautiful incarnadine hue, and their tails, longer than their bodies, resembled half-open fans. They were larger and heavier than eagles. After they had pecked and rummaged in the grass for some time, all three of them took off again and flew rapidly toward the mountain of ice. Having fluttered around it for some time, they flew over the summit, and we lost sight of them. We thought that they probably had nests there. They were very beautiful birds.

IV

While we were sleeping soundly, we were woken up by an impetuous wind, which shook the vessel so much that, for fear that our cable would break, we raised anchor as quickly as possible. We could no longer see the floating island and the beautiful phenomena surrounding it. The sea was very heavy and full of large blocks of ice, which, heaped up on top of one another, formed small floating mountains here and there.

When the weather was better, which was not long delayed, we resolved to make the second overland excursion that we had planned.

Having left two or three men aboard, we took our weapons and set off, taking a different path than the one we had followed the first time. It is necessary to remark that in that direction the coast is very mountainous, but we found a number of little plains and valleys.

At first we were marching through dry and arid rocks, where there was neither grass nor moss; there were frightful precipices there, at the bottom of which gross torrents flowed with a frightful noise. We were obliged to pass along narrow and dangerous ledges. Fortunately, however, we eventually emerged from that region, into which we had moved gradually, and climbed on to a high mountain from which we could gaze in all directions.

We saw summer and winter there at the same time; on the one hand there were plains where everything was frozen and covered in snow; on the other, there were valleys where a cheerful vegetation reigned throughout. The air was so clear and so luminous that, without the aid of the sun, we could easily make out the smallest objects.

We went down there, and found those places carpeted with short slender grass Plants could be seen here and there which put out long serrated leaves. We pulled up a few of them, the roots of which were round and flat, almost as thick as a fist, covered with a very thin black skin. The flesh was white with a hint of red, and had a taste reminiscent of almond. We subsequently found many of them on the coast in the vicinity of the place where we had dropped anchor, and we ate them instead of bread.

The place seemed so agreeable to us that we stayed there for some time. We went on from there between two long mountain chains covered in moss from the foot to the summit, which distilled a kind of odorous gum. The double chain was not straight, but followed a large curve that limited our view, but when we reached the end we suddenly discovered a lake, the waters of which were green and almost warm. An infinite number of wisps of black vapor were exhaled over its entire surface. We thought, with reason, that the heat and the vapors were produce by sulfurized and bituminous substances that must be in its depths. No plants grew on its banks.

After having skirted it for some time, we heard a murmurous noise that was augmented as we advanced. Eventually, we perceived that the extremity of the lake was bordered with little rocks, between which the water, running over the edge, caused the noise that we could hear. We increased our pace, and were surprised to see five beautiful waterfalls, of which the middle one was the largest. It formed three great sheets of water, which fell together on to three almost equidistant steps. The water of all the cascades was gathered together a little lower down, falling on to a great rock that was almost flat, and, precipitating from there, was lost among the rocks below.

It had to be the case, necessarily, that since the lake remained full, although its waters were incessantly flowing away in that direction in such abundance, that there were subterranean channels that furnished it with more, in perpetuity.

As we were reasoning in that fashion, a troop of large and powerful snow-white bears appeared on a hill directly in front of us. We noted that the two or three of them had black patches all over their bodies. One of them came down the hill. Having passed over a little stream at the bottom it slipped between two rocks. Scarcely had it done so than it uttered a certain cry, as if appealing to the others, and, indeed, they all started to follow it, jostling one another in their haste.

We had no sooner lost sight of them than we saw several birds emerge from the midst of the same rocks, soon followed by a greater number, which all took flight toward the high snow-capped mountains to our right. The birds apparently had their nests in the fissures and crevices where they could be seen, but in places so high and steep that it was impossible to reach them.

As we drew away from the five admirable cascades, we descended, with a great deal of difficulty, a mountain whose slope was very steep, into a long and narrow plain, pierced almost everywhere with little holes than spiraled quite deeply into the ground; there had to be an infinite number of animals in that place of a species doubtless unknown to us, but we did not see a single one of them appear. As we walked between the holes we could hear a certain sound, as if there were caves down below, or vaults.

When we reached the end of the plain we came to a kind of great crossroads, where there were five different routes disposed in a star. We hesitated for some time over the choice of which to follow. One extended between two mountains so prodigiously high that they were almost frightening. It entered beneath a broad and high portal, whose structure was a single large piece of rick that, having been detached from higher up one of the slopes, had fallen sideways on to the other and remained suspended here, perhaps for a very long time. That route was sandy; our feet sank into it almost ankle-deep.

We took another, which was much more comfortable. The mountains bordering it were an almost-black rock with broad white and shiny veins, somewhat reminiscent of alum. There we found a very large quantity of a kind of lizard. They were so tame that they were continually running between our legs and over our feet. They had perfectly black heads, reddish bodies and extraordinarily long tongues.

The further we went along that path the broader it became. It finally led us into a very beautiful and spacious valley, where we were able to respire a spring-like air. It was covered with plants very similar to violets; on the majority of them, in the middle of the stem, there was a white flower the size of a ducat coin. That flower had eight dentellate petals, four larger ones underneath and four smaller ones above; the middle was garnished with little bright red seeds. It bore some resemblance to a simple rose, and had a very pleasant odor. The enamel of those flowers, with the green of their stems, had a charming collective effect throughout the valley. A little stream of exceedingly clear water snaked through the middle.

At the extremity of a dip, we perceived something white through the tall herbs. We went closer, and saw, to our great surprise, a small edifice of a singular structure. It was made entirely of white stone; its top was a single large flat stone, triangular in shape, posed on six columns about three feet high, on an oval base that rose some four or five inches above the ground. On the triangular stone an inscription was visible, in bizarre characters, which were unfamiliar to any member of our troop. At the bottom, around the circumference of the base, similar characters appeared at intervals, but almost effaced.

That monument gave rise to an infinite number of conjectures on our part, for we could see very clearly that it was not a work of hazard, but I shall leave the decision to cleverer men than me.

Having left that place, we marched alongside the stream that I have just mentioned, following it toward its source. It emerged from a beautiful spring that was in a grotto hollowed out by nature in one of the slopes of the valley. I was the first to go into it; it was covered with a lovely carpet of moss from top to bottom; at the back, at a man's height, three conduits could be seen in the same line, at equal distances. The water, in running from those conduits, made a pleasant murmur reminiscent of the chirping of birds, and fell into a kind of basin, which was full to the brim and overflowed over the edge, uniting in a large crevice in the rock immediately underneath and flowing away.

The basin was about a foot deep; there were several small flat red stones at the bottom, variously shaped as squares, circles, triangles and hearts. Wanting to take some of them out, I could hardly bear the excessive chill of the spring water. Inside the grotto there was a round and very deep hole about a hand-span broad, which exhaled a vapor so hot that I thought it might burn my face. It was not without an extreme astonishment that I saw cold and heat emerging simultaneously, almost in the same place.

In several places in that valley there were various beautiful and very singular bushes, among them one that shed its leaves in three stages, some distance apart. They were all covered in a kind of down that rendered them as soft as velvet to the touch, and edged all around with the most beautiful yellow color in the world. Above the leaves, at the exact place where they were attached to the trunk, one could see little red seeds the size of a pea emerging at the end of long stalks, which formed a perfect circle; and at the top, they bore a bouquet of the same seeds, very densely packed, in a form similar to that of a pine cone.

V

We saw nothing worthy of note on the route we took to return to the ship. We found a large quantity of birds among the rocks, which almost allowed themselves to be taken in hand, and we took away as many of them as we could.

As the coast were we were anchored was exposed to great tempests and very impetuous winds, we feared that if we stayed there any longer we might be broken against the rocks at any moment. Animated by the desire to make further discoveries, we resolved to depart as soon as possible. We laid in a large provision of the roots I have mentioned, of which there were prodigious quantities in the vicinity, and having raised anchor, with a light south-easterly breeze, we headed westwards, because we thought we had seen some islands in that direction when the air was clear and calm.

After having sailed comfortably enough for twenty-four hours we found ourselves between several dangerous reefs; there were numerous rocks at surface level, but as the wind had almost dropped and we were moving very slowly, we avoided them without overmuch difficulty. There was one rock that rose above the water to a height of about four feet, on the tip of which we saw a large bird with black plumage, fairly similar to a swan. It was perched on one leg, making a fan of its tail like a peacock. It seemed as motionless as a statue on a pedestal. We fired several shots at it without hitting it, although it did not make the slightest movement. The bird must have been transported there by a block of ice, and as waiting for another to pass by in order to return.

Some time after that, the wind having dropped entirely, we were surrounded by a fog so thick that it was utterly dark, which obliged us to drop anchor. The fog was almost hot. I had always believed previously that these climes were uninhabitable because of the great rigor of the cold, but although it makes itself felt excessively, there are frequent intervals when the air becomes milder, and where it is perfectly tolerable.

We remained in darkness for more than twelve hours, after which the weather cleared. The wind began to blow again, carrying us westwards as before. We found that we were then at sixty-seven degrees six minutes of south latitude.

At that level there is a vast number of large flying fish with four wings. The two nearer to the head are very large, similar to the wings of bats; the two nearer to the tail were only half the size. Three of those fish came close to our vessel, leaping and plunging incessantly; they far exceed the girth and length of the most powerful oxen, but soar to a considerable height nevertheless and often remain in the air for a full minute before diving. They are exceedingly greedy and voracious; while flying they always keep their mouths open, in which two rows of short but exceedingly sharp teeth can be seen.

Two of our matelots were sitting next to one another on the poop deck when one of the three monsters, suddenly launching itself to a great height, seized them both from behind and knocked them into the sea. The one who fell first was torn apart and devoured. The second swam around the ship, and we were on the point of throwing him a rope when he was assailed by the other two; one took him by the head, the other by the feet, and, each tugging in its own direction with extreme fury, soon separated that wretched body, whose entrails and blood made a long streak in the sea.

That tragic adventure caused us all a very sensible affliction, all the more so because the men were two of our best sailors.

After those cruel animals had followed us for another half an hour, we lost sight of them. Shortly afterwards there was a great tempest, which kept us alert for more than six hours. As it bore us westwards, however, we discovered four islands, and shortly afterwards three more; all seven were in a line, only short distances away from one another. We immediately decided to land, but it was impossible for us to carry out our plan, for the environs of all the island were replete with sandbanks and closely-packed rocks, full of currents intersecting in all directions, rendering that sea, in the judgment of our pilot, the most dangerous he had ever seen.

We dropped anchor at the point of a huge sandbank facing us, in order to have time to work out what route to follow. Meanwhile, we considered the islands precisely. They were full of small hillocks which appeared at a distance to be vermilion red, and some of them gleamed like rubies. We attributed the cause to some very hot air that was then in the vicinity.

On the eastern side of the fifth island, which was the largest, we saw a cylindrical rock that rose up to a considerable height in a straight line, which, being equal in girth at the bottom and he top, resembled a beautiful column. A little further on there were stout and tall rocks packed closely together, perfectly representing the buildings of a magnificent château. At one of its extremities there was something like a large round tower, from which a thick black vapor was gushing, with rose so high and with such rapidity into the air that it seemed to unite with the clouds, forming a common body with them.

I picked up my binoculars then and discovered large sparks in that thick smoke, similar to stars, which were in perpetual motion. A few moments later I saw torrents of flame emerge from the rock, which, like an impetuous wind, expanded broadly, causing us a general fright. I do not believe that Mount Etna in Sicily or Mount Vesuvius in Italy have ever vomited such terrible ones. Those frightful flames, having endured for some three minutes, vanished, leaving nothing behind but a few sparks ad a light smoke.

We had not been there for twenty-four hours when we perceived that the sea surrounding the islands was freezing. Although we could not feel the slightest chill in the place where we were, we resolved to take to the open sea, and to give the dangerous reefs in the vicinity a wider berth, until we could continue our westward voyage more safely. We came about successfully thanks to a favorable wind, and finally came into deeper water, where we began to see large fragments of ice floating.

VI

In less than two hours the sea was completely covered with icebergs, and we had to maneuver continually in order to avoid them. There was one that came within five or six musket-shots of us, of a grandeur so enormous that it resembled a small island, and which broke into pieces, making more noise than a battery of several cannons all firing at the same time. The blocks of floating ice gradually diminished in number, however, and we eventually found ourselves completely free of them.

A short time later we were surprised by a calm that lasted for fifteen hours; then entire surface of the sea was as smooth as a looking-glass.

A good league from the place where we were constrained to wait for the wind there was a large rock with three points, which we went to reconnoiter in the launch. It was surrounded by a small strip of land ten or twelve feet wide, bordered along the water's edge by tall plants and covered all the way to the foot of the mountain with shellfish, along which we found a large quantity of small oysters, the shells of which were very black. We opened a few of them, and found the taste excellent, which led us to take aboard as many as possible. We were curious enough to climb to the top of the rock; its summit was a kind of platform between the three points, on which we saw several feathers scattered here and there. We discovered a few nests in holes, which were entanglements of moss, grass and feathers. There were two eggs in each one, as white but much larger than hen's eggs. The albumen was pale green and the yolk red-black; but for a certain bitterness that they left in the throat they would have been good enough to eat.

It was not long after we had returned to the ship that the wind began to get up again; we took advantage of it at first, but after a few hours it increased in such a fashion that we feared a rude tempest. It was the same wind that we had encountered previously. We got out of it with a fright. We sailed for a while with so much rapidity that we made a great deal of progress in an hour. On directing the binoculars at the horizon we saw a large dense cloud in the west that seemed to be touching the sea, but when we came closer we discovered a cape, whose cliffs were very high, above which there were thick clouds as far as the eye could see. As we intended, before returning to the old world, to make a few further discoveries, we went to drop anchor in the most convenient place for reaching the land.

There was a gentle slope that we climbed easily; having reached the top we found a large quantity of pebbles and small stones. The whole terrain was sandy and stony, and we were unable to see very far because at that extremity of the cape the land rose up gradually. When we had arrived at a greater height, we discovered great plains extending to the limit of vision, interrupted by several small lakes, bordered in the distance by high mountains covered with snow and very transparent.

Quite close to us, and directly ahead of us, there were two small hills, behind which we could see a jet of water leaping into the sky like huge column, crowned with thick foam, falling back in an infinity of little streams, soon reduced into a dense watery dust. From where we were standing, we could not see where it was coming from; that is why, hastening our steps, we advanced beyond the hills. Three jets of water were then presented to our eyes, emerging from these little rocks disposed in a triangle in the middle of a large mass of boulders and pebbles.

The largest, which was the one we had seen first, rose in the air to a height of about two hundred feet, but the two smaller once scarcely surpassed seven or eight; their water, in falling to the ground, formed a small stream, which, after having snaked for nine hundred or a thousand paces, emptied into one of the lakes I mentioned. The water therein was very clear and quite drinkable. The air was temperate, the intense cold must be felt even later in this region.

It ought to be noted that the lakes were all connected by streams that flowed from one to another; in consequence, we could only advance through the country by making long detours. That is why we left them to one side and veered a little to the right. Everything there was, to begin with, so dry and arid that no grass or bushes grew there.

A great wind from the land then began to blow with such violence, raising up so much sand and dust, that we were constrained to stop from time to time and close our eyes, for fear of being blinded. Fortunately, that soon passed, and we went into a dip where the terrain was very black, covered everywhere by a little thin plant with nodes like canes. It grew by creeping for some distance along the ground and throwing into space a little bouquet of beautiful yellow seeds. That plant was very pretty.

After having taken five or six steps there, we heard a noise like that of a waterfall, and, in fact, we soon saw an abundant torrent emerging from between two high rocks, and then forming a rivulet that flowed with great rapidity, drawing with it a large quantity of stones and pebbles. As we were wondering how to get past it, we perceived a descending path beside a small rise, at the bottom of which there was a kind of thicket of little bushes, tightly aggregated and armed with thorns, with little red leaves. It was partly covering the entrance to a cave.

We hesitated for some time, not daring at first to risk ourselves in a place that might be fatal to us, but two of the boldest of us went in, and we all followed. After having walked for a while in darkness, we suddenly discovered a large and spacious subterrain, divided into various sections with vaults of different heights, all carved out by nature in the rock. Some were high and vaster than those of large churches. Large rocks disposed at unequal distances sustained those heavy and enormous masses of stone. Light entered from above through a large number of openings, some of which were long, like fissures or crevices, and others round or square, from which long-stemmed plants hung down, with leaves as large as fig-leaves. It was apparent that the warm air within the cave contributed greatly to their growth.

The highest and broadest of all those vaults was patterned from top to bottom in black and white. The black patches were much larger than the white ones, but the white ones shone like crystal, and as there was a large round opening at the top, the effect was charming. The terrain was almost flat everywhere except at one of the extremities, where it sloped upwards gradually. We saw an incalculable number of white birds there, like swans but no bigger than sparrows. They thought so little of fleeing or taking flight that they almost let us walk over them. We took as many as we wanted; they were only little balls of fat, but very delicate to eat.

When we reached the end, we found an issue that led into open country. Down below, in a very dark corner, we saw a large round hole reminiscent of a well. We threw a number of large stones into it, which, after having fallen, made no sound. That surprised us. A few moments later, a large black bird suddenly emerged, which, when it extended its wings, frightened us by virtue of their extent. As it emerged from the cavern it emitted three loud cries, with which all the vaults reverberated; it was carrying something long and thick in its beak, but it did not give us time to discern what it might be. The well must have been prodigiously deep and there must have been holes within it, where the bird probably had its nest, or where it found something for its subsistence.

We soon emerged after it, but we had a great deal of difficulty climbing up because the slope was very steep and littered with large pebbles and sharp stones. When we reached the top, we saw that we were beyond the torrent, because it passed over the cavern exactly in the middle.

We were only a quarter of a league from the cavern when we saw two white bears emerge from between two beautiful hills, as green as meadows from top to bottom, whose summits were covered with the thorny bushes with little red leaves that I have mentioned. They went into a narrow path full of sand, along a hillside, which went directly to the sea. At times they dug in the ground with their muzzles, apparently searching for roots. We followed them at a distance, always having our weapons ready in case of necessity, although we had observed several times that they were not inclined to attack humans.

We soon came within sight of the sea. The coast, at that location, formed a little gulf, and the shore seemed to be completely covered by shellfish. By the water's edge we saw three sea-cows asleep on the sand, one of them lying half in the water and half on land. The bears, however, which had made a slight detour, gradually arrived in that place, still digging with their muzzles between the shellfish. They did not seem to be looking ahead of them, but the larger one suddenly found itself next to one of the sea-cows. It attacked it at the level of the neck, and the first bite caused blood to spurt all the way to the ground.

Waking with a start the animal shook itself so violently that it freed itself, and with the large fangs that it had in its lower jaw it pierced the belly of the bear, which, utterly furious, bit it and tore it cruelly wherever it could reach it. The other two came to its aid and the combat between the five animals became general. The first of the sea-cows, however, lost so much blood that it retreated into the sea, and the others immediately followed it, leaving the battlefield and the honor of the victory to the two bears.

There were a great many sea-cows in that region. I saw some that were eight feet long, with a girth in proportion. They are amphibious, and striped like tigers in black, white, yellow gray and red. Their skin is covered with short hair; they have very large heads, four feet with five undivided claws like the feet of a goose, connected by black skin. Their tail is very short; they take great pleasure in lying on the sand on the edge of the sea.

We left the two bears there, digging among the shellfish, and followed the shore, going around the coast to where we had left our boat. When we set foot on the hill that formed the tip of the cape I was very surprised to find the ground very wet, while that we were leaving was quite dry. The cloud that covered it, which had covered it throughout the time we remained there, distilled from time to time a coarse dew similar to a thin drizzle, while the air in the surrounding area remained clear and serene.

I have never been able to understand what might have caused that. It must be the case that there is an occult and attractive virtue in the land, which always retains that gross exhalation above it, in spite of the greatest winds.

VII

After having visited a part of the cape, we wanted to penetrate into the continent, but we did not think it wise to risk ourselves for too long in the mountains of an unknown country whose only inhabitants were wild beasts and a few birds. That is why we resolved to go by sea. To that effect we re-embarked, and with the aid of a slight easterly wind we went along the western coast of the cape. After five or six hours we found so many blocks of ice around us that we feared being constrained to drop anchor, but the wind had doubled in strength and was driving us westwards, so continued our route. We were obliged to veer to the right however, because of a large number of reefs and sandbanks along the cape.

We sailed fortunately enough for forty-eight hours, after which we began to discover a great gulf that entered into the land via a narrow strait about a quarter of a league wide. I named it Bear Strait, because we saw a large number of them.

Something happened at that moment that truck us by its singularity. It is necessary to know that there is a current in that strait flowing from one shore to the other. Twenty or twenty-five of the bears were standing at the water's edge, seemingly waiting for the passage of a large block of ice that could be seen approaching some distance away. Hazard having dictated that as it floated it drew closer to them, they all leapt on to it with incredible speed, and, the current having carried them to the other shore, they immediately leapt on to the land with the same agility. That manner of passing over the water clearly demonstrates considerable intelligence and reasoning in those animals, in spite of the opinion of certain philosophers.

We went fairly deeply into the gulf and anchored, in spite of the presence of the bears, in a place where there were four large blocks of ice that the waves of the sea had carried on to the coast and heaped up there. Everything that we could see around us was covered in snow. About a league away there was a chain of closely-packed mountains, which enclosed a small lake within a ring. On its eastern side, several pieces of rock having been detached over time from below, they had left a broad opening in the form of an arcade, through which the waters of the lake flowed out into the neighboring countryside. The consequence of that arrangement was that it gave the impression of a single-span bridge, all the more so as the rock that remained was flat and even on top. I was curious enough to climb up there. Nothing was lacking to make it a veritable bridge but a guard-rail.

There was an excessive cold then, accompanied from time to time by snow as fine as dust; in consequence, the air was somber and obscure. Afterwards, however, it became clear and very mild; a beautiful luminous exhalation rose in the south, similar to a brilliant aurora, and the cold diminished to such an extent that melting snow flowed down from the mountains. At that point we saw a pretty river form, bordered on either side by reeds similar to bulrushes, which, after having snaked in several twists and turns into the country, came to empty into the gulf a short distance away from us. Having gone up toward its source, we perceived that it was falling from the heights of a broad mountain with a narrow flat top

As the slope was gentle, I soon climbed it, and I found a small lake on its summit, from which the river emerged; it might have been a hundred feet in diameter. Its eastern part was covered in thin ice, and, for all its smallness, it appeared to be extremely deep; its water as fresh and clear. All that would have been ample material for consideration and reasoning for people versed in the science of natural things.

That mountain closed a narrow valley between two ranges of hills, which was covered all the way to the bottom in short and slender vegetation. It ended in a kind of long, broad esplanade of living rock, the edge of which immediately offered the view of a frightful precipice. There was nothing around it but high and rugged rocks, at the bottom of which torrents flowed impetuously into holes and crevices, after having crossed one another's courses, all joining up to precipitate into depths whose immensity chilled one with fear. I can say that the mere thought of it still makes me shiver, and I do not believe that there is a similar precipice in the entire world.

As the terrain in that direction was nothing but rocks, so far as we could tell, we turned to the right—which is to say, toward the gulf. There was nothing there but stones and sand, intercut everywhere by an infinite quantity of little streams very difficult to cross. Finally, however, after a great deal of difficulty, we reached the top of a long, smooth downward slope that took us all the way to the sea. Having reached the bottom, we sat down to rest on the small rocks along the shore.

Half a cannon-shot out to sea from that point, there was a squat mountain of rock, around which there as a thick fog. We had scarcely been resting there for a quarter of an hour when a loud noise like a subterranean wind struck our ears, which seemed to be coming from that mountain. It lasted for about two minutes and then suddenly ceased.

A quarter of an hour later, however, the mountain began to throw off an infinity of little fireballs in all directions, about three feet above the water level. After having spun through the air impetuously, they vanished, as lightning does. A few moments later, a furious din was heard, with redoubled amplitude. Like great claps of thunder.

We saw and heard the same thing four times in succession in the space of little more than an hour. We noticed that the mountain did not emit any smoke, either from the summit or any other place. The fog surrounding it having completely dissipated thereafter, all the air in the vicinity resumed its original serenity.

VIII

As I had seen, by means of my binoculars, that the terrain to the other side of the gulf was much less mountainous and more beautiful, I persuaded some of my companions to make a few excursions with me in that direction, which we did soon afterwards.

At first we found a rather flat and even ground, but stony, and it seemed to me that one would have been able to obtain stones therefrom very appropriate for building. I even saw large holes from time to time that were almost filled in, which might have been taken for quarries.

In front of us there was a large hill that limited our view. I climbed an eminence to see whether I could discover what lay beyond it, and saw three more hills that made an irregular quadrilateral and enclosed a beautiful and spacious plain.

We had no great difficulty descending into it. It was perfectly flat throughout its extent; there was not the slightest rise or dip to be seen. The vegetation with which it was covered was then very wet, as if an abundant dew had fallen shortly before. Along the hills I perceived a large number of long pale streaks, as shiny as quicksilver, which interested in a thousand places, running from top to bottom and from bottom to top.

I moved closer and saw snails four times the size of our edible snails on all the slopes, carrying beautiful green shells on their backs. Their bodies were black; they had long tails and small heads devoid of horns. As they slid over the ground they left a trail of thick white foam, which made the long streaks I have just mentioned.

They were avidly eating a plant that grew on the plain, which is so beautiful and singular that it merits description here. It grows to a height of about an arm's length above the ground, and projects twenty-five or thirty leaves which are very tightly bunched at the base but spread out considerably higher up. The leaves are as broad as a hand-span, with pointed spikes all around as hard and sharp as thorns; they are a very beautiful pale green, full of large veins of the most beautiful golden color one could see.

We uprooted some of them, albeit with difficulty, because of the spikes with which they are armed, and were surprised to see that their roots veritably had the form of a melon, the gray-brown rind divided into sections, as rough to the touch as shagreen. The interior was a soft, pale, spongy flesh with a disagreeable odor, which deterred us from tasting it. If there is nothing in it good to eat, however, there is much to satisfy the eye. I have seen more than a hundred of the snails grazing on a single plant.

In one corner of that plain—the one in the direction of the sea—there was an issue by way of a stone vault, but so low that it was necessary almost to bend double to pass through it. We arrived by that route in a large space paved with beautiful brown stones similar to sandstone, about three feet broad. A hundred paces from there, we saw, in an area full of sand and gravel, the remains of a tower, next to which, as if embedded in the ground, was a huge round stone with a concave face, like a big globe, which had a line of three stars on its surface represented in relief. I could not imagine what it might be.

That stone was at the end of the ruins of a long wall, extending all the way to the sea, which had been at least three feet high and half as thick, but no longer rose more than half a foot above the ground. One waist-high section of it remained near the sea, however, in which a large hexagonal piece of red marble was encased, on which a quadrangle was engraved with kind of serpent in the middle, and various ornaments and bizarre curves all around it.

I noticed that the stones of the tower and the wall were so closely joined that it did not appear that there had ever been any mortar or cement there Although we had not encountered any inhabitants throughout the time we had been in those climes, there was no doubt that there must have been some, all these things being incontestable proof of it, and I am all the more convinced because I saw several places very apt for cultivation, in my opinion, where the cold is not intolerable.

Near those constructions we discovered, by chance, a marvelous echo, for by striking a stone against a rock the sound was repeated as many as six, seven or eight times along the shore. Furthermore, one could make a very good seaport at that place. Still advancing along the coast, we found a large beach that extended for a good three leagues; it were strewn with small sandbanks and there was a little islet in the middle, long and narrow, full of exceedingly green reeds, the edges of which were covered with shellfish.

After that beach there was an inlet of the sea, in the depths of which were three high mountains. The middle one, which was the highest, advanced so close to the shore that there was scarcely three feet of terrain on which to pass by. There was a large hole or fissure on the side facing the sea, like a deep grotto, in which I saw two skeletons of four-footed animals. After examining them carefully I concluded that they must be the skeletons of bears, but which had been monstrous in size. One occupied the entrance almost blocked the passage; the other was at the very back, and I found a large bird's nest between its ribs, with several eggs.

At that place we left the sea and the mountains to our left and veered inland to the right. It was a sandy terrain almost completely covered by a kind of white moss, and at intervals that ground was seen to rise in small hillocks, like those in fields where there are moles, but I could not discover what kind of animal made them. Then we saw a broad stream ahead of us, doubtless forms by melted snow, which flowed abundantly from the neighboring mountains. As it was impossible for us to cross over, we were obliged to make a long detour, and to walk for a long time along a hillside in damp, half-melted snow.

What encouraged us to go on, however, was a beautiful and large prairie that was almost directly ahead of us, strewn with little yellow flowers and bordered by a long hill, where we could see a kind of arbor of green bushes. The flowers exhaled a very pleasant odor, and while I was amusing myself in gazing at them, a large bird suddenly emerged from the bushes. Fearlessly, it came to settle thirty paces away from us. It was about the size of a goose, and walked as proudly as a cockerel, with its head high, lifting its feet ostentatiously at every step. Its claws appeared to be large and sharp. Its plumage was gray and it had almost no tail. There was a thick cluster of long black and white feathers on its head, which broadened out in a circle at the top, resembling a large crown. Its beak was red, short and broad.

After it had rummaged for some time in the grass, it took a few plants in its break and flew away toward the hill. I followed it with my gaze and saw it go into a hole at the bottom. I advanced promptly and found that the hole was deep, turning as it extended into the earth. I inferred that it was the bird's nest, all the more so as I perceived several others, equally deep and similarly fashioned, along the hill—but we did not see the bird again, or any other of its species.

IX

Having resolved to advance a little further into the continent, we set about traversing a large extent full of a kind of
heather, at the extremity of which there were large hills of red
stone. The terrain was almost the same color, with the result
that after we had been walking over it for some time our shoes
and stockings were covered in coarse red dust.

As soon as we had passed the hills we discovered a broad
dry terrain, arid and very sandy, which offered a view in the
distance of frightful rocks, some of which were so high that
their summits were hidden in the clouds.

All of those objects diminished our ardor for penetrating
further forward, to such an extent that we immediately
changed our resolution and turned in the direction of the sea,
with the intention of following the shore all the way back to
Bear Strait, near to which our vessel was anchored. To that
effect we went through a broad valley where the route was
very pretty and easy. We then found a large quantity of birds,
with gray plumage mixed with a little black, about the size of
our pigeons, their beaks hooked like those of parrots. They
allowed themselves to be taken in hand, with the result that we
took as many as we could back to the ship.

Soon after that we talked about returning to the old
world, but by a majority vote we decided first to see the western part of the gulf, because we had noticed that it advanced a
long way on the occidental side. We therefore left the strait
with a good north-easterly wind, and sailed pleasantly for
more than twenty-four hours, heading westwards. The wind
suddenly dropped, however, and we were becalmed for ten
hours.

We had remained near to the land throughout, and we
were then very close to it, but we could not make anything out
at first because of a thick fog that reigned along that coast, the
sea and the mist seeming the same color. After two hours,
however, it had entirely dissipated and we saw, directly facing

us, a vast ring of rocks, which, advancing on to the land, formed an almost perfect circle, into which the sea insinuated itself between two enormous mountains, whose summits touched the clouds. It is undoubtedly the most beautiful natural harbor in the word, where one could easily shelter more than three hundred and fifty vessels from the wind, as in a safe and magnificent port.

The entrance might be five hundred paces wide. The mountains of the ring are mediocre in height, and one almost white rock has all around it, at intervals, holes in the form of church windows, which pierce it completely, through which one can see the country on the other side. All that, seen from the place where we were, made the most beautiful view imaginable. The two large mountains at the entrance seemed to be covered all the way to the summit with green moss.

I went into the beautiful harbor, one of six, with the launch. Around us, we could see numerous birds' nests in holes in the rock. The water was very clear and it appeared to us that it was extremely deep.

The wind, having risen again was blowing directly from the east, and, having continued our route for two or three hours, we found ourselves between two long sandbanks, where there was so little water that we had all the difficulty in the world getting out. Finally, having fortunately extracted ourselves, we found to our left, in the middle of the sea, an assemblage of rocks forming a single large mass. There was one of them which, overhanging extraordinarily, projected a long point northwards. Beneath it, a little above the water level, there was a large fissure or cleft, into which the sea entered to a great depth, and as there was an exhalation as thick as a cloud around the foot of the rocks, it was impossible to see from a distance the part that attached it to them, so that it appeared to us to be suspended in mid-air, until we were able to study it at closer range. That rock appeared to me to be very worthy of attention. It is impossible that, given time, it will not fall into the sea, dragged down by its own weight. I noticed that all around those rocks the water was thick and green, similar in a way to a marsh.

We were scarcely half a league away from there when the wind became much stronger and we began to sail so rapidly that we were soon in sight of a large number of small islets that were very close to one another. With the aid of my binoculars I counted twenty-five of them. They seemed to be as green as meadows. We set foot on the one that was closest to us because we saw a prodigious quantity of shellfish on its shore. We found a great many of the species of small oyster that I mentioned in a previous chapter.

We thought it wise not to risk advancing any further between the islets, because they were so close together that there were a great many reefs and whirlpools, which we assumed to be as many dangerous chasms. We therefore sailed around them, and after fifteen hours we reached the occidental shore of the gulf. The coast was very high, and we anchored in an inlet in order to be shielded from the wind, for there seemed to us to be the threat of an imminent tempest.

Indeed, soon afterwards, thick black clouds obscured the sky so that it became almost black, and as I was considering one that was singular in form it suddenly opened, and offered to my eyes a very bright fire, circular in form, like the sun, but which seemed nearly twice as large. That phenomenon made, in a matter of minutes, three or four precipitate movements from north to south.

At the same time, I perceived on the edge of the horizon a long series of clouds, some of which seemed to be descending perpendicularly all the way to the sea, but without being detached from the others. It was a very clear and transparent vapor, which the wind was pushing gradually toward us.

When it was very close, it seemed to have the color of pale fire, and thus resembled a tall, broad column of fire, which, touching the sea at one extremity and the clouds at the other, was moving over the surface of the waters. After a quarter of an hour it vanished, and nothing remained of it but a light smoke, which soon dissipated entirely.

Meanwhile, the circular fire became visible from time to time in gaps in the cloud, and formed shortly afterwards a very beautiful arc in the sky composed of two colors: a bright yellow and a green that tended slightly toward blue. That arc, reflected in the sea, formed a perfect circle of extraordinary beauty. The wind strengthening enormously, however, the sea became very heavy, and the waves came to break on the coast with a furious impetuosity. It seemed, in consequence, that all the winds had been unleashed, so there was a frightful tempest that caused the beautiful arc and the phenomenon that formed it to vanish in next to no time.

We were very glad to be positioned as we were, covered from the effort of the wind. After the tempest had passed and the air had cleared I climbed up the coast in order to see the surrounding area, but nothing was offered to my eyes but rocks upon rocks and mountains upon mountains, the summits of which and the intervals between them were all covered in snow. In brief, it was a country surprising in its aridity and sterility, where cold made itself felt in an excessive manner.

Having advanced about a thousand paces, I saw a kind of fox, much larger than ordinary foxes, emerge from a hole at the base of a rock. Almost all of its fur was reddish, but the tip of its snout and its four feet, to just above the first joint, were white. It came fearlessly to browse a kind of white moss twenty paces away from me. It was a female, for a few moments later five or six of its cubs, all marked in the same fashion, emerged from the same hole and came to browse round her.

Some of my companions having arrived in the same place, however, the animals took fright and fled precipitately to their lair.

X

Although the various excursions that we had made into the Antarctic lands had not penetrated very far inland, we had nevertheless seen enough to make a judgment on the rest, and as there were several reasons why we could not stay there any longer, we prepared to depart as soon as possible to return to the old world. We resolved to go to the Cape of Good Hope.

We set sail, therefore, with a god westerly wind, which allowed us to emerge in a short time from the gulf and the strait. We were carrying all our sail, and because the wind was strong we covered a good distance in a few hours. We took a bearing and found that we were at sixty-two degrees six minutes of southern latitude. Shortly thereafter we saw the sun again, for the first time. It was about midday.

A little after three o'clock, we found ourselves between two rapid currents, which caused us to fear that there was a dangerous reef in the vicinity. I took my binoculars and saw a large number of rocky spurs above the war level, in the midst of which there were several rapid currents, which, by virtue of their impetuosity, raised a dense and seething foam.

We took all imaginable precautions, but our vessel was nevertheless half-caught by one of those currents. A deft thrust of the tiller took us out of it, however, and we had the good fortune to get through the dangerous pass without any further accident. We arrived safely at the Cape of Good Hope a few days later at ten o'clock in the morning, on the fifth of July 1714.

When I went into the house where I intended to lodge, I learned that a young man had just been buried who had arrived from Batavia four or five weeks previously. When I was told his name I immediately remembered that I had once been acquainted with him and that we had been good friends. I enquired as to the exact details of his death.

Having regaled five or six of his friends, and drunk a little more than was reasonable with them, he had been afflicted at about midnight by a very violent headache, accompanied by stabbing pains in all his limbs. He had gone up to his room and put himself to bed, and about an hour later, when someone went to see whether he needed anything, he was found stone dead. He had been kept for two days, and then buried.

Then I remembered, fortunately, that he had once told me that at the age of ten or twelve, he had fallen into a lethar-

49

gy in his parents' house, and had gone for three days and three nights without showing the slightest sign of life. I therefore went, without losing a minute, to ask for permission to disinter him, which I easily obtained.

I had myself taken to the cemetery and had the grave and the coffin opened diligently; then he was taken to the house, where he was put in a warm bed. I noticed that he did not have the great pallor that dead bodies usually have, and even had a touch of redness in the middle of the left cheek. He remained there for more than six hours without making the slightest movement, but I still wanted to stay by his bedside.

Finally, he uttered a tiny sigh, and I immediately tried to give him a spoonful of an excellent liquor, for which I had gone out expressly, but his teeth were so tightly clenched that I could not introduce a single drop. Shortly thereafter he raised his left arm slightly, and I put the spoon between his teeth again, parting them sufficiently to enable him to swallow— and, in fact, he did swallow something, and opened his eyes shortly thereafter, but without any consciousness. Eventually, however, he came round completely.

After I had told him who I was, and explained to him briefly what had happened, he expressed all possible gratitude for the great service I had just rendered him, and was astonished that his host had had him buried so promptly. He told me later that he had had a servant who, by virtue of his supposed death, had doubtless remained the master of a few jewels, a fairly considerable sum in cash and some merchandise that he had had. Undoubtedly, as soon as he learned that his master might not really be dead, he had found a means to run away, or to hide himself so well that it was impossible to discover him, no matter how scrupulous a search was made. Because of that, the young man found himself stripped of everything, even his clothing not being found.

Fortunately, there was a man of my acquaintance at the Cape with whom I had once had some dealings. He was quite willing to advance him what he needed, on my recommendation. As one of the vessels of the oriental company that call at the Cape was expected any day, on its way back to Holland, we decided to take it together. It arrived three weeks later; a few days after that we embarked, and by the grace of God, returned safely to Amsterdam.

Alexis-Jean Le Bret: *The New Moon*
(1770)

PREFACE

For some matter of business,
One day when the cold was intense,
Four Ladies in a Carriage
Were going along the road shivering.
On the windows of their vehicle,
Humid atmospheric vapors had condensed;
And they saw sketches of Pictures,
Depicting people, plants and flowers.
"In this play of chance," one of the beauties said,
"What an admirable variety there is!
Neither Zeuxis nor Apelles
Would have imitated any better
The touch of the Supreme Painter.
Look, Ladies—be kind enough to follow me,
And if our vision is the same,
Here you will see a King,
He is holding his scepter…a Diadem
Ornaments his majestic head…."
"We do not have the same eyes,"
Said young Aramynte, "and if my sight is clear,
I see in that light Picture,
Not a King but a Shepherd
Who is holding a Crook for a scepter,
I can also see on his hairy head,
For a Diadem or a Crown
A poor battered hat."
The beautiful and playful Clélie,
Gazing, said: "He's neither Shepherd nor King,

And you can put your trust in me."
"But what is he then?" "He's a Fool,
Holding his *Marotte* in his hand
And his *Toque* is in divine taste."[7]
Finally, Chloe, who had kept silent,
Was constrained to speak in her turn.
"What do you see? A Maréchal de France
"Perhaps, or the God of Amour?"
"To speak frankly," replied that beauty,
"I don't have an effervescent brain like you,
And although I look hard I only see features
Formless and without resemblance.
Nothing, in sum, presents objects to my eyes
That have any existence on the Earth."
The last one was right, I think.
For does not one see every day,
In veins of Wood as in the clouds,
Monsters and human beings,
Flames, forests, amours and combats,
Which are, however, only illusory forms.
The proof is that spectators
All make of these deceptive objects
Judgments that are contradictory.

To those caprices of hazard,
One might compare this work,
It is made of vapors, with which a cloud
Grows without design, or model or art.
The critic will perhaps see therein
Various pictures that were never there.

---

[7] In literal terms, a *marotte* is a kind of bauble carried by a
jester, and a *toque* is a little hat, but both terms are used metaphorically, the first to mean a whim or a mania, and the second to refer to madness, especially crazy infatuation. The
second term is subsequently used as a root for one of the text's
key neologisms—perhaps the finest of them.

As it might be misunderstood
By those for whose sight it is expressly produced,
To avoid that misfortune I shall say,
That if you do not have good eyes,
You ought not to try to read me,
For all is jaundiced in the eye of the Bilious.
An ancient put it even better;
These are the words I give you to translate:
Lurida praetera fiunt quaecumque tuentur arquati.[8]
(Lucretius, Book IV.)

---

[8] "Whatever the jaundiced look at becomes yellow."

PART ONE

I. The Origin of Poequilon; his debut in Society.

Selenos is the tutelary Genius of the Planet we call the Moon; that Genius or God was present at the birth of Poequilon[9] and declared loudly that when the child had reached his fourteenth year, he would form marvelous wishes, and that they would be accomplished, but he imposed these conditions: that Poequilon would not make the same wish twice, that he would never request the help of others, and that he could only pass on from accomplished wishes to others after the revolution of two suns; all of which was to satisfy the decrees of destiny and secondary causes.

No one really knows the reason for Selenos' predilection for Poequilon. Some attribute it to the Laws of destiny, others to the favor of his mother Helyone, who, after having increased the number of the Moon's stains, had become the splendor of that Planet. Whatever it was, Poequilon was born in Verticephalia, the Capital of the Empire of the same name and the largest city on the Planet. No one ever said anything about his father, and that is why nothing can be said about him here. When he had reached the fortunate age of fourteen, the advantages of his uterine birth were simply revealed to him, and he was abandoned to his own devices.

Poequilon thought seriously about what he desired; right away, he would have liked to get his teeth into the Moon, but he thought that for a first wish it was necessary to be modest, and only asked for a mountain of gold. Selenos indicated the place where he would find that bagatelle; Poequilon transported himself there, and in no time at all consumed his mountain.

---

[9] Like most of the improvised names in the story, this one comes from the Greek, and might by translated as "Changing" or perhaps "Fickle."

II. Anyone would have done the same,

The favorite of the God, very nearly reduced to mendacity, thought about imploring Selenos again. He recognized clearly that all the mountains of gold and all the mines on the Moon were too few for him; in his embarrassment he consulted a certain Chrysope, an Alchemist, who had helped him to consume his mountain and who had been consuming himself for twenty-five years, along with the coal of the Moon, in the discovery of the Great Work. As one might expect, that lunatic blowhard advised Poequilon to wish for the philosopher's stone. He did, indeed, wish for it, and Selenos granted to him that, for him, all the dust on the Planet would be projection powder.

So there he was, as rich as ever and sheltered from any vicissitude of fortune.

He maintained in Verticephalia a retinue worthy of his inexhaustible opulence; his slaves, his houses, his carriages and his mistresses were innumerable; his Stewards had no accounts to submit, they were merely agents of his pleasures; they had only one concern: that every day, fifty cartloads of dust should be poured out in his palaces. The elegant men and beautiful women of the Moon came from all directions to pay court to him. The Palaces of Kings were deserted, and to amuse his mistresses, he threw the powder in the eyes of Emperors, Judges and Inquisitors—for there are all of those on the Moon, as there are here.

III. Belated but moral ideas; admirable but unfortunate wishes.

In the midst of so many delights, however, Poequilon perceived that he was growing old, and suspected that women cared less for his person than his wealth. On the Moon, reflections are not precocious, and that idea poisoned his happiness; he confided his pains to a Selenopolite, originally from the fourth continent of the globe, a man of great experience. That voyager said to him:

"Seigneur, I am the possessor of ancient manuscripts, which I inherited from my ancestors, in which one learns that half-white men, great drinkers of blood and gold, once carried out fruitless searches to discover a rejuvenating spring, which was called in consequence the Fountain of Youth. If that spring exists, there is nothing better you can do than wish for it."

Poequilon wasted no time in asking the Genius for the Fountain of Youth. As the spring was a long way from Verticephalia, and Selenos wanted to spare his favorite the journey to the waters, he had the spring filtered by invisible channels all the way to Poequilon's Park.

Walking in that place, the favorite discovered the miraculous jet of water, which was only visible to him. He perceived that the precious source followed in his footsteps and fixed itself in accordance with his command, which appeared to him to be a great convenience for the future. He drank the divine liquid several times, and the crystal of its waters produced for his eyes the image of a young and handsome Narcissus.

In that new form he appeared before his slaves, who were unable to recognize him; he presented himself at his Seraglio, but the Guards and Eunuchs threw him out, calling him "youngster."

Embarrassed as he was by his face, he issued threats, speaking as a master. The chief of the Seraglio then took him for a young man driven insane by the love of women; he took pity on him and thought he might cure him of his madness by putting him in a state to guard his own mistresses.

He was captured with so much artifice that he did not have time to invoke Selenos, or even to think of it. As they believed that he had lost his reason, they pretended to recognize him as Poequilon, and, having introduced him into the midst of his most cherished favorites, while he was being stripped of his red robe and was preparing to enjoy his new youth, an adroit hand robbed him in an instant of all the splendor of the Seraglio.

"O Fountain of Youth!" he cried, "Are these the pleasures that you prepared for me?"

He was given an employment in the Seraglio appropriate to his condition, and every time he said that he was Poequilon, two black slaves lashed him with stirrup-leathers.

He was on the point of picking up dust and making gold in order to prove that he was Poequilon, but he thought that all the gold on the Moon would not return what had been taken away from him, and he made the decision to wait in silence for the end of his term, for the unfortunate situation ought only to last for two years, in accordance with Selenos' oracle.

It was very easy to remain a spectator, during his invisibility of sorts, of everything that went on in the Seraglio, and as his reason had returned, he obeyed everyone's commands, so well that he acquired the confidence of the Chief Eunuch, and was appointed to serve the women in their most intimate needs. They often made him sing, because he had a beautiful voice—a talent for which he had not wished, and which the Chief of the Seraglio had procured for him without being Selenos.

It was in the interior of the Palace that he saw and heard things in his new estate that he would never have suspected otherwise.

IV. Very ordinary adventures.

One day, when he was serving Phasea, his favorite Sultana, in her bath and was bemoaning in a low voice that so many charms, of which he had been the master, were forbidden to him in more ways than one, she put her arm around his neck and said to him:

"Handsome Poequilonet"—for that name had been given to him on the day of his sad incarceration—"take this note to Rhetorical, the Chief Steward of the Gardens, and tell him that voluptuousness awaits him in my bosom, that your hands have perfumed me for his delight, and come back promptly to introduce him to my arms."

Poequilon obeyed in spite of the harshness of his role, and Thezorical flew to the Sultana's feet; the young Eunuch was a witness to their infidel frolics.

"Dear Thezorical," said Phasea, "it was you who put me in Poequilon's arms, you who distinguished me among all the beauties of Vertocaphalia, so it is to you that I give the first fruits of amour; was Poequilon worthy to respire the first breath of my tenderness?"

After Phasea and Thezorical had amused themselves at Poequilon's expense, the unfortunate favorite of Selenos retired very pensively. Passing through the women's apartments, he found them all occupied in consoling themselves in his absence, not with parrots, as was customary, but with soldiers, courtiers and, worse still, muleteers. Some were saying the Poequilon would never return, others, laughing: "There he is passing by."

As for the administration of his wealth, Poequilon scarcely worried about it, since he had the virtue of rendering his riches inexhaustible. The secret inspection of his women was his principal concern. There was a kind of anarchy in Poequilon's domains; everyone took what he could. Gold was the prey of the Eunuchs and the women were at the mercy of the Stewards; everywhere there are Eunuchs, the Stewards who have their five senses only play the secondary role in the art of amassing treasures.

Thezorical, unworried about his master and believing him to be at the bottom of a river, thought only of enjoying himself and making his pile during the "interpoequilonat." It happened that at carnival time, at a public ball, he was dancing with a young Verticephalienne, whose graces, intelligence, talents and, above all, beauty turned his head. In order to enjoy fortune with her he thought there was no other means than to court her on Poequilon's behalf, and he convinced her to come to the Seraglio. She was introduced there with all the magnificence of a valet playing the role of his master.

The young and beautiful Fascia—that was the new Sultana's name—did not take long to comprehend that she could not reach the absent Poequilon without smiling at the present Thezorical. Poequilon, charged with the preparations for the feast, was a witness to the Steward's zeal. In his chagrin, he resolved to avenge himself, but, as he was as impotent in that respect as in his person, and everything else, he secretly informed Phasea of Thezorical's infidelity, and the outraged Sultana stabbed the Steward in a moment of privacy. Poequilion gladly threw two feet of moon over the corpse, and everyone thought that Thezorical had gone up in smoke, like his master.

V. Everyone passes this way.

Time went by, however, and the wealth dissipated, because the malicious Poequilon left the dust uncultivated, in order not to augment the prosperity of his ingrate following.

The two years of his Pupation finally expired, and then he asked Selenos to restore that which a barbarian had cruelly removed. He also asked that everything that his slaves had stolen should return to dust, that all his concubines who had betrayed him should become ugly, and finally, that he should be recognized by everyone as Poequilon without quitting the fortunate form that the Fountain of Youth had given him.

All these metamorphoses took place in the blink of an eye. He found himself more brilliant than ever, all his slaves prostrated themselves at his feet; he made a review of all the women of the Seraglio and, showing them the sparkling sign of his authority, he said to them: "I am Poequilon."

Among the six thousand women who composed his delights, however, he did not find one that was not disfigured by an extreme ugliness.

"O Heaven!" he cried. "Am I then the Sultan of she-apes? What! Not one of them loved me sincerely? Selenos! Selenos!"

He reproached Phasea for her shameful weakness, and handed her over to his Eunuchs—an exemplary punishment, the mere idea of which makes the women of Verticephalia shiver.

After the first impulse given to his vengeance, he threw out all that rabble; he had first class slaves recruited, and restored his Palace to its original magnificence. This time, he did not want a Seraglio; he made a stern decision to marry, and to limit his pleasures to a single woman. His principal slaves murmured, but what could they do? He was the master and he was obstinate—I do not say like all great men, but like a great many rich ones.

One day, he was taking the air on his balcony, fulminating against women and cursing celibacy—for experience made him hate them on the one hand, while on the other, the Fountain of Youth made him love them—when he saw the young and beautiful Cyclae coming out of the Temple, whose beauty and majestic figure suddenly inflamed him with the most violent lover.

"There, surely," he said, "is the woman that Selenos has destined for me."

He asked her parents for her hand, and the Superminister married them solemnly in the Temple of the Crescent. (That Temple would have been a bad omen on Earth.)

Poequilon was delighted with his new spouse; he recognized in her intelligence, tenderness and, above all, a good deal of devotion for the great Alma.

"I shall be perfectly happy," he said. "I'm handsome, young and full of vigor. Cyclae, satisfied, will be faithful to me, her virtue and piety are guarantees of her conjugal faith."

He spent two days in the sweetest ecstasy, but one evening, when she imprudently took a mixture of peaches and chocolate, Cyclae lost her life. Poequilon tore out his hair and begged Selenos to return his dear Cyclae to the light, if she had been faithful to him—of which he had no doubt—and, in the contrary case, that she should merely give him a fleeting sign of existence.

Selenos grated that prayer as a merciful gesture; Cyclae opened her eyes and closed them again forever.

"What! In two days!" cried Poequilon. In the bitterness of his grief, he was on the point of asking Selenos for the favor of not being cuckolded again in future, but he thought that the Genius, in spite of his power, could not prevent that which had been from having been.

VI. A Violent Remedy of the Great Men of the Moon, scorned today because that would be incessant repetition.

Notwithstanding his double misfortune, Poequilon found himself still intent on marriage. He did not want to owe everything to Selenos, nor to his fortune; he set out to capture a beauty on his own merits.

He thought he had found the charm of the heart in the tender Semirame; he offered her his hand, and the marriage was concluded in the time prescribed by the law. He lived, the happiest of men, in that sweet engagement.

Semirame, as tender and attentive as she was beautiful, made the days go by in delights.

Poequilon was so fortunate that he no longer thought about asking anything of Selenos, except for another soul in order to feel his happiness more; but he considered that the pains with which life is necessarily mixed would be regulated to the measure of that double faculty of sensing pleasures, and that reflection determined him to be content with one soul.[10]

He cherished his tender spouse with all of his heart, and any pleasure that he had not shared with her would have seemed insipid to him. He would have been only too happy to

---

[10] Author's note: "The humans of the Moon are so feebly provided in the matter of the soul that it seems that Poequilon, by such a wish, might have tempted the power of the Genius, or demanded the property of another, which would not have been in accord with the conditions prescribed by Selenos."

remain in that situation, but the continuous passion to make sure of his happiness devoured Poequilon.

Fatal curiosity! The rapid infidelity of Cyclae presented itself to his memory.

He thought that nothing would be lacking to his joy if Selenos could assure him of the constancy of his dear and tender Semirame.

It was more than two years since he had asked anything of the Genius; he made him this short prayer:

"O Selenos, since I have possessed Semirame, you know that she alone has been my pleasure; I shall be at the peak of human felicity if you can inform me that she is faithful. Give me certain evidence[11] of her love and her constancy."

Scarcely had he uttered those words that he felt himself afflicted by the most agonizing pain in—how shall I put it?—that which Selenos had regrown for him in an instant after two years of privation and servitude.

He understood that certificate of conjugal infidelity only too well. I do not think that it is necessary to be an inhabitant of the Moon to understand what I mean; if one is not unaware of how much analogy there is between our world and that one, one ought to comprehend that Poequilon sensed that he had been struck by the malady known on the Moon as Aphrodise. That name comes very close to the one well known on our world. I shall not give the history of the malady in question here; it will be sufficient for the reader that I inform him briefly that it is a contagious disease communicated in the bosom of pleasure, with which a certain Jason of the Moon has gratified the entire Planet.

When Poequilon was aware of his condition, he did not want to recognize his wife any longer, and he had her swallow

---

[11] Author's note: "*Pignora certa petis, do Pignora certa timendo.* Ovid." [You seek certain proof; I'm giving you certain proof in fear.]

an obedience in a silver-plated cup, by which means he became a widower again.[12]

VII. He who embraces too much grips poorly.

Poequilon spent two years in the pleasures of widow-
hood; that was one benefit that he did not owe to Selenos. Nor
did he have any need of the Genius to cure his infirmity, because a certain Mountebank, very afflicted in his limbs and
who had written a great deal about Aphrodise, made him swallow a good deal of false silver,[13] for which he gave him a considerable quantity of gold in bars.

Nevertheless, in view of the affection that he had for
Poequilon, Selenos might well have had something to do with
that cure, for the Mountebanks of the Moon, when they have
cured someone, employ the formula "with the aid of Selenos,
etc." And to accelerate his convalescence, Poequilon drank a
few drops of the rejuvenating fountain. It must not be imagined that the waters of Youth are a radical cure, but without
that faculty the Moon would fall into stagnation, according to
the Doctors.

Meanwhile, Poequilon made profound reflections regarding the opposite sex; he understood that a woman could not be

---

[12] Author's note: "A vengeance of that nature is not common-
place in Verticephalia, especially in this sort of case, but
Poequilon was then affected by the vapors of the austral lands,
for it is as well to observe that the Earth influences the Moon,
by vertical or oblique ascension, as the Moon does the Earth
by gravitation; there are many people who do not want to believe that, but I give fair warning that I do not stand for any
argument."

[13] I have translated *argent faux* literally, as "false silver," rather than the more usual "false coin" (*argent* also meaning
"money" in French) in order to retain a link with quicksilver,
mercury poisoning being the standard treatment for syphilis at
the time, under the inspiration of Paracelsus.

faithful, because men are sufficient in name only; that is why, when the term of his wish had arrived, he asked Selenos for the vigor of an entire squadron. The prodigal Selenos submerged him with his favors, and the Poequilon ran furiously hither and yon; Priestesses and Loose Women alike, all succumbed to his amorous rage, and he never enjoyed himself but his pleasures were a carnage,

As one can imagine, such a monstrous disposition disturbed the order of society somewhat; the sovereign of Verticephalia used force and skill to make Poequilon stop, and the favorite's erotic vapors were confined between four walls; furthermore, he was alimented in a fashion that when he had furnished the marvelous dispositions of all the heroes of the Mirebalais, his flag was lowered. The Prince thought he ought to administer justice to Poequilon, at the request of all the outraged families. He was put on trial, and his sentence was announced to him; they would cut off his…let us suppose the head…and display it publicly on the "turnip of infamy."[14]

He offered in exchange for clemency more riches than had ever been possessed on Earth by the Peruvians and the Solipses. The Prince held firm and generously refused to yield to that seduction, with the result that, when he was about to go to the scaffold, he begged Selenos with all imaginable fervor to render him invisible and to take away his dangerous and supernatural passion. Fortunately, the two years had expired.

If it seems surprising that two years had already gone by since Poequilon's last wish, take note that on the Moon, where everything is done maturely, legal procedures take a long time, and besides which, Poequilon was a criminal of high status, which required that nothing be rushed.

When they came into his prison to take possession of his person, he was invisible, and realized by virtue of the surprise of the guards that the Genius had granted his wish. He went

---

[14] Author's note: "*Natibus raphano oppletis.*" The quotation is from Lucian; the middle term refers to the root vegetable, the first to the buttocks and the third to ordure.

out in the middle of the escort and was delighted by everyone's astonishment. Singularly enough, the people, who believe so easily in miracles, could not be persuaded that Poequilon had been saved from the scaffold by an entirely divine providence, because of an opinion long credited on the Moon that a rich man cannot he hanged.

In order to appease the people, they pretended to have recaptured Poequilon, and substituted for him a man who had merited the satisfaction of the sentence; the people were not fooled, and it is probable that would have refused to believe it even if it really had been Poequilon—the people of the Moon are like that.

VIII. Good Advice.

The invisible man, attenuated by hunger, fear and detention, first went to his Palace, which had been seized to the profit of the Prince and was in the greatest disorder; he saw his slaves pillaging everywhere, in spite of the oath they sworn to the agents of justice. He let them do it, thinking that confiscation was as good by one hand as another. He went to the kitchen, where he fortunately found what he needed to assuage his devouring hunger. It was a true testament to Poequilon's opulence that after a descent by Officers of the Law, there was still enough to procure him a modest meal.

He amused himself by beating and fustigating the lawyers and policemen who were pocketing things, and everyone cried out that the executed man had returned, which amused Poequilon greatly. Then he drank a few glasses of the water of Youth to get his strength back, for he had no need as yet to be rejuvenated, only being in the fifth lustrum of his second life. However, that little refreshment took him back to adolescence; he wanted to contemplate himself in the spring, and found that he was invisible to himself. He was annoyed to be deprived of the spectacle of his face, but his portrait, which he still had in his pocket, consoled him.

No longer knowing where to rest his head, Poequilon thought that he would only be able to lead a furtive and vagabond life during his invisibility, and that his gold would serve him, at the most, to acquit his conscience for the petty larcenies that he would be obliged to commit in order to live. At least, however, he wanted to take advantage of that rare state of invisibility to observe the secret actions of hypocrites, relieving the unfortunate and consoling afflicted beauties. There was some good in those projects.

He also conceived the plan of seeing at close range what happened in the Palace of Kings, but the elixir of Youth that was seething in his veins deflected him from that serious enterprise.

"Let's respect our Masters," he said. "Anyway, the secrets of Courts are the stuff of Comedy, and I'm bound to find out more than I want to know, and where will that lead me? To journalism. And where does journalism lead? To invisibility. No, no, I want to be seen."

IX. The Difficulty of understanding when one has never read Treatises on the Moon.

The veils of night were spreading over the horizon and Poequilon, having introduced himself into the home of a caterer, to the host's table, sat down next to a Braoca—which is very similar to what we would call down here a Gascon—and in no time at all, the invisible Poequilon has devoured his supper. The Braoca did not know which way to turn,[15] and Poequilon, in order to console him, threw a number of gold coins on to his plate.

"*Cadeselene!*"[16] cried the Braoca. "I believe that I'm Midas, and that everything I touch turns to gold." At least, what he said in Lunar erudition amounts to the same thing.

---

[15] Author's note: "This expression is a Terranism."
[16] Author's note: "An imprecation in the Braocan dialect." It is an adaptation of the French expletive *Cadedieu*.

They laughed heartily at the Brocade. It is worth noting, once and for all, that the erudition of the Moon is almost the same as that of the Earth. You might wonder how that comes about, but it beats me—if all historians were as sincere about many things, they wouldn't do as much harm.

As the heat of the day hadn't yet dissipated, and there was the most beautiful Earthlight that one could ever see, Poequilon did not think of looking for a bed. He was walking tranquilly at the foot of the wall of the Temple of the Vestals when he perceived a tall gaunt man dressed in black running toward a little door in the wall; by his clothing he took him for an Anagogist Rector, which is a edifying profession on the Moon, for which reason that class of men is generally called Edifiants.[17]

Poequilon was not mistaken; the man was indeed a uniformed Edifiant, a kind of Pontiff of the Temple. He was curious to know what business the Edifiant might have at such an hour in the retreat of the Doves devoted to the great Alma, inasmuch as no man, including Edifiants, ought to be able to penetrate into the interior of that sanctuary of chastity. He conceived a scandalous suspicion, but rejected it.

That holy man, Poequilon said to himself, *is probably coming to meditate in silence at the foot of the altar, and to say his prayers to Selenos for the Emperor, the Fatherland and the entire world. Let us not judge an Edifiant recklessly, and let us follow him in his pious exercises.*

Scarcely had he made these reflections than the Edifiant looked around anxiously, to make sure that no one could see him, and, eventually believing that he had not been perceived, he opened the little door. Poequilon slipped in adroitly with the holy man. They traversed several courtyards and entered discreetly into a separate apartment illuminated by a silver lamp.

---

[17] The French adjective from which this improvised noun is derived has the expectable literal meaning of "edifying" but is almost invariably used ironically, as it is here.

Nothing had ever seemed so charming to Poequilon as that little abode; one might have thought that Springtime and Amour were united in that gracious solitude; the heart palpitated there as in the gardens of Flora; the senses were stimulated by delightful perfumes, and by a luxury unknown to men of this century, agitating the soul with an inconceivable disturbance.

Poequilon's inflamed eyes searched everywhere for the divinity of that grotto. His Seraglio had never offered him anything so piquant. He sighed.

The defiant approached a bed that appeared to respire softness and voluptuousness. Poequilon, his diligent and invisible shadow, followed him everywhere. His eyes were struck by the glamour of a Priestess, twenty-five years old and half-naked, who threw her arms around the neck of the holy man and fell back on her bolster in a kind of ecstasy, saying: "Ah, Selenotime! Selenotime! I can already sense the soft ravishment of the soul…already the contemplation of things…"

She did not finish, and her beautiful eyes, overwhelmed by the languor occasioned by a long-desired voluptuousness, closed upon the objects that Selenotime what presenting, as he stripped off his austerity.

The proud and effervescent Rector said to her, delightedly: "Oh, celestial Olibane, incense of just men, let all the dew of the firmament slake the thirst of the field of Selenos, let…."

At that moment, Poequilon, who did not want the Edifiant to plunge any further into sin, taking advantage of the Priestess's ravishment, dragged Selenotime toward the door of the voluptuous bedroom, and said to him in a low voice, in a menacing tone: "Wretch, fear Selenos! Flee this place that you are profaning, forever."

At these words, the Edifiant thought he had been struck by lightning. He gathered his strength in order to obey the command that he deemed to have come from the Heavens, and ran away as fast as he could, thinking at every stride that he could see abysms ready to engulf him.

Poequilon, gripped by an inconceivable charm, thought that he was going to be an honest man, and that it was, in any case, inappropriate for him to abuse Olibane's credulity. He returned, however, to the delightful beside, and contemplated the charming Priestess; her beauty, her paleness, the bosom prepared for the pleasures of a vigorous Edifiant, and the nocturnal adornment of the Vestal, all caused Poequilon to succumb. The Amour of the Moon is no less malign than ours, and is perhaps the same one. In sum, Poequilon reignited the Vestal's fire, and deflected her from desire to contemplation by the force of ravishment.

Finally ceding to sleep, he lay down on a sofa not far from Olibane's amorous couch, and the beautiful Priestess thought that Selenotime had retired with his usual discretion.

If anyone is surprised that Olibane did not testify any surprise at not having seen the caressant object that she clutched to her bosom, it is doubtless the case that the ecstasy of the Priestess did not permit her to open her eyes, or that Poequilon placed between them and the light the gallant barriers of the throne of pleasure; but in addition, the invisible Poequilon was not intangible, and the Priestess of Alma did not believe that she could mistake an Edifiant.

Someone might also think it indelicate that Poequilon, after have chased the Edifiant away, should have established himself on his ruins, but it is not my fault if my hero does not always act like one; it is necessary to depict men as they are. For every Don Quixote, how many Poequilons there are in the world! Anyway, what I'm recounting happened on the Moon.

X. Which is more easily understood than the previous one, although less clear.

When he awoke, Poequilon no longer found the majestic Priestess in her cell; at that moment she was presiding over melodious hymns to the great Alma, and her pure hands were making incense smoke. Poequilon suspected as much, and as he was slightly exhausted by the night's edification, he opened a preciously ornamented cupboard, in which he found excellent restoratives, with which he corroborated. He judged that they fulfilled their purpose perfectly, and, indeed, it was the favorite stimulant of the fortunate Selenotime, prepared by the hands of his chaste Olibane. It was his fountain of youth.

Poequilon, who had found that little research very rewarding, was meditating secretly on his good fortune when he saw the lovely Olibane come back into the apartment, accompanied by two young Vestals, more beautiful than the Graces. Olibane attended to her toilette, and the two young Vestals undressed the Priestess. Poequilon contemplated at his ease all the former beatitudes of Selenotime.

What perfect contours for a claustral beauty! he said to himself. *What a refinement of propriety! What depths of coquetry, for the body of an Anchorite destined for the cilice! What cassolettes of perfumes, for the region of discipline and mortification! O Selenotime! In devoting yourself to chastity, did you know that all the beauties of the Moon were prepared for you, and that you would one day enjoy seigneurial rights over them?*

Poequilon was intoxicated by voluptuousness; he had need of all his reason to contain himself, and was very glad that he was invisible, for the three consecrated individuals would have seen an enormous scandal.

He could not, however, prevent himself from paying court to the charms of the two Angelic Vestals who were serving the Priestess.

"Stop it, Olympia," said one of the beauties. "What a strange thing to do!"

"Stop it yourself, Chlamide," said the other.

"What's going on between you?" said Olibane, then.

"Great Priestess," the both said, in unison. "She...."

At that moment the supper-room bell sounded. The Priestess and the two Vestals of honor responded to it. Poequilon followed them, as stealthily as a wolf, in order to enter with them into the sheepfold, and wreak a little havoc among the delicate dishes of the great Alma—for our invisible

71

man needed, as it were, to employ industry in order to live, but, gallant as he was, he was well able to pay for his victuals.

XI. A very appetizing meal.

He was delighted by admiration on entering the supper-room: fifty beauties modestly seated, dazzling in their paleness and fresher than the dawn, seemingly disputing the Empire of Beauty.

The celestial Olibane, placed under an awning, assuming an important attitude that authority had contracted for her, nominated Olympia to be the anagnoste[18] during the meal.

The young Vestal in question had charmed Poequilon particularly in Olibane's apartment; an expression of tenderness expanded over her physiognomy, combined with a slightly Spanish figure that was much to Poequilon's taste, caused him to remain at the bottom of the steps while Olympia went up to the pulpit; it was stronger than him.

However, he said to himself, *it's necessary to live*. And, standing behind the most beautiful Vestals, he shared the morsels with them, and served them with skill and neatness.

The young women thanked one another reciprocally, as if they were rendering those petty social duties to one another. Poequilon sometimes disturbed the veil of one, sometimes the pectoral of another, and the most ravishing spectacle compensated him for the silence.

Olympia continued her reading, and the sound of her voice was so enchanting that Poequilon, in spite of his distractions, sometimes lent an ear to it.

Olympia recited:

Flee the world and its deceptive lures,
Subdue the flesh and despise fortune,

---

[18] Author's note: "Anagnoste: the person who does the reading." The term derives from the Latin, where it refers specifically to a Roman slave whose job it was to read to his master.

And if you spire to solid grandeurs,
Shun the base pleasures of the Moon.

At those words, Poequilon, forgetting his condition, exclaimed abruptly: "Stupid morality!"

He was then between the Priestess Olibane and the aged Acousta. Everyone attributed the untimely repartee to the old Vestal; she protested her innocence in vain, and was condemned capitularily, during the meal, to give lessons in Selenography to the aspirants for three months, without being able to impose correction on her disciples, and with exclusion from the conventicle during her professorship.

Young Olympia finished the reading and took her meal in her turn. Poequilon contented himself with admiring her beauty and sometimes breathing in her exhalation, which, in lunar style, was softer than a Zephyr. He remembered his last blunder, which determined him to be more reserved in public, in order to avoid disorders that might have raised an obstacle to his amorous projects.

The Vestals retired to their rooms, as did the Priestess, and Poequilon languidly followed Olympia into her cell.

XII. Not every dream is a lie.[19]

The beautiful Vestal took off her sacred ornaments and threw herself nonchalantly on to a sofa. Her cleavage, which she had laid bare, was palpitating in a manner that enabled Poequilon to judge that the beauty's bosom was agitated by some passion; her tender and animated eyes seemed to be expressing amour and dolor at the same time; she sighed, and her

---

[19] The translation cannot reproduce the wordplay connecting *songe* [dream] with *mensonge* [lie]

mouth was immediately embellished by a smile, which Poequilon could not construe.[20]

He would have thrown himself at the Vestal's feet if he had not been retained by the dread of frightening her too much, but he had the idea of taking his portrait from his pocket and offering it to Olympia's eyes.

"O Gods!" she exclaimed. "Who can have put that portrait in my room?"

She got up precipitately, and seized the effigy of Poequilon. She contemplated it attentively, and sighed. Tears flowed from her languishing eyes.

"Oh, inhuman parents!" she continued, groaning. "Cruel people, who have thrown me into this gulf of despair, when I was made for Amour! This portrait that fortune has sent me will be my consolation henceforth; it shall never quit my person, and I shall devour it incessantly, and pretend to animate it by the resources of my imagination."

While Olympia took pleasure in these reflections, Poequilon wrote a note, which he placed adroitly in the frame of the portrait. Olympia took it, and tremulously read these words:

Beautiful Olympia, I have preferred you to all the Vestals. Have no fear of me; I love you and I shall avenge the injustice of your parents, by means of all the delights of Amour. Surrender yourself without terror to the most tender lover; complete the animation of one who only breathes for you. I cannot tell you more, but a thousand secrets will one day be revealed to you. If you cannot see me, at least you can hear me. You can take me in your arms, since I am such as you see me in this painting. Say the word and I shall fall at your feet.

---

[20] Author's note: "*O quantum est in rebus inane!*" The quote is from one of the satires of Persius; it translates roughly as "How much there is that is trivial!"

Olympia's surprise can be imagined, but what was her astonishment when she heard Poequilon sigh, and she felt that charming invisible individual kiss her hand.

"Have no fear," he said to her, in a tender and gracious voice. "I am a man, and the most amorous; feel my tenderness, beautiful Olympia; a Genius protects me; I shall enable to you to share his favors."

"Handsome portrait," said the Vestal, trembling, "I shiver at such an extraordinary event. I believe that I would not be insensible to your love, if I could persuade myself that everything I am experiencing today is not an effect of the enemy of Selenos or the derangement of my reason."

Poequilon washed the Vestal's hands with his tears, and that caused her to succumb. She judged, rightly, that the evil spirit could not push tenderness to that extent.

Olympia allowed herself to be gently drawn to the sofa, and the portrait dropped from her hands.

XIII. Full of equity.

Poequilon was at the summit of joy, at having found the means to console Olympia; the beautiful Vestal had easily given herself to the extraordinary possession of her invisible lover.

The two lovers spent the most delightful days. Poequilon had no other dwelling than Olympia's room, no other bed but her couch, no other wardrobe than his lover's, for it is as well to note that Poequilon's garments were in a rather poor state, and he had taken off his rags and dressed in the Vestal's tunic, which, by a consequence of the accomplishment of his wish, had acquired the gift of invisibility. He had informed the beauty of that; she was delighted to contribute to her lover's well-being.

Poequilon witnessed Olympia's labors and recreations, and the young woman secretly enjoyed the pleasure of knowing that her lover was by her side. Her companions thought her pensive and melancholy, because she never indulged in the frolicsome and sometimes tumultuous pleasures of the Vestals of her own age; she remained tranquilly sitting on the grass while the young ones exercised, sometimes running around lightly, sometimes dancing and playing music—but Poequilon was beside her, covering her with invisible kisses, and rendering the post she occupied precious.

In spite of the sweetness that he savored with Olympia, however, he felt touched with compassion for Olibane, on thinking about the chagrins that the forced retreat of her Edifiant might have caused her; he felt obliged to gather all his strength, for the consolation of the Priestess. Not that he recognized any alteration in her visage; on the contrary, Olibane was fresher than ever; her complexion was rosy and her devout bosom seemed to have taken on a new luster.

Whether it was remorse on his part, or whether it was a sting of voluptuousness that was sharpened by the memory of Olibane, however, he introduced himself into her room at a time that he knew to be propitious to amours, and was about to forget Olympia for a moment, out of pity, when he saw an Edifiant with a short coat come in.

Oh! said Poequilon to himself, immediately. *My commiseration was too hasty. Olibane has no complaints; let's not be unfaithful to my Vestal unnecessarily.*

He left the two lovers and went to take his tribute to Olympia.

XIV. Good men are often dupes.

After abandoning himself to the sweetness of his consolation, he could not help thinking about Selenotime, to whom he had given a moral fright. He had not seen him again in the Temple since the day of that terrible expulsion.

Poequilon thought that it would be kind to put the mind of the Edifiant at rest, who might have attributed to celestial powers a scene that was fundamentally only human. That is why he went out of the Temple early one morning, with the aid of a few slaves who were going for provisions. He directed his steps toward a famous portico where Selenotime made his dwelling.

He recognized him as soon as he emerged, and thought he saw in the holy man's features the imprints of remorse and penitence. He was deeply touched by that. He followed him for a little while, and entered with him into a house that seemed to him to be rather opulent; the slaves showed him a great deal of respect and submission; only the dog of the house barked at him and nipped the tail of his coat.

Selenontime was then introduced into an apartment, into which Poequilon followed him again. A beautiful woman came to meet the Edifiant and said to him, in a low voice: "My husband is in Keraticopolis."[21]

The good man then seemed to catch fire, his eyes sparkling and his complexion animating with the crimson of amour. Poequilon saw them abandon themselves to the transports that certain souls permit themselves: a stolen voluptuousness.

That's the way it is, Poequilon said to himself. *These people are incorrigible. I was stupid to believe that what happened in the Priestess' cell could change Selenotime. But what gave him that contrite expression by which I was so touched? Apparently, these Edifiants have one face for representation, and another for the bedroom.*

XV. One can do good everywhere.

He went out of the house slightly indignant, because he had a susceptible temperament, and before returning to the house of the Vestals he wanted to take a look around and see what was happening in the houses that are known on the Moon as Convents of Joy. These Convents are full of women who are called Plebicoles—a word that has a lot of energy in the Lunar language—and are distinguished from other women of the Planet by a shoulder-knot that they wear. In all the good

---

[21] Author's note: "Which is to say, the City of Horn."

Governments of the Moon, these Convents are protected for the safety of women of honor and for the consolation of shameful paupers.

He therefore introduced himself into one of the most famous Convents in Verticephalia, and he saw people of all ages and estates there, who were giving pleasure and money to the Plebicoles, who were giving them Aphrodise in exchange. He paused particularly to consider two beautiful women who were not wearing shoulder-knots, but who nevertheless had the appearance of being frank Plebicoles.

One of them said to her companions: "It's evident that we've made a good decision in placing ourselves under the standard of old Lusca. Our husbands are in no state to render us homage proportionate to our charms; furthermore, they're misers, and we'll find here what we need to fulfill all our desires, and satisfy the lust that is the passion of our sex. We have, in addition, the advantage of being considered in Society as the most virtuous of wives and of driving a thousand lovers to despair, who are languishing madly with love and respect for us. I will also add that there is no pleasure in good society as solid as that one savors in these places of confusion; today, it's the captain of a ship, whom a long navigation…oh, a mariner!…tomorrow, an escaped Edifiant; another day, a young soldier, as handsome as Adonis, timid and burning with the first fires of amour; a…oh, my dear Demosie, agree that the delights of life consist uniquely in this variety of pleasures, and that there's nothing more fortunate in the Moon than the ever-inexhaustible possession of everything that a fertile imagination can present of sensualities."

"Yes, I agree, my dear Tetratire, but don't we have to fear Aphrodise? What if we make that deadly present to our husbands?"

"Good," said Tetratire. "Do you think our husbands are so well-behaved? We'll see them at our feet after that misfortune, begging our pardon for their incontinence."

"That's all well and good," said Demosie, "but what if jealousy, or the honor of their authority, or even the pleasure that we seek here, brings them to this place, and they take us by surprise? What shield can we oppose to the expressions of their anger?"

"Oh, I've arranged our batteries for that," replied Tetratire. "'So it's to come and see Plebicoles,' I shall say to them, 'that you scorn your wives, barbarians that you are? We're so unfortunate! I have difficulty believing that you would take debauchery to that extent....' Can't you see them already, my dear Demosie, utterly covered in confusion?"

"Oh, beautiful Tetratire, it's a very old trick, that last resource."

"Agreed, my dear friend, but the oldest ruses of war aren't the least infallible...."

Poequilon could not listen to any more; he quit those two infamous Plebicoles in horror, and began to believe that Selenos had created him to know all the iniquities on the Moon.

As he was preparing to leave the Temple of Lupercalia, seeing no object there worthy of his compassion, he went through a corridor in which he heard a few groans. He saw a door that was ajar and slipped into the room from which the plaintive voice seemed to have emerged. There he perceived an aged debauchee in the most pressing attitude, and a young and charming woman who was weeping bitterly and opposing the old satyr's ardor with all her might.

"Cease your pursuits," she said to the man, covered in sweat and overwhelmed by fatigue. "Return me to my parents, from whom you so crudely abducted me. Neither your rank, which you are abusing, nor your wealth, for which I care little, will ever make a prostitute of me. Is it not the ultimate infamy that you have had me brought to this place of horror, in order to deliver yourself with impunity to the unfortunate passion that my modicum of beauty inspires in you? But Heaven will avenge my innocence."

Poequilon could not hold back his tears, nor moderate his wrath. He knocked the old man down and, covering the unfortunate victim with his invisible tunic, he immediately took her out of that odious abode.

The young woman returned at a run to her parents house, to which Poequilon followed her. He enjoyed the sight of their embraces, and, as Jupiter had once done with less pure intentions for the daughter of Acrisius,[22] he let fall an abundant rain of gold in the house of those poor people, which he regarded as an obscure refuge of virtue, and withdrew, content with his generosity.

XVI. Moral Reflections. Nature caught in the act. A Judge does her job, and judges in petto.

Our invisible man, very satisfied with his heart and his day, returned in the evening to the Temple of the Vestals, his favorite lodging. There were so many circumstances that gave a beautiful luster to the nature of the scenes that he could not feel anything but love for Olympia and compassion for the other beauties of that cloister.

He would have liked to be sufficient to all of them, so convinced was he of their inclination for the principle of life and their disinclination for retreat—for I forgot to mention that he had listened to their secret conversations, and as the Vestals confide their adventures to one another sufficiently, he had realized that the beauties were victims of family interests, and that neither their tastes not their reason had been consulted. He even saw that they had been forced to go against their inclinations and that they were all yearning for the secular life, which caused them a mortal anguish. Their institution and their vows excluded them solemnly from any worldly communication. He considered these establishments unjust and unreasonable, since women on the Moon did not participate in the great mysteries at all, and were of no utility to the Selenogal legislation.

---

[22] Danaë, the mother of the hero Perseus, impregnated by Zeus/Jupiter in the form of a shower of gold.

What cruelty it is, he said to himself, *to inlune alive all these turtle-doves of amour, into which Nature seems to have put her complaisance! Who can treat as a guilty party a beauty who carries in her bosom the vehement seed of fecundity, which ought to move a barbarian to compassion?*

He was indulging in these reflections, unfortunately futile but oft-repeated, when he entered Olympia's room, where he found her holding his portrait and bathing it in her tears.

"O Portrait!" she said. "That is the only name I can give you, O charm of my solitary life! You are, therefore, no more to me than a phantom. How have you been able to abandon me? It is not the pleasures that you have procured for me that I regret, it is your heart, which appeared to me so tender, it is your soul, which seemed to me so delicate. What! Was my unfortunate weakness the cause of your inconstancy?"

Poequilon was transported with joy, at the same time as his bosom was torn by his lover's dolor. He approached her and said to her: "Here I am, my beautiful Olympia."

But at that moment, the Priestess and several old Vestals entered precipitately and seized the portrait that Olympia, dissolved in tears, was holding.

"So this is the cause of your long melancholy," Olibane said to her. "What! Lunar soul, you deliver your self to love, after the most sacred oaths! Penitence and mortification shall be your lot!"

The gentle Olympia, to whom Poequilon had recounted the discoveries that he had made in Olibane's cell, could not prevent herself from saying to her: "At least, Priestess, I am only guilty of having a feeble image of pleasure."

Olibane blushed *a bueno entendor paucas palabras*,[23] and then she went away, taking the portrait with her.

Poequilon consoled his lover, and the beauty soon forgot the panting; if similar events often happened in the Vestals'

---

[23] A Spanish proverb usually rendered *a buen entededor pocas palabras*: "a good listener [requires] few words," or, more figuratively, "a good listener picks up implications."

house, they would have less to mourn, and the world would offer fewer attractions to their imagination.

XVII. Uncommon events.

The penance that was imposed on Olympia was not long, and nor was it rigorous—something rather extraordinary in Temples, where hypocrisy believes it can mask its features with virtue by way of intolerance and austerity, but whether the Priestess was rendering justice or showing mildness of character—which it is rare not to find in a beauty with amorous inclinations, as long as jealousy does not trouble her heart—or whether, finally, Olympia's last words had made a singular impression on her, she only condemned the beauty, as if for form's sake, to a few days' retreat in her room, and consoled her there in the most affectionate manner. It is true that what made them seem less welcome to Olympia was the frequent questions that Olibane asked her about the confiscated portrait; but the young woman always affirmed that the trinket had fallen into her hands by chance, and confessed that she had had the weakness to abandon herself to the illusion of those brush-strokes.

Olibane pretended to be satisfied, and said no more about it, but she retained possession of the portrait.

Poequilon had promised Olympia that he would not absent himself again without warning her; that is why, after having spent a few days in delights, he quit the Vestal, swearing that he would come back soon, more amorous than ever.

XVIII. A wife with a head wins a lawsuit without the involvement of intelligence.

Poequilon transported himself by virtue of a sentiment of curiosity—which, as we know, hardy ever quit him—to the Oracle of the Free-Aromatics—which is as if one said among us, the Temple of Themis. He saw an orator there who was discussing in the presence of Archontes the rights of a citizen who had confided his case to him. He was basing his arguments on the documents he had in his hands and on the Emperors' Laws. He had no doubt that the Paraclete would enable his client to triumph. Another Orator rose to his feet, spoke for as long as the first, and made use of the same Laws to destroy what his competitor had advanced.

Poequilon was very curious to know what decision the Archonte would make. By means of his invisibility he slipped into the midst of the Areopage, whose members huddled together in order to collect the votes, and heard it pronounced that the case had the finest varnish and the best springs. He did not understand any of the deliberation and went away.

As he went through the Temple of the Oracle he distinguished in the crowd a beautiful woman who was speaking to one of the Orators with a great deal of vivacity.

"I shall find the Inspirator Archonte," she said.

"That's the advice I would have given you," replied the Orator.

Poequilon followed her. He went with her into a serious apartment, where he saw an Archonte about forty years old, with a cheerful expression, whose eyes became compassionate, to the extent that the beautiful plaintiff merited.

Good, thought Poequilon. *Here's an Archonte who seems to me to be affable; that man loves to render justice, and if I'm not mistaken, he will render it.*

The beautiful plaintiff apologized for having come in person, with regard to a matter that her husband could not explain.

Poequilon expected the beauty to state her case, but the Archonte said to her: "Madame, I know everything; your suit lacks a few documents, which would render success infallible; if you wish, I shall take responsibility for adding them to your file, and your means will then by incontrovertible."

The beauty thanked him appropriately for such a generous procedure, and the Archonte, as she took her leave, said to her: "Be sure now, Madame, that the Oracle will pronounce in your favor, when the votes are cast."

The beautiful Plaintiff went down the steps, and met her husband, who was out of breath, on his way to see his Inspirator.

"Come back," she said to him. "You've had a wasted journey. You always attack the case by twisting and turning; it's necessary to get the machine moving. I only had to say a few words and I won the case. Fortunate are men whose wives have a head on their shoulders!"

"Wife," the man replied, "I know one too well that you have a head on your shoulders, but what has the head got to do with winning my case?"

"You're a fool," said the plaintiff, "And if you argued, the Archon who is protecting me would send you to prison, with no hesitation and no Aromatics."

Ah! thought Poequilon, *this woman isn't obliging with a good grace.* He took her husband aside and said to him: "Although you cannot see me, I'm in a position to render you a service, and I want to do so. You've gained more than success in your case today. It's necessary to console yourself for that; here are the treasures: if your demand is not just, compensate your adverse party for the wrong that your wife's solicitation has done him, be equitable in future, and to begin with, employ the credit that your riches will give you to make it impossible for your wife to plead on your behalf henceforth."

Poequilon found out subsequently that the worthy husband had followed his advice.

XIX. Nature reclaims her rights everywhere.

Poequilon, wanting to call a truce in his errant life, returned to the Vestals' house. He found them in the greatest disorder. Olibane was, it was said, suffering from the most violent pains. Some laughed; others affected to weep; as for Olympia, her compassionate heart did not permit Poequilon to think that there was any artifice in her affliction.

"What news is there?" asked Poequilon, revealing his presence to Olympia.

"I believe," she replied, "that the Priestess is…and I'm very much afraid that before long…oh, I shall die of the shame!"

Poequilon hastened to go into Olibane's room; a Midwife and a few slaves were lending her their assistance, and before very long, the Priestess brought into the world the most beautiful boy on the Moon.

Considering the child, Olibane was struck by astonishment. "He is," she said, "the very image of the portrait I took from Olympia."

The child of penitence was taken away by the family of the Priestess, and Poequilon resolved to make his fortune one day.

XX. Sequitur leviter filia matris iter.
(A daughter gladly follows in her mother's footsteps.)

Meanwhile, what Olympia feared came to pass. Poequilon no longer left the Temple; the dear Vestal had asked him not to leave her until she had given birth to the fruit of his affection. A Midwife covered by Poequilon's tunic was introduced into Olympia's cell and the beautiful Vestal gave a brother to the son of the Priestess.

Olibane, who was beginning to recover, and whom the Vestal Acousta had informed of what was about to happen on Olympia's chamber, came to see the invalid, and was astonished to see a pretty little creature on the Vestal's bed.

"Beautiful Olympia," Olibane said to her, "is it also a portrait that has done that to you?"

Piqued by that mockery, the Vestal replied: "I let you go first, Priestess."

Olibane, being reasonable, took the part of compassion and clemency, and had Poequilon's second son placed with the first.

In spite of the precautions that were taken to keep those two adventures secret, rumor of it circulated in the lay population, but an exceedingly clever Edifiant repaired the honor of the Temple.

XXI. Poequilon and Olympia leave the Vestals' Temple

It was decided that Olympia could do whatever she wanted in her chamber with portraits, and to that effect, Olibane returned the one that she had confiscated, on condition that the dangerous miniature did not make any more children.

Olympia soon recovered, and Poequilon continued to live with her in the greatest security, abandoning himself to the caresses of his Vestal and the joy of being a father.

He spent more than a year in that delightful indolence, without worrying about what was happening in the outside world; the Temple had become his universe, and he had got so used to being invisible that one might have thought it his natural condition. He was surely happy, because the passion for change, that inseparable companion of humanity, no longer agitated in his heart.

He was at the midday meal one day beside his dear Olympia, nourishing himself on the morsels that her delicate hand presented to him, when his invisibility suddenly came to an end and he was perceived by the Priestess and all the Vestals. Terror spread through the bosom of those doves; only old Acousta had sufficient strength to say that it was the phantom of the Vestal Ephialte, who had died sixty years before.

Olibane raised her eyes and, recognizing in Poequilon all the resemblance to her baby, had no doubt that the handsome specter was an incubus, and from that moment on she repented of having abandoned herself to Edifiants, since there were incubi who procured pleasures on the Moon without one having to reproach oneself for having violated chastity.

Profiting from the consternation of the Vestals, Poequilon seized the keys, took Olympia and left the Temple with her. Perhaps Selenos, without being begged, struck the slaves who were guarding the door with blindness, for I have always thought that exit too fortunate not to have a hint of the miraculous about it.

XXIII. Strange metamorphoses, in which the nature of things is nevertheless seen.

Our two fugitives drew away from the Temple and had reached open country when two Stratiotes,[24] well armed and sporting menacing moustaches approached the two Vestals—for Poequilon and Olympia had not had time to change clothes. Poequilon did not doubt that the soldiers had violent designs. That idea gripped him with horror for his dear Olympia, and he begged Selenos from the bottom of his heart that the beautiful Vestal might become a man, in order not to be the prey of those two barbarians, and that he might become a woman, wanting to sacrifice himself for his mistress and arrest their fury by the charm of his beauty.

The two Stratiotes did, indeed, take possession of the Vestals, but Selenos permitted gold to soften their hearts more than beauty, and if that was no great miracle, it was at least fortunate.

Olympia, who took the name Olympius, sensed singular stirrings of jealousy and courage as they approached, and Poequilone, whose name I shall feminize, was not agitated by those emotions—an admirable effect of their metamorphoses!

Poequilone negotiated favorably with the two heroes, who had wanted to honor her passage. She obtained, for Olympius and herself, the clothes of the two Stratiotes, which covered those of Vestals. I do not know what the Stratiotes did, but Olympius and Poequilone continued on their way under the harness of glory.

"What a misfortune it would have been," Olympius said to Poequilone, "if those Stratiotes…."

"They were good fellows," said Poequilone.

---

[24] Author's note: "Soldiers."

"What!" replied Olympius. "You don't seem very upset about it; I hardly recognize you any longer."

"I don't recognize myself," said Poequilone. "Apparently, my change is quite complete."

"O Heaven!" said Olympius. "If those soldiers had had the first fruits...!"

"Dear Olympius, I now sense how difficult it is for a man to encounter that treasure, but my friend, lets enjoy our new being and not love one another any less."

XXIV. Sermons written in the sand

I have not yet said that Poequilone had become as beautiful as a woman as he had been handsome as a man, and that Olympius, in quitting the graces of his first sex, had acquired everything that comprises the embellishments and charm of the second—but one can easily divine that; and the tender Olympius, in considering his beautiful Poequilone, forgot the adventure of the Stratiotes.

Poequilone gazed languidly at Olympius, and thought she felt that she loved him even more since their metamorphosis, but she was a little vexed to find him so delicate, delicacy never have been to her taste; she strongly regretted not having added something to the wish that she had made for Olympius.

However, she said to herself, *since it has turned out that I find myself a woman, I want to be a virtuous woman, which is to say, faithful; I have had so much to criticize in that sex for its inconstancy that I want to put it in the wrong by my example and prove to it that one can be what is known as an honest woman. It's true that those Stratiotes didn't inspire me with enough horror, but that was for want of reflection.*

Afterwards, she swore a thousand oaths to Olympius to love no one but him; her handsome lover made the same protestations in his turn—but Poequilone always found that Olympius expressed his tenderness too feebly.

XXV. An unfortunate encounter, fortunately terminated by an invincible expedient.

Olympius and Poequilone were continuing on their way, in the hope of finding a house in the next town in which they might live in conformity with their fortune, when they were met and arrested by a company of Stratiotes wearing uniforms exactly similar to their own.

They were tied up and taken to the next town, where they were presented to an officer, who looked them over, judged them to be deserters, and condemned them to the final honors of war. Poequilone, who had lost her courage along with her beard, burst into tears and revealed her sex, which was promptly verified in the court. She was then regarded as an errant Plebicole, the plague of armies, and her sentence was commuted to the military lash, without any alteration in the sentence of young Olympius, who protested in vain that he had never served anyone but the great Alma.

The procedure moved at a fast pace, for the Stratiote judges were not like the Archontes, judging as rapidly as they took towns; the birch rods had already been distributed to the ranks and Olympius' head was already circled by the fatal blindfold...oh Heavens! Let us hasten to deliver that innocent couple.

Poequilone prostrated herself in the arena and presented the Stratiote court with such a prodigious quantity of gold that they could not avoid admitting that Olympius was not a deserter, nor Poequilone a Plebicole. Thus they were extracted from that tight spot, where so many others would have failed.

O dust, dust, said Poequilone to herself, *I did well to ask Selenos for you before anything else!*

XXVI. Does good society make for good morality?

They got rid of their dangerous and honorable costumes, bought slaves, carriages and horses, in order to be respected, since everything on the Moon is only judged by its surface, and returned to Verticephalia.

Poequilone judged that a great Lady ought to have big slaves, so she had one that resembled a twenty-year-old Hercules. *It's an ostentation*, she thought, *that befits my opulence; I have no desire to abuse it, for I want to be faithful to Olympius.* Besides which, it goes without saying that Poequilone would have been unable to descend to slaves.

Nevertheless, she had a decided aversion to women, and they fulfilled no other functions in her house than those concerned with her adornment. Poequilone's dressing, undressing and bathing were the service of men, and that honor was only conferred on the most handsome among them.

She sometimes said to herself that it was very flattering for a woman to stir the heart of a slave; that it was the true triumph of beauty; and one might have thought that she was indeed very attached to that sentiment, for she treated with the utmost cruelty a slightly cracked Aristocrat of Verticephalia, who had in his entourage two red elephants, four white camels and twenty black dromedaries, not to mention the eagles and ostriches, and she said to Olympius:

"You see how faithful I am to you."

XXVII. Reprisals.

Olympius was not entirely sure what to think of that fidelity.

I've been a woman like any other, he said to himself, *but it seems to me that I didn't abandon myself to Poequilone's indecencies; what does she expect me to think of those tall slaves who perfume her? If I were to have myself put to bed by her women, what would she say?*

While she made these reflections alone in her room a beautiful hairdresser came in, under some pretext, or for some reason; Olympius, who had only made use of his sex with Poequilone as yet, felt inflamed by the appetite for novelty; chagrin was mingled with it.

"Aha! I've caught you!" said Poequilone, coming in quietly. "It's not only for me, then, that you're brief in compliments; my beauty and my virtue aren't sufficient for you."

"Madame," Olympius said to her, "your beauty is incontestable and your tall slaves are a guarantee of your virtue. In truth, Poequilone, the metamorphosis is very complete in you; if I had remained a woman, I could not have filled the role better. We are both perfect Verticephalian spouses.

XXVIII. Judicious reflections and the return of the natural order.

Poequilone reflected on everything that was passing in her heart; she felt that it was impossible not to be absolute, frivolous, voluptuous and jealous.

If I resume my sex, as I hope to do, she said to herself, *I shall be indulgent to women, for I recognize by my own experience that a woman is not free, and that it is no more just to censure her than the criticize the flow of rivers, the inconstancy of clouds and the waves directed by the winds.*

In consequence of that reasoning, Poequilone allowed herself to be carried away by the irresistible torrent of female constitution. In the midst of that agitation, however, and by a natural consequence of her sex, Poequilone brought into the world a daughter, the origin of whom might have been attributed to many people, but Olympius declared himself to be the father, in accordance with the laws of the Moon: *Pater est quem nuptiae demonstrant.*[25]

The child was named Ephelide.

The two years of the metamorphosis expired, and Poequilone made wishes for Olympius and for herself; while she was harvesting the graces of her toilette she rediscovered her sex, and at the same time, Olympius, in the presence of the

---

[25] "He is the father whom marriage indicates to be so": a principle of Roman law enshrined in many legal codes, including the French one.

beautiful Hairdresser, became Olympia again in a very un-timely fashion. Many men in Verticephalia are subject to al-most similar crises.

By virtue of that rehabilitation, little Ephelide no longer had a father or a mother, but people became accustomed to recognizing Olympia as her mother and Poequilon as her fa-ther.

"Education can do anything," said a Doctor of the Moon.

XXIX. Too true.

Poequilon and Olympia, returned to themselves, blushed at their reciprocal aberrations; they regarded their past conduct as a state of intoxication occasioned by the change of sex, and forgave one another mutually for their infidelities. They also felt parental in their entrails, and sent for their children who were being nourished by Olibane's family. They were, as we have said, two male children, one of whom was the issue of the Priestess and the other of Olympia; the former was named Choripede and the latter Monophyte.

A few days after these arrangements, the beautiful Hair-dresser came into Poequilon's apartment holding a beautiful child to her breast, and said: "Master, since you're reassem-bling your family, allow me to introduce you to this little crea-ture, which your wife gave to me."

Poequilon adopted her and named her Moechocarpe.

It does not always require adventures as extraordinary as those that had happened to Poequilon and Olympia to encoun-ter such mixtures in the posterity of spouses.

The word *spouse* reminds me that our couple, who had not been living together thus far very legally, were finally joined together by the laws of marriage. I don't know whether anyone has noticed that the formula was lacking, in order for them to be honest people.

XXX. Insults in the air.

The four children were raised with an equal distinction, and Poequilon began to live happily with his dear Olympia in the bosom of the family. But he thought that the happiness ought not to be confined to them alone; he opened his door to people of good society, Stratiotes, literary men and parasitic flatterers.

He lived in that entire society, of estimable people who were not esteemed, and *vice versa*; some were unfortunate illustrious individuals, victims of envy and persecution, who had adopted the name of philosophers in order to take their revenge on human injustice. Others were luminous minds, who weighed smoke[26] personally, and always caused the balance to tip in their favor. Each of the latter wanted to be thought the pole star of genius, and their currency was scorn for their brethren.

Poequilon surrounded himself with all these stars, found as if in the midst of darkness; he only encountered enlightenment in the bosom of modest men, and found little of it, but those had all his benevolence.

The majority of Stratiotes rode roughshod over all the other estates of life; one might have thought, on listening to them, that the honor of families was the meanest of pleasures for them.

When the literary men were tearing one another apart Poequilon was far from being able to admire them. He sometimes said to them: "Resplendent stars, why is it that the intelligent have no soul?" And when those confused stars made no reply, he added:

"How can you expect to attain the glory that is the object of all your desires by biting each other like mad dogs, and making a spectacle of yourselves to the public that scorns you,

---

[26] Author's note: "*Dare pondus idonea fumo*." Another quotation from Persius; literally "to give weight to smoke," metaphorically to give too much importance to trifles.

to the extent that it understands you? Do you not sense that you are laboring continually by your baseness to compensate the people for the empire that you nevertheless claim by virtue of your enlightenment? How did you get it into your heads that jealousy, treason, calumny and your crawling conduct could ever constitute human greatness?

"No, the greatest genius on the Moon, who behaved the way you do, would never be anything but the nation's marionette. A man may please by means of wit, but he can only elevate himself by virtue. One esteems the talent of the Musician and the Actor, but when both of them cease to charm our ears, we no longer know the one as anything but a fiddler and the other as a ham. It would have been the same for your class, if you had wanted it; you could, indeed, be pole stars, human guiding lights, if wisdom had had any charm for you, for it is the privilege of intelligence to reveal the springs of the heart.

"It is for Genius to know, and to make sense, and to practice wisdom; but by an effect of your depravity, you intelligence and soul are incoherent today, so your genius lacks fiber, and full of continual combats, your laurels will be withered in your prime."

That was the manner in which Poequilon reproached men of letters for their misdeeds. As for the Stratiotes, he said to them that he would wait for them to attain the age of reason.

With regard to the flatterers, while he found himself unworthy of their eloquence. Her turned his head and pronounced, in a low voice, the judgment that poverty debases people.

XXXI. An admirable ploy to catch reputation on the wing.

Although Poequilon received a numerous company in his home, he sometimes dispersed himself visiting others. He also went to Academies of fine minds and gambling clubs. One day, he was in one of the former when he saw a young man come in who received a hearty welcome, and someone told

Poequilon that he was a wit who had already produced admirable plays for the Theater. He inquired as to the Author's name and was told that it was Amphiluce.

"I've never heard mention of the man," said Poequilon. "What has he written?"

Citation was made of *The Androgynes*, a Tragedy, *The Amphibians*, a Comedy, and *The Somnambulists*, an Opera. He was no more familiar with the works than their author, and expressed his astonishment that he was unaware of productions that were reported to him as having enjoyed success, but a woman in the company explained it to him.

She told him that clever men who were desirous of embarking on a theatrical career, weary of applying shamefully to the Actors of Verticephalia for the performance of their plays, had made the decision to put them on before a small portion of the public, whom they called their society, and by that means, Literary men without favor built themselves a reputation from society to society, which gradually extended its Philacters throughout the nation, since the nation is only composed of societies.

"It's a resource," she added, "that women have found, in order to save their clever friends from the obscurity in which the malice of well-known men and the incapacity of Actors would like them to remain buried."

"Oh! That's very well done," said Poequilon. "In consequence, we shall soon have no more need of the Theaters of the Capital. But where do you find your Actors?"

"We also have Actors in the societies," she said, "whose talents are known in all the good houses, and who put the Emperor's hams to shame. Furthermore, we are bringing forward an excellent project. As not all heads are made for the dramatic genre, and there are productions of every sort, such as Novels, Poems, Madrigals and Philosophical Theories, we have in our societies a number of skillful copyists, with the aid of which we give a prodigious impetus to the works of our friends, in order to substitute by default for impressions that the Printers dare not take on of the work of a man whose reputation is not made."

"My word, you're right," said Poequilon. "I also advise you to have Pantomime societies, in order to enrage the Fairground performers."

XXXII. Offense and reparation made to a bellowing cavern

From that Academy Poequilon passed on to that of the Imperial Tonometry. He saw a great many bizarrely dressed people who were singing, and saw others in a hole who were playing instruments. Poequilon thought he perceived that the singers were off key, and said so to someone.

"Yes, of course they're off key," was the reply, "but they're not going wrong."

At that moment a young Actress appeared on the stage whose tone was in harmony with the dominant instruments. She made a few melodious sounds emerge from her throat, and, suddenly stopping, dared to reproach the recess for having played a false note. Immediately there was a great rumor in the symphonic abyss; a discussion was held, and the temeritous Actress was condemned to make a public apology to the implacable hole and to admit that it had never played a false note. She did so, after a profound reverence, in these terms:

"I departed from the respect that I owe to the pit of the Academy, in daring to say that it had played a false note. I solemnly declare that the gentlemen of the pit never go wrong, and that the tenebrous cavern of the Imperial Tonometry is infallible."

The Actress was applauded loudly, and the audience laughed for a long time at the infallibility of the pit.

XXXIII. The opinion of a desperate man.

Poequilon reflected upon human pride and its ridiculousness. He told Olympia everything that he had learned, and his wife collected the material in order to form a plan of education for their children, because they were convinced that a profound examination of the vices of society is the only thing capable of fortifying the soul and preserving it from contagion.

A Stratiote chief who frequented Poequilon's home took him one day to an Academy of gaming protected by the Governor for the support of a noble family. As they were going there, Poequilon said to him: "So, my dear Monomaque, you sometimes gamble?"

"Yes."

"But do you always win?"

"No."

"So then you're in a bad mood?"

"No."

"But is the man you're playing against always of your character?"

"No."

"Your adversary, in consequence, is sometimes in a bad mood?"

"Yes."

"And when he's in a bad mood, he irritates you?"

"He wouldn't dare."

"But if he dared?"

"I'd kill him."

"But what if he killed you?"

"I'd be dead; but that can't happen; I'm the one who kills."

"Now, you see, my dear Monomaque," Poequilon added, "that it's a great misfortune to kill someone, and an even greater one to be killed. A man of honor ought to gamble less than another, because the slightest offense ought to be more sensible to him than another. Any man who loses has difficul-

97

ty containing himself, and by your estate, you can't let anything pass; even supposing that you're a good gambler, you're often obliged to fight if you play often, and in my opinion, the game, as they say, isn't worth the candle."

As he finished this speech they arrived at the fateful tabernacle. Monomaque started to play against a tall phlegmatic stranger, who lost his money with as much composure as if he were threading pearls.

"See how that man loses," whispered Monomaque to Poequilon. "The fine education he had received! That's how I lose myself." And he continued winning.

From time to time he sympathized politely with his adversary, who made no reply.

However, Monomaque eventually lost all that he had won. He lost it like a well brought up man. Then he lost all the money that he had brought to the table, and the education faltered. The he lost his jewelry, to his chagrin, and he reproached his adversary for not consoling him for his loss, as he had done himself. The foreigner replied, with his customary phlegm, that that kind of civility was not included in the rules of the game.

Having nothing more to wager, Monomaque borrowed a lot of money from Poequilon, which he lost. Poequilon went out several times to pick up dust and furnish Monomaque's losses, but as he wanted to see an end to the scene he finally told him that he could not lend him anymore.

Monomaque offered to play on his word; the laconic stranger replied that he owed a revenge to someone. That was the last straw. Monomaque lost his education, no longer remembering father, mother or preacher; he had the ingratitude to accuse Poequilon of avarice and said that he wanted to stake his blood against the stranger.

"In that case," the foreigner replied, "We need to play that game somewhere else."

All three of them went out, and Monomaque received a wound from the stranger which dispensed him of fighting Poequilon.

Monomaque was taken home, having lost his blood, still wanting to lose the rest of his life in the presence of his wife and children, whom he left in destitution, and whom he urged to die of despair like himself.

Poequilon, a witness to that scene, said to him: "As for you, do what you like; although divine law does not permit a man to take his own life, such a resignation is sometimes a great benefit to society, and it's probably the first act of justice you've ever committed in your life. As for your family, I'll take responsibility for them; be sure in dying that they'll be happier than they have ever been. My fortune will be their happiness, and your memory their salvation."

That speech put balm into Monomaque's blood; he blushed that someone cared so little for his life, and recognized that his vices merited such scorn. He begged Poequilon's pardon and swore by Selenos that he would not gamble again.

Poequilon said to him: "In that case, you won't survive your wound; so, adieu. That's lucky for your children."

XXXIV. A very generous wish.

When Olympia heard about that adventure she wept for humankind, and recounted the tragic event to her children, whose reason was developing. Shortly afterwards, Poequilon returned to Monomaque's lodgings. He found him fully recovered, and it appeared to him that he had as much horror of gambling as he had once had passion, but as he placed little trust in such appearances he wished-for the time of wishing had arrived—that Monomaque would remain in that virtuous disposition for as long as he lived. It required nothing less than a special protection from Selenos to bring about such a change, and Poequilon judged the benefit so rare that he did not think it permissible to asked anything more of Selenos on that occasion.

XXXV. A model to follow.

Poequilon had naturally engraved in his heart the principle that the happiness of fortunate men is to make others happy. He sought every opportunity to spread with discernment the favors that he had received from Selenos, and as dust is a powerful motivating force on the Moon, he distributed with artistry and without affectation, to all those who had need of it, whether to live, to reestablish their reputation, to enter into their rights, to escape a glaring oppression or to avenge innocence, all that interest or favor could heap upon them. He discovered hidden merit, and brought it into the light.

All these transformations were as many miracles, which made the charm of life; when he saw someone unfortunate, he did not set out to determine whether or not it was by their own fault; the thought that a man's duty is to help his brothers, and that it was the sole prerogative of the Divinity to read the depths of their hearts. He regarded with horror the cruel men who seem to take pleasure in seeing a poor wretch palpitate, and pay for their barbaric curiosity with meager alms, the prideful Sermonizers, the supposedly just men whom an unworthy prosperity renders insensible and can only relieve an unfortunate who falls at their feet after "having given the gods their due."

Selenos saw with pleasure his favorite embracing virtue by choice, without ostentation and often without thinking that he was doing good, so the Genius granted the Fountain of Youth to Olympia, because the tender spouse was growing old, and Poequilon, only occupied with virtue and observing people for a considerable number of years, had not asked Selenos for anything.

Olympia was rejuvenated, and became more beautiful than ever. As for Poequilon, he drank so little of the elixir of Youth on that occasion that the liquid only took him back ten years, with the result that he had the external appearance of a man of fifty. One sees few examples of a husband making a wish to eternalize his wife, and one sees even fewer of a man who remains under the appearance of the chill of age, when he could adorn himself with the riches of Spring.

XXXVI. That will not last long.

That is the way that one ought to make use of treasures, but ordinarily, the rich are not Philosophers, and Philosophers are not rich. Poequilon was much more a rich man than a Philosopher, for while he was cultivating the Fine Arts and putting morality into action, he fell into a trap of voluptuousness as simply as a Publican of Verticephalia might have done.

Spectacles were flourishing then, the Sophocles of the Nation occupied the stage, and a beautiful Actress named Chrysophile sowed charm in the eyes and trouble in the heart. Poequilon was captured, like many others by the enchanting bait; the seductive tones of the Siren distracted him from Olympia and philosophy; our sage made love in the wings. He was fifty years old, but he was preferred to the most brilliant youth, because the beautiful Chrysophile was sometimes obliging, and she found in Poequilon the means to exercise the grandeur of her soul. All the handsome unfortunates of Verticephalia experienced her generosity, and Poequilon was delighted to have encountered a mistress so benevolent. He no longer occupied himself with doing good; Chrysophile did it for him, as she understood it. He gave her a palace, carriage and slaves, but she did not quit for that the career of glory; she was too fond of incense and domination to decide to be nothing other than amour in the depths of her palace. Her beauty and her grace subjugated the great; her talents captivated the Public; her imperious humor governed Authors; her favor tyrannized her troupe; and her virtue....

Let us pass on to the next Chapter.[27]

---

[27] Author's note: "We are very glad on the Earth's behalf that not all of our actresses are of that stripe.
To you whose most beautiful work is love,
Beautiful P***, I pay tribute here,

XXXVII. A very accurate portrait.
Morality borrows a pleasant voice.

Chrysophile had enabled Poequilon to experience count-
less sensualities, and her graces were always new to him, her
caresses always varied; so Poequilon's prodigality was proportionate to the love that that Cleopatra inspired in him: feasts,
gifts, magnificent presents, little houses, contracts—for one
can do little with actresses without contracts—nothing was
spared. The courtesan was surprised herself by her lover's
generosity; she could not imagine how Poequilon was able to
subsidize all the expenses that she caused him to make, because he did not tell her the secret of his fortune.

I do not know whether he perceived that the beauty was
astonished by such a durable prosperity, or whether a Philosophical notion passed through his mind, but he took it into his
head to pretend that he was ruined in order to test his mistress'
kind heart.

Poequilon was rather an eccentric Philosopher, to use
that stratagem to sound out an Actress; on the Moon there are
certain Philosophical maxims regarding Actresses, which are
incontestable, among others, one that corresponds to one
known on Earth: no money leads to loneliness.

He appeared one day before Chrysophile looking very
pensive, and was obstinate for some time in hiding the reason
for his melancholy from her; finally, as he could not contain
himself any longer, he said to her: "Adorable Chrysophile, you
love me and I love you, but I'm ruined, and I no longer have
anything but my heart to offer you; I know that you are too
tender and too delicate to think that you could forget a man
who had laid so much at your feet...."

To your virtue even more than your talent.
If you have been able to capture public support.
Charm hearts, and ravish the senses.
You also know the secret of being good."

"What!" said Chrysophile. "You have no more re-sources? Is it really true?"

"But what do I need, if I still have you?"

"If you still have me…but think about it, Poequilon: at your age, married, with children, what can I do? I'll talk to someone, see to it that you can get by, but we can't continue to see one another; that would resemble a marriage of con-science, which would cover me with ridicule. Everyone would say that I'm a model of gratitude, and that I'm returning what you've given me—that would be unprecedented in our world, and I don't want to be the butt of jokes, nor to expose you to it."

"O Heaven!" said Poequilon. "Are you a Plebicole, Chrysophile?"

"Listen to me for the last time, my dear Poequilon," said the beauty, "and don't interrupt. We are Plebicoles before be-ing Actresses, and if weren't, we would never show ourselves in the Theater—not that the Theater is dishonoring; it's our mores that seem to have dishonored it; but it's a business mat-ter, and it only consists, ordinarily, of our accessory. Under the mantle of Thalia, we're sheltered from the research of pet-ty Judges and we render ourselves necessary, on the one hand, by our talent, in order to acquire Protections on the other, which put us above the pettifogging laws that are the torment of devil-led women. So, when a man comes to bring his amour and his purse to an Actress, he's doing nothing but coming to a Convent; our brilliant profession gives an illusion to the senses, and we make him pay dearly for that enchantment; we are, in sum, fashionable women, and you know that items of luxury and caprice are priceless; we are, sincerely, the lovers of anyone who pleases us and the Plebicoles of anyone who can pay; you were in the latter category. You're too old for someone like me, who is young and beautiful, so I couldn't be your lover; but as you were rich and you wanted from me what are known as the pleasures of love, I was quite willing to be your Plebicole, and apart from my heart, which I couldn't give to your meager merit, I've given all the rest to your large fortune."

"But cruel woman," said Poequilon, "haven't you told me a hundred times that you adored me?"

"What a fool you are, Poequilon. Ought you not to render yourself justice, and at the same time consider that I was only playing a role with you? Do you not know that Plebicoles have their affectations, and that that's the objective of their art? Have I not sometimes made you happy, by giving you all the appearances of love, and sometimes by making you drink voluptuousness to the brim? You are even very fortunate that our felicity has lasted as long as your fortune, for if I had wearied of you I could have sent you away. We are free and mistresses of our charms, as Merchants are of their shops. Withdraw, then, to a corner of the world, taking these truths to heart, and convince yourself that we have our maxims, and that is to expiate our disorders that young fools and old debauchees are ruined. In all times and all lands, Plebicoles, and Actresses above all, are the living morality of their century; we cause men to return to their duty in spite of themselves, and we regard ourselves as instruments of the vengeance of honest women. Adieu."

XXXVIII. A frame for the previous picture

One hears the truth when one is poor. Poequilon, convinced of the sentiments of his Chrysophile, went out furiously, because he still loved hr. He was destined for great humiliations. However, Olympia, only too well aware of his misconduct, made him tender reproaches. He promised to be wiser in future, but the project he formed of avenging himself on his impudent Actress closely resembled amour.

He informed Olympia that he was going to rejuvenate himself, and in fact, he gave himself the age of twenty. Handsome and well-built, rich and young, he flattered himself that he would infatuate Chrysophile, and take his revenge on her by passing into the arms of another at the moment when the

Actress' heart was most deeply attained. The plan of an idiot, my dear Poequilon!

In that seductive form he was soon on Chrysophile's breast; the artful Actress improvised new graces; she lavished the caresses of twenty years upon him, and Poequilon, far from avenging himself, dreaded losing favors so precious. Chrysophile made her new lover the foster father of the entire troupe; she wined and dined all those simian individuals, who paid him in gambols: farces, gross epigrams and the vile make-up of a memory in pawn were collected with care to amuse the young magnificent, and those jesting schoolmasters told Poequilon that they were forming him.

Poequilon knew full well the baseness and ignorance of that entire cortege, but Chrysophile compensated him for it; a lover ought to be obliging. For this time, he believed that he was loved, and was not thinking of testing his mistress, when fate procured him the most fortunate of enlightenments. One day, he came into Chrysophile's apartment quietly, believing that that Queen of twenty-four hours was resting; how surprised he was when he saw the Princess's train-bearer substituting for his functions.

"What, Chrysophile!" he cried, "is this the way one carries a train in the dramatic world?"

The train-bearer ran away, and Chrysophile said to the imprudent newcomer: "What! That astonishes you? That poor fellow was pining away with love—should I have let him perish? Do you know that he's a Gentleman of Verticephalia, who entered my service in order to be near to me? Do you know that he's better looking than you? Do you know that he's wittier? Do you know, too, that he has more...but you don't know anything; go away and let me rest."

Poequilon, fearing that if he argued, he would get another fine sermon full of morality and evidence, left Chrysophile, firmly resolved never to see her again.

XXXIX. The consequences of debauchery.

"That's it," said Poequilon. "Adieu forever, abject race. Oh Olympia, how ungrateful I am. How was I able to prefer that unworthy object to you, whose beauty, tenderness and virtue are incomparable?"

He returned to his wife and children; he sensed his love reanimating and his heart elevating in proportion to his appetite for legitimate pleasures; but Poequilon had to do penance for his debauchery; the infamous Chrysophile had caused Aphrodise to pass into his blood, and the imprudent fellow had borne that tribute into the bosom of chastity.

All Poequilon's treasures could not protect him from the long and shameful consequences of a depraved amour. Olympia received the poison in her loins and brought into the world a daughter covered with her father's opprobrium.

Selenos took pity on that faithful spouse and that innocent fruit; he extended his benevolent hand over those two objects of his compassion, but he struck Poequilon with the curse of Job; in vain he implored the clemency of the Genius; he had to wait a year in that frightful condition before being able to make a wish.

The Fountain of Youth did not prevent him from dying, and the Sarcotomes, to arrest the progress of the sores, deprived him of everything that he had employed so much to the prejudice of Olympia.

That year of dolor having finally lapsed, Poequilon asked one morning for a complete cure and obtained it; his body was entirely purified—but what the Sarcotomes had removed did not come back.

He requested it tearfully from Selenos, who caused him to hear these words: "Remember that you cannot make the same wish twice—but if Olympia makes that wish on your behalf, it will be granted, for what you are requesting is more hers than yours; You have been the despoiler of her possession; it was not misfortune that occasioned you that loss, it was vice and a relapse, and destiny has ordered that your re-generation depends on your wife's wishes."

Poequilon ran to his wife's apartment in order to beg her to intercede with the Genius, but he found that she was no longer there. Selenos had removed her, with all her children, and had translocated them to the island of Eutoquia.

It did not take Poequilon long to perceive that he had been abandoned by his family; he regarded himself as a monster, for the protection of Selenos, seemingly accorded to Olympia, did not permit him to suspect that spouse—but the virtuous woman was unaware that Poequilon's reestablishment was in her power. She had no idea that a prayer could work that miracle; she had no examples of it, and besides which, Selenos, in order to punish Poequilon, might well have distanced it from her thoughts.

Olympia lived happily on the island of Eutoquia with her family, although separated from her spouse, because Selenos wanted it thus. She regretted it; she bemoaned it; but that affliction did not surpass the limits that Selenos had put upon it.

Poequilon made ardent wishes to recover his wife and his family; a terrible voice said to him: "You cannot demand the property of another person. Your wife and your children are no longer yours, since you have ignored them for such a long time, and my word is not broken in refusing you that grace; if you discover the island of Eutoquia you can rejoin them, but the voyage will be long and difficult if you are not virtuous and faithful. Nevertheless, do not quit your fatherland until you receive the order to do so in a dream."

XL. How it is necessary to quit one's homeland.

After having heard that oracle, Poequilon made the decision to apply himself to study, for Selenos, whom he had asked one day for the gift of Genius, had replied to him that it could only be achieved by application and long toil. Wanting to leave eternal monuments of glory and beneficence in Verticephalia, he cultivated most particularly the sciences that he did not have. He read a great deal, and frequented old men and great men.

Afterwards, he produced works of intelligence, dramatic plays in which everything respired virtue and sentiment, which acquired him the admiration of his century. He proposed laws and political reforms, which were adopted, and which earned him the name of Legislator. He founded colleges very different from ours, and Hospitals worthy of bearing the name; he established Tribunals, and drew up the statutes of all those establishments, and he was called a Benefactor. He no longer wanted to there to be any poverty in Verticephalia, nor oppression, nor injustice, not ignorance, nor weakness, and in consequence, crime seemed bound to be extirpated.

Forty years had gone by thus since the last oracle, when, one night, he thought he saw Selenos, and heard these words:

"It is time that you abandoned this place to wander all over the Planet until you find your wife and children."

He quit his Fatherland with less regret because he believed that it was happy, and all the Verticephalians mourned him.

PART TWO

I. An Idea of Selenography, or Description of the Moon

As Poequilon is about to travel the world, it is as well that I give you an idea of the Map of the Moon.

The planet is divided into five continents. The first, which comprises the Empire of Verticephalia, is called Taurijove,[28] the second Eliopolia, the third Pyramidustrine, the fourth Peristerique and the fifth Eutoquia, which is an immense island on which no one can land without the particular protection of Selenos. Communication with it is still unknown, because all those who have been fortunate enough to reach it have remained there; it is, therefore, only known by tradition. It is said that one enjoys an eternal Spring there, and a pure felicity, but it is only after having suffered a great deal that one can reach it; it is the infinite recompense for good deeds.

II. A Voyage to Stivalo; Poequilon renders homage to the Prince and experiences his generosity.

Poequilon rejuvenated himself, and set forth, with a great many men, horses and camels, still mourning his wife, whom he could not, as we know, either find or render happy without a miracle.

He arrived in a brilliant nation named Stivalo; his evident magnificence caused him to be welcomed by everyone. He visited the superb edifices with which the country is filled and spread many liberalities.

The Emperor of the country is named the Paterodiple. He is adored like a God; it is generally thought that the Prince in

---

[28] i.e. "Jovian Bull"—the guise in which Jupiter ravished Europa

question has the power to bring about entry into the grace of Selenos, and that he alone can enable someone to land on the island of Eutoquia. Poequilon did not neglect to go and throw himself at his feet. He told him about his misfortunes and begged him to enable him to discover the island of Eutoquia, but to procure him in the meantime the twin characters with which one can pass as the Paterodiple—and he left magnificent presents at the foot of his throne.

The Emperor, touched by Poequilon's misfortunes, received his homage and agitated the air above his head; then he said to him: "Be sure that you will rejoin your family in Eutoquia; as for the rest, I cannot anticipate the resurrection of the flesh. All the Musicians in Stivalo resemble you, and although I am very attached to them, I can only procure them the hope of one day seeing Eutoquia. Console yourself, and sing if you wish in my Catarastes; that will distract you. Those are presents of the Land, which will prevent you from dishonoring young women and preserve you from the malevolences of Venus.

"Oh," said Poequilon, "they are no longer at risk with me."

III. The more than splendid dinner of a Prince of Porphyry

Poequilon thanked the Paterodiple with a great deal of humility. He went to the temples, the spectacles, the baths, the promenades and all the public edifices, in order to seek information about Olympia, but no one could give him any news of her.

He distributed alms to all the wretched, and sometimes thought that he might encounter his family is their midst of the unfortunates who were striving to stir the compassion of the Stivalians at the exits from the temples at Palaces—for Olympia and the children did not have the projection powder, as he did—but the justice of Selenos reassured him.

He visited famous Artistes, was instructed by them, bored by them, and wept. He witnessed the buffooneries of the Stivalians and their much-vaunted Music, and the songs reminded him of his condition. He gave feasts to the Poryphrian Princes who comprised the Paterodiple's Court, and it was there that he amused himself most. He was fêted in his turn by the most highly-placed individuals, and often told them that a God had abducted his wife; he did not tell them the rest, but everyone knew it.

He dined one day at the home of a Porphyrian whose table was splendidly garnished, but the most brilliant aspect of the service was twelve young women of complete beauty; a dazzling paleness, combined with the most regular features, made the charm of the eyes; their semi-naked cleavages and their charming figures guaranteed to the imagination all the delights that can be promised at such moments, in which amour tramples adornment underfoot; all the gleam of his dignity was visible in the Porphyrian's eyes; the sensuality he respired had passed into his veins....

But let us leave that Stivalian Prince, who is not to be mourned, and come back to Poequilon.

IV. Conversations over dessert; beautiful sentiments that cannot be doubted; the sacrifice of self-esteem.

That unfortunate was beside the most beautiful of the guests; he sighed and lowered his eyes; he squeezed her hand and his tears betrayed his dolor.

The beautiful Maggiorana said to him: "Amiable Poequilon, confide your troubles to me; I cannot see you suffering without extraordinary emotions; although I am one of the courtesans of this Porphyrian Prince, I have a tender heart; make no mistake, Poequilon, the most delicate sentiments of love are often in the hearts of courtesans; I have resources for consolation; I think that in the matter of fortune, all your desires are fulfilled, but if I am in error in that regard, don't disdain the services of a friend—I dare not say a lover, for a courtesan, once amorous, is timid, and in that situation the violence of her amour makes her dread the weakness of her charms....

"You have lost a spouse that you adore; is it necessary, for that misfortune, in the finest of your days, to languish like a desiccated flower? Nothing consoles so much as love; if my scant beauty has made some impression on you, well, tender and handsome Verticephalian, forget for a while, in the arms of amorous and present beauty, ingrate and fugitive beauty; I promise you that you will enjoy the sweetness of repose, that your eyes will resume their original fire and your complexion its original glow—those tarnishes roses are already beginning to recover their freshness.

"Oh, handsome Poequilon, the age of a man does not have two Springs; it is amour that is pressing you in my voice."

As she spoke those words, modesty colored Maggiorana's cheeks, and voluptuousness caused her bosom to palpitate; her dark eyelids seemed humid, and Poequilon gave her a kiss.

"I love you, beautiful Maggiorana," said Poequilon, embarrassed by his conquest, "but would I not be guilty of betraying the Porphyrian Prince, whose delights you make?"

"What betrayal?" said the beautiful Courtesan. "I am not the only one who receives the caresses of the Porphyrian. Tell me, I beg you, if there is betrayal, who is betraying his oaths"

Poequilon, vanquished by this reasoning, told her, finally, sobbing, without employing euphemisms: "I am...*ah, che sciagura d'essere sonza coglioni.*"[29]

Maggiorana uttered a profound sigh, and after a momentary reflection, she said to him: "I love you in spite of your infirmities, and as you love me, Poequilon, be sure that you will find with me some compensation. Where would all the

---

[29] The quotation is from Voltaire's *Candide*, where it is similarly given in Italian, supposedly for decency's sake: "Oh, the tragedy of having no balls!"

Orpheuses of Stivalo be if they could not find a generous pity in our sex?"

Poequilon, who had only explored his condition to a limited extent thus far, exclaimed: "Ah! I sense in spite of my shaven surface that I would be glad to hold Maggiorana in my arms."

V. The most deplorable condition is susceptible of consolation.

The Porphyrian having absented himself with one of the guests for speculations that required retreat, Maggiorana stood up and beckoned to Poequilon, who followed her to her apartment. The handsome unfortunate, in spite of the confession of his semi-existence, had inflamed the courtesan, and he felt the devouring fire flowing in his own veins whose explosion, so many times experienced, was then refused to his desires. Maggiorana discovered all the complaisance of her amour to him, but Poequilon could only show her the places *sedes ubi troja fuit*.[30]

Clutching one another tightly, however, the two martyrs lavished the tender caresses of lovers upon one another. Poequilon's eyes wandered over all the charms of his mistress; his unquiet hand seemed to want to compensate her for the tribute that he ought to have presented to her beauty. Maggiorana created an illusion in the eyes of her lover. Her spontaneous arm was lost in the void of despair, and squeezing Poequilon tenderly, whose languor she agitated in her bosom, she cried: "Senza! Senza!"

Nevertheless, Poequilon thought himself less unhappy with that obliging Courtesan; the enjoyment of her charms—limited, it is true, to the pleasure of the eyes and the surface of the senses—nevertheless made felicity possible, with regard to his privation.

---

[30] Approximately "where Troy had once stood," vaguely echoing Virgil's *Aeneid*.

VI. Poequilon is punished for a sophism by a dagger-thrust; the mores of Stivalo. Reflection of Poequilon on his Fatherland.

He made that commerce with Maggiorana last for a long time, and said to himself: *I am offending neither Stelenos nor Olympia; I have not done any wrong to my spouse, since she is stolen from me; I am not unfaithful, since I have no enjoyment; as for the rest, and the sequence lends itself to extension, if one gives it a little thought, Selenos has made me an honest man in spite of myself, since I have only ever been capable of offending him by my penchant for amour.*

These reflections led him to Maggiorana's door, where he was about to amuse his innocent desires, when he felt himself seized from behind and struck with a dagger.

"O Heaven!" he cried. "What treason!"

The murderer, as he ran away, said to him: "*Tal paese tal usanza.*"[31]

The unfortunate Poequilon fell into his blood, protesting that he did not have that which renders jealous.

The Stivalian—for it was one—entered a temple, and after having kissed the altars, was free to commit another murder.

Poequilon asked Selenos to heal his wound, and invulnerability for the future. He sensed the extent to which such a benefit was necessary to him, in a country where Customs were so well observed, and wept for his homeland, where such mores were in execration.

Selenos granted his wish, because the time for granting wishes had come; and by his prompt healing and the hardening of his epidermis he recognized that he was invulnerable.

Proud of that new attribute, he went into Maggiorana's apartment, and told her about his tragic adventure, and the miraculous manner in which he had been healed. That tender

---

[31] "Every country has its own customs."

lover told him that the murder was an effect of the vengeance of the Porphyrian, who had perceived their love, and that that was the customary form of dueling in the nation, where it is a matter of honor not to suffer an affront and prudent not to expose oneself to the consequences of a combat.

Poequilon could not conceive that is a country consecrated to Selenos, atrocious vengeance could be so tolerated.

Certainly, he said to himself, *if Selenos punishes me like that for a slight distraction, after all that I have seen in this world, he ought to exterminate the Moon. O my Fatherland! People make love within your borders, but the altars do not serve as shelters for men thirsty for blood; it is true that the duel sometimes braves the Law there, but at least the man who has armed himself for vengeance risks his life for his honor. O honor, you are the salvation and the glory of my homeland, the security of our Emperor and the thunder of his armies.*

VII. The Unfortunate consequence of an indiscreet wish.

After these reflections, Poequilon sat down at table with his dear Maggiorana. He was very surprised not to be able to taste the flavor of the aliments or the delicious wines. The pores of his palate were so tightly sealed that no juice could penetrate them—O dire effects of invulnerability! Can a man who cannot feel pain feel any pleasure? All his senses were enveloped by an impenetrable tissue, and yet, a profound fire was devouring him, his heart was palpitating and his disturbed imagination was agitating the stone that covered him in vain.

"O Selenos!" he cried. "You pursue me incessantly; render me the senses, render me life; what point is there in being invulnerable if I am insensible? You have removed even the faint tenderness of touch. All the Stivalians armed with their homicidal daggers may fall upon me if, for a moment, so many attractions can become palpable to me.

VIII. A restitution all the rarer for being die to the disinterested wishes of a woman.

Selenos, wanting to punish Poequilon, granted that profane wish; he recovered his original sensibility, and Maggiorana's caresses were a some comfort to him—but how astonished and joyful he was when he recognized that he had all the prerogatives of his sex.

Olympia had finally made that wish on behalf of her husband, whom she judged very unfortunate, knowing his invincible penchant for the pleasures of amour. That very day, thinking about Poequilon and the chagrin by which he must be devoured, she had cried out: "If only he could still...."

That was enough for Selenos to reestablish him in his original nature.

It came at a good moment; as you can imagine, the Stivalienne took advantage of it. The amorous courtesan, seeing that Poequilon had become a man again, as if by a miracle, wanted his pleasure to have a hint of the miraculous too.

IX. Poequilon is accused of magic by the Musicians of Stivalo, whose misfortune is not to be sorcerers.

Poequilon's joy was painted on his face; glorious in having become a member of society again, he raised his head and made himself visible to all the beauties. People were astonished no longer to observe in him that somber and melancholy expression that men separated from themselves—the unfortunate who are a class apart, between the dead and the living—so often acquire. As everyone believed him to be of that number, he was mocked for his temerities, but the beautiful women emancipated thus far soon discovered that he was not an object of derision.

That sudden metamorphosis caused a surprising noise throughout Stivalo. The musicians, even more envious than confused, would have taken a cruel revenge on that renascent phoenix if he had not been under the safeguard of women.

However, the Porphyrians, in making a report to the Paterodiple, represented Poequilon as a magician. He ran away, and with reason.

How can some men, said Poequilon to himself, *and especially some Porphyrians, commit so much injustice? How can someone take offense because an unfortunate man has recovered what he had lost? How can one authorize murder and frightful plots? How can one harvest men in order to make them singers? How can the Paterodiple, who forbids the usage of senses, raise taxes on public constupration? For I know that—and how can Selenos adopt for his favorites men whose mores are so barbaric? Oh, my homeland, you leave to men....*

X. A Voyage to Antopholia; the conversation of Poequilon and a Musician.

He directed his steps toward a city named Antopholia. On the road he encountered a young man who was carrying a package on his shoulders and was singing very pleasantly. He invited him into his carriage and asked him where he was born, where he was coming from, where he was going, what he was did and what he was carrying.

The young man replied sagely: "I'm a Stivalian coming from Stivalo; I'm going to Antopholia; I sing and I have no luggage than what you can see on my shoulders."

"I understand, my friend. You are.... But tell me, please, how you were able to resolve to change for a miserable vocal thread. You know what I mean? Would it not have been better to live without those organ-pipes, sharpened at the expense of posterity? How many homicides you have committed in an instant! Do you know that in my country you might have been hung, for having given yourself a voice?"

"Sire," said the musician, "it was my father who delivered me to the fatal knife, in order for me to live and provide for his own subsistence."

"Your father is a monster."

117

"Almost all poor people would do the same in Stivalo, because a clear voice is a resource without indigence."

"Cannot women be made to sing, if people like clear voices?"

"Oh, Sire, women do something else."

"In my country they do both," said Poequilon, "and it is considered satisfactory. But let's leave it there; it's an evil that it's necessary to bemoan. What are you going to do in Antopholia?"

"I'm going there to join my wife."

"Your wife! That's nice—and your children too, no doubt?"

"Oh, no, Sire," said the young man, smiling bitterly.

"But explain this enigma to me" said Poequilon. "You have been immolated to music since childhood, but you're married? What do you do with a wife? Can your voice, which takes the place of everything, take the place of something?"

"Sire," said the musician, "beauty extends its empire over us, and we are in despair at not being able to obey its laws, but illusion consoles us and the caresses of a beautiful woman, even in redoubling our woes, lighten them...it's a mystery that can only be understood in our situation."

"I understand perfectly," said Poequilon, "the pleasures that you can savor in your condition."

At these words the musician, thinking he had encountered a peer, said to him: "Have you also lost the precious spring of life, Sire? Your last words seem to authorize me to take that opinion of you; however your opulence does not permit me to be convinced of it, unless you are the Doctor of some illustrious Metrotonic Academy."

Poequilon was embarrassed to respond to that naivety. "I cannot criticize your question," he said to the young man, "mine having been equally indiscreet, but there are things so extraordinary in my story that you would not be able to believe it if I told it to you. Let's get back, I beg you, to what concerns you."

Rich people are imposing, and the young Stivalian was reduced to replying.

"So, you're married," Poequilon continued, "but such an engagement in a profanation, which robs society of the productive voluptuousness of your spouse, and these sterile liaisons cannot have the approval of the law."

"Pardon me," said the musician; "the Paterodiple permits us to marry in order to soften our bitterness and prevent us from becoming women."

"What do you mean, becoming women?" said Poequilon. "What obscurity…?"

"Sire," the young man replied, "when you get to Antopholia, you will not take long to discover the thread of that labyrinth."

IX. Mysteries of Antopholia; Poequilon escapes miraculously a misfortune that does not threaten him in the face.

While conversing thus they arrived in Antopholia. Poequilon rewarded the young musician generously. He met his wife, who seemed to him to be charming, and asked her how she had been able….

The beautiful Piastrella interrupted him, to tell him that women engaged in a legally duty-free marriage were dispensed from conjugal fidelity, but that it was a tacit law that it was hidden from the infirm husbands, for the tranquility their minds.

Poequilon understood that marvelously, and made arrangements with Piastrella in order that young Becco, her husband, should remain in ignorance of the tacit law.

As he did not know anyone in Antopholia, he retained the young Becco with him, to company him everywhere. The City seemed so agreeable that he resolved to stay there for some time; he saw the squares, the palaces, the temples, the statues, the libraries and the tombs, and filled his notebooks with numismatic devices and epitaphs.

Meanwhile, he circulated in society, and noticed that his looks had never been so praised as in that city. The men, in particular, exclaimed over his beautiful eyes, hair, etc., and he observed that Becco, who passed for his groom, also had a considerable share in the praises of the Anapholians.

"Becco is very likeable," one of them said to Poequilon, "and I congratulate you."

Another, by contrast, said to him: "I would like you better than Becco."

He did not know what all that meant, and dared not ask the impetuous Antopholians to explain.

He found himself alone one day with the beautiful Cappellugola. She was a woman whose figure and beauty were comparable to the famous Venus of Antopholia. He declared to her in a few words the passion that she inspired in him.

The beauty with a majestic face said to him: "Go find your Becco."

Poequilon took that opportunity to clarify the mystery, and said to her: "I swear to you, beautiful Cappellugola, that Becco is only my groom, and I don't believe that I can do anything else with him, except make him sing sometimes, because he has a beautiful voice."

"What!" said Cappellugola. "Becco isn't...."

"I can assure you," Poequilon said, "that I don't understand what you're saying, and I beg you to instruct me regarding the mores of Antopholia and to regard me as the admirer of your unique attractions."

Reassured, Cappellugola kissed Poequilon tenderly, and told him, without outraging Nature, how the Antopholians insulted beauty.[32]

---

[32] Author's note: "*Ogni medaglia, ha il suo Riverso.*" Every medallion has its reverse side; the Italian proverb in question, usually used in a similar fashion to the English "there are two sides to every question," was famously quoted by Montaigne with reference to questions of sexual hierarchy, although he

When he left that beauty's arms, he met Cappellugola's husband on the stairway, who said to him: "Don't be alarmed to encounter me, young foreigner; I know about the sweet moments you've just spent with Cappellugola, but the Antopholians are of good composition. I could stab you twenty times in the heart, as is sometimes practiced among us when we have nothing better to do, but there are reasons for not always being so malevolent. Your physiognomy touches me, and I want to penetrate you with my good intentions; come with me."

Poequilon, judging this discourse insidious, put up some resistance; soon, twenty servants took hold of him, and after having dragged him into a closet they delivered him in the most submissive state to the jealous Antopholian, who was about to avenge himself in his own manner when Selenos permitted the floor to collapse. Poequilon found himself free and unharmed in the vestibule, from which he ran home.

"That's it," he said. "I'm leaving this infamous nation, which lightning ought to set ablaze one day, this impure cloaca where one sees eagles crawl and rivers flow without sources, and where, in sum, all Nature is overturned.

XII. A Periphanian adventure taken to its conclusion. Recognition that does not flatter everyone.

After that imprecation and a brief rest, Poequilon escaped the Antopholians, sometimes looking behind him, because he feared the pursuit of those furious people. He arrived by night in Periphanes, a large city that was the capital of Periphania.

I say "by night," but that is a manner of speaking, because the day star never ceases to illuminate that great nation;

---

was referring to the supposed practices of Amazons. In the same analogical fashion that Stivalo is Rome, Antopholia is the city of Florence; homosexuality was widely thought to be rife there during the Renaissance.

it finds it difficult to turn its gaze elsewhere, because everything there is so remarkable. There are the serenades that lovers sing under the windows of their mistresses, and combats between bulls and Periphanians, in which there is a great deal of applause when the bull is victorious. The rest of the time is spent killing little insects in the sunlight and massacring enemies in the crowd with the aid of the mantle with which the Periphanians cover their faces. No one pays any attention to these murders; it is only Tauricide that merits the attention of the law.

That species of man comes into the world with the Aphrodise; they are very sober, extenuated by amour, puffed up with pride and flaccid with idleness. The women are beautiful and very voluptuous; they lose their heads at the sight of a Verticephalian; they walk in the shade, their faces covered by a veil, and are imprisoned for the rest of the day behind grilles and bolts, confided to the guard of an old woman known as a Dracona.[33]

All that means, I think, that the Periphanians are very jealous, but so many precautions do not prevent the temperament of the Periphaniennes from harvesting an amiable foreigner from time to time.

Poequilon studied the customs of the Periphanians for some time and went for regular walks at the same time as the women. One day, he noticed the figure and gait of a Periphanienne, and thought he recognized Olympia. In that opinion, he followed her cautiously and discovered her dwelling. He learned that her name was Motacilla, and that she was married to Señor Alto Fronto Balordo Occisero de los Occiseros.[34] He retired very pensively at that news, and was going into his house when an old dracona handed him a letter,

---

[33] Author's note: "They are also hampered by a kind of shackle known as the equestrian zone."
[34] Approximately "High-browed Dim-witted Killer, of the Killers."

saying to him: "Handsome horseman"[35]—that is the usual epithet that given to men in that country—"don't neglect such precious advantages."

Poequilon had nothing more pressing to do than shut himself away to read the letter, which he rightly judged to be gallant. He saw these words, in the Verticephaliam language:

Handsome horseman.
If you have courage and if you love beauty, at the same hour tomorrow you will allow yourself to be guided by the dracona who has handed you this letter, and you will receive the caresses of the most amorous of Periphaniennes.

Motacilla

On reading this, Poequilon was confirmed in the belief that Motacilla was none other than Olympia, who had recognized him, but, living under the tyranny of Balordo Occifero, she could not employ any other means of seeing him than the customary stratagems of the women of the nation. That she had not declared herself in the letter was doubtless to procure him an agreeable surprise. On the other hand, a certain impulse of jealousy troubled him. He thought that Olympia might not have recognized him, but had become amorous at the sight of him, and he judged that he ought not to miss the rendezvous, whether it was to encounter an unhappy and faithful wife or to convince him of her perfidy.

The moment came and the dracona came to find him with two men laden with a harpsichord case; he allowed himself to be put inside it, and he was carried in that fashion all the way to Motacila's room. When he was liberated, the beautiful Periphanienne offered herself to his eyes and revealed her charms to him, which are easier to represent than describe. She was in the most voluptuous state of undress, and the most

---

[35] I have translated "*homme de cheval*" brutally, as intended; if the author had wanted to say *cavalier* (or *caballero*) he would have done so.

comfortable for a climate in which the heat causes the bitter and subtle fire of an inexhaustible sensuality to flow through the veins, and which plunges into a delicious languor those who carry it in their bosom.

Her wavy hair flowed over her bare shoulders, and over her delicate midriff a light garment of dazzling whiteness outlined her magnificent waist and the curve of two widespread hips, which announced the girdle of Venus. A light abundantly-pleated skirt, in which amours seemed to be hiding, allowed the sight of two slender and elegantly turned legs, the gracious contours of which were revealed by attitudes that seemed involuntary. From that ravishing base, Poequilon returned his gaze to a pale and agitated bosom, which no veil concealed, and the visage of a Goddess, whose alabaster was only differentiated from that cleavage by the nuances of the subjugated modesty that flatters even at the moment of amorous delirium.

Two large dark and languid eyes appeared to take pleasure in Poequilon's delight, and two beautiful arms wound tenderly around the amorous Verticephalian.

"Handsome Hyppicos,"[36] she said, in the Periphanian language, "I can see that you love me; don't languish any longer; let's take advantage of the sweet moments that love accords to us.

Burning with amour, Poequilon soon said to himself: *I came here expecting to find Olympia; it isn't her, but ought I to offend the beautiful Motacilla, who prefers me to all the distinguished men in Periphanes? No, there is no man capable of such firmness; I shall make the most adorable of all women happy; our felicity is common. Oh, forgive me, Olympia; I am dying of amour, and Motacilla is tearing me away from you and from myself.*

He savored inexpressible pleasures, and in the transports of joy and gratitude he said to the beauty: "Never have the pleasures of amour seemed to me so seductive, so vivid; I thought I might die twenty times over of languor, fury, senti-

---

[36] Author's note: "Horseman."

124

ment, voluptuousness and tenderness. I had only ever experienced such sweetness with Olympia."

The beautiful Periphanienne, her eyes moist with tears, said to him: "Recognize Olympia, Poequilon, and see that the true pleasures are only in the knots that we have formed."

Poequilon was nonplussed by these words. He considered the beauty attentively, and as if the scales had fallen from his eyes, he recognized Olympia. He bathed her with his tears and covered her with the most tender kisses—but the memory of Alto Fronto Balordo Occisero de los Occiseros came back to mind.

Olympia smiled, and told him that the Occisero in question was only one of the women of her retinue in disguise, that she had used that stratagem for safety's sake in all the places where she had traveled in search of him since leaving Eutoquia, where the children she had left there had multiplied considerably.

"I begged Selenos so much to permit me to search for you," she added, "that he granted me that favor, but on condition that if you were unfaithful to me after having found me again that I would return immediately to the Island of Eutoquia and that you would only see me again on that Fortunate isle—which you will reach one day, it's true, but only after many difficulties.

Poequilon swore the most constant fidelity to her, and asked her for details of her travels and her sojourn on the happy Island.

Olympia replied that Selenos had forbidden her to satisfy his curiosity in that regard, and that he would be informed when destiny ordained it.

Poequilon contented himself with that response, but he wanted to make sure that Occisero really was a woman; the slave in question was summoned, and Poequilon was soon librated from his anxieties.

He asked his dear wife then how she had subsisted since leaving the island, and learned with abundant joy that Selenos had granted her the projection powder in the four known and arid continents of the Moon.

XIII. A Voyage to Pitho

Poequilon wanted to leave Periphania and enjoy the company of his beloved Olympia in a nation where the mores were more to his taste, and he decided on the famous city of Agathokrine, the capital of the Empire of Pitho.

Olympia, who had been traveling for a long time, fruitfully, said to Poequilon: "The mores of Pitho would not have suited you any better than those of Periphania. However, there have been fortunate changes in these estates. The Emperor of Periphania has established laws that ought to change the face of government and assure the tranquility of the people; he has destroyed the monsters that were ravaging the nation, and by virtue of a generous firmness that cannot be to highly praised in this climate, he has put all the Periphanians under his personal protection.

"The Emperor of Pitho merits equally great praise; he has triumphed over the blackest conspiracies and has profited from that glorious success to put limits on the severity of the Fecracy,[37] by making himself the High Fecrat of his Empire; but I don't like lands where changes are so recent; there always remains some germ there fatal to foreigners, and if you take my advice, we won't remain there for long."

They eventually arrived in Agathokrine. Poequilon was surprised and edified by the extraordinary piety of the people. "In truth," he said, "these people inspire me with a singular confidence, and I could easily take them for Angels."

---

[37] Although Fecracy is derived straightforwardly from Fecracy—i.e. the rule of the faith, all the more appropriate given the importance in both Spain (Periphania) and Pitho (Portugal) of the Auto-da-Fé—Le Bret would also have been conscious of the echo that the name contains of the root Fec (as in Feces).

"Suspend your judgment," said Olympia. "Appearances are very deceptive under a Fecratic government. In fact, the fear of losing their property and the terror of torture renders some secretive and throws the others into a lethargy far from the piety that Selenos desires.

"These people that you believe to be so Saintly, if they have the slightest suspicion of you, will go to denounce you to the Fecrats, for you to perish cruelly. I cannot blame them, for if one does not do that, another will accomplish that dire function, and the unfortunate Pithonian who has spared you will be enveloped with you in the deadly sentence."

These warnings frightened Poequilon, who noticed that the Fecrat Edifiants imposed authority upon families. He was afflicted by that, for he had known that breed for a long time.

"If the Fecrats are part of the government," he said, "should they not remain in their Tribunals to await the complaints of Individuals and judge cases within their competence? Nothing is so indecent as to be both Judge and Emissary."

It was thus that they reasoned on the mores of Pitho, and they resolved to conduct themselves with so much circumspection that the Fecracy could not get its teeth into them.

XIV. A prompt exit from Pitho, and for good reason.

In spite of Poequilon's precautions, a Fecratic storm gathered over his head, and he had no suspicion of it. He learned by chance that a woman from Stivalo, with whom he had once been acquainted, was living not far from Agathokrine. He wanted to see her, and having found out where she lived, he saw the shoes of an Edifiant at the door. He did not think that such footwear ought to prevent him from going in, and as an old friend of the mistress, he went into the apartment. He was very astonished to catch the Edifiant in a function opposed to his ministry; however, he made his apologies and left.

On the way back he met a bearded man who usually turned his ingots into coin for him, and told him about that adventure.

"You're lucky that I'm a Lipodermist, and in consequence incapable of denouncing you," he said, "but believe me, run away with your wife if you don't want to be reduced to ashes at the next Good Work of the Fecracy. You've committed an irremediable profanation in not going away on seeing the Edifiant's shoes. The chamber into which you penetrated was a sanctuary. Flee, I tell you; I tremble for you and or me. The crime committed by my father, who was burned after being ruined, was trivial compared with yours."

"But my wife told me," said Poequilon, "that since the day when the Emperor made himself High Fecrat, the Fecracy had become less severe."

"That's all well and good," said the Lipodermist, "but as long as the word Fecracy subsists, fear for your skin; there are indeed some Fecracies less dangerous than others; the Fecracy of Stivalo, the Fecracy of Periphania and the Fecracy of Gondola are not as terrible as Pitho's, and Pitho's is less terrible than Zinzibri's, but in that matter it's the same as diseases; it's commonly said that there are no good diseases, and the same is true of Fecracies.... Shh! The Pithonians are already watching us. The Fecrat has spoken; I'm sure of it. Save yourselves, quickly. I'm running too, since I've been seen with you."

Poequilon went back to his house in the grip of fear, told his wife everything, and asked Selenos for the grace of getting him out of Pitho, with Olympia. He asked that the same favor be accorded to the good Lipodermist who had given them that advice.

They embarked on a ship that was leaving for Heliopolis—when one is running away, one is not the master of one's route.

"Since we're constrained to go to Heliopolis," Poequilon said to his wife, "let's go there without complaining, but when we've gained moon[38] and are safe, let's make arrangements, my dear Olympia to return to our homeland. I'm already very weary of traveling the world. I've found you, so I ought to be at the end of my journey."

"Your travels are not yet over," Olympia replied. "Remember that Selenos condemned you to travel over the entire Planet until you had found your wife and children; the task is not yet complete, as you see. Submit yourself to the Oracle."

"O Heaven!" said Poequilon. "Is it still necessary to lead an errant life?"

XV. Shipwreck; a fortuitous scarification, which causes a great error.

After some days of fortunate navigation, such a furious tempest blew up that the vessel was broken on rocks. With the aid of some debris, Poequilon and Olympia saved themselves, and were pushed by the wind to the port of Zinzibri with no further accident except that Poequilon, who had escaped the shipwreck almost naked, was wounded at the extremity of a very delicate part of his body, by means of a fatal nail on which it was caught. Olympia put a balm on it, however, which cured the wound in a few days.

The two spouses, recovered from their fatigues, drank from the Fountain of Youth, and by means of their Projection Powder they established themselves magnificently in Zinzibri. They were esteemed by the Fecrats for their wealth, and by the Zizinbrites for their good morals, for Olympia often said to Poequilon: "Let us be careful, for this baneful moon into which the tempest has thrown us is a turbulent country. The Fecracy loves gold, and we are rich; I would rather have lived here in obscurity, and it would be even better to go and breathe air less heavily laden with the vapors of hypocrisy.

---

[38] The French *terre*, for which Le Bret naturally substitutes *lune* [moon] can mean "ground" and (as in the next chapter) "land," as well as "earth."

Even if we were in Heliopolis, my dear Poequilon, that city is a Pithonian colony. Believe me, let us cross the golden river and set ourselves at liberty."

Poequilon shared that opinion strongly, but a stubborn humor that afflicted him in the abdomen obliged him to postpone his departure; they had recourse to a famous Sarcotome, who cured him.

That Operator, while examining Poequilon's malady, noticed that the body-part I mentioned, which had been injured in the shipwreck, conserved a certain scarring that the nail had caused. The man, who was a devotee of the Fecracy, having observed that scar, judged that his patient was a Lipodermist, and thought he was obliged by conscience to inform the Vice-Fecrat.

The day after that officious denunciation, Poequilon and Olympia were seized, and after all their treasures had been confiscated, they were placed separately in the most frightful dungeon of the most magnificent Palace.

XVI. Terrible judgment and infernal clemency

They were interrogated frequently; it did no good to prove that they were from Verticephalia and the best Selenites on the Moon; they were convicted of at least having Lipodermitized, and Poequilon's fatal excision condemned him, along with Olympia, to be added to the victims who had to incessantly immolate in the Pious Works of the Fecrats.[39]

---

[39] This incident, reminiscent of a much more elaborate one in Simon de Tyssot's account of *Voyages et aventures de Jaques Massé* (c1715; tr. in *The Strange Voyages of Jacques Massé and Pierre Mésange*, q.v.) is presumably inspired by the same source, an account given by Gabriel Dellon's *Histoire de l'Inquisition de Goa* (1649; tr. as *An Account of the Inquisition of Goa*), which was cited in numerous later texts. Zinzibri is, therefore, the Portuguese colony of Goa.

However, Olympia, who was beautiful, ignited a fire in the heart of a certain Fecrat, while the latter was preparing Poequilon's pyre. That Edifiant announced to the unfortunate spouse that there could be no mercy for her husband, but that for her, there was a sure means of saving her life.

What a means! Ardent and barbaric Fecrat, could you not accord mercy in its entirety? That was in Olympia's eyes. *What demon is breathing amour and cruelty into your bosom?*

The chaste and generous spouse pretended to yield to capitulation, and as she had not asked Selenos for anything for a long time, she hoped for a success that her husband was at risk of not being able to obtain, his last wish having been made in Agathokrine less than two years before.

XVII. A marvelous event that was very necessary

After making that wish, Olympia was not set free, but she was treated with distinction and lodged comfortably. The Edifiant came to see her frequently, and pressed her to make good on her promise.

The day indicated for his triumph arrived, and it was the very same one that Poequilon was due to expiate the injury he had received during the shipwreck—but Olympia's wish having penetrated Selenos, she emerged from her prison without anyone stopping her, and went to the bloody square where Poequilon, surrounded by Guards and Judges, was only expecting death.

She went to her husband and said to him: "Follow me"—which he did without encountering any resistance. Selenos, having not judged it necessary to confound all the elements in order to save innocence, had contented himself with turning that entire homicidal Cortege into statues, and the metamorphosis was all the more in accordance with natural law because their hearts were already made of marble.

That marvelous event, the physics of which could not be explained, as with the moonquakes that occurred in Agathokrine, ought to have corrected the Fecrats sternly.

Poequilon and Pympia embarked in the port of Zinzibri and crossed the golden river. When Poequilon saw that infamous shore from a distance he cried: "O my homeland, where shall I see you again? When shall I breath gaiety and virtue, honor and repose in your bosom?"

XVIII. A voyage to distant lands.

In order to accomplish the Oracle, the errant Poequilon and his wife travelled the moons and the seas. Olympia, who had acquired a good deal of knowledge during her travels, instructed her husband and tried to console him for the harsh necessity he had of traveling. They traversed the nations of the White Heads and the Red Heads, governed by the great Jugular Sash; the nation of the Blue Bodies, which the Taurijovians have metamorphosed into beasts; that of the Anthropophages and Pyramidustrine.

What a source of reflections for Poequilon the mores of those various nations was!

The first thing he noticed in the country of the White Heads and the Red Heads was slaves, who, it was said, had no tongue, and who were carrying in veneration a long silk sash. Olympia told him that the sash was destined for a Great Man.

"It's doubtless a new mark of honor," Poequilon replied, "with which the Satrap in question is going to be decorated?"

"Undeceive yourself," said Olympia. "That fatal sash will put an end to his days."

"O my Fatherland!" cried Poequilon. "You too are governed by a sash, but what a difference! My master's sash, with which he draws the entire nation effortlessly, is resplendent with glory."

"The Emperors of these countries and their Satraps," said Olympia, "cut off the heads of men here as if they were the heads of poppies."

"I believe that things are getting worse and worse," said Poequilon. "The more we travel, and the longer we live, the more horrors we see. Let's flee."

They escaped from that frightful despotism, and, going along the coast, they reached the summit of a crag from which they could see the sea covered in Ships. The most horrible carnage was offered to their eyes.

"All the elements," said Poequilon, serve as receptacles for human crimes; why does Selenos not change their hearts? Or, if it depends on them not to be wicked, why does he not exterminate at a stroke that race rebellious to the cries of virtue?"

"Respect the decrees of Selenos," Olympia said to him. "In that confused mass of murderous men there are many virtuous people; it is the supreme will of the man who commands that is probably criminal; slavery is always innocent; it is only disobedience and rebellion that can render it culpable."

"What!" sad Poequilon, shivering. "Can humans not make use of their reason?"

"Force subjugates them," Olympia said. "The idea of death chills them, and they cease to have reason, so they struggle against an authority that they have recognized as legitimate; such are the abuses of Society, my dear Poequilon. Selenos permits that Society, for the improvement of humans; and those who hold the scepter answer to Heaven for the injustices of their designs, for the Masters of the Moon have been created for justice, the happiness of peoples and the glory of Selenos."

"I'm convinced of those verities, beautiful Olympia," said Poequilon, "but O my Homeland…!"

The nation of the Blue Bodies wrenched tears from Poequilon. It is situated in the Peristerique; the proximity of the Sun has given that color to the natives of that climate. Poequilon noticed a large quantity of Whites, and perceived that the latter were the masters; what caused him to make that judgment was that the Blues were employed, some in digging mines and the others in extracting the substance from reeds; the Whites were only occupied in beating the unfortunate forced laborers with sticks. He protested against that injustice, and Olympia told him that the Periphanians had been the first to discover that Nation, fertile in precious metals and rare foodstuffs, which they had conquered by surprise and enslaved by force; that all the Nations of Taurijove had marched in their bloody footsteps, that Verticephalia herself had not been exempt from that odious cupidity.

"I was unaware," said Poequilon, "of that stain on my country, but politics excuses it, and the balance of Empires has drawn it into that crime of necessity. Let's get out of this place of despair, however, since it isn't possible for me to save these unfortunates from the oppression under which they're groaning, and let's redouble our prayers to Selenos that they might recover their liberty and happiness.

The Anthropophages, whom they discovered by chance at the top of a mountain that appeared to form the border between two countries, occasioned a host of ideas on Poequilon's part.

They perceived in all directions a multitude of men armed with clubs, who, after killing their fellows, roasted them and made a meal of them.

"You see," said Olympia, "two Nations that are not civilized; they are what we call Savages. Notice the cruelty with which they tear one another apart and make use of their enemies' remains. However, these Barbarians have laws, they are submissive to the man they have elected as their leader. They do not know Selenos, but they worship in the religion that they render to the winds and the storms. Like us, they live in a society; like us, they wanted that; for their common interest and their public and individual security, they have formed a kind of government; but they are less fortunate than us, although fundamentally, they are no more wicked; their misfortune consists of being unable to improve themselves by greater communication, and the proof of that is the antiquity of their principles; nothing is more invariable than ignorance; it is the mother of invincible prejudice. These limited people, being unable to work to reform their barbaric institutions, remain exposed to reciprocal cruelties; nature itself is, for them, a sterile field, and the temporary rigors of temperature are features to which they can only oppose blasphemy or the fear of death. They envy the strength of animals, and do not suspect that the latter are their inferiors."

"Ah!" said Poequilon. "May they remain as they are; improvement might cost them very dear; is not the liberty that they enjoy more precious than all the enlightenment of Taurijove? They do not know misfortune; war alone can complete their misery, but at least they fight for themselves; it is their country that they defend, their wives and children that they snatch from the enemy. What wealth have those unfortunate Savages collected whom the Periphanians have subjugated? What use have they made of the discoveries procured for them? What good have the elements of urbanity done them, acquired in being the slaves of their perfidious Instructors? Politics, civilization, deadly cargo of Taurijovians, you will always be the misfortune of savage and innocent Nations!"

"But that is not the way that I would like you to see the Savages civilized," Olympia said to him. "It is by gentle and humane ways; I would like the civilized Nations that penetrate into their lands to give them idea of virtue, lessons in humanity and principle of government. I would like them to be educated in the Arts, their Nature to be developed, in order that they should be enabled to know the Creator, the purpose of their existence—and, finally, that they should be allowed to collect the fruits of that new doctrine."

"Nothing is so fine and so generous, my dear Olympia," said Poequilon, "but it's necessary to begin by vanquishing these ferocious creatures, and when one has vanquished one takes possession of the enemy's soils with pleasure. Destroy cupidity and ambition among civilized men, and then they will do good for the pleasure of doing good—which is to say that one will have seen the birth of humanity."

In Pyramidustrine, they saw people wandering incessantly over the surface of that Moon; frightful deserts where wretches were perishing of thirst, into which avarice or poverty had cast them; and public markets where human beings were sold like camels. They shivered in horror on seeing the indecency with which naked women were exposed and sold to the Seraglios of Emperors. The majority of those unfortunates deplored their sad fate; some had been snatched from their mothers' arms; others, victims of naval combat, had been the prey of the victors.

"O barbaric mores!" cried Poequilon. "What! I also see Taurijovians making this unworthy traffic! My dear Olympia, to what are we exposed if we are confused with these infamous men? Let us admit with pleasure that our homeland is a celestial abode by comparison with those we have seen since we left it. If Selenos has sworn to exterminate the wicked people of the Moon, he ought to show mercy to Verticephalia."

XIX. Return to Verticephalia

Poequilon wept; everything that he saw filled him with sadness.

"Life, dear Olympia," he said, "is beginning to displease me; there is only you who can make me taste some sweetness in it. Men are ferocious animals who devour ne another; the interest that guides them causes them to forget the most sacred duties and neglect the most tender consolations. Shall I never see my homeland again?"

However, they set sail thereafter for Taurijove, where there still remained many countries to travel, including those of the Amphibia, who, with the aid of a demigod, had shaken off the yoke of the Periphanians; the Staussachers, who are perched on top of a rock, the simulacrum of liberty; the Syndikocrates, who carry their deity in their bosom; the new kingdom of the Stratiotes; the proud empire of the Cyclamors, who present lightning on the Standards and all the attributes of the Gods; the Karalkadeskis, who worship Discord as the Romans once raised altars to Fear; the Icy States; the Caesarist Isles, which the last sigh of the great Caesar plunged back into torpor; the nations governed by the wise Queen Herogyne; and finally, the Triangles, which cupidity and the spirit of independence have plunged into Anarchy and which, by virtue of an opinion of liberty, lacerate their own hands.

The Amphibia compose a Democratic nation where people live in complete liberty, observing good mores; it is the refuge of persecuted innocents, and even of guilty exiles.[40]

"You will doubtless be happy on these shores," said Olympia to Poequilon, when they arrived there. "The empire of commerce ensures all the security and the politics of this nation. Almost everything it possesses is exotic; it takes products of every sort from all over the Moon, which it trades very lucratively with the Nations. One could call this country the Shop of the World; by their continual expeditions the Amphibia excite the luxury and stimulate the appetite of all the Empires."

"Properly speaking, then," said Poequilon, "they are the tempters of the human race."

"They have been obliged to resort to that recourse," Olympia replied, "to maintain their liberty, after having shaken off the yoke of the Periphanians."

Olympia was still speaking when Poequilon saw a troop of young men passing by, surrounded by soldiers who were taking them to the Port and throwing them violently into vessels.

"They're doubtless criminals," said Poequilon.

"No, Sire," replied an Amphibian. "They are vagrants who have no recommendation, and we take possession of such men, to fight on the Ocean and populate our Colonies, because we do not want vagabonds or beggars in our Government."

"But are those men yours, to disposed of in that manner? The action of buying men in order to make slaves of them is already very barbaric, but that of stealing them is even more so."

"We don't steal them; they have come, and it's the right of windfall."

---

[40] i.e., the analogue of Holland.

137

"Make them work on your continent; at least consult their inclination and take advantage of their talents, if compassion does not lead you to general relief; but to violate the rights of hospitality—that only belongs to Anthropophages."

"All our citizens have their place here, and we leave foreigners free, so long as they have money, even if they are scoundrels escaped from the Tribunals of their homeland; we even protect the latter against the research of those they have offended or injured. I know that there are often honest men among those we embark, and the proof of their probity extracts them from their poverty, but what do you expect? It's the Law of the Land."

"A horrible Law," said Poequilon. You, who have been on the point of preferring death to slavery, how can you treat your brethren thus? In my country, we do not punish misfortune; we relive the indigent in or to prevent him committing a crime; we give him time to make use of his talents; if he is an honest man, he lives; if he is a monster, he dies in an exemplary fashion."

Poequilon added: "Adieu, Amphibian nation, where, without money, I would be sent to the galleys. You are only good to serve as a refuge for apostates, lipodermists, bankrupts, rapists, murderers and rebels. Let's go."

The country of the Staussachers is bristling with mountains and snow-covered rocks. Poequilon found the laws of that nation admirable; he recognized that it was a perfect democracy, where the equality of conditions was almost observed among the Citizens;[41] he was delighted by that discovery, believing that he as seeing liberty, but he soon revised that judgment when he saw those free men selling their neighbors as slaves, either to fight in armies or to guard Princes.

"What!" he said. "The commerce of these inhabitants is to traffic in their persons? They sell their blood and lives at auction to foreign Princes? They have neither friends nor enemies? Simultaneous stipendiaries of several opposed Crowns,

---

[41] The analogue of Switzerland.

their duty is a continual civil war. Does that Nation merit occupying a corner of the world?"

"But they're poor," said Olympia. "Their country doesn't produce enough to nourish them; it's necessary that they make a profit from their bravery and their fidelity; they posses those two virtues to such an eminent degree that they are admired all over the Moon."

"I respect them in that regard," said Poequilon, "but their commerce is a shameful traffic; their liberty is merely a disguised slavery, and the Laws that govern them are nothing but interest and a pragmatic sanction with the coffers of pompous warrior Emperors. On the other hand, it is shameful for Nations to suffer that foreigners guard their masters; that ought to be the employment of loyal subjects."

"One can't satisfy everyone," said Olympia, smiling. "You find something to criticize everywhere."

When Poequilon was in the free country of Syndikocratia he immediately exclaimed: "Here are free people; they maintain themselves here, if they can; their Laws are good, their mores mild. I am annoyed, however, that their dogma is erroneous and that they have against them a confederation, which seriously threatens their liberty."

He wanted to see one of the most illustrious Citizens, whose reputation had extended throughout Taurijove, particularly in Verticephalia.[42] He was told that the great man had been proscribed by his nation because of the underhand maneuver of a celebrated Verticephalian jealous of the exclusive property of public suffrage. Poequilon was indignant at the methods of the incendiary of sorts, who had declaimed throughout his life against maleficent genii and persecutors.

---

[42] Georges May identifies Syndiokratia with Greece, but that seems unlikely as it was still under Ottoman rule when *La Nouvelle lune* was written. It is conceivable that it refers to the Republic of Corsica established by Pasquale Paoli, which was toppled by the French conquest if the island in 1768, forcing Pasquale into exile.

He had also been told that the Syndikocrats had been punished, in a way, for having fallen into the trap of seduction, for the Verticephalian who had deceived them and found a refuge among them had blackened them shamelessly since.

"In truth," said Poequilon in the Lunar language, "the spirit of that man is the shoe of Theramenes. What! After having received hospitality in this Nation, where he found shelter from his enemies, after having lavished the praise on it that it merits, he is perverse enough to attack it? But what puts the cap on this malignity is that he only launches his darts against that Nation, which was kind to him, when he thinks that it is on the brink of ruination. Can it not say in its misfortune—even though the ingrate is illustrious—*certe bis videor mori?*[43]

Straticratia was next to be observed by Poequilon. The Prince who then reigned assembled all the qualities of a great man: an equitable Sovereign, conquering Warrior, impartial Legislator, protector and cultivator of the Fine Arts, a sublime Philosopher and a virtuous man.[44] Poequilon studied the character of that Hero, and the maxims of his government, for a long time. Ready to leave his estates, he wanted to throw himself at the feet of that new Solomon.

The Monarch received him with a welcome truly worthy of the grandeur of his soul, and then asked him what he thought of the Laws of his Empire and the manner in which they were observed.

"Prince," Poequilon said to him, "you have followed all the glorious careers, you have had all crowns and all triumphs of public admiration, but you have shrunk the soul of your subjects by confounding the classes and giving the administration of Justice to your favorite Stratiotes. You have aged as if

---

[43] The quotation is from the last line of one of Aesop's fables, known in English as "The Old Lion"; it translates roughly as "give death a double sting."

[44] Frederick II, also known as Frederick the Great, king of Prussia,

you were immortal, in a short while there will no longer be and great man in your Empire but you."

Poequilon withdrew having said that, and went with Olympia into the land of the Cyclamors.

He was very surprised to see that the chief of that Empire had neither a seat nor authority, and that nothing was carried out without the consent of ten Senators, vassals and servants of the Emperor, assembled around thirty thousand geometric paces. But what surprised him even more was to see qualified Edifiants wearing the Sovereign Crown, making war on Kings, and often on their master. He realized that there were three Religions in the Empire; and what struck him was to see an Edifiant Prince who had two himself, by virtue of a convention that was called the famous Treaty.[45]

"One can see," he said, "that politics absorbs faith."

Furthermore, he found that the police were admirably exercised in all those States, but he groaned to see Serfs in a country where the word liberty had been pronounced.

On entering the homeland of the Kavalkadeskis,[46] Poequilon and Olympia saw an election decided by saber-thrusts, and took flight.

Beyond that they passed into the icy Empire of the Caesarists; they discovered nothing there but a deformed monument, which made them regret the great Caesar.

"If the cold has condensed the animal spirits of his successors," said Poequilon, "may his example warm them up again."[47]

---

[45] The King of Poland was also the Grand Duke of Lithuania by virtue of the Confederation of the two nations (one Catholic and the other Orthodox). Le Bret could not know that the commonwealth was to break up in 1772.

[46] The Russians

[47] If the "Caesarist Empire" is an analogue of Sweden (as Georges May asserts), the much regretted Caesar would Gustavus Adolphus, but the earlier reference in this chapter was to the "Caesarist Isles," and it was separated by a semi-

The Estates of Queen Herogyne excited Poequilon's admiration. That great Princess governed for Empire with as much wisdom as magnanimity and enjoyed a peace that she had acquired at the price of the blood of her subjects, and almost their last resources. Her misfortunes and her constancy had rendered her even more commendable than her noble qualities, which had caused her to be given the title of King, as if the denomination of her sex were beneath such a masculine and heroic princess.

Poequilon, full of admiration for that Sovereign and admiration for a Government in which everything announced the entrails of a tender and august mother, would willingly have settled in that abode, but he loved his own country even more, which is forgivable.

The sea surrounds, so to speak, the nation of the Triangles, and those people have in consequence the empire of that element, to the great regret of their neighbors, because the former abuse their situation, and, in spite of the most sacred treaties, they cannot help committing hostilities, opportunity favoring their rapines and their forces on the Ocean rendering reprisals impracticable.

Poequilon did not look kindly on that. He noticed that the power of the Sovereign was very limited, and that the government depended on the tumultuous waves of a miry marsh agitated by saltpeter. He observed also that the Triangles were naturally antagonistic to Verticephalians; he was obliged several times to make use of his strength with men of the people, because someone had recognized that he had the features of a Verticephalian, although he had taken care to abandon the costume.

Nevertheless, he found excellent qualities in the distinguished Triangles. That Nation had no music, and Painting

---

colon from the realm of Queen Herogyne, undoubtedly Christina of Sweden, whose official title throughout her reign was "king." If the Caesarist isles are, in fact, an analogue Denmark, then the regretted Caesar must be Christian IV

142

and Sculpture were unknown to it, but it had a great deal of Selenometry, Economics and Physics, and one profound Philosopher of great ideas and an elevated style, but little amenity in general and even less compassion.[48] As for their personal afflictions, nothing equaled their sensibility or their resignation in overcoming the evils of life by the barbaric effort that is known as Roman on Earth.

He thought himself constrained to form that judgment by the most frightful and bizarre spectacle that he had ever seen. He was strolling one day on the edge of the Sieve,[49] his eyes fixed upon that river, when he perceived several boats filled with Triangles; but how astonished he was when he saw all the passengers suddenly dive into the water! He had scarcely recovered from his surprise when he encountered a Triangle to whom he related that tragic event.

The latter replied, with as much phlegm as he had listened: "Doubtless the men were unfortunate, or their life was a burden; if ever I am vexed I shall terminate my career by means of a similarly generous action."

Poequilon concluded from this speech that the nation of Triangles was truly the land of Suicides. He subsequently told Olympia about the adventure. She attempted to justify the Triangles by attributing that inclination to despair on the influence of the river that irrigates their country.

"It is a vile river," said Poequilon, "since it is the river of death. Why do you think that the Author of Nature has presented humans with a poisoned element that contributes to the destruction of people? If the river really is such, Selenos ought to have put up insurmountable barriers, as to the volcanoes of Stivalo and the precipices of Caesaria. But whatever the truth is, I'm forced to admit that the Triangles have a good deal of honor and few prejudices. I hold in the highest esteem that

---

[48] Presumably Isaac Newton.
[49] The author uses the term *Cible* here, but French also has another word for sieve, *tamis*, whereas their term for the River Thames is Tamise.

strength of soul in them, which establishes the shame of crime in the individual, and does not render hereditary to a posterity the infamy of one's ancestors. I would like to be able to cultivate that maxim in my country."

While he was living thus among the Triangles, he was informed of an order obliging Verticephalians to leave the Kingdoms—which is to say Verticephalians who were on moon, for those who were in a port or at sea were declared free. He seized that opportunity to return to Verticephalia with pleasure; he embarked with his dear spouse and wept with joy on seeing his bell-towers. He kissed the natal moon three times, and was purified.

XX. Verticephalian naiveties

"I have traveled all over the Moon," said Poequilon, "and have not encountered either Eutoquia or my children, but I am seeing my homeland again, and the clemency of Selenos is making itself felt in my heart. What a novel charm has seized me! O my Fatherland, how can one detach oneself from your bosom?

On arriving in the great city of Verticephalia, Poequilon and Olympia were quite astonished not to recognize it at all; nothing remained of it but the great city that traverses it, which is named the Alkoulouthetique, and which seems, in dividing it to the right and the left, to be tightly embracing that capital of the Moon; all that the immense city contained was for them a new spectacle.

As it had been more than three centuries since they had left, they found an extraordinary magnificence there, and it had grown by more than two thirds. As for the inhabitants, they were also unrecognizable.

There were entirely different mores, the garments no longer conserved the slightest trace of the past, and the language had changed so much that Poequilon and Olympia had difficulty understanding their compatriots, and they were only understood by scholars, and only those who had been led by an interest in literature to leaf through old Verticephalian books.

Poequilon's first concern, after having learned the language and the customs of his country, was to seek information as to what had become of its beautiful establishments, its foundations and its legal institutions. He was told that people were entirely unaware of those things, and that nothing more ancient was known in Verticephalia than a certain school whose founder was very equivocal, an old bridge that was still new and a bronze statue without a cravat, which was worth its weight in gold, and before which one took off one's hat without thinking about it—which proves the existence of innate ideas.

At this naïve account, Poequilon burst into tears and said to himself: *This man*—he meant his informant—*is definitely of his country and mine.*

"Embrace me, my dear compatriot," he said. "It is thanks to you that I recognize my Fatherland. It has changed in my eyes but you have conserved it in your bosom. Verticephalia will never be destroyed. But tell me, have you not sometimes read the writings of a certain Poequilon, or seen his beautiful plays performed?"

"Poequilon?" said the Verticephalian. "I don't know him. Poequilon is not even our language. There has never been a Poequilon in the world. The theater of Poequilon! You're joking. In what Dynasty did he live, this Poequilon?"[50]

"He lived under the Empire of the Prince who avoided being subjugated by the Triangles, and who owed his salvation to a peasant girl as chaste as she was simple, but who handled a sword well, who was subsequently captured and burned by the Triangles."[51]

---

[50] Le Bret is presumably bearing in mind, ironically, the fact that the Molière's real name was Poquelin.

[51] i.e., the time of Jeanne d'Arc—the early 15th century—as implied by the earlier remark that more than three hundred years have elapsed since Poequilon left his homeland.

"Oh, I know, I know—you're talking about the Virago of Scirachryse…good, good, apparently, the theater of Seigneur Poequilon was burned with that Heroine," said the Verticephalian, "for I never heard mention of it." And he went away, bursting into laughter.

"So," said Poequilon, "you have to kill yourself to have a reputation among these blockheads."

XXI. A bad joke.

A few paces away he encountered a man who seemed to be desperate, who was crying: "I'm ruined! I'm doomed!"

Poequilon went to him and said to him: "Calm down, Monsieur, my fortune is immense and I can repair your losses…."

"Never, never!" relied the desperate man.

"What!" said Poequilon. "Have you lost your wife or your children?"

"Yes, Monsieur, I've lost my children. I left them on a table next to the fire, with the design of correcting them on my return. My drunken valet upset the table, and everything was consumed in an instant…!"

Poequilon, shivering, could not help interrupting the man to say to him: "Monsieur, does one leave one's children on a table? And what great misdeed had they committed, to prepare them for the meditated punishment?"

"Well, Monsieur," replied the unfortunate father, "when I say my children, I mean my Manuscripts; on them I had founded all my glory, and the hope of a durable renown."

At these words, Poequilon breathed out. He told him an abridged version of his own history, without forgetting his pretentions to immortality, which the night of time had buried before him.

"Console yourself then, Monsieur," Poequilon said, as he concluded his story. "Amuse people, and don't ever worry about it again, if that's all that is making you unhappy. It's sufficient that you love glory in order for me to be your admirer; you are, from this moment on, a distinguished man in my eyes, and if you want to share my fortune, we'll do good together; the example is worth more than the precept, don't you think?"

The burned Author was touched by Poequilon's sentiments; he forgot his children, with difficulty, and associated himself closely with that rare man, for the good of his century, leaving the suffrage of the future to the men of the future. It is said that he disposed of the treasures of his generous companion with so much wisdom and humanity that he made, with trying to do so, a reputation that has lasted several centuries and perhaps still endures.

XXII. Mistaken identity, or innocent crime.

Poequilon was not longer thinking about anything but living like an Epicurean philosopher in his delightful homeland, with the reservation nevertheless of being faithful to his wife, for he had not forgotten that at the first false step, she would be taken from him. One singular adventure, however, gave him a great deal of chagrin.

On returning from a journey, Poequilon went back into his house as dawn had scarcely illuminated Olympia's apartment. He got into his affectionate wife's bed, and although she seemed to him to be asleep, he wanted to give her proof that he had been good during his absence. He acquitted himself as a faithful and amorous husband, but, daylight having finally penetrated as far as the nuptial bed, he was very surprised to find in his arms a beautiful slave of Olympia's.

The girl informed him that her mistress had been in the country for two days, and that she, having remained in the City, had occupied Olympia's bed by virtue of a temporary appetite for softness. She added that she had certainly suspected that Seigneur Poequilon was in error, but that she had not dared to dissuade him.

The truth was, however, that the beautiful Slave had fallen in love with Poequilon, and having heard him come in, she had slipped into Olympia's bed in order to profit from an error, if her lucky star could bring about that fortuitous encounter. Her plan, as can be seen, had been as fortunate as it was well-imagined.

Once, Poequilon would have been charmed by that adventure, but in the conditions on which he was allowed to be with his wife, he was in despair, because, although he was sensible to the charms of all beauties, he adored Olympia sincerely, and he would not have wanted to be separated from her for all the pleasures in life. However, that recent infidelity caused him to shiver, and he regarded Olympia as lost to him, when that beautiful Spouse returned from the country and threw herself into his arms.

Then he thanked Selenos in secret, and thought, with reason, that the equitable Genius had thought that he ought not to punish an involuntary infidelity.

XXIII. Criminal innocence. Many people are guilty without even suspecting it.

The beautiful Eclipsis, however—the clever slave who had substituted herself for Olympia—often came back to Poequilon's mind, in thoughts of the charms of which he had been the master and which he had used without enjoyment, since his imagination had then been extended toward another object than the one he held in his arms. The idea that he formed, rightly, that the beautiful young woman had fallen in love with him, inflamed his heart and his senses.

While he was plunged in these tender reveries, Olympia came to find him in his study, and after a few caresses, Poequilon, burning with amour, threw himself on Olympia's bosom, while directing his fires toward the image of Eclipsis.[52]

---

[52] Author's note: "*Te tenet, absentes alios suspirat amores.* Tibul. I*"* The quotation is from one of the elegies of Tibullus.

He had scarcely ceased to be happy when a great noise was heard, and Olympia disappeared.

That's it, Poequilon thought. *Olympia has been taken from me. Selenos has read my heart, and judged the infidelity manifest. He did not find me criminal in the involuntary act, but he has punished me for the voluntary one. How many husbands are guilty in the Tribunal of Selenos, if he condemns distractions in the imagination!*

XXIV. That is the way it is necessary to do penance.

Deprived once again of his dear Olympia, Poequilon lived in affliction, and, wanting to appease Selenos, he devoted himself to abstinence. Still full of vigor, having charm and beauty, and having the treasures of life at his disposal, the daylight displeased him. Devoid of ambition, devoid of passion, people appeared to him what, in fact, they are. Then he ceased to hold them in esteem; prejudices fell at his feet, hypocrisy was unmasked in his gaze, brilliant exteriors of dissimulation vanished at his approach; the politeness of Courts made him see nakedly the perfidy and vanity of honors; only misfortune and indigence fixed his sentiments and attached him to society; he became by virtue of that fact a friend of humankind—which is to say, of the unfortunate, for the majority of fortunate men are not human.

He wanted to show his century and his country that wealth ought only to be lavished on the head of a Citizen for the relief of his fellows. He considered, maturely, that, an Emperor being the father of his people, all the rich men who were closest to him by virtue of their opulence and credit were Substitutes for the Sovereign; hence, he concluded that any man in abundance who was unjust, inclement and devoid of compassion was a monster and a tyrant: a monster who devoured his fellows by depriving them of assistance; a tyrant who robbed

In the context of the original, it translates roughly as "Holding you in her arms, she sighs after other absent loves."

them, by the abuse of his wealth, of the compassion of an honest man, in whose hands the fortune would have been better employed.

It is easy to see that, with these reflections, Poequilon attached himself solely to bringing the wretched out of the grip of their poverty, of turning them away from the slope to crime by a prompt assistant that returned the indigent to the road of virtue, and obtaining graces for those citizens gone astray, whom hunger or the sustenance of their family had led to neglect of social conventions. All these acts of benevolence were accompanied by recommendations to Judges on the inflexibility of laws that did not take any account of circumstances, and the natural revolt of humanity in a state of lesion, injustice, opprobrium or merely calamity.

His success in these virtuous enterprises was his joy and his consolation, and he often sighed when he thought that he had only reached that level of improvement after seven or eight centuries of existence and the experience if misfortune.

Is it necessary, then, he said to himself, *to be unhappy, or to have been unhappy, in order to be able to shed tears? Alas, if it's necessary to see unhappiness at close range to understand it, how many unfortunates are reserved to perish!*

XXV. When one goes to sleep like Poequilon, one can hope for a fine awakening.

A great Emperor governed Verticephalia, and that Prince had all Poequilon's respect and admiration.

If our August Emperor lives for a long time, he thought, *Verticephalia will be happy. What a multitude of abuses he is destroying! With what firmness his is resisting the torrent of prejudices and the murderous interests of seductive enemies of the nation! He has achieved in a few years what the greatest Princes were unable to do in half a century; he is the literal model of Kings, for others have imitated him, even his enemies; he is a conqueror, a pacifier, a friend of justice, an avenger of oppression, as well as the father of his people, a*

good father of a family. O Selenos, conserve our August Mon-
arch, that is my ultimate wish.

Selenos, who read the heart of his favorite, was touched by these virtuous dispositions, and judged that it was time free that errant life from evils.

And, indeed, Poequilon had scarcely finished that prayer than he was gripped by a profound torpor; the friends and slaves surrounding him thought that he was dead, and while the former prepared to bury him and the latter to dig a hole in the moon, to render him the last duties, Selenos transferred him invisibly to the shores of the Isle of Eutoquia.

XXVI. Poequilon arrives in the isle of Eutoquia

When he woke up, Poequilon saw a multitude of men wandering on a riverbank; a large boat came toward them and all of them jumped into it impetuously. Poequilon did the same, and in a next to no time, the boat traversed the river. All the passengers got down on the fortunate Island, and a host of inhabitants who were waiting for them on the other shore took them to Queen Elephantide.

That Princess was veiled, but her majestic figure imposed respect and delight. She was seated on an ivory throne, holding an olive branch by way of a scepter, which she made all the stranger kiss when they were presented to her.

She opened a bronze tablet on which the names of all those who had just landed on the Island were engraved, admitted them to the rank of citizens of Eutoquia and distributed employments and fields of cultivation to them. Some were to be dignitaries associated with the Queen, with vast moons and châteaux. Others only received a tiny quarter of moon and were destined to cultivate the fields of the Great and important men.

There were some in whom the necessity was imposed of serving the Queen or the Great, without any other retribution than for little pieces of ivory per day. Poequilon was in that number and was aggregated into the Queen's retinue. I say "retinue" because in Eutoquia the Princes have no need of Guards for their security; they only have a retinue for the splendor of the throne. Poequilon was paid one day's wage in advance, and then the Queen made a speech.

"Strangers who have just landed on this Island, do not complain about your share, if it does not appear equal; it is assigned on the number of your good deeds, and the time that you must pass in mediocrity is affixed by destiny, after which you will rise in rank and enjoy greater fortune.

"You are sheltered from indigence and injustices; make good use of your fate and without murmuring; that is the means of expiating your past sins promptly and enjoying the perfect happiness of this Island."

She extended the olive branch over their heads, and each of them took up his post.

The Queen presented her gloved hand to Poequilon and said to him: "You will emerge from obscurity one day; it is necessary to appease Selenos."

The whole Court perceived that the Princess's voice had suffered some alteration in speaking to that Stranger, but as the Isle of Eutoquia is devoid of crime, no suspicion is excited there, and the reflections of the Great went no further.

XXVII. He is very much a stranger in this Realm.

You will obviously have suspected that the Queen was none other than Olympia, who, by her virtues and her fidelity, had reached the supreme rank in the Isle of Eutoquia. She had recognized her husband, for whom she had been waiting a long time, and her heart suffered at not being able to liberate him from the laws of Destiny or the justice of Selenos.

Poequilon was far from thinking that Olympia governed that great Empire. Since Poequilon's arrival, the Princess had made it a rule only to appear veiled, and even changed her voice when she spoke in public or issued decrees, in order that Poequilon would not suspect her of being the Queen, so that thought never entered his head. He only suspected that she was on the Island and that she was living happily there.

He was burning with the desire to find her, and his embarrassment was great, because his functions did not permit him to devote himself to search for her. He thought, therefore, that he might engage some Eutoquian less busy than him to carry out the investigation for him, but the Island was immense, and in Eutoquia one only has the opportunity to accomplish one's desires in proportion to the rank one occupies.

He was not yet instructed in all matters, and, having the art of making gold, he was unworried about the state of mediocrity to which the Queen had reduced him.

If I give a great deal of gold to Queen Elephantide, he thought, *she will send her hemerodromes all over the island in search of Olympia. It is necessary that I show to her eyes all the riches of the Paristerie.*

XXVIII. Misers and usurers, you have changed mud into gold, now the gold becomes mud again.

Occupied with that thought, he saw men cleaning the streets, who were making heaps of filth in order to load it into carts. He asked an old Eutoquian why those men were condemned to that vile profession.

"Those men were Lipodermists before arriving on the Island," the old man replied, "which is to say, Misers and Usurers; on the Moon they were the nurturers of prodigal youth, and in this métier they are expiating the crimes they committed in their former estate."

Poequilon advanced toward the muddy men and said to them: "All the mire that is the object of your care I shall convert into gold"—which he did right away.

The muddy men were very surprised by such a miracle; they leaned on their shovels and forks to contemplated the metal, and vestiges of their ancient avidity could still be seen in their physiognomy.

"What a pity it is," one of them said to Poequilon, "that you've come to this Island with such a marvelous talent. But what do you expect to do here with that heavy and durable mud?"

"My intention," said Poequilon, "is offer it as a tribute to the Queen, in order to incline that Princess in my favor, so that she will mount searches all over the Island to discover my wife."

The muddy men burst out laughing, and one of them said: "Gold is worthless here, and what you've just produced will be thrown into the sea. That's why we beg you to make it into mud again—we'll have less difficulty in purging the island of it."

Poequilon sighed, on seeing that he was poor.

What! he thought. *This metal, so precious, after which Paterodiples, Kings and Women sigh...but let's not think about it anymore.*

"Have you been collecting mud for a long time?" Poequilon asked the men.

"Four hundred years."

"Four hundred years! You haven't been corrected of your vices, then?"

"It's because we're well paid," said one of them. "It's the most lucrative employment on the Island."

"That may be so," said Poequilon, "but it's vile work."

"Yes, yes, I've heard it said, by a Factor who had studied: *Lucri bonus est odor ex re qualibet.*"[53]

XXIX. How many people would be bathed!

Meanwhile, someone told the Queen what Poequilon had done, and the Courtiers laughed long and hard at his magnifi-

---

[53] "Money smells good no matter what its odor." The quote is attributed to the Roman Emperor Vespasian, after his son criticized the tax he had placed of public latrines; it is often paraphrased in the dictum "money has no odor."

cent present, as well as his adored Olympia. Elephantide, touched by Poequilon's sentiment, was nevertheless obliged, in accordance with the laws of Eutoquia, to condemn the gold-maker to an exemplary three plunges in the river, after having submerged the metal he had produced by himself. The sentence specified that in case of recidivism, Poequilon would augment the impure number of Lipodermists who were breathing in the mire of the Island.

Poequilon satisfied the sentence in front of the assembled people and he was given four pieces of ivory.

O pieces of ivory! said Poequilon. *Sacred money of the fortunate Isle! Symbol of candor! You have taught me that only virtue is rewarded here; you are the representative signs of human worth.*

After that honorable recompense of sorts he went back to his post, his mind occupied by the most sublime ideas, and only thinking about acquiring virtues.

XXX. Poequilon is proclaimed king of Eutoquia.

Poequilon distinguished himself so well in his employment, by his assiduity and his aptitude for virtue, that Elephantide appointed him chief of her retinue; then he was given fields and palaces, but the privation of his beloved spouse rendered him insensible to his elevation, and to his new fortune. He employed a large number of Eutoquians in working to find Olympia, and as he was just and generous, he dispersed all his fields, palaces and ivory; his fortune was so depleted that he could no longer fulfill his duties with the dignity that they required.

The Queen, who knew how he had employed his wealth, sent for him—he was reaching the term of his perfect felicity—and, affecting a severe manner, she said to him: "Poequilon, I know that you have dissipated your wealth. This is the first time that a fortunate citizen of this Island has fallen into poverty; all eyes are upon you. No one knows to what such a reversal of fortune can be attributed, in a realm of innocence, into which, by virtue of immutable laws, crime and debauchery cannot penetrate. What, then, have you done to lose your fortune? It is not to relieve the wretched, for there are none on our island, and everyone here can subsist on what he possesses, since passions are unknown here and the only competition between our Islanders is to reach the ranks that virtue provides and which attract the consideration of Citizens of the lower orders, without pride being able to poison their hearts."

"Great Queen," said Poequilon, "Selenos, in enabling me to reach this Island, has not deprived me of all my passions; he has left me one that will be eternal: the love of my wife, my dear Olympia, whom I counted on rejoining in this Isle of Felicity, which will never be anything for me but a abode of misfortune if I do not encounter here the object of all my prayers. I am very guilty in her regard, but I have always adored her and I have only consumed all my wealth in the vain attempt to find her. I thought she was here with my children, Selenos having promised me that, but I can see that his justice is still pursuing me."

Although the Queen was veiled, Poequilon perceived that she had softened. "You sympathize with my woes, great Queen," he said to her.

"Yes dear Poequilon," said Olympia. "I approve of your love. Your constancy flatters me more than you think. Console yourself; your woes are at an end. Always love your Olympia, but be sensible to Queen Elephantide, who loves you."

"O Heaven!" said Poequilon. "Can this abode of innocence permit...? Great Queen, you're deceiving me; you want to sound the depths of my heart. Can Selenos be inspiring you...but no; if you are the Queen of Eutoquia and talking to me in that fashion, you must be Olympia."

At those words, the Queen lifted her veil, and Poequilon recognized in Elephantide his tender Olympia.

The august visage of that Princess was bathed in tears. Poequilon, who was on his feet, threw himself into her arms.

She summoned all the Nobles of her retinue and said to them: "This is Poequilon. This is my husband, whom Selenos has returned to me. The term of his happiness and mine has arrived; let him share the Empire with me. And you, Nobles of my retinue, who are my children, this is your father; this is the stem of our family."

Immediately, they prostrated themselves, and Poequilon embraced them all, one after another. Olympia introduced him to the children that they had had in Verticephalia, who were the heads of families and in the foremost dignity.

The people were summoned and the Nation assembled; Poequilon was proclaimed King, and Queen Elephantide resumed the name of Olympia, in accordance with the decrees of Selenos.

I shall not attempt to give any idea of that sage government; everyone will form an image of it in conformity with the elevation of his soul. It is sufficient to know that people there are happy, because the throne is sacred and just, the authority paternal, innocent and pure, and the Religion inaccessible to contradictions.

Henri Delmotte: *A Voyage to Paraguay-Roux and the Austral Palingenesia by Tridace-Nafé Théobrôme de Kaout't'chouk, Breton Gentleman, Subassistant at the Establishment of Elysopumps, etc., etc., etc.*

(1835)

On 31 February 1831, after having hauled in the mooring-ropes and unfurled the shrouds, we set forth for the port of St. Malo, all sails down, under a south-east-north-westerly wind. It was blowing freshly; the waves and breakers splashed silently and came to play around the flanks of the corvette *La Calembredaine*,[54] in which we were sailing; it wove its knot, in naval terminology, and in no time at all we were doubling Cape Finistere, the place where the end of the world begins, as its name indicates, and we soon reached the island of Madeira.

We took on water there, and as the exotic natives of the island were occupied at that moment in making dry Madeira, we thought we ought to assist in that operation, unknown to our vintners, whether in Champagne or Burgundy. It takes place toward the end of winter, when the sun, shining over the roofs, causes those rounded and elongated icicles to form, the thousand angular faces of which reflect the prismatic rays so brilliantly.

Men experienced in the métier put the icicles into the necks of bottles of sweet Madeira, and when they are certain that the extremity of the block of ice has reach the bottom of

---

[54] *Calembredaine* means "nonsense," usually applied in the context of talking; the word is etymologically related to *calembour* [pun], with which the text is so richly larded that there is only space to footnote a few of those that do not translate.

the bottle they cut the base of the icicle adhering to the roof, very subtly, without pressing too heard, and then seal the bottles hermetically.[55] The cut is carried out by means of red-hot pincers, in order not to alter the color of the wine. Nothing is simpler than to imagine the cause and the effect of that procedure; the icicle, dissolving promptly in the liquid, thus communicates its dryness to the wine, which absorbs it entirely and retains it until it is drunk.

We raised anchor with the pulley-blocks and took to the open sea along a strait of whose name I have forgotten to make a note in my journal. We had to weather a few storms, as many large as small, which caused the most superstitious matelots to take advantage of the opportunity to tell their rosaries.[56]

In the evening, the sails having broken down, I was walking on the deck with the officer of the watch. After a time the conversation became intimate, and he communicated to me, under the seal of secrecy, one of the most important discoveries he had ever made, and which he planned to make known to the Admiralty.

"When a vessel," he said, for I let him talk, "has arrived at a degree of longitude whose figure is the same as that of the degree of latitude it has reached, no longitude or latitude is any longer possible, since the measure of the two different degrees is equal, one of them can no longer be broader or longer than the other, and vice versa."

The astonishing simplicity of that discovery, which has nevertheless only been made in the nineteenth century of the

---

[55] Author's note: "Whence it comes about, by onomatopoeia, that a wine jug is known as a *carafon*, or *car il a fond*. The *il* was subsequently omitted by lexicographers, and people said, by corrupting the primitive and primordial root, *carafon*; it is a trope by which a word is minimized—cf Demessis, *Traité des tropes plus ou moins usité dans la langue française,* p. 143."

[56] This sentence is a series of puns on the word *grain*, which can mean "bead" as well as "storm," and, of course "grain."

Christian Epact, struck me by virtue incalculable results of its application to the section of the angles of the arc of the meridian, and especially by the light it was going to cast on the equipolation of the Zenith and the Nadir.

When I went back to my cabin I was so preoccupied with what I had just heard that I bumped by head on one of the corners of my hammock, and exclaimed involuntarily: "Who would be astonished, after that, if it were not Adam who discovered America, Cain gunpowder and Babel the printing press?"

Inarticulate and harmonious sounds, similar to those of a thousand bird-organs playing a tune in Italian *tutti* announced to us that we were approaching the Canary Isles. An acrid and incisive odor of ripe millet (*Fourcroyana pimeloides*, Linneaus) and hard eggs left us no doubt on that subject, even if we wanted to conserve any. We finally set foot on the native soil of those lovely birds (*Acanthis lutea*, Buffon, *viridis*, Cuvier, or *fusca*, Lesson), which are the ornament and charm of our aviaries, where they savor the pleasures of captivity so joyfully.

I devoted my every moment to them, and this is the result of my observations and the information I received about that pretty species of soliped annelids. The canary of the Canaries, the veritable canary—in a word, the autochthonous canary—is born white all over, whatever zoologists might say. When, like a young child that has just seen the light of day, that newly-hatched animal, urged by nature, disgorges the viscous fluid that pathologists call *meconium*, it tries to do so in vain, because its structure—its *habitus*, in technical terms— mounts an obstacle to it, and this is how:

The intestinal system of the canary has the particular feature that the primordial extremity of the large colon is not connected, as in other pachyderms, to the sphincter of the ovoid rectum by the small intestine; furthermore, the latter does not even exist in the species, and its place is taken by a non-secretory and amorphous laryngeal membrane of a soft and spongy consistency, but the extremely compact cellular tissue of which, not permitting any stercoral detritus to fray a path to the exterior, forces it, by a very pronounced phlogistic and diagnostic movement, to flow back into the interior. The animal, in that period of its existence, suffers and languishes, but soon the chelos, driven back in very small angular globules into its vital economy, penetrates all the orifices, and colors its feathers in yellow if it has only thus far eaten eggs, or green if it has already tasted lettuce.

You will easily understand, after that exceedingly clear explanation, why the canary's feces are white. The chemical analysis, according to Klapproth, Hufeland and Freytag indicates that they are composed of albumin silicate, manganese subcarbide, sulfurous oxygenated phosphate and pyritic hydrosulfuric acid.

The canary's malady, known in all climates under the name of budding jealousy, does not originate, as Guyton de Morvaux[57] has asserted, from the resemblance between that lymphatic tumor to a window-catch, but from the abdominal structure inherent to the species, which we have just described. Its determinate and rational cause is the infiltration of the urinary duct into the parenchymal phlogoses of the membrane that we mentioned—an infiltration that occasions the edema of the internal walls, determines the petechy of the diseased organ and dilates it while contracting it upon itself, a morbid situation that leads to hydropsy, and finally gives birth to the death of the individual.

We did not want to abandon the Canary Isles without having visited the famous peak of Tenerife, visible to the naked eye at a distance of fifty-seven leagues, and from two hundred leagues with a telescope, provided that the latter is good and, especially, brings objects much closer. We hired guides for fear of going astray on the summit of that giant lump of chalk.

---

[57] Louis-Bertrand Guyton de Morveau (1737-1816) was a notable French chemist who played a significant role in the 1789 Revolution.

On the way, while climbing, we admired the fissures in the bare and uncultivated rock as well as the productive fertility of the celebrated mountain. Having finally reached the ultimate extremity, we first went straight to the habitation of an opulent American negro industrialist who, understanding very well that only communications can establish relationships between producers and consumers, in order to add proof to that axiom—so true but little appreciated in political economy—had just established tilted sluice gates on the culminating point of the peak, to which, by means of a very ingenious improvement, he had applied the Watt system. That is steam, by which he has succeeded in obtaining a force equivalent to at least two hundred thoroughbred Arab horses, which raises and drops the seesaw forming the lock-chamber of those sluice-gates, the upstream and downstream of which are preciously finished.

The officer I mentioned before objected to the American that the inequalities of the terrain as well as the mass of snow that accumulated on the mountain would oppose insurmountable difficulties to his hydraulic works.

"Not at all," the industrialist replied, smiling. "With regard to the first point, you must understand that it would be physically impossible to establish tilted sluice-gates—note the expression—on absolutely flat ground. As for the second difficulty, this is how I resolve it…."

He introduced us then into a vast courtyard surrounded by spacious buildings, in which hundreds of workmen were occupied in different tasks. Immense heaps of snow were piled up next to one another, like grain-mills, and workers were carrying them away in little baskets to throw them into enormous coke furnaces similar to those that Monsieur Cockerill uses for cast iron.[58]

We could not hide our surprise at encountering in the Canary Isle an establishment similar to the one in Seraing, and

---

[58] The reference is to the British industrialist William Cockerill (1759-1832), who emigrated to France and built textile mills in Verviers and Liège.

we enquired urgently as to what the snow became in those ardent furnaces.

"Marine salt!" replied our host.

At those words, our astonishment no longer knew any limits, but he soon convinced us of what he was telling us by giving us the following explanation of the manipulations that were being carried out before our eyes.

During the waning of the August moon, when the last quarter of that planet is at its perihelion, the snow is carefully collected; it is mixed with a very compact volatile alkali as hard as one can find; then it is submitted to the centripetal action of an extremely violent reagent, such as chalk, in order to separate the heterogeneous particles from the homogeneous molecules, in such a fashion that, the absorption being complete, the snow is eventually ready to undergo the proof of fire. The energy of that fire, for the latter operation to succeed, must be equivalent that of refractory rays reflected by the isosceles prism of the mirror with which Archimedes set fire to the fleet of Scipio Africanus in the port of Syracuse.

The extreme ardor of that prodigious heat seizes the snow when it is introduced into the furnace and prevents it from melting, which could not fail to happen if the heat were less intense. The snow, hermetically enveloped by the flames, solidifies by crystallizing, and is taken out red hot from the furnace; it is then thrown into tubs filled with a dilute solution of alum and animal saltpeter, and it is in that preparation that it recovers its primitive whiteness.

We tasted that marvelous salt; it was very sapid, lightly teasing the nervous buds of the tongue, and superb to look at.

We finally took our leave of the negro industrialist after having offered him a copy of a work on pebble-oil by Dr. Cloetboom,[59] born in Strépy-Bracquegies, a circumstance un-

---

[59] Author's note: "*Iconoclastic observations on the various methods employed in the manufacture of pebble-oil and the manner of making use of that metallurgical substance in the*

known until now to contemporary biographers. He received the book with pleasure and promised, in view of the abundance of the raw material, to add an exploitation of pebble-oil to his factory, with the result that before long, he would be able to boast of having turned the famous peak of Tenerife into salad, since the mountain already produced vegetables, that its oaks and other woods could furnish vinegar, its rocks oil and its snows salt. As for pepper, unfortunately, it would be necessary to import that from Cayenne.

We went back on board, braced the mizzen, hoisted the jibs, raised the royals and not long afterwards, pushed by a favorable wind, dropped anchor in a bay in the Cape Verde Islands. We made no observation there more curious than that of the famous geologist Schwartzeberg, who was accompanying the expedition. He submitted the land of Cape Verde to metallurgical analysis, and found that it was composed in equal proportions of Naples yellow and Prussian blue, which produces the Venice green tint with which it is colored—the tint that gives the islands their name, just as the colors of their waters give their names to the Black Sea, the Red Sa the Blue Sea, the White Sea, etc.

As we were about to go back on board, a Malay cicerone offered to show us the Royal Museum of Antiquities. We accepted the offer and immediately went to that interesting establishment. Various objects captivated our attention there, including a phial still containing the elixir that Garus, king of the trans-Rhenian Propontide, sent to Anaximander, King of Thrace, when the latter contracted jaundice under the walls of Thebes, then defended by Pisitratus. The two most curious rarities in the gallery, however, are two Roman earthenware vases discovered recently almost at surface level in the island's interior.

Those vases both have the form of a truncated cone resting on it point; one the upper part of the first one observes a

---

cure if cutaneous infections of the pibus, Brussels 1832, octavo."

hemispherical swelling crowned by a strangulated circular neck. The inscription on the first vase is:

DIV. IO. N. EN. S. M. — S.P.Q.R.

which was initially translated as:

DIvii JOvis Nepotis ENnius Sacravit Manibus

and that of the second vase was conceived in these terms:

NI. GER. A. N. T. — S.P.Q.R.
which was interpreted as:

NIlo GERmanicus Aquas Nubiae Traxit (or Traxulit)

But since then, Hellenist scholars well-versed in the lexicography and lapidary chirography of ancient peoples have proved that the former signifies:

DIVIONENSis MULTARDA

and the second;

NIGER ANTuerpiensis

a version evidently confirmed by the shape of the vases.

The importance of this discovery for archeology and the history of the ancient peoples of Italy is incalculable, for it demonstrates evidently that Rome, the mistress of the entire world, nevertheless paid that tribute to the manufacturers of Dijon, for their mustard, and those of Antwerp for their boot-polish, long before the Phoceans[60] came to settle in Marseilles.

---

[60] Author's note: "Paludanus—'of the marsh,' or 'of the fishpond,' in English—an Epiote by birth, was the chief of the Numidian tribes that irrupted into the Marais-Pontins to found

The polish of the capital of the Marquisate of Antwerp and the condiment of the main town of the Duchy of Burgundy undoubtedly reached the subjects of Caesar by way of the Brunehault causeways, which were the locomotives of the day.

The curator of the museum, a descendant of the illustrious Gronovins,[61] had recently married one of the great granddaughters of the Benedictine scholar Montfaucon.[62] He showed us the very interesting manuscript of a treatise that he intends to publish. The treatise will form four folio volumes, ornamented with plates, three of notes and one of tables. The author proves conclusively in that work, which he permitted us to read, that obscene lamps representing the phallus are lamps that were set alongside culpable Vestals when they were buried alive. Roman law intended by that measure that the corrupt Vestal should have before her eyes until death, and beyond, the instrument of her dishonor. That explains in a very rational manner the large quantity of those lamps that one finds every day in digs.

Here the author adds a very simple and just reflection: "If the Romans had been familiar with German tinder, the number of Vestals executed would have been much reduced, for their lovers would have made use of that means, which they would have had to hand, to relight the fire on the altar of

---

Marseille. When the excavations were carried out of the places where the foundations of the city to be were laid down, he cried, in order to encourage his workers: "Quel fosse, ein!" [What a ditch, eh!] In commemoration of that remark, his tribe took the name of Phoceans, by which it is still known today."

[61] According to François-Xavier Feller's *Dictionnaire historique* (1818), Jacques Gronovins (1645-1716) published a dissertation in 1684 proving that the story of Romulus, the legendary founder of Rome, was completely fictitious.

[62] The Benedictine monk Bernard de Montfaucon (1655-1741) was one of the founders of modern archaeology and the great pioneer of paleography, the study of ancient handwriting.

Vesta when it went out." What an even greater influence might have been exerted on the mores of the dwellers of the Tiber by the modest phosphoric match, which was, alas, unknown to them!

We were continuing the course of our voyage placidly when, one morning, we were woken up with a start by a salvo that made the hatches shake. We went to the lower deck in haste, and there we found the crew, under arms, arranged in a circle around the captain in his full dress uniform. The latter announced to us in a grave and solemn tone that we were on the equator and, in consequence, the ceremonial baptism was about to take place.

I will spare my readers the details of that holy rite, so familiar to all good Christians. I submitted to it with unction and humility, and the almoner was delighted by my pious sentiments. I ran on to the deck as soon as it was finished in order to see the famous line that divides the world into two hemispheres, but it was a waste of effort, for, less solid than the pyramids of Giza, it had disappeared so completely that I was unable to discover the slightest trace of it. I retired, discontented, and cursed the carelessness of mariners—adventurous and insouciant folk—who had neglected the simple precaution of placing a few boundary-markers to indicate to future navigators the precise place where the line had once existed.[63]

We doubled, without stopping, the island of Saint Helena, the celebrated island where the spouse of Constantin Porphyrogennete, founder of the race of Peleologues,[64] discov-

---

[63] Author's note: "'It is doubtless to the continuous motion of the waves that the disappearance of the line, along its entire length, must be attributed.' *On the Influence of Tides on Sea Level* by Charles, Prince de Ligne, Duc de Lorraine et de Bar. Nivelles: Chez Letrait, 1816.)

[64] Constantine Palaeologos was the last Byzantine Emperor. Porphyrogennetos was an honorific title given to a son born after his father had become emperor.

ered the wood of the true cross, and where the secular man who set fire to Europe in our days became a heap of ashes.

I shall say a little about the Cape of Good Hope, so devoid of interest, according to Levaillant,[65] one of the members of the expedition of the unfortunate Captain Cook. All the indigenes of that region are English or Dutch. We ate a galantine of filleted elephant trunk *à la Soubise*, and a delicious *vol-au-vent* of giraffe in tortoise. We went to digest it on Table Mountain, covered with expanses of water, and from there we admired the beautiful view that extended before our eyes, for Cape Town is situated directly under the table.

We did not neglect to visit the astronomer Monsieur Herschel, a worthy son of his famous uncle, who has come to install himself to the Cape for three years in order to verify whether the reverse of the stars whose other side he had observed from Greenwich in England was identically similar.[66] He offered us coffee, and we then presented him with a glass of starry aniseed from the Maldives, and he bid us farewell, after having shaken our hands cordially and wished us good luck for the rest of our voyage.

By means of his famous telescope, which brings objects twelve times closer than they are away, he has convinced himself that the stars are species of celestial animalcules that nourish themselves on pure ether. Those that we call shooting stars are stars that are disgorging the superfluity of their luminous matter by way of urinary or gastric tracts, and comets are species of voracious stars that engulf myriads of invisible stars in their passage. They seem to be particularly fond of those that compose the Milky Way, doubtless because their taste is more agreeable. Those kinds of planets play a role within the armillary system very similar to that played by conquerors on out terraqueous globe; the female individuals of the species have thick capillary systems; they are the hairy comets; and indi-

---

[65] The African explorer François Levaillant (1753-1824)

[66] John Herschel (1792-1871) arrived in Cape Town to study the stars of the southern hemisphere in January 1834

viduals of the other species, known as tailed comets, are re-markable for the enormous dimension of their reproductive and regenerative apparatus. These discoveries annihilate entirely the systems of Tycho Brahe and Copernicus, and we shall soon envisage the sun, and even the moon, in an unfamiliar light.

The captain was alerted to an exceedingly lively and precipitate oscillatory movement of the compass two days later, when we were in the vicinity of the Cap des Aiguilles, where all the wool of the great and small Namaquois and Caffrerie is knitted.[67] We then entered the Sunda Strait, into which are discharged, drop by drop, the impure and miry waters of the canal that Busiris, the sin of Nimrod, hollowed out in the Urethra.[68]

We also called in at the Île Bourbon, so called because Hugues Capet, chief of that royal branch, was born there. We passed through the Molluskan islands, formerly called the Moluccas, a formless and indigestible mass of hymentopteran and tetrapteran crustaceans whose formation does not date back beyond the creation of the globe.[69]

I shall not talk about our incursions into the Caroline, Philippine, Marianne, etc. Islands, all inhabited either by laundresses, ironers or dressmakers, uniquely occupied in the fabrication of Persian fabrics and Indian nankeens, nor the Île de la Trinité, all of whose inhabitants are idolaters, which surprised us strangely. The only interesting thing we saw in this phase of the voyage was the rice-mines of the Carolines. That

---

[67] The Grand et Petit Namaquois and the Caffrerie are African tribes referenced in Levaillant's 1797 account of his travels in southern Africa.

[68] The basis of this pun, continuing the general theme, is that Sonde [Sunda, in geography] also means "sound," "probe" or, most relevantly, "catheter."

[69] Tetraptera, here construed as if it meant "four winged" by analogy with the insect order of hymenoptera, is only used in biology in the Latin names of plants.

substance is found in schistous and granitic rocks mingled with chalk; it affects the form of agglomerated masses, like puddings, and not that of tabular veins, like marble or copper, or that of salmon, like lead. Manual labor alone extracts the rice, in which the mines are very rich, but before it is separated from the mica and fatty quartz that are inherent to it and it can become granular, as we receive it in Europe, it has to be subjected to a sequence of exceedingly complicated metallurgical manipulations, too long to describe here, which will be the subject of an *ad hoc* paper that I shall publish in due course.[70]

We finally reached Polynesia, the unique goal of our voyage. Polynesia! That marvelous country newly invented and "unknown even to its inhabitants," to make use of the beautiful expression of Ptolemy Porphyrogenete, reproduced word for word by Racine. We saluted it with cries of joy, and, without wasting a second, we headed for the Viti islands.[71]

The first, on the beach of which we descended, is named Vanona-Leboli, and is entirely deserted, to such an extent that one often finds immense villages there in which one does not encounter a single house.

A few human bones confirmed that that of Kandabon[72] had once been inhabited by cannibals who had nourished themselves on human flesh. They had devoured one another, and the last of them, having no more fellows to sink his teeth into, had eaten himself. He had recorded that circumstance in is epitaph, engraved with the point of a nail on a piece of liana, the text of which read:

D.O.M.
Emêm-iom

---

[70] Author's note: "*De ritibus missis à Carolind.*" The crucial phrase means "spoken rites"

[71] i.e. Fiji.

[72] Author's note: "From Kan, in Latin *campus*, field, and the English *bone*: Field of Bones."

Regnam em rap rinif ed ia'j
Rerovéd à neir sulp tnaya'n
Emèrtre miaf am de emitciv
R.I.P.

I have attempted the following free translation, although no one in the crew knows the language of such uncivilized savages any more than I do:[73]

D.O.M.
A victim of extreme hunger
Having nothing more to devour
I have ended up eating
Myself.
R.I.P.

We went back aboard, and were heading straight for an island whose mountains crowned with verdure offered a magnificent sight when a dense fog hid it from view. We looked for it on the marine charts but could not find it. We took possession of it in the name of France, and after having visited it we called it Civilization Island, a name fully justified by the astonishing marvels that we witnessed there, and of which I shall try, if it is possible, to give you a faint idea.

The ligneous railways that the natives once built have been completely abandoned, because the speed of the trains was not great enough. Those railways nevertheless had the advantage over the ones in Europe that, being made of wood, they were considerable less heavy and cheaper. Steam engines have been forsaken as much too slow, and the electric fluid has been adapted as a motor. The locomotive machine, entire-

---

[73] As the narrator evidently has not noticed that the text of the Epitaph is simply his own French translation written backwards, I have left it in the original, while translating his translation into English, although that does spoil the symmetry somewhat.

ly made of metal, has the size and form of a saddle-pistol, which led to it being given the name of a Voltaic pistol. That new kind of wagon is attached by means of an iron ring to the casing of a glass carriage, in which the traveler takes his place. That apparatus flies with an immeasurable rapidity along a metal wire that serves as a conductor.

That new vehicular system offers immense advantages over the ancient mode of transport; firstly, the modesty of the price, for this is the estimate for the establishment of one of these paths along an extent of a kilometric league:

Two iron hooks.................. ....40 fr. 37½ cm.	
Iron wire............................ 2511	
Hammer to attach the hooks............<u>107</u>	
2658.37½	

Secondly, the facility of establishing them: a child would be sufficient for that operation, and as the routes do not damage in any way the terrains over which they pass, there is no point in expropriating them. If the route hinders the riverside proprietors, the wire is removed and placed elsewhere, with no further ceremony or expense.

A very great advantage of these metallic causeways is that at night they are brightly illuminated by numerous sparks or fiery showers that scintillate and escape the iron wire impregnated with electrical fluid. We would, however, like to hide—but in vain—one very serious inconvenience of this recent discovery, if which it is necessary to make the painful confession: one cannot place more than one passenger at a time in the carriages, because the latter, according to physicists, must be isolated, or else he would be struck by an electrical commotion while inside. It is hoped, however, that further improvements will soon allow this obstacle to be overcome.

The constitutional system is the mode of government adopted by the Civilization Islanders. This is how they apply it. A king is nothing, they say, since he is not responsible, and yet, as he the one who governs, one is necessary, for without him, no government would exist. Now, a king of flesh and bone eats, drinks and consumes; consequently, he requires a civil list, which encumbers the budget and generates debt; since kings die, their deaths give rise to disturbances, and if there are no children, lead to changes of dynasty. They have warded off all these inconveniences with the prudence of Nestor, the companion of Telemachus, and this is how: they have fabricated a very fine king in encrusted jacaranda-wood.

That king is moved by clockwork, and with his right hand, when the spring is tightened and the weight reset, can sign at least twenty or thirty documents without stopping. The monarch, whose signature is very well calligraphed in English, only figures in the budget at a sum of fifty francs, employed for the purchase of oil and grease; that is the whole of his civil list.

The royal signature is only placed in the presence of all the assembled ministers, and it is the President of the Council alone who enjoys the privilege of turning the monarchical handle, the kingpin of state. He is the depository of that instrument, by the entitlement of his functions. As for the responsibility of the ministers, it is real; they cannot take off, night or day, a rope attached around the neck by a slip-knot. Any elector has the right to tighten that knot with impunity, to the extent of perfect strangulation, if he can then furnish proof that the minister he has just slain had committed any infraction of the charter. Among the islanders, that simple hempen cord, so modest and at the same time so useful, replaces as an insignia of power the ostentatious red morocco portfolio of our statesmen.

The greatest abuse of deliberating chambers, they say, with great common sense, is that they can deliberate. They have got rid of that inconvenience, for their chambers are composed of deaf-mutes, the only qualities necessary in order to be eligible. A mute delegate cannot sell his voice; also being deaf he is even more inaccessible to seductions, and as the laws have to be voted conscientiously, it is sufficient to put them before the eyes of the representatives for them to emit their opinion for or against, disengaged from any species of influence. Let no one imagine, in our decrepit and enfeebled Europe, that eloquence is banished from these mute chambers; I have witnessed some of their deliberations, and I can assure you, after having seen the gestures of several delegates, that—to use the apt expression of one of our most illustrious generals—"Their silence speaks for them."

Their legislation is a model. I shall only cite one example. Shortly after our arrival on the island, duels were the order of the day. What did the legislators do? They immediately voted this law, admirable in its clarity and conciseness:

No one may fight duels, except alone.

And duels ceased, as if by magic.

One finds savings banks on that island in the most wretched hamlet, and the laborer without work, the individual who lacks everything, the indigent proletarian and the millionaire reduced to living on alms thus find the greatest facility for depositing in those banks the excess of their needs and the fruit of their economies.

Thanks to progress in chemistry, taken on that island to a very high degree of perfection, gas lighting has just been replaced by another mode, much more portable, the discovery of which is owed to Cueu-Mani-Chou, Thénard of the country. After numerous and repeated experiments he has found an extremely subtle substance, deleterious and inflammable, to which he has given the name phosphoriculine. He had noticed that chelos (*stereus* in Latin, *lulle* in German) emits many pyroform and phosphorescent essences; he needed no more than that. He set to work and this is the apparatus he invented:

The nozzle of a serpentine tube is fitted to the external orifice of the rectal ring of the individual who desires illumination, and the other end of the tube is adapted to a bagpipe, which affects the form of the bustle that our elegant ladies wear. The apparatus placed in that bag receives the raw material, decomposes it and extracts the phosphoriculine therefrom, by means of a highly ingenious method, which flows through another conduit of narrow dimension, made of ebony wood, which curves forward between the thighs up to the height of the hyoid bone of the navel. That tube is terminated by a system similar to that of an Argand lamp, in which that new conquest of chemistry is consumed. The itching occasioned by the operation, far from being painful, causes extremely agreeable sensations, and the machine does not hinder the march of its wearer at all.

If you nourish yourself on onions, turnips, peas, lentils and other monoandrous polygynous bulbous plants, you obtain a brighter and more intense light because the phosphoriculine is purer, but if the bomborax within you is in a morbid and anemic state, you obtain little or no light. That observation has determined the application of the ausculator in question to medicine, where it serves to indicate the idiosyncrasy of gastroenteritis, whether chronic or acute, tenesmus, puerperal colics, borborygmus, etc. The character of the fuligiphorous individual also causes variations in the color of the flame, for which I cannot make a better comparison than the fireworks employed in the Italian theater. Thus, lymphatic temperaments give a white light, nervous ones a blue-tinted flame, bilious ones a yellow light, sanguine ones a red flame, etc.

Since I am on the topic of medicine, I ought to add that the art in question, like the others, has made frightening progress on the island. The country's physicians loudly make fun of Hahnemann's homeopathic theory, and cure their patients with nothing, all medicaments, they say, being harmful. This is a specimen of their cures: A man is afflicted with dysentery? They make him do the forked tree (*poirier* in Walloon, *pyrus japonicus* in Yeddo)—which is to say that they place him head down, supported by his hands. That treatment, perfectly well reasoned, is always crowned with success.

"But what about the blood that rises to the invalid's head and chokes him?" we objected to the doctor who described that cure to us.

"What?" he replied. "How can blood rise to the head when the latter is at the bottom?"

We remained confounded.

The island is as favored in relation to the products of the soil as with regard to industrial and scientific products. We undertook a few plant-gathering expeditions there; the richness of the vegetation is such that we could not discover any simples; all the plants there are double, and we even found a few triples, which, with very little....

At this point, the exceedingly interesting journal is abruptly interrupted.

It was found in a carefully-corked bottle in Persia, at the height of the Himalaya, with gives rise to the fear that *La Calembredaine* has perished and that the unfortunate Kaout't'Chouk has shared its unfortunate fate.

Edmé Rousseau: *The Aerial Journey*
(1859)

PART ONE

I

I am delivering this new work to print because I consider it as a sequel to my work on the grandeur of the works of God,[74] the beauties and marvels of nature, in which I only speak, as it were, about the globe that we inhabit, and did not say very much about those we see traveling so distantly, rotating and circling in the zodiac. I thought that a description of other worlds might serve to complete the work on the grandeur of God's works.

The idea made me smile at first; then I was frightened by the great difficulties that I would have to vanquish; but the great difficulties did not stop me; there was an idiopathy in me, an inclination that brought me back incessantly to the desire to know all the heavenly bodies, great and small, that I saw in the immensity; scientific astronomers have given us descriptions of them, of course, but many of those descriptions are only based on appearances, and I desired ardently to know the reality. But how could I succeed in discovering that reality?

---

[74] *Grandeur des oeuvres de dieu, ou L'Ouvrage des six jours.* The Bibliothèque Nationale catalogue gives its initial publication date as 1867, three years after the first publication of the present text; Barbou might have published the works out of sequence, but the phrasing of the sentence suggests that there was an earlier first edition.

There my embarrassment was augmented to such a point that I was almost discouraged. However, my idiopathy did not weaken; I thought, day and night, about how I could attain that reality. I thought that there was no other means to employ than that of balloons I have invented and with which one can navigate in the air without running any risk. However, I thought, when I arrive on a planet, how will I be received, if it is true, as it is said, that they are all inhabited and that even the sun has its inhabitants?

All these reflections occupied my mind continually; and then another very important difficulty presented itself: how would I live on an unknown world? I am not a geophage. I thought then of filling the nacelle of one of those little transport aerostats with food, water and everything that I thought necessary for a voyage of several million leagues. One travels quickly by way of the air, and that reflection encouraged me a little.

But another difficulty presented itself: that of going to visit globes or worlds of whose inhabitants I knew no more than they knew of me. How would they receive a being of which they doubtless had no idea? If it was as an enemy, my situation would become very embarrassing; how could I defend myself, alone against a crowd whose members might be led to insult or maltreat me by the curiosity of such a novel spectacle?

By precaution and prudence, two things essential to voyagers, I thought of filing one of the nacelles of the transport aerostat with weapons and ammunition, in order to prepare for defense when I approached the planets I wanted to visit.

This is the itinerary had had the intention of following: the Moon, Venus, Mercury, Iris, Flora, Parthenope and the Sun.

I was very preoccupied with the voyage I was planning, and in which I had already glimpsed many difficulties that seemed to me to be insurmountable, but which did not take long to disappear completely, as you shall see; a benevolent genius was watching over me.

178

On a beautiful day in the month of June, the atmosphere was warm, the air was embalmed with the perfumes of odorous flowers coming from a long way away. Flora had triumphed over cold winter, and appeared in our gardens. Zephyr had succeeded the Aquilonian frosts; everyone was breathing a mild, warm air. The body abandoned itself to a lazy nonchalance, and thought drifted, abandoned to a gentle reverie. One could taste a wellbeing that made one love life.

After my dinner, the air was refreshed, and the sunset reminded me of those I had admired so much in America. I went down to take a stroll in the little wood that is twenty paces from the house in which I live, and, as the heat of the day had fatigued me slightly, I sat down on a couch of grass and stretched myself out delightedly. I did not take long to fall into a reverie while contemplating the firmament, which was soon strewn with stars that I had long desired to know at closer range. But what could I do to visit them? I saw the impossibility of it, but I was dreaming of it at that moment more than ever.

My reverie caused me to fall into a torpor that numbed my senses, and I went to sleep. I had a dream that is still present in my memory, and this is it.

I felt myself being lifted into the air; how and by what I did not know, and I was not overly anxious about it, for I felt quite well; it was as if I were cradled in an invisible hand. I fell into a somnolence, from which I as soon extracted by the cold I felt; I have learned since that I was then in the high regions of the atmosphere, which are cold and damp. I made a few movements, and felt that I was covered by a warm and light fabric.

A soft voice said to me: "Have no fear; you're in my care. I am your good genius, and I am charged with taking you wherever you want to go and protecting you there; such is the order I have received from Zadir, our chief.[75]

"Ah!" I said to him. "You fill me with joy. How will I be able to thank you for your care and devotion?"

"You do not owe me anything," he replied. "Zadir has an affection for you, even a tenderness, and everything that I shall do for you is only owed to Zadir. As for me, I am only carrying out his orders, which I fulfill with pleasure."

"But at least permit me to shake your hand as a sign of gratitude," I said to him. "Hold it out to me, for I can hear you but I cannot see you; you're invisible to my eyes."

"I always will be," he replied. "But if you have need of me, pronounced three times, aloud: *Za, Za, Za*, and I will immediately be beside you. Now, where do you want to go?"

"I'd like to commence my voyage with the Moon," I replied.

"Very well," he said. "You'll be there in a few minutes, for it's no more than ninety-three thousand leagues distant from the Earth."

I was amazed to hear him say that, but I thought that his speed was probably as rapid as that of light, which travels seventy-seven thousand leagues in a second. We set off, and a few seconds after our departure we arrived on the Moon, a planet that is sixty times smaller than the Earth.

My arrival on that planet produced an extraordinary effect on its inhabitants. I say *my* arrival because Za—that was the name of my genius—could not be seen, since he was invisible. The news of what was for them a phenomenon spread rapidly, and a numerous crowd of inhabitants soon gathered in order to see me. I saw nothing hostile in their attitude, howev-

---

[75] In the interplanetary fantasies cited in the introduction, those by Tiphaigne de La Roche and Madame Robert both feature genii with names beginning with Za—as do several other fantasies of that period, so Rousseau is following an established tradition, albeit a trifle belatedly.

er; they doubtless saw me as a being of their species who only differed from them in the matter of costume.

I thought that, and made no reparation for defense, since I was not being attacked, and, on the contrary, I hoped for a favorable welcome. I had judged well; son I saw an innumerable host of curious people coming from all directions, in the midst of which I could distinguish individuals of high rank, to judge by their brilliant escort. Several of those individuals were mounted on small horses, others were being carried in palanquins of a sort.

When they arrived nearby, one of the important individuals approached me and asked me who I was, where I came from and what brought me to their country. Za, on quitting me, had left me the gift of understanding all the languages spoken on the planets that I wanted to visit, which he did in accordance with the order that his chief, Zadir, had given him. I was therefore able to reply to the important individual, who appeared to be satisfied with my responses and withdrew, followed by his escort.

About an hour after that visit I received another of greater importance; it was that of an ambassador or minister of King Dirzali, who addressed himself to me in order to invite me to accept an apartment in his palace. I accepted his offer with alacrity, because I saw it as a good means of being respected in the country of which King Dirzali was the sovereign, and obtaining more easily all the information that I desired to collect.

I therefore departed with the minister, and in less than an hour we arrived at the King's palace, situated in the center of the city of Enul, the capital of the realm. During the short journey I had made with the minister I had asked him to instruct me regarding the ceremony that it was necessary to observe when he introduced me to the King.

"On entering the Throne Room," he told me, "You must make three genuflections; then you approach the king, who will be waiting for you, sitting on his throne; you should prostate yourself at his feet, and remain in that posture until I say to you: 'Alazati.' Then you get up, and the King will offer you his hand, which you should place on your head, and then kiss respectfully.

"When that ceremony is complete, the King will invite you to dine at his table, around which are couches of a sort with cushions, on which you stretch yourself out and support yourself. Then, after the meal, you will be taken into a neighboring room, which is the desert room, where Queen Dirzali will be present, and the queen's mother, whose name is Douri. The presentation is made in that fashion, and then you will be recognized as one of the palace guests, because the horses and litters of the court will be at your disposal."

I thanked him for his kindness, and he told me that he was glad to have been useful to me.

The beginning of my voyage commenced under good auspices, for, on the very day of my arrival, I acquired powerful friends. The generosity of the King, and the sympathy that the Ministers seemed to have for me, assured me of tranquility during my sojourn on the planet, where the inhabitants are generally good. Their stature is slightly less than ours; the women there are similar, although a trifle plump in the face and too gross in a certain part of the body, which probably comes from their being inhabitants of the Moon, for in certain regards they had a hint of the Hottentot Venus about them What would be a deformity among us is a beauty in the inhabitants of the moon; everything is for the best.

I took advantage of the privileges that my title as a guest of the palace gave me, and asked that I might be given some kind of vehicle and a guide in order to visit the realm. I was given a kind of litter carried by two small horses and I set out.

II

The landscape of the Moon is very hilly and mountainous. I saw mountains there of a considerable height, very steep and terminating in a peak. Crags of enormous size can be seen there, and precipices of great depth, which is doubtless why people think they can see eyes, a nose and a mouth on the Moon. The effect that it produces on our eyes when one gazes at it from Earth only comes from the parts of it that are illuminated by the sun, and those which, being are deprived of it, form shadows, and those shadows might come from profound cavities that do not receive any light. In addition to those cavities there are also seas, gulfs, lakes and rivers, which cannot transmit any light; they can, in consequence, be placed at the rank of shadows; and by a bizarrerie of nature, those different parts give the Moon, seen from our Earth, the appearance of a human face.

Seeing nothing very remarkable in the part of the realm that I visited, I climbed into my litter again and continued my journey on a less rugged road. The country was quite pleasant, but monotonous for me; I only saw things similar, or nearly so, to those of Earth. The vegetation and trees were beautiful; some were covered in flowers, others with fruits that were still green. A few birds animated the landscape somewhat; a few inhabitants were occupied in rustic labor, others were grazing flocks of small animals with some analogy to our sheep, and other, larger animals that had no resemblance to any of ours.

I therefore saw nothing that could interest me, or distract me from the ennui that I was beginning to experience, and I resolved to continue my great voyage. I asked my guide to take me back to Enul, from which I would depart to visit the planet Venus, where I hoped to find agreeable distractions

We set out, and that night I slept in my apartment in Enul. Before going to bed I received a visit from the Minister and announced my imminent departure to him. It was still daylight, whereas it was night in my homeland. I asked the Minister whether it would be possible to take my leave of the King; he replied affirmatively. And I followed him to the King, employing the same ceremony as I had on my arrival. I added my thanks for the royal welcome that he had made me, and told him that I was leaving penetrated by his generosity toward me.

When the ceremony was concluded I went back to my apartment and made my preparations. Night had fallen and, in a hurry to depart, I called out "Za, Za, Za."

My good genius did not make me wait, for a soft voice said to me: "I know what you want of me. You want to leave."

"Yes, I replied, and as soon as possible."

"This very instant," he replied. "Where do you want to go?"

"To Venus."

"That's easy, but it's rather late, and to enjoy the beauty of that planet, it would be better to wait for daylight. Rest tonight, and tomorrow morning, before sunrise, I'll deposit you near Venere, which is the capital city of that planet."

"I'll follow your advice," I said. "I abandon myself entirely to you."

I went to bed, but fully dressed, and slept so profoundly that I did not feel my good genius lift me up when, responding to my request, he carried me through the air, whose freshness woke me up.

"We'll arrive momentarily in Venere," my good genius said to me. "The Sun is about to appear and illuminate the monuments of that charming city, the most beautiful capital in all the planets. The Sun is rising and lighting it up; look and judge."

I looked, and remained ecstatic in contemplating all the beautiful things offered to my gaze. I was enchanted.

When Za thought that my admiration and curiosity were satisfied, he said: "I shall now deposit you in the pretty summer-house that you can see from here, near to which are groups of young women lightly dressed in white; some are singing, others playing various instruments and others dancing. Those charming young women are the maids of honor of Queen Vénusté,[76] thus named because of her grace, her beauty and the generosity of her mind. The Queen's maids are quite

---

[76] "*Vénusté*" means charm, in the sense of sex-appeal, in French.

curious; they won't take long to see you in the summer-house and hasten to inform the Queen, who will come to visit you. All that will happen as I predict, and soon. I won't leave you, although I shall still be invisible. Have no fear of anything; whatever happens, I shall always be nearby to protect you, and to defend you if necessary."

In fact, I soon heard soft music full of harmony, which filled my heart with a keen emotion. I ran to the window of the summer-house and saw a numerous cortege approaching, preceded by richly-dressed individuals. They were followed by young women whose physiognomy respired pleasure and sensuality. They surrounded a palanquin in which a woman of great beauty was seated. She had a young child next to her, who was entirely naked; he was crowned with various flowers, which were in perfect harmony with the curls of his blond hair. He had wings attached to his shoulders and was carrying a quiver full of arrows; he was holding a bow in his left hand. He was the son of Queen Vénusté.

The cortege stopped at the door of the summer-house where I was stationed. One of the important individuals then approached, and I ran out to meet him. He came in and sat on the sofa. He told me that he had come on the Queen's order to ask who I was and for what reason I had come to her estates. I answered all his questions and he left to make his report to the Queen, who descended from her palanquin shortly thereafter, at the door of my summer-house.

I went to meet her and received her with all the marks of respect due to her rank. She took her place on the sofa and did me the honor of asking me to sit next to her. I was delighted by admiration next to that Queen, so beautiful, so benevolent and so full of graces. She perceived my delight, and capped it by inviting me to go and live in her palace—and offer that I accepted gladly, for I would have at my disposal all the means of visiting the planet and discovering the customs and mores of its inhabitants.

However, a thought crossed my mind and darkened that brilliant dream of happiness slightly. Honored as I would be by the generosity of the Queen, would I not become an object of jealousy and envy for the important people she had with her? Would I not be the target of hatred, calumny and the dangers that might result therefrom?

Those thoughts were darkening my mind when a soft voice said to me: "Don't worry; have no fear of hatred. As for calumny, a good man ought not to dread it; the testimony of his conscience ought to suffice for him. Don't torment yourself; Zadir has put you under my protection, and I shall fulfill my mission."

I therefore departed with Za, who transported me, without my being able to say how, to the door of the Palace, into which I entered. A man suddenly appeared, who excited my curiosity, and several people approached me. Among those people I recognized the man who had come to the summerhouse. I asked him to present me to the Queen, which he did with pleasure.

I approached Vénusté with all the external signs of a profound respect. She greeted me graciously, without any other ceremony. We were alone, and she said to me with her characteristic bounty:

"I was waiting for you, and I have prepared an apartment for you in my palace, where you will find everything necessary, and everything that might be agreeable to you, I hope. You meals will be served in your apartment until further notice. My apartment communicates with yours by means of a secret passage and I shall come to see you in order to learn from you many things that I do not know, but which you ought to, for you must have as much science as courage to have succeeded in penetrating into this land, where no stranger has ever appeared before."

I thanked her for the confidence that she was testifying and told her that I would be glad to be able to give her proofs of my gratitude and devotion. She held out her white hand to me, which I pressed lightly in mine, and I was bold enough to raise it to my lips. She was not offended, and from then on, a sentiment of amity reigned between us.

When I saw the Queen, she said to me: "I have thought that, in order to put an end to the conspiracy that is being woven, you would do well to visit my realm, which you desire to know. An officer will accompany you and provide everything that you might need during your journey. When you return, all the fuss will have died down, and you can remain tranquil next to me."

I accepted the proposal the Queen had made and left.

III

The country was beautiful. The trees were laden with fruit, for it is hot on that planet, and everything feels that influence. I admired the beauty of meadows enameled with flowers, tall trees in the shade of which handsome young men were lying beside pretty young women, who were laughing as they listened to their affectionate words. I judged that they were affectionate because the couples seemed very animated, and their faces bore the imprint of joy.

All is amour and sensuality on that planet. At the commencement of the journey everything appeared to me to be very reminiscent of Tuscany; afterwards I saw locations that bore a strong resemblance to those one sees between Rome and Naples As much by virtue of the landscape as the heat, there is a good deal of analogy between the planet Venus and the southern part of Italy and Sicily.

Further away, the scene changed, but it lost none of its beauty. Mountains presented a magnificent aspect of waterfalls, cascades and torrents, which reminded me of those of Terni and Tivoli. Those waters alimented a beautiful lake in which pretty young women were bathing: beautiful women with contours as pure as statues by Phidias and Praxiteles. Some were shining whitely in the sunlight by virtue of the beauty of their skin; others were sheltering from the Sun, protected by large rocks and the huge braches of trees that grew among their fissures. They enjoyed an agreeable freshness there. They frolicked in the water like swans; their laughter and great hilarity testified to their happiness.

Further on, I saw beautiful hills covered with trees and bushes, among which I glimpsed a few pretty fabrications formed like little temples. I assumed that they were dedicated to some local deity.

From a bend on one of the hillside I perceived a certain number of buildings, including a few large edifices. I judged that it was a town, and asked my guide. He told me that it was Cyprine, the second city of the realm, and more beautiful than the capital. I wanted to see it and my guide took my carriage into it, which attracted a great deal of curiosity. When they perceived me, that intensified greatly. The news promptly spread through the entire town, and a large crowd surrounded my litter.

They found out from my guide who I was, and the distinction with which the Queen honored me; that was enough for me to obtain the highest regard, so it was not long before I saw the governor of the town arrive; he invited me to dinner and offered me an apartment in the palace where he lived. I thanked him for his courtesy, and accepted.

While waiting for dinner time, I continued my visit to the town and the port, which was known as Porto Venere. I was singularly surprised by that name, which is that of a small Italian town on the shore of the Gulf of Spezia, between Genoa and Livorno. How had that name reached the planet Venus? I don't know. My genius Za might have known, but I did not want to disturb him merely to satisfy my curiosity.

A short distance from the port I noticed a little island, the sight of which charmed me, and I experienced a desire to visit it. I said so to my guide and he summoned a kind of launch. In very little time we arrived at the island of Cythera—not the ancient isle of Cythera, nowadays known as Cerigo. The interior of the little island was charming; myrtles that were still green, and rose-bushes covered with roses surrounded a little temple of elegant form, which I assumed to have been constructed and educated to the goddess whose name the planet bore.

I was confounded by astonishment. How had all those names reached that planet? How had they been able to construct a little temple in conformity with Greek architecture? I could not get over my surprise—or, rather, my amazement. I had therefore delivered myself profoundly to my reflections when my guide came to inform me that it was time to return to the town in order to respond to the governor's invitation.

We left, and as soon as we arrived in Cyprine he took me to the governor's palace, where he received me with distinction. He led me into the dining room, where I found everything prepared for dinner. Around the room there was a sort of vast sofa on which several women of distinction were sitting, all of ravishing beauty. The one who occupied the principal place was the governor's wife. He introduced me to her.

I saluted by bowing deeply and placing my hands on my head. She replied to my salutation by placing two fingers of her right hand on her forehead and extending her left hand, which was very beautiful, toward me. I took it and bore it to my forehead, in accordance with the instructions I had received from my guide.

When the presentation was complete, a whistle-blast was heard, and all the ladies took their places at the table, each placed in accordance with her rank. The seats were three-legged stools; those which had a back were occupied by women of superior rank.

Dinner was served; it comprised several kinds of meat, principally that of large birds similar to pigeons, which are very numerous in that country, and a few fish, which includes a cyprian fish whose flesh is highly esteemed in the realm, which is very similar to our carp. Afterwards came vegetables, some cooked and others raw, which were seasoned with a kind of cream or piquant juice; that was the salad. It was cleared away, and a kind of dais that seemed to be part of the ceiling descended on to the table, and by that means brought a well-

189

ordered dessert composed of various fruits, compotes and preserves.

During the dinner there were no other beverages than water, but during dessert jars were brought full of a spirituous but sweet liqueur, which I drank with pleasure. The cup that I had before me was filled with it. Because glass is unknown in that country, all liquids are drunk from vessels of fine clay, a sort of kaolin, which, when baked, takes on a transparency equal to our porcelain.

After dinner we went into the garden to an arbor covered in verdure, through which the sun's rays could not penetrate; one enjoyed a mild coolness there, and breathed the air pleasurably, gently agitated by light breeze. A lady sang; her voice was soft and harmonious. Another lady accompanied her on an instrument similar to a mandolin , and another on a kind of harp, which she plucked with fingers as slender and delicate as those of the Medici Venus.

The agreeable evening was terminated by a few refreshments, brought to us by pretty young women with the gracious and delicate figures with which almost all the women of the planet Venus are endowed; then everyone retired.

When I woke up the next day, I thought that it was time to return to the capital and to Queen Vénusté. I hoped that the absence would have calmed jealous minds. A vain hope. I arrived in the presence of Queen Vénusté, and I read in her eyes that she was glad to see me; when we were alone she told me that the greatest tranquility had reigned since my departure and that she had taken the measures necessary to maintain order, but among the important people of the realm I noticed many somber faces. I pretended not to notice them and made polite advances, to which they responded coldly.

In sum, I read on many faces that they were not pleased to see me again. I had been convinced of that in advance and was not disconcerted. I had no fear of those people but I feared their secret plots, either to have me murdered or to irritate the people and excite them against me. I recalled what my good genius had said on that subject and was no longer anxious, but I expected to see some conspiracy burst forth.

Three days later a crowd of the people presented themselves in large square of the palace, loudly demanding the expulsion of the foreigner, and the leaders of the insurrection demanded to speak to the queen, who permitted the three principal chiefs to be admitted.

The Queen received them in the throne room, sitting on the throne. She was full of grace and majesty. Her throne was surrounded by guards, some of whom were guarding the entrance to the room in order to subdue the noise and ensure that there was no disorder. The three principal leaders of the insurrection were brought in, and the Queen, standing up, asked them what they wanted.

The men, however, dazzled by the Queen's majesty, the splendor of the throne and everything surrounding them, were nonplused, and were only able to stammer that they had come to beg their gracious sovereign to send the foreigner away.

"Those who sent you," the Queen said to them, "do not know this stranger. I know him, and I am informed as to the motives that brought him to my realm. What I can tell you, in order to testify to the confidence that I have in you, is that he only came here to ensure your wellbeing. Go tell those you have brought to lack the respect and confidence that you owe your Queen that I shall not send the foreigner away, and that I know how to make myself respected. You are the dupes of schemers who have abused your good faith. Go inform them of my reply. I know those who have prompted you to take this offensive step. Go; I forgive you and think only of making you happy."

The three leaders withdrew after having sworn devotion and respect to the Queen.

Shortly after their departure, cries of joy were heard in the palace square, provoked by the report of the three envoys, who told the people about the fine and noble reception that the Queen had given them. But the nobles were not content and were already weaving a new plot.

They decided to accuse the foreigner of seeking to take possession of the throne and become their king; to that effect they hired a number of commoners to affirm, as witnesses in the lawsuit they intended to bring, that the foreigner had promised them large rewards if they would associate themselves with his project, which was to overthrow the Queen's government, and recognize him as their King. The men who had woven the plot denounced me to the Chief Justice, and I was summoned to appear in three days at the Supreme Court. All the hired witnesses were obliged to appear before the judges at the same time as me.

When the Queen learned that I was to be brought before the judges of the criminal court she came to me and said: "Is the news that I have just heard really true, my friend? You have been accused of being the author of a plot against me? Can that be possible? I can't believe it."

"You're right, my friend; I'm incapable of it, and you have judged me correctly—but let them do it. I'm tranquil on the subject that obliges me to appear before the judges. Be present at my trial on the appointed day, and you will see my calumniators confounded."

IV

The day of my judgment arrived. There was a great stir in the town; people were coming and going in all directions and there was a confused murmur of voices. The sun's rays only illuminated the day lugubriously; large clouds announced an impending storm; everything was somber and sad.

The Queen had come to my apartment at an early hour; anxiety had kept her awake all night. "Well, my friend," she said, when she came in, weeping. "It is today that you will be tried and perhaps convicted unjustly; I will not permit that. My guards will be at the tribunal, ready to act at my first signal."

"Thank you, my Queen, my good friend, but, as I've already told you, let them do it. I shall be convicted, without a doubt, but promise me that you will remain a tranquil spectator of everything that happens, for it is then that you will know me better and will be assured of my perfect innocence."

"I promise," she said. "I see you so full of confidence that my fears die down and you reanimate my courage."

"I shall be convicted, as you say, but don't worry, I implore you."

"You will be content with me, my friend."

"And come to see me this evening, my noble friend, so that I can thank you."

"I will come," she said.

The palace square was covered by the people, curious to see me pass on my way to the tribunal. I went there alone; I had not wanted an escort. The crowd opened a passage for me, and I went through the middle of it without having heard the slightest murmur. For her part, the Queen went there carried on a palanquin by her servants; she was followed by her maids of honor and escorted by guards.

I went into the tribunal hall; an usher indicated the seat that was reserved for me on a platform facing the judges. The Queen was on a platform surmounted by an awning. On the opposite side were the dignitaries of the State and the commoners called as witnesses. Some of the Queen's guards were placed beneath the sovereign's platform, while others were posted at various points in the hall and others at the entrance door—for the room was vast. The air circulated freely, for glazed windows are unknown in the realm; people are only protected from the insults of the weather and the sun's rays by means of large curtains opened and closed at will; on cloudy days all of them are open.

The greatest silence reigned in the hall. At a sign given by the Great Judge the usher told me to stand up, and the interrogation commenced.

"Who are you?"

"I'm a foreigner."

"Where do you come from?"

"The Earth."

"What is your name?"

"Pcer."

"Why did you come here?"

"To educate myself."

"You have no other designs?"

"No."

"You are accused of wanting to take possession of the throne."

"It is a false accusation."

"However, there are witnesses that you have tried to suborn."

"They are false witnesses."

"How can you prove that?"

"By confounding them."

"How will you confound them?"

"By putting them in my presence and making them identify the true suborners, for I know who they are."

Then there was a murmur among the noblemen of the realm; several of them approached the Great Judge and spoke to him in a low voice. The Great Judge said to me: "Accused, your defense is inadmissible, and in any case, we are enlightened by witnesses worthy of faith. We shall return to the deliberation room, and I shall return to inform you of the result."

The judges retired, and reappeared a short time afterwards. The Great Judge read the result of their deliberation and said to me: "Accused, you are convicted and judged guilty of the crime of lèse-majesté, and as such, condemned to the penalty of death by the torture of scatole."[77]

A stifled exclamation departed from the Queen's platform. I was standing up; I looked at her, and my calmness reassured her.

---

[77] The word *scatole* usually signifies a product of putrefaction that has the odor of feces. Its employment here is a trifle enigmatic, as is the protagonist naming himself as Pcer. It is possible that both are the result of typesetting errors, but if so, it is not obvious what the intended formulations might have been.

"Jailer," said the Judge, "take possession of the guilty party, take him to the tower and guard him there until the time of his execution."

The jailer approached and made as if to take possession of me, but at that moment, the collision of the electrified clouds produced a flash of lightning. Thunder crashed, and already the jailer had fallen at my feet, struck dead.

Great was the astonishment and consternation that reigned in the hall; terror was painted on the faces of a few highly-placed individuals. The thunder was still rumbling. The crowd was prostrated, fearful of great misfortunes. The Queen was calm.

The Great Judge, at the instigation of my enemies, had a turnkey summoned from the tower, and ordered him to take possession of me, to take me away and guard me until further notice. The turnkey approached me, but, at the moment when he was about to take hold of me, I disappeared from all eyes. My good genius Za had rendered me invisible like him and had transported me to the apartment I occupied at the palace, where I thanked him sincerely for the further service that he had just rendered me.

"It will always be the same, every time you are in danger," he told me, in his soft voice. "You were accused unjustly, and I must protect your innocence; I would not have done it if you had been guilty. Such are the orders I have received from Zadir. If you do not deviate from the conduct you have maintained thus far, your good genius will not cease to protect you—but if you were weak enough to cede to the insinuation of the few evil genii who are our enemies, Zadir would abandon you and forbid me to be useful to you. I cannot give you advice—that is forbidden to me—but the one thing I am permitted to advise you to do is always take your honor as the guide of your conduct."

I assured him that my conduct would always be exempt from evil actions.

"If that is so," he said, "and I believe you to be sincere, you can always count on my protection, wherever you are; you

195

know the three words that you must pronounce to summon me to your aid. Pronounce them in case of need and I shall be with you immediately. Now, when do you want to continue your voyage, and what planet do you have the intention of visiting?"

"Mercury," I told him.

"It isn't far from here," he said, "and you can be there in a few moments. Inform me when you are ready."

I thanked him and he vanished. Left alone, I ate some food that was on my table, and then lay down on the sofa to reflect on the events of that terrible day, which had terminated so well for me.

Suddenly, the Queen appeared in my apartment, and said to me: "You can be tranquil now."

"It's necessary to hope so, at least," I replied.

"What!" she said to me. "Don't you believe that the sedition is appeased?"

"I think it has relented," I replied, "but in suspense, for the same ferments exist. It will not take much to excite the people again, and believe that they are working on that at this moment. It's me that they want and it's on me that the hatred and jealous of the nobles will pour. For myself, I have no fear—you've had the proof of that—but I fear the annoyances and torments that my presence here will cause you. It's necessary, for your tranquility, that I go away for a time."

Scarcely had I finished speaking that we heard a roar similar to that of waves violently agitated by a tempest and breaking into surf against reefs.

"What's that noise?" she asked me.

"It's the voice of the people," I replied.

Immediately, a horrible cracking sound was heard.

"What's that?" she asked.

"It's the doors of your palace being broken down. Go back to your apartment; they won't abuse you and no harm will come to you; it's only me they want. You can see that I'm an obstacle to your tranquility."

And as the mob had invaded the palace, and was approaching my apartment, I urged the Queen to return to her own. Scarcely had she gone than I summoned Za. He appeared immediately. I asked him to render me invisible to the crowd that was about to irrupt into my apartment and, once it had gone and I had made sure that the Queen was safe, that we should depart for the planet Mercury.

"Very well," he said.

The crowd precipitated into my apartment, and remained mute with astonishment at not seeing me there. A powerful voice made these words heard: "The one you seek is not here; he has gone. Go away, or fear the effects of my wrath."

Consternated by that superhuman voice, the crowd withdrew in silence. Then I asked my genius to let me go to the Queen's apartment to make sure that she was tranquil and in no anger.

"Very well," he said. "Go; I'll wait."

I went to the Queen's apartment, still invisible to all eyes. Everything was calm. I went in without being seen; I found her sad and pensive, and said to her: "Have courage and hope; adieu, my noble friend."

That adieu pierced my heart, but I had a sacred duty to fulfill: a duty and sacrifice that honor ordered me to fulfill.

V

I returned to my good genius Za, and we departed immediately for Mercury, where we arrived in a few moments. The heat is excessive on that planet, where it is seven times stronger than in our hottest summers, to the extent that it liquefies metals. The inhabitants are extremely lively and frolicsome; one might think that they were afflicted by calenture, a species of delirium to which Europeans are subject in the tropics.

It was on that planet that Za set me down, and as soon as the inhabitants perceived me they ran to look at me, some on their hands instead of making use of their feet, others turning cartwheels and other uttering fearful cries.

I thought that they were all afflicted by madness, and said so to my good genius, who had not quit me.

"You've judged them accurately," he told me, "And I doubt that you'll like it here—or that you'll obtain any pleasure from visiting the planet, which is covered with saltpeter, and where the excessive heat might make you uncomfortable. I think it might be better for you to leave."

"You've divined my desire and anticipated the request that I was about to make for you to transport me to another, more habitable, planet."

"I'm entirely ready to do so," he replied. "Where would you like to go?"

"First, to Iris," because I believe it's not far from here."

"That's true," he said. "You'll be there in five minutes."

Indeed. Five minutes later he deposited me on the planet Iris, beside an elegant summer-house in the garden of the Queen of that planet.

The Queen's maids of honor perceived me and hastened to inform her that there was a stranger in the garden near the summer-house, and that they could not understand how the man in question had been introduced.

The Queen sent one of the ladies of the palace with her maids of honor to find out who I was. They soon arrived in my presence, and after having examined me for a few minutes the lady of the palace told me that the Queen had sent her to find out who I was, where I came from and why I had come to her realm.

I answered all her questions, and she seemed to be satisfied with my replies.

"I shall go report the extraordinary things you've told me to our Queen," she said, "and she will doubtless want to see you."

"I am at Her Majesty's disposal," I told her.

She returned to the palace, and a short time later, I saw a person arriving whose clothes were gaudily adorned. He came toward me placing the back of his hand on his forehead, told me that the Queen desired to see me and invited me to follow

198

him. During the journey I asked him what ceremony I ought to observe.

"On entering the throne room, you bow, crossing our arms over your chest; then you advance toward her, put one knee on the ground and say to her: 'Great Queen, dispose of your servant,' And when she says to you: '*Ben venuto*,' you get up and bow profoundly.

"That ceremony concluded, she will doubtless invite you to dine at her table, and then you will become a commensal or guest of the palace, for the queen likes to learn, and as you appear to me to be very knowledgeable about things that are unknown here, it's probable that she will want to you to be close to her, in order to profit from your instruction."

At that moment, another officer came to inform me that the Queen was waiting for me, and that he had been instructed to take me to her. I got up and followed him. On entering the room, I saw Queen Irisa on her throne. She was clad in a long white dress of a very light fabric, striped in various places with the colors of the rainbow.

I approached her, observing the ceremonial custom of which I had been informed. She observed me with great curiosity. She was young and very beautiful, but unlike Vénusté, who had blue eyes and blonde hair, Queen Irisa had brown eyes and chestnut-colored hair. Her face was both noble and piquant; she respired bounty.

"According to what I've been told, it appears that you come from a long way away and have come here to learn—but I'm also told that you appear to be very learned."

"I am, in fact, educated, but Your Majesty knows that there are no limits to science; the more one possess, the more one can acquire."

"I like to hear you talk thus," she told me. "I think exactly the same. But what learning do you think you can acquire in this land, where it is non-existent?"

"Forgive me, Madame; I wanted to acquire the knowledge of your planet and judge the reality of something that I had only seen at a distance of thirty-three million leagues, with the aid of our binoculars and telescopes."

"You are talking about things that are entirely strange to me, which excite my curiosity to the highest degree, and the desire to satisfy it. Would you like to instruct me regarding the marvelous things you have just mentioned?"

"I will do that with great pleasure, Madame, and to facilitate that instruction, I will draw you a plan of the planetary system, which will help you to understand easily what the heavenly bodies are, the place that they occupy in the firmament, and how they circulate there."

"You throw me into an astonishment that I've never felt before. And you have the ability to teach me all these beautiful things, which seem so marvelous?"

"Yes, Madame."

"And when will you commence my instruction?"

"Whenever it pleases Your Majesty."

"Tomorrow," she said, swiftly. "The apartment will be prepared that I invite you to occupy in my palace, in which you will be perfectly free. Your meals will be served at the times you indicated, and all the things necessary to you. One of the rooms in your apartment will be your study; it is far away from noise and perfectly suitable for study and meditation. You will find everything there that might be useful to you in your scientific studies. It is in your study that I shall receive your precious lessons. That study communicates with my apartment, which is above yours, by a secret stairway constructed between two walls, and it's by means of that stairway that I shall come to your rooms to collect the knowledge that I lack and that I have a great desire to possess."

That secret stairway reminded me of Vénusté's passage, and I sighed profoundly.

Queen Irisa did indeed, come down to me apartment the following day, to examine the various rooms, especially the one intended as my study.

"How do you like this room?" she asked. "Do you think it will be suitable? What objects do you need for your work?"

"What is indispensable," I replied, "is paper, ink and a pen."

"But I don't know what paper and ink are. Tell me."

"Paper is a composition made of old linen, which is allowed to soak in water for a long time and reduced to paste; one then lays that paste very thinly over frames in the shape of the paper, and when it has dried out one peels it away, and the sheet of paper is made. If the paper is to be used for ink drawing or painting with water colors, it is soaked in gummed water in order to prevent it from being absorbent, and then laid out to dry. You have here a tree-bark that is analogous to the papyrus whose internal bark once served as paper, but that papyrus was only used by the ancient Egyptians to write in hieroglyphs on subjects of religion, the scientists and the arts."

"But I've never heard mention of any of what you've just told me. Will you be kind enough to teach me about all these things, for the more I hear the more my desire to learn increases?"

"I have the honor of telling you, Madame, that I will do so with great pleasure, for I am entirely devoted to your orders."

"My orders?" she said. "But you have none to receive from me, for I consider you as a friend."

With those words she extended her hand to me, which I pressed in mine.

"Where shall we commence with my instruction?" she asked.

"With the planetary system," I replied. "But I shall precede that with the knowledge of God, who is the author of nature—which is to say, of all created things. God alone is uncreated. God exists by virtue of himself. God is a pure spirit, a divine essence that extends in everything and penetrates everywhere. That is why God is the immensity—which is to say that he is present everywhere, that he sees everything and can do anything. God is eternal wisdom. God is all of eternity. God is prescience. God alone is infinite—which is to say that his power is limitless."

VI

Irisa stared at me with an indescribable astonishment.

"Oh, my friend," she said. "What emotions, what hitherto unknown sentiments your instruction causes me to experience! Continue, I beg you."

"When God created the world, chaos existed—which is to say that everything was in confusion. At his omnipotent voice, light succeeded darkness; chaos disappeared. In six days God, created the universe—which is to say, the entire world, al the celestial bodies, the Earth and its inhabitants. Now I will give you an idea of the position of the celestial bodies, comprising the sun and all the planets that God has placed in the firmament, in the zodiac, which is divided into two equal parts by a line known as the ecliptic, which the sun seems to travel.

"Now, Madame, with this planetary system, which I have drawn as best I can, you will understand with greater facility all that I have told you about the celestial bodies, and these planets, which are all the works of God."

"So, my friend, the sun is not a God?"

"No, Madame, it is only a creature of God, which has been formed in order to fecundate the Earth by the heat of its rays and to ripen the fruits that produce the vegetables that serve as our nourishment and that of animals. But let us leave that subject and go back, if you are agreeable, to our conversation about the things you desire to know."

"You could not give me a greater pleasure, my friend, for since you have talked to me about God and creation my mind has been working hard, and it seems to me that the subject is not exhausted, and that you have many interesting things to teach me."

"You have thought correctly, my friend, because we have to talk about the celestial spirits."

"What do you mean by celestial spirits? Are they other gods?"

"No, Madame, for there is only one God. The other celestial spirits are spiritual creatures, created by God to announce and carry out his orders; they inhabit heaven and surround the throne of God, all resplendent with glory, from which he dictates his laws to the entire universe.

"But what is heaven, my friend, and what are the names of these celestial spirits?"

"Heaven is the empyrean: that is the highest sky, in which God has placed paradise. Under the empyrean is the firmament, which appears to us to be a beautiful azure blue; that color is apparently produced by the ether, a very subtle fluid that is assumed to fill the space above the atmosphere, and which is not breathable. The ether is the firmament; it is what is known poetically as the azure vault; it is there that the stars circulate sand accomplish their rotation or revolution. The celestial spirits are called Angels. God created them entirely out of divine substance; each one is an entirely spiritual creation, a spirit with which the immortal soul that God has given them is united, whereas the immortal soul that God has given to humans is united with a material body—that is the only difference. The number of angels is several million."

"Thank you, my friend. But tell me what Paradise is, and what an immortal soul is. I've never heard mention of either of those things."

"Paradise is in heaven; it is the city of the blessed, where they enjoy an eternal felicity, if they have merited it. God formed humans out of clay. When humans had been formed from that material substance, God gave them an immortal soul, which is the divine breath; it is principally by means of the soul that God gave us that humans are created in the image of their Creator. It is thus that God, the Supreme Being, has rendered humans masters of the animals, and made them monarchs of the Earth. Our soul is spiritual, since it emanates from God; it is of the same nature as that of the angels, who are created like us, except that their soul is united, as I said, with a spiritual nature, while in humans the soul is united with a material nature. An angel is the noblest of creatures. Our soul

203

possesses admirable faculties, at the head of which it is necessary to place thought, which is an operation of the intelligent substance and free will, which is the operation, or rather the faculty, that the soul possesses in making a decision.

"A human being contains one thing that is certainly not material, and that is a spirit, the soul, the image of God, as the matter that forms humans is the image of earth. Animals have a soul that is nothing but intellect, and at death it returns to oblivion, while ours, much more perfect, has a higher, eternal destiny. Humans are intermediate between animal and intellectual nature."

The Queen seemed to be plunged in a profound reverie. She came round and said: "Everything that you have just told me has thrown my mind into a strange agitation. I need to meditate in order to conceive and analyze the elevated things that you have told me—too elevated for me, who had no idea of them. I hope that you will help me to draw my mind out of the obscurity in which it is still enveloped."

"I am entirely at your discretion, my good friend. Tell me what the matters are that you would like clarified, and I will write you notes that will help you to interpret what you have found obscure in all that I have just told you."

"That is an excellent idea, my friend, for I can study your notes in my hours of solitude and we can continue in your study my instruction on the celestial bodies, in accordance with the planetary system that you have drawn for me."

VII

The next day, the Queen came to my study and I began my lessons in astronomy.

"Astronomy is the knowledge of the celestial bodies and the sky. Physical astronomy explains its phenomena.

"Uranography is the description of the sky.

"Uranometry is the art of measuring the heavenly bodies.

"The Sun, the torch of the world, occupies the center of the universe, where it is motionless. Mercury rotates around the Sun, in such a way that the Sun is at the center of the circle described by Mercury. Above Mercury is Venus, which similarly rotates around the Sun. The Moon is sometimes close to the sun and sometimes further away, and it is the same with the other planets, which all rotate around the Sun. Only the Moon rotates around the Earth and illuminates it by night. After Venus come the Moon and the Earth, which, being higher than Mercury and Venus, describe a larger circle than those plants. Finally, Mars, Jupiter and Saturn, describe even greater circles around the sun than all the others. That is why the other planets take longer to complete their revolution.

"The Sun is luminous by itself, by reason of the substance that composes it, and whose continual incandescence is the cause of the luminosity. English astronomers claim that the center of the Sun, which they call "the stone" and we call the nucleus, does not produce the heat. That opinion already existed among French astronomers, who have compared the heat of the nucleus with the most brilliant part of the solar disk, which they call the photosphere, and from which the sun's rays depart. In addition to the five hundred planets discovered by Herschel in 1802,[78] other planets exist around the sun: Iris and Flora, discovered in 1847; Metis in 1848. Hygiea in 1849, Parthenope and Victoria in 1850, Irene and Eunomia in 1851.[79]

---

[78] 1802 was the year when William Herschel suggested the name "asteroid" for the minor planets, following his observations of Ceres and Pallas, but the figure of five hundred must refer to the additional items he added in that year to his catalogue of "nebulae" and other stellar objects, far outside the solar system.

[79] The minor planets Iris and Flora—the seventh and eighth to be named—were discovered by J. R. Hind in 1847; Hind also discovered Victoria in 1850 and Irene in 1851. Metis was discovered by Andrew Graham in 1848, Hygieia, Parthenope and Eunomia by Annibale de Gasparis in 1849, 1850 and 1851 respectively. All the bodies in question orbit between Mars

"The Sun takes more than twenty-five days to rotate on its axis; the Earth takes twenty-four hours. The days of Mercury are twenty-four hours three minutes, the days of Venus twenty-three hours twenty-one minutes. On Mercury the heat is seven times more intense than in our hottest summers; it is so strong there that it even liquefies metals. On Saturn, by contrast, it is twenty-four times colder than in our most rigorous winters; everything there is frozen. Saturn is a very long way from the Sun, which seems very small there, only appearing as a small pale star of very feeble heat. The cold there is excessive, as I said, which renders the inhabitants unsociable by their phlegmatic humor and the absence of all gaiety. The distance of Saturn from the Sun is three hundred million leagues.

"The Sun is one million four hundred thousand nine hundred and twenty times larger than the Earth, from which it is thirty-eight million leagues distant—some say thirty-three, other thirty-five; once it was thirty-six million. On Mercury, the character is opposite to that of Saturn.

"The stars are, in general, celestial bodies that shine by night. The stars are fixed in relation to the Sun; wandering stars are planets; falling stars are luminous meteors.

"A constellation is an assemblage of neighboring stars designated by a single name; one says, for example, the constellation of Canis Major, Taurus or Virgo.

"Sirius is a star in the constellation Canis Major, the brightest in the firmament.

"The distance of the stars from the Earth is about two hundred and six thousand times the distance that separates the Sun from the Earth, about thirty billon leagues.

"Light travels seventy-seven thousand leagues per second. With the most powerful telescope one can discover more than forty million fixed stars of fourteen different magni-

---

and Jupiter, and none goes anywhere near Mercury, as is alleged when this list is repeated a little further on.

tudes. Three thousand stars are visible to the naked eye in a single hemisphere.

"The light of the star nearest to the Earth, which arrives in the evening, departed three years ago from the start that sent it. The light of the most distant stars needs three or four thousand years to reach us, traveling, as I said at seventy-seven leagues a second, and beyond those stars one assumes that there are others more distant, which could only be seen with more powerful instruments than the ones we possess.

"A comet is a kind of planet that rotates around the Sun in a greatly elongated circle. As they get closer to the sun their tail extends further, and when they draw away, their tails gradually shorten, and end up disappearing. The tail of a comet is its atmosphere, which becomes luminous and visible in separating from the opaque body of the planet. Heat is produced by the interaction of solar rays with the atmosphere.

"The center of the Earth is the center of gravity of the objects on its surface. But as the Earth rotates around the Sun with all that it contains, it follows that the Earth's center of gravity or point of support is in the Sun.

"Vortices are masses of matter whose parts, separate from one another, all move in the same direction. A whirlwind is an infinity of particles of air which spin around together and envelop those that they encounter.

"The planets are borne in the celestial matter, which is prodigiously subtle and agitated; that entire great mass of celestial matter, which extends from the Sun to the fixed stars, spins around, carrying the planets with it, causing them to rotate in the same direction around the Sun, which occupies the center. Our great vortex is composed of sixteen planets, of which we can only see seven. Uranus and Neptune are in the same category as Saturn with regard to cold; everything there is frozen.

"The Chariot is composed of the Sun, the Moon, and five planets, Mercury, Venus, Mars, Jupiter and Saturn. The planet Jupiter is situated between Mars and Saturn. Jupiter is a thousand times larger than the Earth; that planet is a hundred and sixty-five million leagues distant from the Sun; it is illuminated by four moons, little inhabited planets; seen from the closest of those little planets, Jupiter is six hundred times larger than our Moon appears to be to us. Saturn has five moons.

"The air that surrounds the Earth only extends to a certain height, about twenty leagues. That air follows the Earth and rotates with it, both in its rotation and its revolution.

"The Earth is sixty times larger than the Moon, which has neither dawn nor dusk, nor does it have rainbows.

"In addition to five hundred planets discovered by Herschel in 1802, Iris and Flora were discovered in 1847, Metis in 1848, Hygiea in 1849, Parthenope and Victoria in 1850 and Eunomia in 1851. These latter planets are all situated around the circle described by Mercury.

"Thus you see, Madame, that the planet Iris, of which you are the Queen, has been known to us for twelve years."[80]

"I can see that, my friend; but I would like to know by what means it was discovered at such a great distance from your Earth."

"As I have told you, it was with the aid of our telescopes."

"But I do not know what they are; will you explain them to me?"

"A telescope or long-view, is a tube fitted at each of its two extremities with a glass lens, which magnifies distant objects. There are also large reflecting telescopes, which enlarge objects and make them seem closer. An astrolabe is an instrument for calculating the height of stars. A heliometer is an instrument for measuring the diameter of the Sun and of planets. A helioscope in an instrument for looking at the Sun."

"But tell me, I beg you, what glass is, for I have no idea."

"Glass is a fragile transparent substance that is obtained by the fusion of a mixture of sand and an alkali salt, caustic soda, extracted from the ashes of ferns, a kind of plant that grows in the woods."

---

[80] Thus indicating a date of composition of 1859.

"I understand that, but I don't understand how it magnifies objects."

"To magnify or make objects seem smaller on makes use of concave lenses—which is to say, hollowed out roundly, and it is by that means that the lenses placed in telescopes obtain the approach or distancing of objects.

"In order to measure the diameter of stars, astronomers employ a reticule, which consists of wire placed in the focal plane of the telescope in the form of a network or lattice, and it is by the distance between the wires that one can judge by calculation the distance of objects."

"In truth, my friend, you augment from day to day not only my astonishment but also my admiration, by means of all the marvels that you relate to me. But tell me: this glass to which you attribute so many marvels; is it only used by astronomers for their telescopes?"

"It serves several other purposes. When the glass is molten, and can be blown, one makes it into vessels from which liquids are drunk, carafes and bottles to contain liquids, panes to garnish frames that are fitted into windows to provide protection from bad weather. Mirrors are made from it—looking glasses that reproduce the resemblance of objects presented to them, which appear behind the mirror. The ancients did not know glass, they used oiled paper, or obsidian stone—a translucent stone—to replace widow-panes. Oiled paper is translucent, but one cannot see through it."

"But my friend, that discovery would be of great utility here. If the plant you mentioned exists on this planet we might, perhaps, with the precious information that you can give, succeed in making glass. If you are agreeable, we can go to explore my realm together and visit its woods, to try to discover fern there and other plants whose ashes we might use to make glass."

"I consent to that willingly, my noble friend; you know that I'm entirely devoted to you. But do you have in our capital, or elsewhere, a man who has some knowledge of Phytology?"

"I don't know that science."

"It's that of knowing and describing plants."

"I don't know, my friend, but I will have enquiries made, and if I discover a capable man, he will be brought here, and if he can give us satisfactory information, that will spare us a good deal of perhaps futile research."

VIII

The next day, a man was brought who was said to know plants. The Queen summoned me, and I questioned the man in her presence. It was difficult for me to refer to ferns in his language, because I did not know the word; I therefore made the decision to draw one, and he told the Queen that he had seen them in a wood near the village of Baleno.

Furnished with that information we hoped that our journey would not be fruitless, and the Queen decided that we would leave when the heat was less intense, for we were close to Mercury and we know how hot that planet is.

In the meantime, I continued giving the Queen lessons, and sometimes went to walk in her gardens, which were vast and well planted with flowers; that was a great attraction for me, because I had the intention of drawing a flower.

One day, when I was very occupied in examining the flowers, I heard the cries of several women, shouting: "Elpo, Elpo!"—which is a cry of distress, appealing for help. The cries were coming from a nearby grove of trees. I ran in that direction—or, rather, flew, because the cries were getting louder—and launched myself into the little wood, and in a few seconds I reached the edge of a pool where I saw the Queen's ladies, frightened and sobbing, only able to express the subject of their desperation to me by signs.

Finally, I understood that the Queen had disappeared in the middle of the pond. Throwing myself into the water and diving was the affair of an eye-blink, and I reappeared almost immediately on the surface, holding the Queen in my left arm while using the right and my feet to swim.

Cries of joy were uttered by the maids of honor, and when found my forting I hasted as much as possible to reach the bank, carrying my precious burden.

I laid the Queen down on the grass. She had lost consciousness, but her heard was beating quite regularly, and the cares that I lavished on her brought her round. She opened her eyes, and a sweet smile was my recompense.

I advised the ladies-in-waiting to change the Queen's garments quickly, and when everything was ready for the change I left the grove, but I stayed nearby in case I was needed. I informed the maids of honor of that, and allowed my clothes to dry on my body. I was not in any danger; the heat dried them out rapidly.

I was fortunate, glad to have saved the lady's life; I experienced all the happiness one feels on accomplishing a good deed.

I had asked the ladies-in-waiting to send me news of the Queen, and, indeed, they did so twice during the night. The Queen was feeling quite well, experiencing no distress except for a slight lassitude, and she was generous enough to ask for news of me.

The next day, the Queen came into my apartment by the door to the secret stairway; she was a little pale, but not in pain.

"I have come, my dear friend," she said, "to assure you of my gratitude for the service you rendered me. You have saved me from an imminent peril by which I was threatened; without you I would no longer exist."

"I give thanks to God, my good friend, for having been good enough to choose me to extract you from danger. He deigned to grant my prayer, and it's to him that you owe thanks, not to me; I am only the instrument of which he made use."

"And you believe," the Queen said to me, "that it is to God that I ought to be grateful? But I'm not of your religion, and I have no right to the protection of your God, whom I only know imperfectly and who does not know me."

"Forgive me, Madame, but my God is yours as he is mine; his bounty and his divine providence extend over everything that breathes; he protects all human equally, whatever their religion might be, for he considers them all to be his children. Doubtless he must have a certain predilection for those attached to his worship, but the God I adore is not a jealous God; he excuses those who worship imaginary gods, idols that are the image of a false divinity, fetishes, which are the idols of negroes, various beliefs such as those that still exist in the Oriental Indies, and the Egyptians, who adore the sacred bull Apis, animals and even reptiles.

"The savages of America adore the Great Spirit; they are more reasonable, living in tribes in their age-old forests, always in the presence of nature, their thoughts fermented, and they understood that that beautiful nature, and the resplendent stars, must have been created by a superior being. They were unable to conceive of an invisible God, Bossuet has said, and they called him the Great Spirit, but since that time, the majority have been enlightened by our missionaries."

"But my friend," said the Queen, excitedly, "can you not enlighten me as well as these missionaries have done for the savages? For all that you tell me ignites within me a keen desire to know the beauties and verities of your religion."

"I will do gladly, my noble friend. I will do more; I will give you the knowledge of God, the definition of the divinity, by means of convincing proofs that only I can give. Others before me have sought to resolve that great problem, but in vain. Even Simonides, the celebrated poet of antiquity, who lived five hundred years before Jesus Christ, failed in that definition, which was demanded of him by Hieron, King of Syracuse,[81] but I will give you proofs, and verbally, because I do

---

[81] The lyric poet Simonides (c556-468 B.C.) did spend some time at the court of King Hieron of Syracuse. This anecdote, originally related by Xenophon, appears—among many other places—in Pierre Bayle's *Dictionnaire historique et critique*, where Rousseau might well have found it.

not want to offend the opinions of others, which might give birth to controversies, and I am opposed to all contestation, either verbally or in writing."

"I approve, my worthy friend."

"When you're disposed to listen to me, we'll take a walk to the most remote corner of your gardens, where I can speak to you without fear of being overheard, and there we shall be in view of a part of the marvels of creation whose divine author I will make known to you."

The next day, the queen said to me: "My friend. I'm awaiting a great service from you. I cannot put off asking you for it any longer."

"Whatever it is, great Queen, I agree to it in advance."

"My friend, I desire ardently to know, to possess, what you promised me: the knowledge of the true God, the one that you adore."

"Today, my Queen, you shall be satisfied. When the ardor of the sun is less fierce, we shall go, as I said, into a solitary place in your gardens, and I will unveil the great mystery, the immensity of God. Your mind will be suddenly enlightened; you will understand then how God can be present at the same time throughout the universe, how he sees everything, and knows everything."

"How grateful I shall be to you, my worthy friend. Come to dinner with me today, and after dinner we shall go into the most isolated garden, where, without any other witness than God, you will make me know him and we shall adore him together. My heart enjoys in advance the happiness that awaits it. Oh, my friend, how dear you have become to me!"

I went to dine with the Queen, and did not perceive any sign of jealousy in the physiognomy of those present; everyone knew that the Queen's conversations with me were merely concerned with instruction. I had the reputation of being a scholar and I did not excite envy.

After dinner, I accompanied the Queen into the isolated garden, and after we had made sure that we would not have any indiscreet witnesses, I communicated to the Queen all my science regarding the knowledge of God, in his immensity and his infinite power. I explained how God was manifest in his works; I invited her to admire the beautiful vegetation that was around us; I told her how that vegetation was made, how the fruits succeeded the flowers, how the nucleus was formed inside them, enclosing the nut or the pips that served for reproduction.

Our conversation went on for a long time, and I perceived that the Queen was absorbed in her thoughts.

"I think, my noble friend," I said to her, "that that's enough for today with regard to vegetables. You would be too tired if this first lesson were prolonged, for there still remains a great deal for me to tell you about the marvels of nature; it's an inexhaustible subject."

"So much the better, my friend; I would have liked to listen to you for longer and to enjoy the pleasure that your precious lessons procure me; I'm delighted by today's, for it promises me a series of others that will be no less interesting and instructive."

""We're getting close to dusk," I said. "The sun is about to disappear in the Occident; we'll enjoy the beauty of a sunset."

"What do you mean, my friend, by the Occident?"

"The Occident is one of the four cardinal points, with are the north, the south, the Orient and the Occident. I shall mark them on the planetary system, that I drew for you."

"My friend," she said, "I would like to know one thing, but it might be a great indiscretion that would abuse your generosity."

"Have I not told you, my noble friend, that I'm entirely devoted to you."

"Yes, and you've given me proof of it, but I dare not demand this new thing of you."

"Dare, my noble friend, for it would offend me and cause me a good deal of pan if you doubted my willingness to satisfy you. Oh, I beg you tell me what you desire."

"What I desire, my worthy friend, is something that you possess and that I would like to possess too."

"Speak, my noble friend; everything that I have belongs to you—do you not know that in friendship, all property is common?"

"Oh, I know that. Well, what I desire is to know the language that you speak."

"But what you are asking me, my noble friend, would give me the greatest pleasure. We can commence right away, with the worlds and short familiar phrases that the most commonly used. That the way to learn a language quickly: first the practice and then the theory. Begin right away by asking me the names of things. Have no fear of questioning me, for it's by asking questions that one learns promptly. You have a great deal of perspicacity and a vivid conception; in very little time you'll understand everything that I tell you in my language."

IX

The Queen did, in fact, follow my advice, and a few days later, she knew a quantity of words and we already pronouncing a few short sentences that I had taught her very competently.

I was delighted with my royal pupil's progress; rapid success was certain.

I was fortunate enough to find, in a remote part of the gardens, a block of marl, or calcareous earth, which had doubtless been thrown there by a gardener who had found it while digging in the garden. The marl was quite soft and beautifully white; I thought that I might make sticks of chalk out of it, so I summoned one of the gardeners and asked him to carry the block to the palace for me.

I departed with my discovery and had it deposited in a cellar with the intention of going down there the next day in order to break the block into fragments similar to our sticks of chalk. In order to have a black marker I might be able to burn some wood, which I could extinguish in time to produce charcoal. I thought that during my expedition to Baleno with the Queen I might perhaps find charcoal, or some substance with which I could make black pencils, and perhaps find galls on oaks or other trees produces on the leaves and stems of certain trees by the injections of certain hemipterous insects; then I would be able to make ink. Quill pens were not difficult to find, and in any case, I would be able to make more.

The next day, when the Queen came to my study, I told her about the block that I had discovered and what I hoped to get out of it while hoping to find something better, but I needed an intelligent man to cut the block for me. She told me that she would send me a skillful man who could do the work. I also told the Queen that when we went to the wood at Baleno I hoped to find a substance with which to make ink, after which we would be able to write.

"So much the better!!" she said, enthusiastically. "I am longing to know how to write, because I believe that my progress in your language would be more rapid."

"I agree with you, my noble friend, and it's also to help you with that task that I shall try to make paper."

"In truth, my friend, I admire you, but I recall that you need old linen for that, and I shall give the order to find some. Then, whenever you want, we'll go to the wood at Baleno to look for the plants for the glass. The man who has seen the plant will go with us to show us the place. The weather is less hot, and will be favorable to our expedition. If nothing prevents us, we'll leave tomorrow.

We did, indeed, leave the following day. We passed through Arco, which is the planet's capital, without pausing, because the Queen wanted to remain incognito. Baleno is very close to the city, and we soon arrived at the wood where the man who was to go with us joined us.

We went into the wood and found the ferns, and other analogous plants. The Queen instructed him to cut all the plants and send them to her residence, taking care to separate the species, especially the fern.

I asked the men whether he knew of any place in the wood or its surroundings where there were minerals. He replied affirmatively that there were granite rocks and stones the color of lead. I asked to see them and he guided me to them. I examined the stones and put some of them aside in order to be sent to the royal residence along with the plants. He promised that he would do so, and kept his word.

I rejoined the Queen, who was sitting at the foot of a tree waiting for me, and told her about my discovery, and the hope I had, by cutting up the stones, of obtaining pencils like those of plumbago.

We returned to the residence, where, when we arrived, the Queen went up to her apartment—but as she was turning a corner on a stairway her foot slipped. She uttered a loud plaintive cry, followed by groans; her women ran to help her, but the Queen's dolorous plaints, which augmented when they touched her, threw them into a quandary. Alarm and consternation were general; they did not know how to soothe the Queen or what to do in order to transport her to her bed. Couriers were sent on horseback to Arco and Baleno to bring back physicians and surgeons, with orders to go and come back at a gallop.

The wait for assistance was an overwhelming anxiety for all the palace personnel. The queen was still lying on the stairs, and no one could touch her without her uttering frightful cries. After some two hours, two physicians arrived; they went to the Queen, but she was in such great pain and prostration that they could not get any information out of her as to the pain she was experiencing. They consulted with one another and decided to have her carried to her bed in order to palpate her and discover where the seat of the trouble was.

It was a terrible moment when the Queen as transported to her bed; it was a heart-rending spectacle, and all the witnesses were penetrated by a sharp distress. The Queen's screams were frightful, and yet she could not have been left any longer where she was. The greatest pains were taken to minimize her suffering, and they finally succeeded in moving her to her bed, where she lay completely inert for some time. The physicians made her breathe in different odors, which calmed her somewhat, and started searching for the source of the trouble.

The queen had broken her thigh and the great trochanter at the head of the femur. It was incurable! The thigh was already swelling up and the swelling was getting worse; all hope was lost. The heat was intense and gangrene was to be feared; the condition was visibly deteriorating.

The Queen was endowed with a great strength of mind; she understood her situation and wanted to be instructed positively by the physicians. She summoned them and asked them to tell her frankly what they thought of her prospects.

The physicians were nonplussed, and stammered a few words, but the Queen said to them: "Have no hesitation in replying to me, Gentlemen. I need to know where I stand, and how long I still have to live."

"Your Majesty might live until tomorrow, but if she has dispositions to make, she had better make them today."

"That you, Gentlemen, That's sufficient."

The doctors withdrew, and she had one of her ladies-in-waiting summon me. I immediately went to her. She smiled at me and held out her hand.

"Come closer, my friend; I need to talk to you. I have to thank you for your kindness toward me, your devotion and the great and useful instruction that I received from you, of the knowledge of God, and the great truths and maxims of your holy religion. You have not sown in barren ground; those seeds have borne fruit, and I want to die a Christian, but I lack one thing for that, which I desire ardently, and that is to receive baptism. But who can confer that sacrament on me, my friend."

"Me, my noble friend."

"What! You have the authority to do that?"

"Yes, every Christian has the right to baptize by pronouncing the sacramental words."

"And when can you baptize me?"

"Right now, if that is your desire."

"Yes, my friend, right now."

"Yes, my sister—for we are about to be brother and sister in Jesus Christ. You are thoroughly penetrated, my sister, with all the verities that I have revealed to you?"

"Yes, my brother."

Then I took a little water, which I poured over her head, saying: "Angélique, I baptize you in the name of the Father, the Son and the Holy Spirit. So be it."

The Queen was admirable in that solemn moment, which rendered her a Christian. I made the sign of the cross and said to her: "Angélique, my sister, you are now a Christian."

"What joy! And it's to you that I owe it!"

The Queen died during the night. I watched over her with her women, and toward midnight she was able to recognize me. She said to me, in a very faint voice: "Adieu, my friend, adieu." She held out her hand, which went cold in mine. Her soul returned to God.

Unable to bear the sight of that abode, I resolved to leave as soon as possible.

X

I summoned Za; he arrived beside me almost immediately.

"You're grief-stricken," he said, "and I understand why you want to leave this place. Where would you like to go?"

"To the planet Flora," I replied.

"Very well; you'll be there in a moment, for it isn't far away."

We did, in fact, arrive a few minutes later.

As we approached the planet, Za said to me: "That edifice you perceive in the residence of Queen Flora, sovereign of this planet. Look closely at her palace; you will see an arbor covered with large leaves decorated with flowers; at this moment. At this moment the queen is sitting in that arbor, where her nymphs are presenting her with baskets and flowers; others are singing their sovereign's praises; their charming chords are accompanied by instruments that produce a soft and agreeable melody.

"It's in the presence of the sovereign that I'll deposit you. Your appearance will surprise her, without a doubt, but don't worry about it and have no fear; I shall be nearby."

These words had scarcely been pronounced when I was already at the feet of Queen Flora, who uttered a cry of fright on seeing me.

"Have no fear, great Queen; I mean you no harm—on the contrary. I am a man who has come thirty million leagues to visit your planet, and who hopes to obtain a favorable welcome from Your Majesty."

"You see me disposed," he Queen said to me, "but where do you come from? Who are you? Why have you come to my estates?"

"Great Queen, I come from the Earth, which is a planet like yours; I am a man always occupied in scientific research. I thought that your planet ought to produce flowers unfamiliar to us; my design is therefore to acquire a knowledge of the flowers you possess here, to draw and to paint them, if I can procure colors."

"What! You know how to draw and paint?" she said to me. "If you could teach me your talents, it would give me the greatest pleasure. Can you instruct me in those arts?"

"Undoubtedly, Madame, if Your Majesty has the desire."

"If I have the desire, you say! But it would be a joy! We have tried in vain to draw our flowers, but have been unable to succeed. That is probably because there are means to employ of which we are unaware."

"Your remark is very just, Madame. Those means consist of a knowledge of rules and principle."

"And you know these rules and principles?"

"Perfectly, Madame."

"And you will be kind enough to teach them to me?"

"I shall make it a duty."

"What expression are you using there? I would have preferred it to be out of amity."

"You Majesty does me much honor, and I shall be able to recognize her bounty toward me with my entire devotion."

"That's very good, my friend. I see in you a man endowed with distinguished sentiments, and from this moment you are a guest of the palace. I will have an apartment prepared for you, where you will be served everything that you require. You shall indicate the times for your meals, and choose in our apartment the most convenient room to make into your study and work-room. You will dine with me today, in order that everyone will know how I regard you, and that you possess my esteem."

"Thank you, Madame. My conduct will prove to you that I merit it."

"I'm convinced of it, my friend. Now, what shall we do about the lessons in drawing and painting?"

"We'll begin with drawing, which it is necessary to know before painting. From the very first lesson Your Majesty will understand how important it is to know how to draw before commencing painting; a painter, no matter how careful he is, is always detestable if his drawing is poor; a good drawing, made simply in black pencil, is a thousand times preferable to a bad painting."

"Good! I shall follow your instructions exactly, my friend."

"It will be to your benefit, for Your Majesty will understand promptly how important drawing is to the rapid progress she will make when she commences painting."

I went to dinner with the Queen. Her reception was very gracious, and simultaneously testified to her deference for me. People gazed at me curiously, some in a kindly fashion, others with a jealous eye.

The Queen gave each of her nymphs the name of a flower, which it is necessary to translate as Primrose, Pansy, Clematis, Violet, Daisy, Marguerite, Wallflower, Hyacinth, Eglantine, Rose, Hortensia, Convolvulus, Tulip, Lily, Heliotrope, Jasmine, Camellia and Dahlia.

The number of her nymphs was not fixed. She had three for whom she had more affection; they were her confidantes; she therefore confided to them that I knew how to draw and paint, and that I was going to give her lessons to teach her that art. Their joy was great, and they testified to the Queen the desire they had also to receive my lessons.

"I don't know, my dear friends, whether he will agree to give them to you, but I will ask him, and will tell you what he replies."

Soon, the whole troop of pretty nymphs had the same desire, when they knew that I would soon begin giving my lessons to the Queen, who came to visit me in my apartment to see whether there were any changes I wanted to make.

I asked for a curtain, in order that I could obtain the level of light that was necessary to me.

"One will be put up for you," she told me. "When would you like to commence my lessons?"

"When it pleases Your Majesty—but what we lack is pencils."

"I have some, and I think that you will be able to make use of them."

The Queen came the next day and had all the objects of which she made use for drawing brought to me. You will understand in advance that none of it was of much use to me. There was a kind of paper in use in the country that, strictly speaking, might serve for drawing, and soft stones of various colors to serve as pencils. I carved some of the latter, giving them the form of pencils, and the lesson commenced.

I asked the Queen to draw a vase that I placed in front of her on the table, in which I put a flower. It was a lily.

She began with the lily; I made her begin with the vase. She began with the mouth of the vase; I made her draw a line perpendicular to the horizontal, and then divide up the vase into sections—which is to say, to indicate the planes of the neck, body and foot of the vase, and then to indicate the contours of the vase on the indicated planes, commencing on the left.

She did as I said, and understood immediately the great advantage of the facility that one finds in following the rules of an art. She trembled with joy at having been able to draw a vase so rapidly and so accurately.

"How content I am, my friend. You have just made me understand instantly the importance there is in knowing and following the principles of an art. I also understand why one must not start painting until one understands drawing perfectly. Thank you, my friend, for that good lesson, which is of great importance for me. Now I have something to ask of you which might perhaps be indiscreet on my part."

"Speak, Madame, and if what you have to ask me is within my power, you will find me disposed to satisfy your desire."

"How good you are, my worthy friend. Well, if you are agreeable, we will go to visit Florina, which is the capital city of my realm. That will enable to you get to know a small part of my realm, and during the journey I shall tell you what I have to ask of you."

"I accept your offer with great pleasure," I told the Queen, "for I desire to know the interior of your planet."

"If this journey interests you we can, if you wish, go to Floresca the day after, which is the second city of my realm."

"Very gladly, Madame. I shall go with you wherever you wish."

What the Queen might have to ask my worried me; it was a vague anxiety, to be sure, but it troubled my mind nevertheless.

I departed, therefore the following day, with the Queen in her litter, carried by two small horses.

XI

I did not see anything remarkable on the route that we followed, except that almost all of the countryside was covered with flowers that embalmed the air; there were few picturesque locations, nothing but the flowers. I like flowers a great deal, but seeing nothing else everywhere became tedious.

We arrived in Florina, through which the Queen wanted to pass incognito. The city is quite pretty but has nothing worthy of remark.

We came back that same evening to the residence. During the journey the Queen did not speak to me about the request she had to maker of me, and I did not prompt her. I thought that it would do as well the flowing day.

The next day, we went to Floresca. The landscape was almost identical to the one I had seen the previous day; always flowers.

The Queen was pensive. Finally, she said to me: "My friend, this is what I have to say to you. You know that among my nymphs there are three for whom I have a marked predilection; I have confided to them that I am receiving lessons in drawing from you. They have mentioned it to their companions, and several of them desire to receive our precious lessons. What do you say?"

I received that confidence rather coldly, and I replied: "I'll think about it, Madame, and let you know my answer tomorrow."

As I was not enthusiastic to give lessons to anyone but the Queen, I made the most prudent decision, that of going away. I summoned Za, who arrived immediately.

He said to me: "I know what's worrying you and the decision you've made; I can but approve. Where do you want to go?"

"To the planet Parthenope," I told him.

"Very well; we'll leave tomorrow morning. Prepare yourself: go to bed fully dressed and at sunrise, I'll wake you up within sight of Parthenope.

I thanked my good genius, and he disappeared. I made my preparations, ate a little and went to bed fully dressed, as my good genius had told me to do.

He woke me up at sunrise within sight of Parthenope.

"Look," he said.

I looked, and was astonished to see a planet whose topography was not unknown to me; the more I gazed the more locations I recognized that I had seen before: the city that I perceived recalled memories; I recognized a few monuments—if, at least, thought I recognized them, because it could only be an illusion, since I had never come to this planet. Perhaps it was a kind if mirage, like the one that exists in deserts, and even at sea; I did not know which conjecture was the most probable. Finally, weary of conjecturing, I decided to wait.

My good genius undoubtedly saw what was happening within me, for a voice said to me: "Everything you see is agitating your mind, but don't worry; you'll soon know the reality. Can you see a great cortege accompanying a woman dressed in rich garments?"

"Yes," I replied.

"That's Queen Partha, who is going to take a stroll on the shore of a bay that you ought to be able to see; it is there, in her presence, that I shall set you down. Respond to the questions that she asks you. She's a little hard of hearing, but that comes from the language of the planet, for the Queen is good and I hope that she'll give you a good welcome. In any case, as always, don't worry about anything; I shall be nearby."

At that moment, a delightful music became audible; it was coming from the cortege, and my good genius set me on the ground directly in front of the Queen. My sudden appearance caused her a certain alarm, and stopped the progress of the cortege.

"What do you want with me? Who are you?"

"Great Queen," I replied, "I have come to your realm to learn and to assure myself of the reality of things that I have only seen thirty million leagues from your planet."

"What is he saying?" the important individuals who were with her asked her. "He's mad, I believe."

225

"No, great Queen, I'm not mad; I'm telling you the truth."

"But how is that possible?"

"An individual approached the Queen, and by this gestures—which are frequently employed in that country—I was able to determine that he was talking about me. He often looked at me, and with interest. Perhaps he took me for an astronomer, or at least for a man knowledgeable about astronomy.

The Queen said to me: "*Siete il ben venuto, Signore.* You will be lodged in my palace, and I shall come to see you in order to obtain an explanation of the things that you have said to me, which pique my curiosity."

The Queen seemed benevolent. I thought that my sojourn with her would be pleasant and useful.

The Queen came to see me the following day, asked me how I found my apartment, whether I was well cared for, and if I lacked anything.

"I'm perfectly comfortable here, great Queen, and I have only to thank Your Majesty for her kindness toward me."

"But tell me, Sire, how you have been able to discover my realm at a distance of thirty million leagues? That seems impossible to me, and it excites my curiosity as well as that of the other people who heard you."

Then I told the Queen about the means of telescopes, of which I gave her an explanation. The Queen manifested great surprise as she listened to me, and only expressed herself in exclamations of astonishment."

"*O che cosa bella, o che maraviglia!* Tell me, *caro mio*, is it possible for you to procure such instruments? I would be charmed to see things so far away. One of the people who heard you when you arrived told me that you appeared to have knowledge of astronomy. What is that science?"

"It's the knowledge of the stars."

"And you possess it?"

"Yes, Madame."

"*Va bene*. Come to dine with me today, and after dinner I shall take great pleasure in hearing you talk to those people. Perhaps the knowledge you possess will be useful to them."

"I desire to be, Madame, and I shall be very glad to have been agreeable to you in something."

"*Benissimo mio caro*. Someone will come to fetch you at dinner time, *sitate pronto. Si maestro io lo saro*."

One of the Queen's officers came to notify me, and I went down immediately. The Queen received me with distinction, and had me seated next to her. Although flattered by that preference, I feared that it might excite the jealousy of the nobles present at the dinner. At dessert, however, the frowns cleared.

The Queen was uniformly cheerful and showed a great deal of natural wit. Behind her there were two of her maids of honor to serve her; one of them gazed at me with sustained attention and seemed to be examining all the guests. She found an opportunity to say to me: "*Ho da parlavi, do poprenzo*."

What could she have to say to me?

After diner, as everyone withdrew, and the Queen was accompanied by the nobles, she seized a moment when she was not observed and said to me: "*Badate*."

I looked at her in surprise. What had I to fear?

She indicated a passage to me with a gesture and said: "*Siguitemi*."

I followed her, and when she saw that she could talk to me without being overheard by the nobles, she said to me: "The marks of distinction that you have received from the Queen have awakened the jealousy of the noblemen. Be prudent, and never go out without being armed with a stiletto, which is the offensive and defensive weapon of this country—for it's to be feared that someone might seek to murder you."

I thanked the charming young woman, and she disappeared rapidly.

What I had just learned gave me pause for thought, and I resolved to procure a stiletto—but to whom should I address myself in order to obtain that weapon?

The domestic who served me and who appeared to be attached to me seemed to be appropriate to fulfill that task, and I decided to talk to him about it that same evening. To buy anything, however, I needed local money, and I only had French. I emptied my purse, and to my great surprise, several small gold coins fell out whose value I did not know.

I summoned my domestic. "Gennaro," I said. "I desire to have a stiletto."

"That will be easy, *Excellenza*."

"How much does a stiletto cost?"

"*Se condo la grandezza at la bellazza*."

"I'd like a simple one to carry inside my coat."

"*Un buone stiletto, costera due ducati con lo stucio*."

I took out my purse and asked him what the little gold coins were.

"*Sono ducati*," he replied.

I took two of them, which I gave him to buy the stiletto, and gave him one to keep the secret. He brought me a stiletto without a sheath, which suited me perfectly, and I put it inside my jacket, with the intention of always carrying it on my person, because I saw in the young woman's warning and the gold coins that I had found in my purse another precaution of my good genius, who doubtless approved of that prudent measure.

XII

That existence of always being on the alert became intolerable to me, however, and I resolved to continue my voyage and conclude it with the Sun. I was not tempted to go to Jupiter, Saturn, Uranus and Neptune; those cold regions made me tremble in advance.

Before quitting the planet Parthenope, however, I desired to see the capital city and its surroundings. One morning, therefore, I set out toward the capital. On the road I encountered a vehicle that was going in that direction—a kind of cabriolet called a *coricoli*.

I soon arrived in the great city, the sight of which caused me a great astonishment, because it seemed to me that I knew it. Its monuments, which I could see from a distance, I had certainly seen before—but where? I could not succeed in remembering.

Having arrived at the city I asked my driver to take me to a good hotel, and he took me to the hotel *del Sole, sulla piazza del Sole*. It was then that my astonishment reached its peak; I was in a city exactly similar to Naples, in the same hotel, and in the same room, that I had occupied twenty years before. I was in the city that I loved so much, and whose surroundings had so many attractions for me.

I did not waste a moment. I went out armed with my stiletto and headed toward *Chiaja*, going past the beautiful San Carlo theater, and did not take long to arrive *al giardino reale*, at the end of which is the grotto of Posillipo. I stopped at the entrance to the grotto, next to the tomb of Virgil, nicknamed the Swan of Mantua, where he was born. He was, it is said, a pupil of Parthenius.

Parthenope was a siren whose body was found on the sea shore. A Greek colony was established on that shore, known today as the Bay of Naples. They founded a city there, which they named Neopolis or Neapolis, which means "new city." It received the name Napoli in Italian, doubtless borrowed from Napoli, city of Greece. The French call it Naples.

Sitting next to Virgil's tomb—or, at least, the place that it really occupies in Naples—I had before me the whole extent of the bay, the beautiful bat identical to the Bay of Naples, and for a horizon Vesuvius, and the Somma, at the foot of Vesuvius. I admired a pretty town similar to Portici, to my left, Castel Sant Elmo, and to my right, an island similar to Capri, celebrated for the shameful debauches of Tiberius, which he called his delights.

I took a coricoli to visit the environs of the capital of Parthenope. I collected a few souvenirs of my youth there, by virtue of the resemblance of a few locations to those in the environs of Naples, or, at least, I took pleasure in imagining

229

that the resemblance existed. Satisfied with the excursion, I asked my driver to take me back to the Queen's palace.

There I thought about all the annoyances and torments that awaited me occasioned by the jealousy of the nobles, and I took the firm resolution to leave. I summoned Za, and told him that I intended to quit Parthenope in order to visit the Sun.

"Very well," he said to me. "We'll leave tomorrow at daybreak. Go to bed fully dressed, as usual, and we'll arrive at the Sun in no time at all—but you won't be able to stay there for long, for although the Sun has its inhabitants, you won't be able to live with them. Content yourself with visiting them for your instruction, and we'll leave the same day to go wherever you please."

"That will be to France," I told him, "my dear fatherland, where I left a beloved sister that I'm in a hurry to see again, and who is doubtless anxious, awaiting my return impatiently, for he has no idea where I am."

I went to bed fully dressed, and the next morning, Za deposited me on the edge of the center of the Sun, before the immense ocean of fire, which I consider to be an igneous substance whose heat rises to the photosphere, from which the Sun's rays depart.

It was on the edge of that sea of fire that my good genius set me down, and I stayed there without being inconvenienced by the heat, because I was protected from it by the Sunspots, some of which are of very great extent.

I was sitting down and contemplating the immense hearth that I had before my eyes, which wearied them slightly. I turned to look in another direction and perceived two men, who could see me but who did not pay any attention to me. The men were enormously corpulent and had muscular limbs; they were naked, and their skin was red. The sight of them reminded me of the Patagonians that I had seen in America, and were very nearly the same height, which is said to be seven feet, although it is necessary to remark that their feet only measure eleven inches.

The two men drew away from me; left alone, and experiencing the need to take a little nourishment, I was wondering how to appease my hunger when I perceived a basket some distance away, which I hastened to visit.

What joy! It was filled with provisions. It was an attention that I doubtless owed to my god genius, and I shouted "Thank you, Za."

Having nothing more to see on the Sun I summed him, and told him that I desired to return to France, to the very spot where he had raised me up on my departure.

"And when do you want to leave?"

"Whenever you like," I relied.

"At this very moment—and you'll sleep at home tonight."

I did, indeed—and without anyone having noticed my absence.

PART TWO

Introduction

I had just concluded my voyage to the Moon, the other planets and the Sun when my good genius Za transported me from that star to the Earth, to the very spot from which he had lifted me up.

"Before you go," I said to him, "I have a request to make of you."

"What?"

"I desire to go to visit the space beyond the fixed stars, where I suppose there are others much more distant, which our astronomers have not yet discovered; it is that space, which I shall call *imaginary*, that I desire to visit, in order to know the truth."

"What you are asking might be difficult for me to obtain, for it's very far away, and it will take many years to get there. But other imaginary spaces exist, of which your scientists are perhaps unaware, although they are much closer at hand, to which it would be possible for me to transport you.

"I'll go talk to our chief Zadir about it, and I'll accompany you, if he permits it. If not, I'll have you accompanied by two genii of the air who are subordinate to me: a sylph and a sylphide, his sister. They'll be very useful to you, without a doubt, in those spaces, where everything is so different from the planets you have visited, where many events probably await you; but I'll give them the order and the power to protect you throughout your voyage, and when it ends, they'll bring you back here. When do you want to go?"

"Whenever you think it appropriate."

"I'll go warn them to collect provisions sufficient for the journey."

My good genius informed me when everything was ready for the voyage, and we left the following day.

Three days after our departure we arrived in the imaginary spaces.

I

The imaginary spaces are situated in different parts of the immensity; they are unknown to scientists. They are not planets that rotate on their axes and circle the zodiac; their only movement is oscillation, like that of a pendulum. They are islands, flat on the upper surface and round underneath, which gives them the form of the drums known as kettledrums, used by the cavalry. The inferior part, being higher than the Sun, receives the light of the star, and the upper part receives that of the fixed stars, which are as many suns.

In nebulous times, those islands are illuminated, in part, by birds like those in America which are called Firebirds. These birds are very abundant around the islands, where they find their nourishment. The islands are numerous; the majority are nameless, because they are small and uninhabited; they form Cyclades, and atolls in archipelagos.

The best known of these islands are those of Reveries, Fictions, Illusions, Tricks, Prodigies and Marvels. In addition to those there is a gathering of islands in the form of a delta, of which the three principal ones, which occupy the angles, are the Isles of Chimeras, Metamorphoses and Visions. Other islands also exist in a nearby space—I say nearby because it is only five thousand leagues distant from the one where we are now. I learned that from my sylph, but as a veridical voyager, I shall only speak about those islands when I have visited them.

On our arrival in the imaginary spaces we descended on the Isle of Reveries, where we saw beings of human form that were marching or strolling in silence. They could probably see us, but they did not appear to be astonished; their thoughts, if they had any, were doubtless wandering in the waves of the air. Their taciturnity did not make them very amiable hosts. The men and women appeared to be of the same humor; only

233

the children seemed more alert. The men, woman and children were all naked; only the women had, for a girdle around the midriff, a liana bearing a few leaves. The people did not seem very hospitable.

I made those remarks aloud; my sylph heard them, and, as the brother and sister thought as I did, they transported me to the Isle of Fictions in a matter of minutes

There were saw beings of human form, to be sure, but with elongated heads, and double eyes on each side, like the fish called *Anablepsis*. Others had bird-like beaks instead of jaws, like the animals of that name which exist in New Holland.[82] Others had only one eye in the middle of the forehead, like certain crustaceans called *Polyphemus*. Others had a mouth so small that one could scarcely see it, like the animals knows as *Anostomes*. Others, in large numbers, resembled monkeys, with the exception that they had no tails. Others had heads like horses. Others, finally, had muzzles like lions, like the leprosy of Arabs known as *Leontiasis*. All these beings were frightening in their appearance, all the more so because they had the cries of monkeys, the whinnies of horses and the roar of lions.

I regretted having undertaken the voyage, but I was *en route*, and I hoped to find people less ugly on the other islands. Then I asked my sylph to transport me to the Isle of Illusions.

When we arrived on that island, I found that everything had a very agreeable appearance; the men were good enough, at least in appearance; the women seemed to me to be pretty. We were given a good welcome by the islanders, who received us in their huts, which were constructed of branches and mud, but I found the interior very neat.

The atmosphere was thick; the air was laden with large clouds, which the light of the stars could not traverse entirely; one only received at intervals the fugitive light of firebirds and that of glow-worms, which were in the grass and in the bushes

---

[82] i.e. "duckbills"—the Platypus.

by which the hut I was in was surrounded. Those glow-worms emitted as much light as a candle, and the multitude of those insects produced a considerable clarity, at least sufficient for us not to be in complete obscurity. When dawn appears,[83] however, all that lighting is soon replaced by daylight, in which one can judge things better.

I had thrown myself down on a kind of bed on the floor in the corner of the hut. When I awoke I found myself lying on a coarse mat, with my head placed on a bundle of dried plants. In spite of the hardness of that couch, I had slept very well. An agreeable dream had transported me to my own bed, with its flexible mattress and mahogany frame, surrounded by curtains suspended from a crown attached to the ceiling and ornamented with elegant drapes.

I no longer saw anything in their place but a host of insects and little animals, all stirring, running, agitating crazily, jumping and capering; and in order that everything should be in keeping, I heard on the floor below the hiss of reptiles and the croaking of frogs and toads. There was a complete cacophony, when, suddenly, all those discordant sounds gave way to a gentle harmony, a delightful symphony that ravished my senses and drew me out of my torpor.

I awoke entirely, therefore, and no longer saw anything of what I had seen, or heard anything of what I had heard, and was convinced that I had been the victim of an illusion.

I got up from my bed, already dressed, and I went out to breathe in the morning air and stroll around the island, where I hoped to encounter my sylph or my sylphide in some form— for I did not know them; they were invisible to me, as my good genius Za had been. It was probable, however, that my sylph would speak to me in order to ask whether I had anything to ask of him. I could not summon him, because I did not know his name, or that of his sister; I had forgotten to ask.

---

[83] It is not obvious how dawn can appear on the imaginary worlds, given the configuration previously indicated, but there appears to be a cycle of day and night on all of them.

I went out, therefore, and at the door of my hut I found myself face to face with my host and hostess, who saluted me by putting their hands on their head and saying: *"Salamicadi!"* I replied to their politeness, and recommenced my stroll.

About half an hour after my departure from the hut, I sat down at the foot of a tree. The subtle air of the island was stimulating my appetite when I saw a charming woman suddenly appear, with gracious manners and gestures, who reminded me of Fanny Elssler in her role as *La Sylphide*.[84]

"Is that you, Fanny, that I can see once more?"

"No," she replied. "I'm the sylphide who is the sister of the sylph accompanying you. My brother has asked me to bring you this basket, in which you'll find your morning meal."

"I'm very grateful to you, but I beg you to tell me your brother's name."

"My brother's name is Zico. That is the name that you should pronounce three times when you have need of him."

"And may I ask yours?"

"Mine is Zica. My brother has a sympathy for you, and will acquit with pleasure the orders he has received from his chief, the genius Za."

"By what title should I address you when you give me the pleasure of coming to visit me?"

"None," she said. "Simply Zica. When you have need of my services you call me by pronouncing it three times: *Zica! Zica! Zica!*—and I shall be with you immediately. But it's late and you must need to eat. I'll leave you in order to return to my brother, but before leaving you, tell me how you spent the night."

"I sleep well, although rather poorly couched."

---

[84] Fanny Elssler (1810-1884) was an Austrian ballerina who first came to France in 1834. She danced *La Sylphide* in 1838, apparently in an attempt to outdo her great rival Marie Taglioni, for whom the role had been created, but she failed.

"Would you like to change island? I'll notify my brother."

"I'd like that, but will you accompany us?"

"We've received orders to accompany you wherever you desire to go."

"In that case, I desire to go to the Isle of Tricks."

"Very well. I'll go tell my brother, and it probably won't take us long to get there. While awaiting our departure, rest in order to repair the fatigue caused by a sleepless night."

With those words, she disappeared. I ate, and after the meal, which I needed, I leaned back against the tree at the foot of which I was sitting and went to sleep.

II

I do not know how long my sleep lasted, but I was wrenched out of it by a sudden brightness that struck my heavy eyelids. I woke up with a start, and my eyes were dazzled by the glare of a bright light coming from a flock of firebirds that were passing beneath us.

Then Zico said to me: "We'll be on the Isle of Tricks shortly, the capital of which is Lutèce."

"Lutèce!" I exclaimed. "How has that name reached all the way here? That ancient village composed of huts? Those huts, it's true, have mostly become sumptuous town houses and palaces: the Tuileries, the Louvre and Notre Dame have been built in the place once occupied by those miserable huts!"

"Look, here's the Isle of Tricks. Can you see its capital?"

I looked, and was stuck motionless by surprise on seeing before my eyes all the admirable monuments that embellish the modern Lutèce, Paris, admired by all strangers, where the science and arts flourish and appear to have arranged a rendezvous. I could not get enough of the pleasure that I experienced in contemplating that city, over which I love to run my eyes.

But is it an illusion, then? For I no longer recognize the majority of its streets; in their place I see, either spacious squares or new streets lined with magnificent houses, and they are all sculpted, ornamented with balconies; all those streets are broad and magnificent; I can no longer see the labyrinth of narrow and dirty little streets lateral to the Rue Saint-Martin; that entire miry quarter has disappeared, to give way to beautiful and airy streets. The Rue Saint-Martin itself has disappeared; in its place I see a superb boulevard traversing that great quarter of Paris; everywhere I see nothing but embellishments. The Louvre, which was already so beautiful, is now admirably sumptuous, where the great and the beautiful are combined in exquisite taste. It needed a genius to complete that beautiful work, worthy of the Parthenon of the new Athens.

If the beautiful garden of the Tuileries, the Champs-Élysées and the beautiful palace that I see there, the Hôtel-de-Ville, the Bibliothèque and so many other monuments that I perceive are only a trick, an illusion, I cannot complain—I owe them a few moments of joy!

Shortly afterwards, Zico deposited me in Lutèce, at a house in the Chaussée d'Antin, where I lived with my family for several years. He set me down in the garden—the garden that I had embellished so much, having an excellent gardener care for it. Night had fallen, and I hastened to go into the house, where I found many dear objects of my tenderness, and my amour.

When I went into the drawing room, there was a unanimous cry of joy. I was surrounded by cherished individuals, who lavished their caresses upon me. The sweet and intense emotion that we all experienced prevented us from expressing ourselves other then in abrupt, inconsequential remarks, but the tears of joy and happiness that we shed spoke for us. It was the eloquence of the heart, easily understood by any sensitive soul.

We dined *en famille*—what a joy for us, who had not savored it for a long time! The dinner was long and peaceful; we did not say much, having too many things to say, but our eyes expressed all our thoughts better than words could have done.

Finally, the time arrived to go to bed, and everyone retired, regretfully to their bedrooms; but none of us savored the pleasures of sleep. How could we sleep after so much emotion? So we got up early.

I was unaware of all the disasters, all the changes that had overtaken the house. After our ruination, it had been sold to entrepreneurs; all the lovely things that I had had constructed had been taken out or demolished. I experienced a constriction in the heat, but I did not allow it to depress me; my courage did not abandon me, and that of my wife and sister did not weaken. We had embarked on a new enterprise, which prospered to begin with, but was destroyed by a revolution in Paris.

I spent the day with my family, but the next morning, when I woke up, I saw none of the members of my family around. I thought, and was convinced, that everything pleasant that had happened to me was a dream, an illusion that had vanished; only the misfortune was real, and had remained. That house, that place of joy for me, was no longer anything to the eye but a skeleton that reminded me at every step, at every moment, of the happy times, so regrettable, that I had spent there. I could no longer bear it there, and I decided to leave.

I summoned my sylph and told him that I desired to go to the Isle of Prodigies.

"Very well," he said. "We'll leave tomorrow before sunrise. Make your preparations go to bed fully dressed, and we'll transport you to the Isle of Prodigies."

III

The next day, at sunrise, we were within sight of the Isle of Prodigies. I was profoundly asleep. Zica woke me up, and my sylph said: "There's the Isle of Prodigies, whose capital city, which you can see from here, is called Prodigium.

I contemplated the island, which appeared to me to be very singular, in that all the houses, all the monuments and all the edifices were inclined, but my astonishment did not last long. I remembered the leaning tower of Pisa, opposite the Baptistry, and the leaning tower of Bologna, known as the Asinelli, and then I found nothing surprising in it, although it was singular, fantastic and capricious, because for me it was not a phenomenon, something extraordinary. I expected, however to find bizarre and eccentric inhabitants.

Zico, as he had been instructed to do by my genius Za, had given me the faculty of understanding and speaking the languages of the islanders of the imaginary spaces. He set me down at the portal of a house of grandiose appearance, which was not inclined. When they perceived me, the servants of the house approached me. Some were black, others a very pale white, like the albinos that are regarded in India as degenerate beings and only go out at night; they are called *kakerlak*,[85] and also known as white negroes. Others were of different hues. Night was falling; I was surrounded by all those people coming to see me; for them I was an object of curiosity.

The noise they were making was overheard by the mistress of the house, who wanted to know the cause of it. She was told that it was a man such as had never been seen, that he was a stranger and seemed to be expecting to be offered hospitality. The lady, whose name was Belladone, belonged to a great family of the city of Prodigium. She wanted to see me and gave orders that I was to be taken up to a small room adjacent to the one she occupied.

Her order was carried out, and someone came to invite me to go to see the lady. I went up a magnificent staircase, very similar to ours. I was shown into the small room indicated by the lady, and soon afterwards, I saw a woman come in whose beauty dazzled me.

She doubtless perceived my disturbance, for she said: "Don't worry; you're in my house; you'll receive all the assis-

---

[85] Literally, cockroaches.

tance and cares of hospitality; but may I, without offending you, ask who you are? For you're a stranger, from a land that I doubtless do not know. By your distinguished manners, I judge that you're of a good family."

"You're not mistaken in our judgment, Madame; I am, In fact, of a very good family; the education I received gave birth in me to the desire to know everything that exists in the immensity. I was born on a planet that is in that immensity, and which is some thirty million leagues distant from your island."

"What!" she exclaimed. "You have been able to come from so far away?"

"Yes, Madame."

"But how did you do it?—you have no wings."

"No, Madame, but I was transported to your island by a superhuman power, which protects me and has given me the means of visiting several planets, and even the Sun."

"The Sun!" she exclaimed. "What, you have been to the sun, and you were not burned there?"

"No, Madame."

"But you are saying things that are marvelous."

"I agree, Madame, and, before having visited that immense globe of fire, I would have thought like you; but the observations made by astronomers have taught me that the center of the Sun is not burning, since it is inhabited, and that the heat that comes to us from its disk, where the heat of that sea of fire rises to what astronomers cal the photosphere—that is the most luminous part of the Sun, from which its rays depart, which illuminate, fecundate and heat everything that exists in the universe, and bring about the maturity of the fruits that vegetables give us.

"On your island, you do not enjoy all the benefits of the sun in their entirety, because it is situated beyond its elevation, and it only illuminates it from underneath, but that underside is not far away, and receives its rays almost horizontally—principally its vertical rays, which give the center of your island a heat almost equal to the volcanoes that we have in the center of our planet. You thus enjoy the same advantages that we possess in that regard, but it is not the same for the upper surface of your island; it is scarcely lit by the sun, but it receives from below the warmth necessary to the vegetation, which must be very beautiful. The upper part of your island receives the light of the fixed stars that are around the Sun. You have, in addition, the multitude of firebirds that surround your island and illuminate it by night, and the other multitude of glow-worms, which illuminate the countryside. Those advantages are not, without a doubt, comparable to those we possess on our planets, which all rotate on their axes and around the sun, which alone remains motionless at the center of the universe."

Belladone, whom I shall call *Belladonna*, paid the closest attention to what I was saying. She did not take her eyes off me, and seemed astonished by the things I said—which she was doubtless hearing for the first time, for she uttered a profound sigh and said to me:

"Everything that you have just told me interests me a great deal and gives me the greatest pleasure. I can see that you possess a great deal of learning; perhaps it would be agreeable for you to augment it with a knowledge of the island that I inhabit."

"That is my intention, Madame, and I propose to explore it."

"If such is your intention," said Belladonna, "I offer to accompany you in your research; that will give you the means to examine everything without fatigue, because we can make the little excursion in a barouche, and you will be free to stop at all the places you would like to examine. If you wish, we can go to visit Prodigium, the capital city of the island."

"I accept your offer with great pleasure, Madame, and even with gratitude."

We set out the following morning in a little caleche drawn by two animals of the deer genre, a kind of reindeer, very light in running.

The landscape of that island is charming; the vegetation is prodigious in the beauty, the variety and the freshness of its plants, which were all unknown to me, but nevertheless attracted my admiration. I asked Belladonna their names but she did not know them. The trees were surprising in their beauty, their fruits admirable.

We arrived at a little wood, which it was necessary to traverse. We found ourselves at a crossroads, where Belladonna proposed that we stop in order to rest our animals. We got down from the barouche, and sat down at the feet of two of the large and beautiful trees by which the crossroads was surrounded. We savored the pleasure that the soul experiences in contemplating the marvels of creation.

"Don't you think," I said to Belladonna, "that thoughts are sweetest when one is confronted by the works of God?"

"What do you mean by God?" he asked.

"I mean by God," I replied, "the Sovereign Being who created everything that exists in nature: the beautiful sky that we are contemplating, the earth we inhabit, all the plants with which it is ornamented, all the animals, and these charming birds whose delightful songs sing the praises of their Creator!"

At that moment we had the harmonious concert of numerous birds that were in the trees at the feet of which we were sitting.

Belladonna took my arm and squeezed it, saying: "What you have just told me, my friend, causes me an impression that I have never felt before. And you believe that it is God, whose name you have just pronounced, that created all these beautiful things?"

"I am convinced of it, Madame, and in the 5864 years[86] since he created it, everything has remained in the same state. After having created the heavens, God created the angels to announce and execute his orders; then God created the Firmament, in which he placed the Sun, and created the planets and stars in the same way. Then he created the fish and the

---

[86] Indicating a date of composition of 1860, if the author is employing James Ussher's calculation of the creation having occurred in 4004 B.C.

birds. On the sixth day he created the animals and man, and concluded with the masterpiece of nature, by creating woman!

"The wisdom of God is so profound that everything he has created is subject to his supreme law. The sun is motionless at the center of the universe where God has placed it; the planets rotates around it and receive light from it, which some of them, called moons, transmit to other planets by reflection during the night.

"For humans and for animals his divine providence had foreseen and provided for their needs; for God, by his immensity, is present at all times in all the parts of the universe. That is why God sees everything, knows everything and provides everything; that is what is called Providence.

"All the animals find on land the nourishment appropriate to them. Who gives them that nourishment, if not the one that created them? The fish find their nourishment in the waters; the birds find theirs on land and in the air; the insects find it everywhere.

"The quadrupeds find it in vegetables and in animals.

"The humans who inhabit lands where agriculture is unknown receive their nourishment from flocks of birds of passage that pause over their territory, but their principal nourishment is that of synagelotic fish—which is to say, fish that swim on shoals, especially herrings, whose fecundity is prodigious.

"The peoples who take their nourishment from fish are called icthyophages; others are acridophages; they eat grasshoppers. Carnivores nourish themselves on flesh.

"The inhabitants of the kingdom of Siam, in India, nourish themselves on the flesh of raw fish. The inhabitants of the Bavis Strait, in North America, which separates Greenland from New Brittany, nourish themselves in the same way.

"Geophages are a few savage peoples whom hunger reduces to eating earth. Anthropophages are savages who eat human flesh.

"The peoples that I have just mentioned are part of the peoples known as barbaric—which is to say, uncivilized: idle, devoid of industry, sagacity and intelligence.

"Humans are born without industry, it's true, but they have to profit from the ideas of God, the type of which are seen throughout nature; they can also profit from the instincts of animas, which gives them at birth an industry appropriate to them. Only humans are born without instinct and without industry; they are obliged to acquire that industry, but always by imitation; it is only after a great deal of time, toil and reflection that they have succeeded in surpassing the animals. Aerostatic inventions, hydraulic machine team engines, astronomical instruments, ships with propellers, railways, clocks, watches, the fabrication of cloths, machinery, etc., the science and the arts, prove that humans possess a portion of divine essence, the immortal soul."

Belladonna listened to me with the greatest attention, and said: "Everything that you have told me transports me with admiration and astonishment. I admire the bounty of God, his divine Providence—but I'm astonished that he does not protect all humans equally."

"Your remark is just, Madame, but your astonishment will cease when you know that humans, whom God created good, went astray and became wicked and ingrate toward their creator. Their iniquity became intolerable, and God resolved to annihilate them by means of the universal deluge, in the year of the world 1536 or 1606. A single man was saved with his wife and children, three of whom were sons: Shem, Japhet and Ham. The last of them was cursed by his father, along with his posterity.

"The peoples that I have mentioned to you—the barbarians, the savages—are the posterity of Ham, and were abandoned by God. However, among those men soiled with crime and iniquity, there are good ones whom God protects, for God is just and good."

"I can easily understand what you have just told me, but I will need to be instructed and to be able to meditate profoundly on the beings and things that you have mentioned, which I only understand imperfectly. Will you be generous enough to instruct me in the knowledge that I lack?"

"Have no doubt of it, Madame; I shall do so with pleasure."

"Thank you, my friend. Now, would you like to go to Prodigium?"

"Willingly, Madame."

We climbed back into the little caleche and set off. I admired all the plants over which the luxury of the vegetation extended. I noticed a few animals that were unknown to me, but which were extraordinary. I decided to visit the island alone and on foot, in order to be able to draw the plants and animals.

IV

The city of Prodigium had a very bizarre, incongruous appearance, owed equally to all its aspects. All the inclined buildings were eccentric in appearance, caprice having played a greater part in their construction than taste, but that was certainly not a prodigy of art. We went into the city, where I was extremely astonished to see that all its inhabitants were lame, all having one leg shorter that the other, with the consequence that couples walking arm in arm, if they were not lame in the same leg, bruised their shoulders and their heads by virtue of their proximity. It was truly bizarre to see that unsteady movement, which often degenerated into grotesquerie, everywhere.

Belladonna stopped the caleche at the door of a beautiful house inhabited by one of her relatives, who received us cordially. We stayed there the next day and the day after that, and then we returned to Belladonna's house.

On the way, I told her that I had the intention of traveling the island alone and on foot; what had fortified that resolution was that I had discovered in Prodigium a kind of paper and stones that I could carve into the form of crayons. But Belladonna did not want to let me depart alone, because very singular events sometimes occurred on the island.

"But I have nothing to fear, my good friend—and besides, I still have my stiletto, which I habitually carry on my person to defend myself in case of need."

"Nonetheless," she said, "I shall accompany you everywhere. We'll travel the island together in the barouche; I'll have it stop in any place you indicate; the barouche will be furnished with provisions, and in the evening we'll come back here, to recommence the following day, if you wish. All the time that you're occupied with your drawings, I'll wait for you in the barouche, or remain beside you. What do you say?"

"I say that you're as good as you're beautiful!"

The following day we put the plan into execution; Belladonna no longer left me; we ate in the barouche, where the servant prepared everything; then I went to draw, and Belladonna remained sitting next to me watching me work. Such was our plan of campaign.

I began by drawing a few plants and small animals. Then a larger quadruped, a kind of kangaroo, arrived in front of us. I was about to sketch it when it hurled itself upon Belladonna. To draw my stiletto and strike it was the work of an eye-blink; it fell dead. Belladonna whistled for her domestic, who came running, and she ordered him to put the animal in the barouche, in order to take it away as a trophy of my victory. Belladonna was excited by the scene that had just unfolded; she squeezed my hand and kissed me. That was the first time, and for the first time, I reciprocated. The kisses were those of gratitude and the purest amity.

"You see," I said to Belladonna, "that my precaution was not futile."

"No," she said, "I probably owe it to you that I was not disfigured by that vile animal."

The next day I did not want her to get down from the barouche. I went on my own to the place where I had killed the kangaroo. Then I went a little further on, where I saw some enormous fruits similar to pumpkins. I was examining those products when I noticed that they were moving. What could be causing that movement?

In accordance with my habit of seeking the causes of effects, I wanted to know. I took out my stiletto and struck the fruit with it, making an opening, from which a thick smoke emerged. I kicked it forcefully with my foot, and it split; a hideous animal came out of it, which fixed sparkling eyes upon me and opened a menacing maw. I was still holding my stiletto, and I struck at it so effectively that black blood escaped from the wound, and soon afterwards it died in convulsions.

I put off until the next day visiting other products. I went back to Belladonna, to whom I made a tribute of the new trophy. She was frightened by the sight of the hideous animal, and told me that she did not want me to expose myself to danger again, or else she would accompany me.

Even so, I went back the following day, and she remained in the barouche. I went to the same place and cut into another fruit, from which emerged, in the mist of blue-tinted smoke, a multitude of butterflies, with variegated wings in the most beautiful colors.

A burst of laugher that I heard behind me caused me to turn me head, and I saw Belladonna, followed by her domestic, armed with a stout staff.

"Luckily," she said to me, "today's hunt is more agreeable and less dangerous that yesterday's."

That adventure amused Belladonna and made her want to attempt another. The following day we returned to the same place, but I went alone to the location of the big fruits. I noticed one of them whose form was different from the others and I thought that it might contain different things. Its shape was an elongated cube, the top of which was slightly curved. With my stiletto I traced two fairly deep lines in a cross on the top, extended slightly along the sides.

Immediately, the surface of the fruits split into flaps of a sort, which rose up about a meter and a half, and formed a kind of aviary filled with birds, resembling canaries, warblers,

linnets, nightingales, colingas with rich plumage and hum-
mingbirds, the smallest and prettiest of all birds, with found
themselves enclosed in that improvised cage.

I heard a cry of joy, and saw Belladonna a few paces
away, marveling at what she saw. Her domestic was following
her at a distance, still armed with his staff, in order to help me
in case of need. I offered my new conquest to Belladonna,
who accepted it with great pleasure. Aided by the domestic, I
carried the aviary to the barouche, and we left.

Belladonna was ravishingly beautiful; the pleasure that
she experienced gave her a new shine. The evening was cheerful, and we planned to return to the same place, but I begged
Belladonna not to come, because it was not certain that we
would have butterflies or birds to deal with.

"Nevertheless," she said, "I'll go, and if there's danger,
I'll share it with you."

It was necessary for me to consent, and the following
morning, we set forth as usual. I got down alone and advised
Belladonna to stay in the barouche, telling the domestic not to
leave her for a moment.

I went further than usual in the area where the fruits
were. I soon found myself between two banks, in the middle
of which, at the bottom, a little stream was running, which
gave the plants bordering it a prodigious exuberance of vegetation. Among the plants I discovered a few large fruits like
those I have already mentioned. One of them attracted my
attention by virtue of its enormous size. I approached it and
examined it attentively; its color was a very pale yellowish
green, but its stalk was surrounded by a beautiful black areola.

I experienced something singular as I contemplated that
extraordinary vegetable. Finally, I wanted to know what it
contained. I made a circular cut with my stiletto around the
areola, which made it into a kind of lid, which separated noisi-
ly from the spherical body of the vegetable and the opening.
First of all the head of a man emerged, and then the entire
body, which was very tall. Then he said to me:

"Who permitted you to trouble my repose and destroy the dwelling I had chosen? Have I done you any harm? Why did you do that to me?"

"Sire," I replied, utterly nonplussed, "My intention was not to do you any harm, but to learn all the knowledge that I might be able to acquire in these spaces."

"I know what the motive is for your voyage in the imaginary spaces; if it were to do harm I would already have pulverized you. Zadir, whose friend I am, as well as that of Za and Zico, give you the best of recommendations. You can, therefore, count on my good offices in case of need. My name is Dizzaca."

With those words, he disappeared. For my part, I was about to rejoin Belladonna in the barouche when I met her, coming to look for me, tormented as she was by my long absence.

I reflected during the night on the day's events, and thought it might be prudent to abstain from all curiosity, and especially of seeking to delve into extraordinary things, for that curiosity, although innocent in itself, since it had no other motive than my instruction, was nevertheless indiscreet and blameworthy, as had been seen. To avoid any recidivism that might be unpardonable, I judged it necessary and prudent to leave the Isle of Prodigies.

Having made that decision I summoned Zico and told him that I wanted to visit the Isle of Marvels.

"That's easy," he said. "When do you want to leave?"

"Whenever you like."

"Then we'll leave tomorrow morning before sunrise, in order that you can enjoy the admirable effect that its rise produces over the old capital of the island, which is called Mirabilis.

V

The next day, my sylph and his sister having transported me to within sight of the Isle of Marvels, Zico said to me:

250

"Look at Mirabilis, the marvelous city with which no other in the entire world can be comparable."

I looked, and thought once again that I was the victim of an illusion; I could not believe my eyes. I rubbed them in vain; it was not an illusion; what I was seeing really was real. My astonishment as I saw, and was able to contemplate, that vast and beautiful city is comprehensible; instead of being built on the ground, all of its houses, all of its monuments and all of its edifices were suspended in mid air, sustained and supported by an atmosphere that was probably particular to them.

All those constructions formed streets or surrounded squares, but that surprising city was subject to considerable movements caused by the wind, which often changed the location of constructions and made Mirabilis, in consequence, a city that was always new.

Zico set me down at the gate of that marvelous city. I went into it with the intention of exploring it and getting to know its inhabitants; the men were handsome ad well-built; the women were marvelously beautiful, as much for their facial features as for the perfection of their bodily figures, which attained excellence in the majority.

I was marveling at everything I saw and so absorbed in my contemplation and my thoughts that I did not notice the effect that I was having on the inhabitants, some of whom were following me while others were observing me curiously.

I arrived in a place in the city where I saw several benches placed in front of the entrance to a house. I sat down on one of them, because I was tired, and a few minutes later an exceedingly pretty woman came to invite me to go into her house. At that invitation, made so cordially, I got up and followed her.

She took me into a room where I saw a large table covered with different foodstuffs that were unfamiliar to me, but which simultaneously flattered sight, the sense of smell and the stomach. Benches were placed around the table and several people were already sitting there. The lady of the house offered me her hand and led me to the top of the table, where she sat me down beside her, which I did with pleasure. Immediately, she covered my plate with morsels of food, which I ate with a hearty appetite, because they were good and I was hungry.

The lady seemed benevolent and showed considerable interest in me. She asked me who I was, where I came from and what was the motive for my voyage to their country, where no man like me had ever been seen before. I answered all her questions; she seemed amazed by my replies.

The astonishment they caused her was noticed by the other guests, who did not take long to enquire as to the cause of her astonishment, and it was supposable that I would soon be known throughout the city—a supposition that was promptly verified. The news of the presence of an extraordinary man in Mirabilis reached the governor, who came to see me and invited me to be his guest, which invitation I accepted.

I thanked the lady who had given me hospitality and went with the governor, who took me to his palace, where I was splendidly lodged and served perfectly, with regard to my meals and everything else that I needed.

On the first day the governor invited me to dine with him, but before dinner he introduced me to his wife, who welcomed me graciously. She was in a sumptuously decorated drawing room, sitting on a sofa of which she occupied one end; she was marvelously beautiful. All the ladies who were sitting with her did not cede anything to her in that regard. I bowed respectfully, to which she responded with a nod of her head, and offered me her hand.

The governor then took me into a large hall, where several seats were arranged in a circle in the middle. The ladies I had seen in the drawing room came into the hall, preceded by the governor's wife, and took their places in the circle of seats. At a sign from the governor, a domestic blew into a stout pipe that passed through the floor, and the part around which the ladies were gathered sank, soon to be replaced by a table covered with the most appetizing dishes. Then the governor's wife drew her chair closer to the table that had risen up through the opening in the floor; everyone else followed her example.

The carver fulfilled his function, and when everyone had eaten, the table sank down and was almost immediately replaced by another, laden with the dessert. Then everyone returned to the drawing room, where some of the ladies sang, in a delightful manner. Then we went for a stroll in the gardens, which were admirable. The evening was very beautiful, although the air was slightly agitated, and finally, as the wind increased, everyone went back indoors.

Toward the middle of the night, however, a storm broke out; we were tossed around in the palace as if we had been on a ship at sea, rolling and pitching. There were gusts of wind that caused considerable damage in the palace, and caused almost all its residents to pass a sleepless night, because beds were thrown in various directions, and items of furniture followed the same movement. There was an upheaval, and general turmoil.

The next morning, I went out in order to go and see the hospitable lady, but I could no longer find her house; all of them had changed places. I no longer recognized the streets along which I had passed the day before, new streets having been formed by the upsets of the night. However, I was not tempted to explore that new city, because I feared that if I got lost in the labyrinth I might not be able to find my way back to the governor's palace. That is why I retraced my steps and succeeded, although not without difficulty, in finding it again.

I saw the governor, who was coming back after going to see the King, in order to give him an account of all the changes occasioned in the city by the hurricane, and to receive his orders. He had spoken to him about me, and had depicted me as a man endowed with extraordinary knowledge.

"I would be very glad to see this man," the King had said to him. "He might be able to indicate to us means of repairing, if not everything, at least a part of the disasters and upheavals that occurred last night. Tell him that I desire to see him, and bring him to me."

"You Majesty will be obeyed. When does he want me to have the honor of introducing this stranger to him?"

"As soon as possible and without ceremony; I desire to judge in advance my fashion of introducing myself to him."

The governor asked me if I was ready to yield to the King's desire.

"Your expression is very just, for a King's desire is an order, a summons. I can't refuse, and we'll leave whenever it pleases Your Excellency."

"That's good," he said. "We'll have lunch and then set off."

We ate, and immediately afterwards we went to see the King, who gave me a very generous welcome. Then he asked me a great many questions about matters concerning me personally, about my homeland, and, principally, the knowledge I had acquired—which occasioned his astonishment, manifested by exclamations of enthusiasm. Then he spoke to me about the night's events, the disturbance of his capital, which had been so beautiful and had now lost its beauty in the confusion—a misfortune that caused him a great deal of chagrin.

"Your Majesty can be reassured," I told him. "The evil is not without remedy."

"What!" said the King, excitedly. "You believe that the damage is not irreparable?"

"I do believe that, Sire, and if Your Majesty will give me the means, I hope to be able to return his capital to him, not merely as beautiful, but more beautiful than it was before."

"More beautiful!" cried the King, at the peak of astonishment. "You have the power to do that, my friend?"

"Yes, Sire; but my power is nothing but the intelligence and the experience I have acquired by my studies, my observations and my imagination."

The King appeared to be enchanted; his handsome features expressed the happiness that he was experiencing internally. He took my hands, shook them, and lavished the most affectionate names and expressions upon me.

"But how will you achieve this miracle, my friend?" he asked me.

"There will be no miracle, Sire, for the power to work miracles is the attribute of the Divinity. I shall only employ my intelligence, which I owe to God and to profound studies. I shall begin by drawing a plan of the new Mirabilis, which I shall submit to Your Majesty's examination. If he accepts it, then I shall put my best foot forward to carry it out. To accomplish that task, Your Majesty must put at my disposal the men who will be necessary to the operation, such as carpenters, locksmiths, blacksmiths, rope-makers and ditch-diggers—in sum, all the workmen I need—with the injunction of obey my orders."

"That is just and indispensable," the King said, "and I beg you to accept the title of Director General of Works in Mirabilis."

"I accept it, Sire, because I hope to merit it to your entire satisfaction."

"I don't doubt it, my good friend. You've rendered me very happy, and as I want everyone to know the high esteem in which I hold you, and the amity that you have inspired in me, come to dinner with me today."

I accepted his invitation; I was announced by the usher under the title that the King had given me, which surprised all the people who were present. The King received me with distinction and introduced me to the Queen, who gave me the most gracious welcome. All eyes were fixed upon me. Even the governor, who was present, seemed astonished by the great favor that I enjoyed with the King, because he did not know the reason for it. At dessert, however, the King addressed his guests and made the following speech:

"Sires, the extraordinary man that you know by the title of Director General of Works in Mirabilis seems to us to have been sent by the heavens in order to repair the upheavals that occurred last night in our beautiful city. I therefore call upon your collaboration to procure him everything that he will need

255

to cry out this vast and useful enterprise, which is for the good and the wellbeing of all."

The dignitaries stood up and held out their hands as a sign of acquiescence. After dinner they came to congratulate me, shake my hand and offer me their services and their amity.

The next day I made the plan of the new Mirabilis, which I went to present to the King the day after. I left it with him so that he could examine it at his leisure. I had made a duplicate of the plan, which I kept for myself. I was busy studying it when the governor came to see me, in the apartment that I occupied in his palace.

"My friend," he said to me, "the King has asked to tell you that he is impatient to see you to give him an explanation of the plan you handed to him, which he does not understand very well. He desires to know the significance of all the lines you have traced."

"Excellency, I am under the King's orders, and we shall go to see him whenever you think it appropriate."

"The let's go right away. The King will dine more cheerfully, and will be glad to understand your projects, which interest him so keenly."

We immediately went to the King's residence. He seemed delighted to see me. He took me into his study, where I saw the plan that I had drawn displayed on his table.

"I thank you," the King said, "for having come to my aid; for without you, it would have been impossible for me to understand what all these lines signify."

"Your Majesty will understand it very soon. I beg him to follow me in the explanation that I shall have the honor of giving him. The circle that you see in the center of these lines is the location where Your Majesty's palace will be; the double circle represents the space left free between the palace and the city. All the lines that end at the circle that surrounds the palace are the streets of the city; the small circles in the lines of the streets are for squares or for monuments that Your Majesty might like to erect there. In accordance with his plan,

256

Your Majesty will be able, without leaving his palace, to see all the principal streets of the city."

"Oh, what an excellent idea you have had, my friend! Will you consent to my showing your plan to my engineers? I believe that kind of deference will dispose them to assist you in all your operations, and I think their collaboration will be useful to you, in furnishing you with all that you will need to carry out your great and noble design."

"Your Majesty thinks wisely, for there will be no offended self-esteem, and I gladly renounce the title of author of the project in order to avoid any species of jealousy. The most difficult thing now if the execution of the gigantic project; that is my concern, but the cooperation of engineers will be very useful to me and accelerate my execution, in that they will furnish me, more easily than I could achieve, with all the necessary and indispensable things that I have already listed for Your Majesty; they can procure me the carpenters, smiths, rope-makers and ditch-diggers they know, and I can have the machines that I need for the execution built by those artisans. When the operation is finished, I plan to make all the houses safe from a further upheaval."

"What?" said the King. "You can neutralize the terrible effects of the wind, and storms?"

"Yes, Sire."

"But, my friend, you are acquiring new rights to my gratitude every day."

"You do not owe me any, Sire; I am acquitting, as best I can, the generosity that Your Majesty has shown to me, and which I hope to retain."

"It is acquired in advance; you have my royal word on that."

The King summoned the engineers to a room in the palace, and presented my plan to them. They thought it perfect, but did not understand the means of execution. Then the King proposed to put them in communication with me, which they accepted unanimously and promptly. The King arranged our meeting for the following day, in the hall of public sessions, in order that no one would be unaware that I was the author of the plan and the project of execution. I thus found myself at that session, presided over by the king, the next day.

The hall was filled with the notable people of the city; the engineers were gathered around the King. When I entered the hall they came to meet me, and we went to the King together. He was seated at a table on which my plan was displayed. After having examined it, the engineers complimented me, but they did not understand the means that I would employ in its execution.

"It is for that execution, Gentlemen," I replied, "that I need your cooperation, to give me the workers that I need to construct the machines whose designs I shall supply to them, and of which, if necessary, I shall make a small model. When all the machines are ready, I shall indicate their employment to each of you, and in a matter of days, Mirabilis will be rebuilt on unshakeable bases."

Unanimous applause greeted my last words.

The next day, the engineers brought me the artisans that I needed to build my machines and carry out other tasks. From the carpenters I ordered horizontal and vertical capstans, all with their hand-spikes. From the blacksmiths I ordered large iron rings and pitons, hooks of different shapes and strong chains of different lengths. From the rope-makers I ordered ropes and cords, from the mechanics, jacks.

I explained to all the artisans, not only in words but also by drawings and small models in wood and clay, all the machines that I needed, and gave them the dimensions that they had to have. I supervised their work, and four days afterwards, I was able to bring together the large fraction of my machinery. Only the mechanics did not succeed, but I had the means of substituting for the jacks by means of a scaffold that I set up, pulleys that I had attached to it, ropes, capstans and levers.

On the sixth day I assembled the engineers to trace the double circle for the placement of the royal palace, and the points at which all the city streets were to terminate. That work was completed in a day.

On the seventh day, all the artisans succeeded in bring the machines that I had ordered into the double circle, and I had them placed at the locations they were to occupy, facing and by the sides of the palace.

On the eighth day, I asked the engineers to furnish me with two hundred men and fifty horses.

On the ninth day, everything I needed was ready. I went to inform the king, and told him that my operation would commence the following morning. The King, intoxicated by joy, shook my hands and embraced me, lavishing the most flattering and affectionate expressions upon me.

On the morning of the tenth day, an unusual stir reigned all over the city; the news that I had conveyed to the King was soon known to all the inhabitants, whose joy reached a peak. They were all mounted on their houses—if I might be forgiven the wordplay—impatient to enjoy the success of my operations.

It was a curious spectacle to see all those houses, covered by their inhabitants, who were manifesting their joy with animated gestures, songs and the sounds of various musical instruments; it was a general joy caused by the imminent re-edification of their city, once so lovely, which they would soon see more beautiful still, by virtue of its regularity. Soon, the labyrinth would disappear; chaos would give way to a new creation.

I was at the palace at the hour that I had indicated; I saw the engineers arrive; we shook hands. We were all in perfect accord, all animated by the finest spirit; they were all ready to carry out my orders. We went into the enclosure traced by the double circle, where I had had the artisans place my machines. I explained the properties of each one to the engineers. I had the iron rings attached to the facades and the sides of the palace. I put ten men in service at each capstan, explaining to them the use of the hand-spikes, and five men at each of the iron rings on the façade and sides of the palace; the horses were placed behind the capstans, in order to have them all to hand in case of need.

Everything was ready, and I sent one of the engineers to inform the King that I was about to commence my operation.

The King appeared on his balcony with the Queen, and we saluted them with cries of "Long live the King!" and "Long live the Queen!" They waved their hands.

Then I shouted, loudly: "Pay attention!" I checked that everyone was at his post and shouted to the engineer I had placed at the capstans: "Start up the facing capstans!"

The palace advanced majestically as far as the line, and I shouted: "Halt!"

The same maneuver was carried out at the sides of the palace, which was positioned regularly on the base that I had had the diggers and the masons prepare for it.

The King and the Queen seemed very emotional, and testified to their joy and happiness with the salutes and hand-kisses that they sent to us. The same testimonies and acclamations came to us from the ladies and the dignitaries who were occupying all the windows of the palace. But my work was not finished; it still remained for me to anchor the palace to the position that it now occupied. Everything was prepared for that operation. I had chains fixed to the iron rings that I had attached to the framework of the underside of the palace, and the other ends of the chains were sealed in massive blocks of stone that I had prepared. The masons and the blacksmiths did their work, and the palace was secured against the blasts of the wind.

The engineers and I then occupied ourselves with the task of future days, with would consist of organizing the streets of the city. That was now the engineers' affair; they had my plan and the machines that I had set up, and they could operate them as they had seen me do for the palace. However, I did not abandon my post as Director General, and on the eleventh day I was one of the first there; I intended the most beautiful houses to be placed on the circle, facing the palace or at the ends of the city streets, and the other house to be relegated to more distant positions. The important thing, for the moment, was to clear the quarter neighboring the palace, in order to be able to begin tracing out the streets.

After having given my orders, I went to visit the governor. As soon as I came in he said: "You've arrived at a good time. Here is a package that King instructed me to hand to you personally. I'm glad for you, for it must be something very important. Read the message, and you'll be as impatient as I am to know what it contains.

I opened the package, which contained two documents. One was a handwritten letter from the King, which complimented me on the success of my operations and expressed his satisfaction with them; the other was a kind of parchment, at the head of which was written:

Title of nobility and property given by us, Mirabilo Premiero, King of the Isle of Marvels, to out Director General of Works in Mirabilis, whom we name Duke of Maraviglia and owner of the land that we establish as his Duchy.

Made at our palace in Mirabilis, on the, etc.

The governor congratulated me on my success and I left him in order to go to my post. I saw with pleasure that all my orders were being executed perfectly, and testified my satisfaction to the engineers, whose zeal was augmented to such a degree that, on that same day, everything was ready for the streets to be traced, along with the squares, public gardens, fountains, columns and so on.

On the twelfth day, the tracing of the streets, squares and gardens was executed, and the thirteenth, fourteenth and fifteenth days were employed in placing the houses along the lines.

The sixteenth, seventeenth, eighteenth and nineteenth days were employed in preparing and surrounding with temporary wooden fences the public gardens, squares and areas that were to be occupied by the fountains.

I went to see the King to tell him that we were approaching the end of the essential work, and that His Majesty could visit the new city the following day if he so desired.

"It's my most ardent desire," the King said to me. "I'll go to admire your work tomorrow."

"However, Sire, it's not yet perfected; the essential work is done, but I'll need a few more days to complete the embellishment of Mirabilis. I shall have the honor of acquainting Your Majesty with all the ornaments with which I have the intention of decorating his capital."

"In that regard, my good friend, as in everything that I judge you capable of doing, I leave you complete liberty."

"Thank you, Sire. Your Majesty will be satisfied."

"The following day, the twentieth, the King and the Queen, carried in a litter by two horses, came to visit the new Mirabilis, which they entered by the Royal Road that terminated in front of the royal palace. Their Majesties were followed by a numerous cavalcade composed of dignitaries and the King's guards. Their Majesties were received by the inhabitants with shouts of "Long live the King!" and "Long live the Queen!" The long Royal Road resounded with the acclamations of the multitude.

Their Majesties seemed happy and manifested their joy by means of gracious salutes, which they addressed to the people, to the engineers, to the artisans and to the laborers, among which cries of "Long live the Director General!" were uttered. When Their Majesties arrived at the locations destined for the gardens, squares, fountains, etc., they could not dissimulate their joy and admiration in imagining what they would look like when they were finished.

The King and the Queen, wanting to testify their satisfaction with my endeavors immediately, summoned me; I was not far away, for I was desirous of judging for myself the effect that the execution of my plan produced on Their Majesties. I was easily found and I went to them.

On seeing me, the King said: "Come my good friend, come and enjoy the pleasure that you are procuring us by the admirable success of your operations. Come to dine with us today, and explain to us your intentions for the perfection and embellishment of the locations that you have prepared.

At dinner time I went to the royal palace. The usher announced me, presumably in accordance with the King's order, under the title of "His Lordship, the Duke of Maraviglia, Director General of Works in Mirabilis." Those titles did not appear to cause any surprise to the people present, because they had been witnesses to the success of my operations and shared the general enthusiasm.

After dinner, I made the King and Queen party to the embellishments that I intended to execute on the plans that I had prepared, and on which I would established gardens, squares and fountains, explaining that the wooden fences, being only temporary, would be replaced by others in iron; that I was about to occupy myself with the ornaments and designs, and that everything would be finished in eight or ten days.

The King and Queen were delighted, and manifested their happiness in their gazes and affectionate words.

The next day, I designed my fountains and their ornaments, which I had already composed, as well as those of the fences.

On the twenty-second day I had the gardens and squares traced out, in the middle of which I traced the plans for the fountains.

I charged an engineer with having the stone carved for the fountains in accordance with the drawings and sections that I gave him, and also for the bases that were to support the iron railings. I indicated the places where the gates were to be placed, and provided the design of the railings, each of which would be surmounted by a gilded spike; the metal was not very rare on the Isle of Marvels, but its use in gilding was unknown. I instructed artisans in gold-beating and the technique of applying it to the objects to be gilded. The engineers seconded me so well that a week later, the fountains were constructed and the railings placed.

I had the gardens and squares dug, and the paths traced in accordance with the designs that I gave the engineers, whose zeal and activity rivaled that of the artisans and laborers.

On the twenty-third day, I had the trees, ornamental bushes and clumps of flowers brought; they were planted in the placed I had marked, while the gilders applied their gold leaf to the spikes of the railings. I had had two large temporary reservoirs set up near the fountains, and had them filled with water, in order that they would be able to flow at the moment when the King and Queen came to visit my works the following day. Then I went to see the King in order to announce to him that my works were concluded and that Their Majesties would do me the greatest honor by visiting them.

"We cannot render you too much honor, my dear Duke. Come to lunch with us tomorrow, and then we shall go to admire your new works."

After that lunch, I went in all haste to the square that I had completed in order to make sure that everything was in order for the arrival of the august visitors. Everything was as I had instructed. I placed a man next to each reservoir with orders to open the taps when the King and Queen arrived. Everyone was at his post, and I waited impatiently for the royal cortege.

Soon, the acclamations of the multitude announced it, and I saw Their Majesties' litter coming into the square. They made a tour of it. I was in the garden, near one of the gates, from where I was able to judge the effect that my work produced on the King and Queen. They seemed surprised, astonished and wonderstruck by all that they saw.

The King perceived me, stopped his litter and beckoned to me. I opened the gate near which I was standing and approached Their Majesties.

"Enjoy your work, my good friend," said the King. "You are making our tears flow, but they are tears of joy and happiness. I am too emotional to express to you all that I am experiencing; I will do that later; give me the pleasure for the moment, of accepting this slight testimony of my gratitude and the title of Excellency, Minister of Public Works."

With those words, he detached his gold chain, which he placed around my neck, and the Queen offered me her hand to kiss.

At that moment, applause burst forth from all the windows of the beautiful houses with which I had had the square surrounded. Women waved their handkerchiefs and the men cried: "Long live the King! Long live the Queen!"

"You hear that," said the King. "*Vox populi*. They are sharing all the happiness that you have given us."

I could not find words to reply to the King; the emotion I was experiencing had taken away the faculty of speech. The King perceived that and held out his hand; a silence followed, and the King and Queen invited me to dine with them.

At that royal banquet, I found a gathering of all the high dignitaries of the State, of which I was now a part. All those gentlemen gave me a very gracious welcome. Was it sincere or was it simulated? That did not worry me very much. I possessed the amity of the King; that was all I desired.

The next day, I went to visit the King, who received me with open arms.

"I'm delighted to see you, my good friend, for I have to renew my thanks for the happiness I'm achieving. I've never been as happy as I am now; that's why I have the intention of establishing an annual celebration of the re-edification of Mirabilis."

"To that effect, Sire, I also have another project."

"What is it, my friend? It must be good."

"It would be, Sire to erect a column in the square at the end of the Royal Road; it would be an agreeable viewpoint, and a beautiful perspective, seen from the royal palace, of the long convergent lines."

"Your idea is superb, my friend."

"But sire, the column would be a rather long endeavor, because of the ornaments with which I want to decorate it, the principal one of which can perhaps only be sculpted by me. It would eternalize Your Majesty's reign, and the epoch of the re-edification of Mirabilis, which its inhabitants, and those of the Isle of Marvels, owe to you."

"And also to you, my dear friend," said the King, swiftly. "But tell me, my friend, what will be the ornaments of this column? Excuse my curiosity, but I can't resist."

"The shaft of the column will be placed on a pedestal whose four sides will be ornamented with sculptures related to the subject, and the summit of the column will be crowned with a statue of Your Majesty."

"What!" said the King, trembling with emotion. "We can accomplish such a fine project?"

"Yes, Sire, and tomorrow I hope to be able to give you designs of the column and its ornaments. If our Majesty approves of them, I shall have the stones carved, as well as the cladding of white marble, which I shall sculpt. For the statue of Your Majesty, I shall have a block of white marble taken from a quarry, which I shall also sculpt myself, and I shall execute that work in Maraviglia, because it will not be seen by anyone before being placed on the column. Your Majesty alone shall see it in my studio; he will be able to judge better than anyone else the difference that exists when it is put in the place that it is to occupy. When I have deposited by block of marble, Your Majesty might be kind enough to come to Maraviglia to grant me the sittings that I shall need to make his resemblance—or, in order not to disturb him, I shall model the head in Mirabilis in clay, which I shall copy in the marble."

"I will do as you wish, my good friend; dispose of me in complete liberty."

"Thank you, Sire, for this final work will complete the beauty of the splendid Mirabilis."

"Oh, my good friend, you will put the crown on my happiness!"

The King shook my hands, and tears of joy inundated his noble face.

Shortly afterwards, I took my leave of His Majesty in order to go and sketch my column, so that I would be able to present a final version to him the following day. My project was so well imprinted in my imagination that it was terminated the following morning. I went to take it to the King, who thought it marvelous, and asked the Queen to come to his study in order to show it to her. The Queen was delighted on examining my project, which she thought admirable. I took my leave of Their Majesties, and announced to the King that I would leave the following day for Maraviglia in order to prepare all the marbles of which I had need.

VI

I therefore left for Maraviglia the following day, with three domestics. It was a charming property, which was unfamiliar to me, but of which I took possession with great pleasure.

The building comprised a principal residential block, with two wings in the form of pavilions. Behind were the supplementary buildings: garage, stables, poultry-yard, etc. I was astonished to see that these constructions were not sustained by the air, like those in Mirabilis, and was content with that—but that contentment did not last long.

The next morning, when I woke up, I went to open the window of my room, and I saw that all the buildings had risen into the air to a height of ten or twelve feet, which annoyed me a great deal. A short time afterwards, however, I noticed that they were drawing closer to the ground. That observation caused me to reflect, and I thought that the Sun, which illuminated and warmed the underside of the islands, must produce vapors that elevated the houses, and that when those vapors expanded in the air, the houses descended toward the ground again.

I had remarked from my window a hillock that I wanted to visit. Desiring to get to know my property, I descended to the ground and set forth into my terrain. I arrived at the foot of the hillock, which I climbed. It was covered in ash and bituminous volcanic material, lava, pumice stone, etc.

I arrived at the summit of the hillock; the ground was dry and hard; it seemed to me that I could hear it resonating beneath my feet. I stamped my foot hard, and there was a frightful cracking sound; that was the dry cap of the hillock splitting, cracks running in all directions. The crust gave way at the place where I was standing and I fell into the precipice that it was covering.

My fall was not rapid; it seemed to me that I was sustained by an invisible force. A voice said to me: "Have no fear; I'm watching over you."

It was the voice of my sylphide, Zica.

I descended thus to the bottom of the precipice, where I was greeted by my sylph, Zico, who said to me: "You've fallen here into the midst of our enemies, the gnomes, who want to dispute with us the treasures that this precipice contains, and which belong to us. Look at everything and have no fear. Your good genius Za has confided you to my protection and has given me the power to defend you—power and orders that he has received from Zadir, the chief of us all. So, act without any dread."

Then I got up from the stone on which I was sitting in order to explore the subterrain, where I received no other light that what reached me through the hole into which I had fallen. That light was very faint and diminished as I advanced into the subterrain. Eventually, it suddenly disappeared. I found myself in obscurity.

I was continuing to march when my eyes were struck by a dazzling light coming from a large fissure. I was approaching it in order to go into it when the passage was disputed by a monstrous animal. It was an enormous dragon, whose eyes were like two carbuncles, and whose frightful mouth was vomiting flames.

I was trying to continue going forward when the furious animal launched itself upon me to devour me; even more promptly, however, I drew my stiletto and drove it forcefully into its skull. It collapsed, uttering a long roar, which, repeated by all the echoes of the subterrain, resembled a rumble of thunder. It deployed the long coils of its tail, which was terminated by two darts, in order to pierce me, but the blow that I had struck was mortal; it fell in convulsions, executing frightful somersaults, but I was still on my guard.

Finally, exhausted by that terrible agony, it died, vomiting thick black blood with a fetid odor, which spread through the subterrain.

Meanwhile, I entered resolutely into the grotto that had suddenly illuminated with bright light. I was dazzled by the glare of the radiance that was departing from all the sides of the grotto, which was filled with precious stones and numerous vases in gold or silver, of incalculable value.

I summoned Zico, who arrived immediately, and said to me, in a soft voice: "I congratulate you on your victory, and you've now become the richest man in the universe."

"No," I replied, "this treasure belongs to the corps of good genii, and I'm glad to be able to return it to its legitimate owners."

"Very good, my friend. Za and Zadir will be informed of your brave and noble conduct."

With those words, he left me, but a short while afterwards I received a visit from Zica, who appeared to me as she had done on the Isle of Fictions.

"I've been sent to you by my brother," she said, "in order to get you out of this precipice, so that you can return home and devote yourself to your affairs."

She remained with me for some time, and in spite of the pleasure that her presence gave me, I was unable to resist an imperious need for sleep, which she had doubtless provoked— for when I awoke, I found myself transported on to the hillock, from which I perceived my house. I immediately returned to it, and was astonished to see it decorated with a staircase in order to go up and down when the house was sustained and supported in mid-air.

My domestics had been worried by my long absence, and had searched for me in vain; they testified their joy on seeing me again.

I went up to my apartment, and was very surprised to find it richly decorated and filled with magnificent furniture of a refined taste. I understood that my good genius Za was the author of the metamorphosis, and was glad.

I then started work on the Column of Mirabilis. I summoned the owners of marble quarries from the small town of which I was the seigneur, and they furnished me with the marbles I needed. I designated the most suitable of the outbuildings to be converted into a studio. Fortunately, those buildings remained on the ground and were not, like the others, lifted up into the air during the night. That made it much easier for the miners to bring in the marbles and stones that I needed in order to sculpt them. Afterwards, I sent for a locksmith, to make me tools of which I provided him with models, and a carpenter to build me a scaffold, a step-ladder, a stool and a pedestal.

While waiting for all these things to be brought, I visited my habitation in detail, inside and out, examining it minutely and very attentively. I especially admired the exquisite taste of the ornaments and the beauty of the furniture in my apartment. I sat down in an exceedingly beautiful armchair, the soft cushions of which, along with the silence and the feeling of well-being I was experiencing made me drowsy, and I eventually fell asleep.

I dreamed that I was in the grotto in the precipice, and, although profoundly asleep, I sensed that my eyes were struck by the glare of the radiance emitted by all the precious stones that it contained. All those stones were, however, in the state of cabochons—which is to say, polished—so why were they gleaming as if they had been cut into facets? The eyes would have been unable to sustain it for long without being wounded. It was a very seductive sight, but I did not regret the sacrifice I had made. On the contrary, I was glad to have done my duty. I slept peacefully, like a just man whose conscience is pure.

When I awoke, I experienced the pleasure of contemplating my apartment. Were all those furnishings, so beautiful, really mine? I noticed, for the first time, that the keys were in the doors and drawers of each item of furniture. The desire gripped me to see inside. I began with the one that was closest to me; it was a beautiful writing-desk. I opened it and saw a set of drawers to either side, all garnished with golden rods; the handle of each drawer was formed by a large diamond cut into facets. The square section between the two sets of drawers was occupied by a box of precious wood incrusted with arabesques in gold thread, which had emeralds for leaves ad diamonds rubies, topazes, amethysts and aquamarines for flowers. I opened the drawers first, and was surprised to see that they were filled with gold coins, with were stamped with my head seen in profile, with the legend: *Russo, Duce Maraviglia et civita bellina*, and, for a exergue: *Mirabilis annus MVIIILX.*

Then I opened a chest of drawers; I pulled out the drawers. The top drawer was filed with precious gems, and the other three with silver coins bearing the same date *MVIIILX.*

Then I opened the cupboards; the upper shelves were garnished with linen of the highest quality, in shirts, sheets, etc. The bottom of each cupboard was filled with boxes containing silver coins of various values, struck with the same image, the same legend and the same date as the gold coins. The undersides of the wardrobes were occupied by boxes containing small change.

Then I opened two larger cupboards or wardrobes, furnished with a considerable number of garments, as many for my everyday use as for social occasions; the latter were ornamented with rich embroideries and with court mantles, which were of great magnificence. In a richly ornamented box I found my ducal crown.

A few days later I received my marbles, which I had deposited in my workplace. I charged the men with bringing me, as soon as possible, potter's clay or marl, in quantities that I indicated, and to be careful to wrap it up in large damp cloths.

While I was waiting for the clay, I bought two horses and a litter.

I went to visit Civita Bellina, of which I was the seigneur, and had the satisfaction of being given a very good welcome by the inhabitants.

When I returned to Maraviglia, I saw with pleasure that the miners had brought the clay, and the next morning, I left for Mirabilis with two of my domestics. I stayed with the governor, who received me as a friend. I occupied the same apartment, and asked him for a ground floor room in his palace, which I needed for a work of sculpture and in which I could receive the King, who would sometimes come to visit me there.

"You know, my friend," he said, "that my palace is at your disposal. Choose the room that suits you."

I visited the palace, and chose a room appropriate to my work.

I sent for one of the engineers, whom I charged with making me a step-ladder, a pedestal and a stool. He promised them to me for the next day. Then I went to visit the King, who received me as usual, with the same generosity. I told His Majesty that everything was ready for the commencement of his statue, the head of which I would make in Mirabilis, although it would be better, for the body of the statue, to model it in the studio I had established in Maraviglia.

"Very well, my good friend; I shall come to your residence, and for me it will be a pleasure trip."

"And for me, Sire a day of joy."

The head was modeled the same day, but I asked the King to give me a second sitting the following day in order to apply the finishing touches. The King consented with pleasure. The next day, the head was finished, and the King decided that he would come to Maraviglia a week later.

"But Sire, if the sitting is prolonged, will Your Majesty deign to grant me the favor of accepting the hospitality of his humble subject's abode?"

"Say the abode of a friend," replied the King. "But my dear Duke, the hospitality of a friend's abode is too pleasant and too agreeable to be refused. I therefore accept your invitation with great pleasure."

Having no assistant, I was obliged to carve out my block of marble myself and to sketch the head in accordance with the clay model that I had made of it. That work, although laborious, was completed in six days; on the seventh, I rested and went to stroll by a small lake that I had on my property.

The atmosphere was warm; the limpidity of the water gave me a desire to bathe in it. I took off my clothes and jumped into the beautiful lake, surrounded by trees and bushes that were reflected on the surface of its waters. I was swimming back and forth in all directions when I encountered a whirlpool that I had noticed from the bank and had been imprudent enough not to avoid.

The rule in such circumstances is to go with the movement until one is two or three feet below the surface and then, with a mariner's kick, to cleave through the whirlpool and emerge from it. I neglected that movement and was drawn into a subterranean tunnel where, very fortunately, I collided with a rock on to whose cracks I was able to cling. I climbed swiftly up its ledges, and was fortunate enough to arrive in a hole into which the air penetrated. I was just in time; that moment of respiration reanimated my strength. I succeeded in entering the hole, which broadened out as I went further; soon I was able to stand up.

I continued advancing, but instead of rising toward the surface of the earth, as I had hoped, I sensed that I was heading in the opposite direction. I was in profound darkness, when my eyes were dazzled by a bright light, toward which I headed, and I entered into a space where the bright glare of luminous rays blinded me and forced mine to close my eyes for a few moments.

I was in a crystal enclosure, through which sunlight penetrated. In fact, I was above the sun, and hence beneath the superior surface of the Isle of Marvels, from which I could perceive the recently discovered planets that I would visit later.

VII

I found myself in a very embarrassing situation inside my crystal rock. How could I get out? I could not climb up to swim through the subterranean channel because of its rapidity and the weakness I was experiencing because of lack of nourishment. I therefore had recourse to Zico, to whom I appealed, and almost immediately heard his soft voice, which nevertheless scolded me slightly for my imprudence.

An instant later, I found myself transported to the shore of the lake, where I found my clothes, which I put on. After having thanked Zico, I went home, where I put everything in order to receive the King, who was due to arrive the following day.

I sent to Civita Bellina to buy the provisions that we needed for the King's sojourn. Apartments were prepared to receive him and his entourage. My studio was carefully cleaned, and I had a beautiful armchair placed where the King would need to sit. Everything was ready for his reception.

The next day the King arrived, without an escort and only accompanied by three domestics. I went to meet him as he got down from his litter. He shook my hand affectionately, and I took him to the drawing room, which he examined attentively, seemingly marveling at the beauty of the ornaments, all the merit of which he attributed to me. He did not permit me to dissuade him; it was necessary for me, reluctantly, to remain silent.

The same day, the King gave me a sitting for the head, and I showed him a drawing of the statue, of which he approved.

The next day, I prepared the last phase of the marble head, which was concluded the day after.

The King departed for Mirabilis, and I promised him that the statue and the white marble plaques would be transported in a fortnight's time. I asked His Majesty to have the engineers set up a tent near the area that I had marked out for the column to occupy, in order to deposit therein all the objects that I was fabricating. He promised to do so.

Left alone, I carved out the body of the statue, prepared the ornaments for the cladding, and occupied myself with means of transporting all those objects. Those means were supplied by the kind inhabitants of Civita Bellina, who hastened to respond to my appeal, which was for the service of the King and my own.

On the designated day, twenty-five men arrived at Maraviglia, leading twelve horses and three sleighs, on to which they loaded the statue and the marble plaques, which I had covered with stout cloth.

The convoy set out for Mirabilis; I followed it in my litter, and everything arrived at its destination in perfect condition. The engineers had prepared the tent, in which the statues and the cladding were deposited, after which I went to visit the King, who welcomed me generously and invited me to stay for diner. He seemed delighted to learn that all the things I had made had arrived in Mirabilis intact and had been deposited in the tent, where no one would see them before the erection of the column. After dinner, I went to visit the governor, who informed me that my apartment had been prepared to receive me, and that he begged me to treat his home as if it were my own.

I spent a very good night, and the next day, I went to the placement of the column, where I found the engineers gathered, in accordance with the orders they had received from the governor. They all came to shake my hand and seemed to be pleased to see me again. I asked them to send me stone-carvers and masons as soon as possible to establish the stone block for the foundations of the column, the pedestal of which would rest on that block. I traced out the dimensions of the hole that they were to dig in order to establish solid foundations.

They were diligent, for when I arrived at the work site the following morning, I found all the workers occupied, each with his own concerns. I had the hole for the foundations dug out to a depth of about twenty feet; the stone-carvers worked ardently, and I lavished words of encouragement on them. The next day, the hole was dug and the masons were ready to commence the block. Then I gave the engineers the diameters of each rounded block for the shaft of the column, and the breadth of the stones for the square pedestal.

In sum, everything proceeded at such a rapid pace that, for days later, the pedestal could be placed on the foundations. Every evening, I reported to the governor on the progress of my work, perfectly understood and seconded by the engineers, the artisans and the laborers, and asked him to keep the King informed.

"I shall do so with pleasure, my friend, because it is just that the King testifies his satisfaction to them, in order that they will attribute it to the report that you have made, and they will assist you with greater ardor."

That is what happened a few days later; I had the base of the column put in place, on which the engineers would super-impose the other stones of the shaft, the diameter of which I had specified.

Finally, a fortnight later, the column had reached the height that I had designated for its crown; the pedestal of the statue was placed upon it, lined with marble at the base, on the faces and the cornice. Then I employed carpenters to build the scaffolding around the column in order to lift the statue. I employed the same means that I had seen employed in Paris for the column in the Place Vendôme.

Everything succeeded perfectly. I went to inform the King that everything was ready for the inauguration of his statue on the column, and asked him to designate the day that suited him for that inauguration.

Transported by joy, the King said: "As soon as possible, my friend."

"In that case, Sire, it will be tomorrow."

All the inhabitants were notified in no time. Delight spread throughout the city.

The next day, the square and the Royal Road were covered by inhabitants, all palpitating with trepidation and pleasure. The moment was solemn. Everyone was experiencing a certain anxiety, but when they saw the statue of the King elevated above the top of the column and it was posed majestically on its pedestal, rid of the cloth by which it had been covered until then, the deathly silence that had reigned during the operation gave way to the acclamations of the crowd, which manifested its joy and its happiness with shouts of "Long live our good King!" and "Honor to the Director General!"

The enthusiasm was at its peak.

The next day, I had twelve boundary-stones set up, surmounted by balls of gilded copper; I placed three of them on each side of the column's pedestal. Those boundary-markers were linked together by chains with oblong rings, whose ends, attached at will to the copper balls, formed a kind of garland hanging between them. The ground was flattened and smoothed, and covered with a fine gravel.

The King and Queen came to visit and examine my work, which they had only seen imperfectly the day before because of the vast crowds of citizens and the emotion they experienced. They congratulated me on the beauty of my work and invited me to dine with them. I accepted their invitation. I received the congratulations of the King, the Queen, and all the dignitaries.

Then I addressed the King and Queen.

"I receive your Majesties' felicitations with thanks; that is my sweetest recompense. But it remains for me to complete the ornamentation of the pedestal of the column, which have only been sketched out. When that work is terminated, I shall have another project."

"What is it, my good friend?" exclaimed the King.

"Sire, my project will be to establish fountains in the square that I have made, and by that means, to supply water to all the quarters of your capital, for the needs of its inhabitants.

For public health and hygiene I shall establish public baths and wash-houses, in order to maintain the cleanliness no useful to health."

"Excellent!" exclaimed the King. "But my good friend, how will you do it? We have no water here."

"I shall bring it, Sire."

"Sublime!" the King exclaimed.

And my project was welcomed by all the guests at the royal banquet with the sound of their applause, to which that of the King and Queen was joined.

The next day I gave orders to an engineer to have mobile scaffolds placed, decked with cloth, around the pedestal of the column, in order to be able to finish the ornaments.

I returned to the governor's palace, but as I passed along one of the new streets I saw a pretty woman, on the doorstep of a house, who saluted me with her hand, smiling. I recognized her immediately; it was the hospitable lady who had welcomed me when I had arrived in Mirabilis. I expressed the joy I felt at that encounter, after having searched for her in vain.

"But I've seen you several times during our great works as Director General of Works in Mirabilis," she told me. "I didn't dare speak to you, for the King has made you a great lord, and you certainly merit it."

"But you were wrong," I said, "for if I had been able to be agreeable to you, I would have seized the opportunity gladly to recognize the hospitable welcome you gave me without knowing me. If you ever have need of my services, address yourself to me, either at the residence of the governor of Mirabilis, under the title of His Excellency to Minister of Public Works, or at Maraviglia, under the title of the Duke of Marvaviglia, and be sure that I shall employ all my credit to be useful to you. Have no fear of importuning me, for you would be giving me the greatest pleasure by accepting my offer. You know my titles and my residence; would you care to give me your name and address?"

"With great pleasure. My name is Kissa, Via Grande."

Having returned to the governor's palace, I asked him to summon the engineers, in order to communicate my plans to them and my instructions for the machinery to manufacture and the works to be carried out in order to bring water to Mirabilis and establish fountains, baths and public wash-houses. I had already drawn up the plans.

The engineers assembled the following morning in the apartment I occupied in the governor's house. I explained my plans and the means of their execution. They understood them all, with the exception of the fire-pumps, which they could not comprehend. I explained to them that it was by means of the motive force of steam that the pump was activated; they were amazed, and told me that they did not think that their mechanicians were capable of fabricating such an extraordinary machine.

"That's unfortunate," I told them, "but we'll substitute windmills of which I'll give you the design. They'll understand that better."

The engineers came back to see me the following day. I have made drawings of the fountains, baths, wash-houses and the windmill, which was to be constructed on the shoe of my lake, the beautiful water of which would aliment the fountains, baths and wash-houses of Mirabilis. I had designed the windmill on the model of those I had seen in Holland, which serve the same purpose. Then I made a second plan, which was similarly aimed at my objective, which was to fill the large elevated reservoir that I intended to construct with water. The means employed for that would be the Archimedean screw.

The engineers ended up understanding me perfectly.

Then I ordered them to excavate a small canal between Maraviglia and Mirabilis for the passage of the waters. I went to Maraviglia with two engineers to map out the placement of the windmill, the reservoir and he canal. I told them to employ the kind of heavy plow that they employed to work the land in order to give more depth to the trace, and then have it excavated by the number of men they judged necessary for the accomplishment of our works.

I had almost finished the ornaments on the pedestal of the column.

After a month, the fountains, baths and wash-houses were terminated, as well as the windmills, the reservoirs and the canal. I went to inform the King, and told him that the waters would arrive in Mirabilis the following day.

The King experienced such emotion that he could not articulate any words to express his satisfaction. He hugged me in his arms and invited me to come to the morning meal the next day, so that we could go together afterwards to admire my new marvels. Those were his words.

Early the next day, all the inhabitants of Mirabilis were up and about; they know that the water was due to arrive in the city that day; they joy was inexpressible.

I went to the morning meal with the King and afterwards, I climbed into his great litter, where he made me sit next to him. The Queen followed in another litter accompanied by her first maid of honor. The entire Royal Guard and all the dignitaries of the kingdom were on horseback, escorting the two royal litters. The cortege was brilliant. Joy appeared to be animating all the faces. The people were enthused. Cries of "Long live the King!" "Long live the Queen!" and "Long live the Director General!" burst forth from all directions.

All the fountains that I had had constructed functioned very well; the baths and the public wash-houses were filled with water. In sum, everything succeeded in accordance with my desire.

When we returned to the palace the King stopped the litter in front of the column, which was now clear of all the mobile scaffolding and cloth that had masked the ornaments. He admired them, and shook my hand as a sign of satisfaction. Then he told me that, in order to conclude such a fine day, he was giving a feast for the important people of his Court, and he invited me to take part in it.

I thanked him for the signal honor that he had deigned to give me, and went to the royal feast. I was welcomed there with distinction. All my works were concluded. I had abandoned, for the moment, the project of going to visit the three isles of the Delta; I would do that later.

Deciding to return to my family, I took my leave of the King, who dissolved in tears in bidding me farewell.

SF & FANTASY

Adolphe Alhaiza. *Cybele*

Alphonse Allais. *The Adventures of Captain Cap*

Henri Allorge. *The Great Cataclysm*

Guy d'Armen. *Doc Ardan: The City of Gold and Lepers*

G.-J. Arnaud. *The Ice Company*

André Arnyvelde. *The Ark; The Mutilated Bacchus*

Charles Asselineau. *The Double Life*

Henri Austruy. *The Eupantophone; The Olotelepan; The Petitpaon Era*

Barillet-Lagargousse. *The Final War*

Cyprien Bérard. *The Vampire Lord Ruthwen*

S. Henry Berthoud. *Martyrs of Science*

Aloysius Bertrand. *Gaspard de la Nuit*

Richard Bessière. *The Gardens of the Apocalypse; The Masters of Silence*

Chevalier de Béthune. *The World of Mercury*

Albert Bleunard. *Ever Smaller*

Félix Bodin. *The Novel of the Future*

Louis Boussenard. *Monsieur Synthesis*

Alphonse Brown. *City of Glass; The Conquest of the Air*

Émile Calvet. *In a Thousand Years*

André Caroff. *The Terror of Madame Atomos; Miss Atomos; The Return of Madame Atomos; The Mistake of Madame Atomos; The Monsters of Madame Atomos; The Revenge of Madame Atomos; The Resurrection of Madame Atomos; The Mark of Madame Atomos; The Spheres of Madame Atomos; The Wrath of Madame Atomos* (w/M. & Sylvie Stéphan)

Félicien Champsaur. *Homo-Deus; The Human Arrow; Nora, The Ape-Woman; Ouha, King of the Apes; Pharaoh's Wife*

Didier de Chousy. *Ignis*

Jules Clarétie. *Obsession*

Michel Corday. *The Eternal Flame*

André Couvreur. *Caresco, Superman; The Exploits of Professor Tornada* (3 vols.)*; The Necessary Evil*

Camille Debans. *The Misfortunes of John Bull*

Captain Danrit. *Undersea Odyssey*

C. I. Defontenay. *Star (Psi Cassiopeia)*

Charles Derennes. *The People of the Pole*
Georges Dodds (anthologist). *The Missing Link*
Charles Dodeman. *The Silent Bomb*
Harry Dickson. *The Heir of Dracula; Harry Dickson vs. The Spider*
Jules Dornay. *Lord Ruthven Begins*
Alfred Driou. *The Adventures of a Parisian Aeronaut*
Sâr Dubnotal *vs. Jack the Ripper; The Astral Trail*
Odette Dulac. *The War of the Sexes*
Alexandre Dumas. *The Return of Lord Ruthven*
Renée Dunan. *Baal; The Ultimate Pleasure*
J.-C. Dunyach. *The Night Orchid; The Thieves of Silence*
Henri Duvernois. *The Man Who Found Himself*
Achille Eyraud. *Voyage to Venus*
Henri Falk. *The Age of Lead*
Paul Féval. *Anne of the Isles; Knightshade; Revenants; Vampire City;*
The Vampire Countess; The Wandering Jew's Daughter
Paul Féval, *fils. Felifax, the Tiger-Man*
Charles de Fieux. *Lamékis*
Fernand Fleuret. *Jim Click*
Louis Forest. *Someone is Stealing Children in Paris*
Arnould Galopin. *Doctor Omega; Doctor Omega and the*
Shadowmen (anthology)
Judith Gautier. *Isoline and the Serpent-Flower*
H. Gayar. *The Marvelous Adventures of Serge Myrandhal on Mars*
G.L. Gick. *Harry Dickson and the Werewolf of Rutherford Grange*
Delphine de Girardin. *Balzac's Cane*
Léon Gozlan. *The Vampire of the Val-de-Grâce*
Jules Gros. *The Fossil Man*
Edmond Haraucourt. *Daah, the First Human; Illusions of Immortality*
Nathalie Henneberg. *The Green Gods*
Eugène Hennebert. *The Enchanted City*
Jules Hoche. *The Maker of Men and His Formula*
V. Hugo, P. Foucher & P. Meurice. *The Hunchback of Notre-Dame*
Romain d'Huissier. *Hexagon: Dark Matter*
Jules Janin. *The Magnetized Corpse*
Michel Jeury. *Chronolysis*
Gustave Kahn. *The Tale of Gold and Silence*
Gérard Klein. *The Mote in Time's Eye*
Fernand Kolney. *Love in 5000 Years*
Paul Lacroix. *Danse Macabre*
Louis-Guillaume de La Follie. *The Unpretentious Philosopher*

Jean de La Hire. *The Fiery Wheel; Enter the Nyctalope; The Nyctalope on Mars; The Nyctalope vs. Lucifer; The Nyctalope Steps In; Night of the Nyctalope; Return of the Nyctalope*

Etienne-Léon de Lamothe-Langon. *The Virgin Vampire*

André Laurie. *Spiridon*

Gabriel de Lautrec. *The Vengeance of the Oval Portrait*

Alain le Drimeur. *The Future City*

Georges Le Faure & Henri de Graffigny. *The Extraordinary Adventures of a Russian Scientist Across the Solar System* (2 vols.)

Gustave Le Rouge. *The Dominion of the World* (w/Gustave Guitton) (4 vols.); *The Mysterious Doctor Cornelius* (3 vols.); *The Vampires of Mars*

Jules Lermina. *The Battle of Strasbourg; Mysteryville; Panic in Paris; The Secret of Zippelius; To-Ho and the Gold Destroyers*

André Lichtenberger. *The Centaurs; The Children of the Crab*

Maurice Limat. *Mephista*

Listonai. *The Philosophical Voyager*

Jean-Marc & Randy Lofficier. *Edgar Allan Poe on Mars; The Katrina Protocol; Pacifica; Robonocchio; Return of the Nyctalope;* (anthologists) *Tales of the Shadowmen 1-11; The Vampire Almanac* (2 vols.)

Ch. Lomon & P.-B. Gheuzi. *The Last Days of Atlantis*

Xavier Mauméjean. *The League of Heroes*

Joseph Méry. *The Tower of Destiny*

Hippolyte Mettais. *Paris Before the Deluge; The Year 5865*

Louise Michel. *The Human Microbes; The New World*

Tony Moilin. *Paris in the Year 2000*

José Moselli. *Illa's End*

John-Antoine Nau. *Enemy Force*

Marie Nizet. *Captain Vampire*

Charles Nodier. *Trilby and The Crumb Fairy*

C. Nodier, A. Beraud & Toussaint-Merle. *Frankenstein*

Henri de Parville. *An Inhabitant of the Planet Mars*

Gaston de Pawlowski. *Journey to the Land of the 4th Dimension*

Georges Pellerin. *The World in 2000 Years*

Ernest Pérochon. *The Frenetic People*

Pierre Pelot. *The Child Who Walked on the Sky*

J. Polidori, C. Nodier, E. Scribe. *Lord Ruthven the Vampire*

P.-A. Ponson du Terrail. *The Immortal Woman; The Vampire and the Devil's Son*

Georges Price. *The Missing Men of the* Sirius

Edgar Quinet. *Ahasuerus; The Enchanter Merlin*

Henri de Régnier. *A Surfeit of Mirrors*

Maurice Renard. *The Blue Peril; Doctor Lerne; The Doctored Man; A Man Among the Microbes; The Master of Light*

Jean Richepin. *The Crazy Corner; The Wing*

Albert Robida. *The Adventures of Saturnin Farandoul; Chalet in the Sky; The Clock of the Centuries; The Electric Life; The Engineer Von Satanas*

J.-H. Rosny Aîné. *Helgvor of the Blue River; The Givreuse Enigma; The Mysterious Force; The Navigators of Space; Vamireh; The World of the Variants; The Young Vampire*

Marcel Rouff. *Journey to the Inverted World*

Léonie Rouzade. *The World Turned Upside Down*

Han Ryner. *The Human Ant; The Superhumans*

Frank Schildiner. *The Quest of Frankenstein*

Pierre de Selenes: *An Unknown World*

Angelo de Sorr. *The Vampires of London*

Brian Stableford. *The Empire of the Necromancers (1. The Shadow of Frankenstein; 2. Frankenstein and the Vampire Countess; 3. Frankenstein in London); Eurydice's Lament; The New Faust at the Tragicomique; Sherlock Holmes and The Vampires of Eternity; The Stones of Camelot; The Wayward Muse.* (anthologist) *News from the Moon; The Germans on Venus; The Supreme Progress; The World Above the World; Nemoville; Investigations of the Future; The Conqueror of Death; The Revolt of the Machines; The Man With the Blue Face; The Aerial Valley*

Jacques Spitz. *The Eye of Purgatory*

Kurt Steiner. *Ortog*

Eugène Thébault. *Radio-Terror*

C.-F. Tiphaigne de La Roche. *Amilec*

Simon Tyssot de Patot. *The Strange Voyages of Jacques Massé and Pierre de Mésange*

Louis Ulbach. *Prince Bonifacio*

Théo Varlet. *The Castaways of Eros; The Golden Rock.; The Martian Epic* (w/Octave Joncquel); *Timeslip Troopers* (w/André Blandin); *The Xenobiotic Invasion*

Pierre Véron. *The Merchants of Health*

Paul Vibert. *The Mysterious Fluid*

Villiers de l'Isle-Adam. *The Scaffold; The Vampire Soul*

Gaston de Wailly. *The Murderer of the World*

Philippe Ward. *Artahe ; Manhattan Ghost* (w/Mickael Laguerre); *The Song of Montségur* (w/Sylvie Miller)

Victor Margueritte. *The Bacheloress; The Companion; The Couple*

MYSTERIES & THRILLERS

M. Allain & P. Souvestre. *The Daughter of Fantômas*
A. Anicet-Bourgeois & Lucien Dabril. *Rocambole*
A. Bernède. *Belphegor*; *Judex* (w/Louis Feuillade); *The Return of Judex* (w/Louis Feuillade); *The Shadow of Judex* (anthology)
A. Bisson & G. Livet. *Nick Carter vs. Fantômas*
V. Darlay & H. de Gorsse. *Arsène Lupin vs. Sherlock Holmes: The Stage Play*
Séamas Duffy. *Sherlock Holmes in Paris*
Paul Féval. *The Black Coats (The Parisian Jungle; Heart of Steel; The Sword-Swallower; 'Salem Street; The Invisible Weapon; The Companions of the Treasure; The Cadet Gang); Gentlemen of the Night; John Devil*
Émile Gaboriau. *Monsieur Lecoq*
Goron & Émile Gautier. *Spawn of the Penitentiary*
Paul d'Ivoi. *Around the World on Five Sous* (w/Henri Chabrillat)
Rick Lai. *Shadows of the Opera: Retribution in Blood; Sisters of the Shadows: The Curse of Cagliostro*
Steve Leadley. *Sherlock Holmes: The Circle of Blood*
Maurice Leblanc. *Arsène Lupin vs. Countess Cagliostro; Arsène Lupin vs. Sherlock Holmes (1. The Blonde Phantom; 2. The Hollow Needle); The Island of the Thirty Coffin; 813; The Many Faces of Arsène Lupin* (anthology)
Gaston Leroux. *Chéri-Bibi; The Phantom of the Opera; Rouletabille & the Mystery of the Yellow Room; Rouletabille at Krupp's*
Richard Marsh. *The Complete Adventures of Judith Lee*
William Patrick Maynard. *The Terror of Fu Manchu; The Destiny of Fu Manchu*
Frank J. Morlok. *Sherlock Holmes: The Grand Horizontals; Sherlock Holmes vs Jack the Ripper*
Jean Petithuguenin. *The Adventures of Ethel King*
Antonin Reschal. *The Adventures of Miss Boston*
P. de Wattyne & Y. Walter. *Sherlock Holmes vs. Fantômas*
David White. *Fantômas in America*
Pierre Yrondy. *The Adventures of Thérèse Arnaud*

SCREENPLAYS

Mike Baron. *The Iron Triangle*
Emma Bull & Will Shetterly. *Nightspeeder; War for the Oaks*
Gerry Conway & Roy Thomas. *Doc Dynamo*
Steve Englehart. *Majorca*
James Hudnall. *The Devastator*
Jean-Marc & Randy Lofficier. *Royal Flush*
J.-M. & R. Lofficier & Marc Agapit. *Despair*
J.-M. & R. Lofficier & Joël Houssin. *City*
Andrew Paquette. *Peripheral Vision*
Robert L. Robinson, Jr. *Judex*
R. Thomas, J. Hendler & L. Sprague de Camp. *Rivers of Time*

NON-FICTION

Stephen R. Bissette. *Blur 1-5. Green Mountain Cinema 1; Teen Angels*
Win Scott Eckert. *Crossovers* (2 vols.)
Randy Lofficier. *Over Here*
Jean-Marc & Randy Lofficier. *Shadowmen* (2 vols.)

ART BOOKS

Jean-Pierre Normand. *Science Fiction Illustrations*
Raven Okeefe. *Raven's L'il Critters; Rave's Faves*
Randy Lofficier & Raven Okeefe. *If Your Possum Go Daylight...*
Daniele Serra. *Illusions*